TERNS OF ENDEARMENT

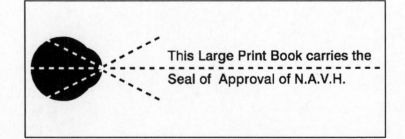

This Large Print Book carries the
Seal of Approval of N.A.V.H.

A MEG LANGSLOW MYSTERY

TERNS OF ENDEARMENT

DONNA ANDREWS

THORNDIKE PRESS
A part of Gale, a Cengage Company

Farmington Hills, Mich • San Francisco • New York • Waterville, Maine
Meriden, Conn • Mason, Ohio • Chicago

Copyright © 2019 by Donna Andrews.
Thorndike Press, a part of Gale, a Cengage Company.

ALL RIGHTS RESERVED
This is a work of fiction. All of the characters, organizations, and events portrayed in this novel are either products of the author's imagination or are used fictitiously.
Thorndike Press® Large Print Mystery.
The text of this Large Print edition is unabridged.
Other aspects of the book may vary from the original edition.
Set in 16 pt. Plantin.

**LIBRARY OF CONGRESS CIP DATA ON FILE.
CATALOGUING IN PUBLICATION FOR THIS BOOK
IS AVAILABLE FROM THE LIBRARY OF CONGRESS**

ISBN-13: 978-1-4328-6689-1 (hardcover alk. paper)

Published in 2019 by arrangement with Macmillan Publishing Group, LLC/St. Martin's Publishing Group

Printed in Mexico
1 2 3 4 5 6 7 23 22 21 20 19

ACKNOWLEDGMENTS

Thanks once again to the wonderful team at St. Martin's/Minotaur, including (but not limited to) Joe Brosnan, Hector DeJean, Jennifer Donovan, Melissa Hastings, Paul Hoch, Andrew Martin, Sarah Melnyk, and especially my editor, Pete Wolverton. And once again I am spoiled by David Rotstein and the Art Department for another beautiful cover.

More thanks to my agent, Ellen Geiger, Matt McGowan, and the staff at the Frances Goldin Literary Agency for handling the business side of writing so brilliantly and letting me concentrate on the fun part.

Many thanks to the friends — writers and readers alike — who brainstorm and critique with me, give me good ideas, or help keep me sane while I'm writing: Stuart, Aidan, and Liam Andrews, Chris Cowan, Ellen Crosby, Kathy Deligianis, Margery Flax, Suzanne Frisbee, John Gilstrap, Barb

Goffman, Joni Langevoort, David Niemi, Alan Orloff, Art Taylor, and Robin Templeton. Thanks for all kinds of moral support and practical help to my blog sisters and brother at the Femmes Fatales: Alexia Gordon, Aimee Hix, Dean James, Toni L.P. Kelner, Catriona McPherson, Kris Neri, Joanna Campbell Slan, Marcia Talley, Elaine Viets, and LynDee Walker. And thanks to all the TeaBuds for two decades of friendship.

Shortly after I came up with the idea for *Terns of Endearment* I realized that it probably wasn't very smart to write the book without ever having been on a cruise — and if it hadn't been for cruise veteran Dina Willner's expertise and organizing efforts, I would probably still be waiting on the docks.

James Walker, of Walker & O'Neill, PA, Maritime Lawyers, answered some of my questions about the legal aspects of crime on the high seas, and his website CruiseLawNews.com is fascinating reading for anyone interested in shipboard travel.

I owe special thanks to the folks who tried valiantly to educate me on nautical matters and on the U.S. Coast Guard. My Walsingham Academy classmate Rear Admiral Joel R. Whitehead (retired) gave generously of his time. And my writer friend Shari Randall enlisted both her husband, Commander William Randall (retired), and Bill's friend, Captain Brian Kelley (retired), to straighten out many of my landlubber's misconceptions. Any errors that remain are obviously things I failed to ask any of them about.

And above all, thanks to the readers who continue to enjoy Meg's adventures!

CHAPTER 1

Thursday afternoon

"Do you really think there's room for all this luggage on the boat?"

"Ship," I corrected. "I know it's only a cruise ship, but I understand it demoralizes the crew when you call it a boat. And don't worry, the porters will handle everything."

Trevor Ponsonby-West sighed and looked put-upon. Well, he was put-upon. Being put-upon was more or less his job. He was my grandfather's personal assistant, which meant Grandfather delegated to him anything he didn't want to bother with himself and couldn't cajole his friends or family to do. Trevor's job was demanding under normal circumstances and almost overwhelming when Grandfather traveled. And he traveled a lot. After all, even though he was now in his nineties, the world still expected to see Dr. J. Montgomery Blake rescuing endangered species, leading envi-

9

ronmental protests, and appearing in the nature documentaries that had become such a staple on television channels like National Geographic and Animal Planet.

Trevor did a great job of getting Grandfather where he had to go, when he was supposed to be there, and equipped with whatever he needed to bring. If only he could do it without quite so much sighing.

"Oh, dear — I shall have to tip the porters." He hunched his narrow shoulders anxiously, making him look more than ever like a tall but malnourished vulture, and stifled another sigh as he pulled out his wallet. "I should check to make sure I have some small bills."

"I think you'll need large bills to reward them for hauling all this." I waved at the sea of luggage.

"True. And — Oh, there's my phone buzzing again." He pulled it out and glanced at it. "Oh, dear. I need to run an errand for him. Do you suppose . . ."

"Go keep Grandfather happy," I said. "I'll hold down the fort here."

Trevor dashed off, looking anxious. This was his only other expression.

"Yes, it should be a wonderfully educational cruise!" Grandfather's booming voice rang out from somewhere a little farther down the pier.

"You'll be giving lectures on board?" A man in a sports coat and pristine dark blue denim jeans was scribbling in a small notebook as he stood near Grandfather — though not so near that he interfered with the efforts of the woman with the camera, who was circling constantly and occasionally snapping a picture or two.

"And leading nature walks on shore when we get to Bermuda," Grandfather went on. "Due to its isolation from the mainland, it's a unique ecoregion. Alas! We won't have time to visit more than two of the islands — Bermuda's not a single island, you know, but a chain of one hundred and eighty-four islands, although only twenty of them are inhabited."

Evidently Grandfather had been boning up on our destination.

"And I'm hoping to get enough footage for a documentary on Bermuda," he added.

"Planning to save any endangered species while you're there?" the reporter asked.

"Well, I do hope to look into how the Bermuda skinks are doing." Grandfather's expression became solemn, as if the fate of the Bermuda skinks had dire implications for the rest of the universe. "It's a species only found in the Bermudas, and the International Union for Conservation of Nature has it on its Red List of Threatened Species."

"Is it a rodent?" the photographer asked. From the way she wrinkled her nose slightly I deduced she had scant sympathy for endangered rodents.

"A reptile — to be precise, a lizard about this big." Grandfather held his thumb and forefinger about three inches apart.

I could tell by the photographer's expression that reptiles were not an improvement over rodents. If the Bermuda Tourism Authority were listening in, they'd probably worry that Grandfather was undermining their promotion efforts.

"The Bermuda skink is threatened by habitat destruction, of course, and predation from introduced mammals like cats and rats. But oddly enough, one of the biggest threats to their survival is litter."

"Litter?" the reporter asked, thus saving me from having to.

"Many small lizards have friction pads on their feet that let them stick to surfaces they walk on, but Bermuda skinks have tiny claws instead. So if they crawl into an empty glass jar or a discarded soda can — something with a slick interior surface — they can't get out again. They starve or die of heat stress or dehydration."

Was he serious? Probably. Damn him. I could see that once I got to the island, instead of relaxing and enjoying the scenery, I'd be restlessly scanning my surroundings for stray jars and soda cans that might contain forlorn Bermuda skinks in need of rescue.

"Can you face that way for a few minutes?" The photographer pointed to the right. "At the moment, the sun is at your back, and it's almost impossible to get a good shot."

Grandfather obliged and lifted his head, assuming the triumphant pose he usually reserved for that moment in his documentaries when he succeeded in rescuing something, or at least not getting eaten by something. The photographer began to click in double time.

"How dreadful!" came a voice from behind me. "Even here I can't get away from those ghastly paparazzi!"

I turned to see an older red-haired woman in a billowing orange floor-length caftan, holding a matching orange paper parasol. She was an imposing figure, only an inch or so shorter than my five foot ten, and while the caftan flowed rather than clung, I could tell she wasn't particularly skinny. But not fat, either — stately. Her deep red, almost maroon, hair clashed with the color of the caftan. If I were her, I'd have chosen a different dress — or a different and more plausible hair color. Maybe she thought the garish red roses painted on the parasol tied the whole ensemble together.

The photographer had stopped clicking her camera, and Grandfather looked annoyed. The reporter was staring at the caftan lady with a frown on his face, as if trying to figure out who she was. The photographer was watching the reporter, no doubt waiting for him to indicate whether she should aim her lens at the new arrival or go back to Grandfather.

The woman — the diva, as I mentally dubbed her — looked at me with an expression I recognized — the look of someone who is accustomed to having minions to do her bidding, and thinks she's found a promising one.

"Is it *The New York Times? The Washington Post?*" Her voice was high, rather affected, and pitched so loud I was sure people on the next pier could hear her. "Well, it doesn't really matter. Shoo them away for me, will you?" All the while she was standing up straight and holding her parasol at an angle that did more to frame her face for the photographer than to protect her from the sun.

"It's *The Baltimore Sun,*" I explained. "And I think they're here to interview Dr. Blake. Dr. Montgomery Blake, the naturalist," I added, seeing the puzzled look on her face. "The one who's giving lectures on the cruise."

"Of all the — *Hmph!*" She strode off, looking highly indignant.

The reporter and the photographer were looking at me expectantly. I shrugged to indicate that I had no idea who she was. They turned their attention back to Grandfather.

"Dr. Blake, can we move a little way down the pier?" the photographer asked. "I think we can get a better background over there."

Actually she seemed to be pointing not to another part of our pier but to a point farther along the waterfront where the tidy world of the cruise ships gave way to piers clearly designed more for utility than looks. Knowing photographers, I was willing to bet she wanted to pose him in front of a particularly dilapidated tugboat — or was it a fishing boat? — with the name *Scurvy Rogue* painted on its bow. Grandfather would love it.

"Excellent!" He began striding in the

15

indicated direction, with the reporter and photographer, who both had much shorter legs, almost running to keep up with him.

"Shouldn't he be boarding already instead of showing off for the press?" I turned to see Caroline Willner, a longtime friend who, to my relief, was joining us on the cruise. As the owner of the Willner Wildlife Refuge and an expert zoologist herself, she rivaled Grandfather in knowledge and far excelled him at communicating her knowledge to the public without sounding condescending or confrontational. More to the point, she was the only person I knew who could get away with addressing Grandfather as "Monty, you old goat!" — and one of only two people in the world who could make him behave. Since Mother, the other one, would also be aboard, I was guardedly optimistic that they could prevent his worst faux pas.

For the moment, I was even more relieved to see that Caroline seemed to have made it her next mission to ensure that the reporters didn't distract Grandfather from boarding before the ship sailed.

"How much longer before they pull up the gangplank, anyway?" Caroline asked.

"Twenty minutes," I said, after a glance at my phone. "And yes, he really should board soon. I'm more worried about whether the porter's going to show up to deal with our luggage."

Caroline studied the luggage with narrowed eyes before pulling out her own phone.

"They need more porters," she said. "Or more efficient ones. I'll sic your mother on the luggage. Then I can focus on chivvying Monty on board." With that she strode off, phone in hand, toward the rather distant pier where Grandfather was happily posing next to a pair of gulls.

Feeling a sense of relief, I sat down on one of the sturdier suitcases, closed my eyes, and did some of the deep breathing exercises my cousin Rose Noire always recommended for times of stress.

After a few rounds of breathing, I gave up. I certainly hoped the all-natural herbal anti-seasickness remedies she was bringing along worked better than the yoga breathing. I opened my eyes, and began studying my surroundings. Which were not encouraging.

"Why Pastime?" I muttered, not for the first time. When Grandfather had let it be known that he was interested in doing the cruise ship lecture circuit, he'd gotten offers from several lines, including several of the top contenders in the educational and environmental cruise market. Pastime was a relatively new company, and from what I'd seen, they didn't have their act together yet. Farther down the waterfront I could see passengers bound for other ships dropping their luggage off with eager, attentive baggage handlers and strolling on board. Those other cruise lines had it together. Why didn't Pastime? This didn't bode well for the rest of the cruise. And besides —

"What's all this?"

I glanced up to see that the long-awaited porter had arrived and was inspecting our sea of luggage. He looked up at me and scowled.

"There's a limit, you know," he said. "Two suitcases per person."

"I know." I waved a thick wad of Pastime paperwork at him. "There are sixteen passengers in our party. I think you'll find only thirty-two items of baggage there. Unless someone else has hidden their bags in with ours, hoping to weasel out of tipping you."

That didn't seem to improve his mood — even with the suggestion that I was not unfamiliar with the concept of tipping porters. And his surliness wasn't helping my own mood, either. I had the sinking feeling that some or all of our bags were about to disappear into the luggage-handling equivalent of the Bermuda Triangle, never again to be seen by mortal eye. I could imagine sighting the *Flying Dutchman,* its shredded sails inspiring a feeling of dread as its phantom crew hauled frayed ropes and stared balefully at the forlorn mountain of increasingly faded and battered suitcases tumbling carelessly about on its decks.

I shook off my wild imaginings, fixed my attention on the porter, and summoned up what Rob called my Mother Voice — the one that usually got results.

"I'm not boarding until I see these safely loaded," I said. "They're all properly tagged and ready for you." I refrained from adding that they'd been ready and waiting for him for two hours, and me with them. He was glancing at some of the tags as if hoping to find a problem. Good luck with that, I said to myself. I'd made sure of the proper tagging. Attached to each suitcase with a stainless-steel loop was a sturdy plastic luggage tag holder containing the appropriate brightly colored slip of paper listing the suitcase's owner, the deck and cabin number, our sailing date, our destination, and several sets of letters and numbers that were meaningless to me but presumably would help the porter deliver each suitcase safely to its destination. It had seemed an admirable system when I read about it on the Pastime Cruise Company's website. But that was before I'd met this porter. He was a sallow, surly fellow, about my height but much wider and burlier. His white Pastime uniform, with all its shiny gold buttons, bars, and miscellaneous bits of trim, seemed cut for someone slightly shorter with a much smaller beer belly. In his red-rimmed and slightly watery eyes I saw — a lack of intelligence? No, more a warning that whatever intelligence he possessed would be enlisted to ensure not the safe arrival of our luggage, but his own immunity from blame for any disappearances that might happen.

On impulse I pulled out my phone and opened the camera app.

"I almost forgot — I'm supposed to be keeping the family back home posted on everything that happens," I said. "All those exciting moments that will make them feel as if they're right here with us. Smile!"

As I spoke, I took a step or two backward, to ensure that I fitted all thirty-two bags into the frame with the porter. Who did not smile as requested — instead, he looked put out, as if by documenting his proximity to our luggage I'd foiled his plans.

Or maybe I was just attributing sinister motives to a man who was overworked,

20

underpaid, and tired of coping with temperamental passengers.

Still, just in case, I also took what I hoped was a subtle glance at the employee badge he wore on his left shoulder and committed his name to memory. Actually, it was such an oddly international combination — Gianpiero Mulder — that I'd probably find it hard to forget.

Just then Trevor scurried back. I was surprisingly glad to see him. Normally having Trevor around was rather like finding oneself suddenly in the midst of a swarm of gnats. But as long as I could transfer the gnat infestation to the annoying Gianpiero . . .

"Oh, good — you're back." I beamed at Trevor. "Perhaps you could help make sure Mr. Mulder here doesn't encounter any problems sorting out our luggage and getting it to the right cabins. If it takes more than one trip, I can stay here and guard anything left behind."

As I'd hoped, the mere request made Trevor visibly anxious over the possibility of the luggage going astray. He'd attach himself to Gianpiero like a starving leech. Whatever sinister plans the surly porter had in mind for our luggage were almost certainly foiled.

And to my relief, all thirty-two items of

21

luggage fit — just barely — on the porter's cart. I was free to board.

And about time. Caroline and Grandfather had already boarded while Gianpiero was loading the luggage. The Pastime employee at the foot of the gangplank had begun glancing at her watch and then frowning at me. The ship wouldn't sail for several hours, but I knew from reading the pre-boarding instructions that they wanted all the passengers aboard as soon as possible so they could get the mandatory safety drill over with, to avoid delaying our sailing time.

I paused on my way to the gangplank and looked up at what would be our floating home for the next week. The *Pastime Wanderer* was a graceful, gleaming white ship, several hundred feet in length with half a dozen decks. Tiny compared with some of the enormous cruise ships I could see farther down the waterfront, where Carnival, Royal Caribbean, and the other better-known lines were docked. But those enormous ships carried enormous crowds — three or four thousand passengers for the bigger ones. The *Wanderer,* thank goodness, only had room for about two hundred.

And nearly all of them were already on board. I tore my eyes away from the ship and stepped forward to present my ticket and passport to the young woman in the white-and-gold uniform who was standing by a lecturn at the foot of the gangplank.

Finally!

CHAPTER 2

"I hope I'm not the very last one," I said as the young woman inspected my documents.

"Oh, that's okay," she said. "Someone has to be."

Oops. But her smile was genuine, though it probably revealed more relief that all her charges were present and accounted for than pleasure in seeing me in particular. Still, I felt bad.

"Sorry," I said. "I was waiting for the porter. Call me a worrywart, but I wanted to see the family's luggage go on board with my own eyes."

"I'd call it smart," she said. And then, as if realizing she'd committed the cardinal sin of saying something negative about the company, she hastened to add, "Not that you'd have to worry about your luggage getting left behind on a Pastime Cruise, of course! But not everything in life's that reliable, is it?"

"Exactly." Nice save, I added silently. Maybe I should have said it aloud. Or something more encouraging. After all, she was a welcome change from the porter.

"Do you need anything else?" she asked. I shook my head, and she gave me a quick smile before hurrying back into the Cruise Maryland Terminal building. She probably had a lot to do before we set sail.

I stopped at the foot of the gangplank and studied the ship — after all, it was my last chance to get an outside view of it for at least a couple of days. A few people were standing on the upper two decks. A few more on the individual balconies that graced nearly every cabin. It all looked very peaceful and elegant — let the relaxation begin!

At the top of the gangplank I found myself in the boarding lobby, a brightly decorated area that ran the width of the ship. Pastime's decorators had gone in for bright tropical colors here — turquoise, lemon yellow, and salmon pink, with painted murals of exotic fish and shells. On the far wall, a sign with a large arrow pointing to the right announced the passageway that led to the main dining room. Along the right wall was a large alcove that held an upward-bound stairway and an elevator. Along the left wall, an open door with a STAFF ONLY sign beside it revealed a rather narrow corridor.

Odd and rather annoying that there was no one inside to greet me and give me a hint about what I was supposed to do next. Maybe it was because I was the last to board — although that was the porter's fault, not mine. I heard a door open somewhere to my left, but when I turned to look — nothing.

"So sorry," came a voice from behind me. "May I help you?"

I turned to find a shortish man whose gleaming white uniform was festooned with enough gold-colored braid and buttons to decorate a small Christmas tree. He was smiling, but it didn't really seem like a joyful smile — more the smile of someone having a rather trying day but determined not to show it.

"I'm First Officer Martin." He extended his hand.

"Meg Langslow."

"Dr. Blake's granddaughter," he said. "Delighted to have you aboard."

He actually looked as if he meant that. I was relieved. I knew some of Pastime's management weren't entirely thrilled at having so many of our family on board. But it was their own fault — they'd offered Grandfather a substantial discount for any friends or family who wanted to accompany him. If it was going to be a problem for a dozen or so of us to take advantage of it, they should have made it clear how many discounts they really wanted to offer.

Clearly Martin knew nothing about those rather testy discussions. Or perhaps didn't care. He glanced around with a faint frown, then looked back at me and smiled — but a little uncertainly, as if greeting arriving passengers wasn't part of his job these days and he was trying to remember what it involved.

"Just wondering where to go next," I said. "Our cabins are on deck four, but I gather we're not supposed to go there immediately." I suspected they wanted us out from underfoot, so the feckless Gianpiero would have plenty of time to misdeliver all of our luggage.

"Oh, right." He glanced at his watch. "You should be okay to go to your cabin by now. Although you might enjoy using the time to explore the ship."

"What I really want to do is walk all the way around the ship on the outside decks," I said. "The way people always seemed to be doing in movies set on cruise ships, like *Shall We Dance, An Affair to Remember,* or even the Marx Brothers' *Monkey Business.*

But I gather these days it's all private balconies."

"Actually, you'll find a few areas of open deck," he said. "Including very nice sun decks in the stern of decks four and five. And if you ask me, the best place to watch the scenery when we set sail is deck six — it's all deck, no cabins, so you get a great three-hundred-and-sixty-degree view."

I thanked him and pushed the up button on the elevator. He strode off as if he had several hundred things to do. Yes, sailing days were clearly stressful for the crew.

I took the elevator up to deck four and stepped out into the middle of a corridor that ran the length of the ship. I saw a sign that said SUN DECK with an arrow pointing left, so I headed that way. On both left and right, outside most of the doors, were small clusters of suitcases — though not outside either 420 or 422, the two staterooms Michael and I would be sharing with the boys. Well, Trevor and Gianpiero did have twenty-eight other suitcases to deliver. I'd hold off on worrying yet.

Just beyond our cabin was the doorway to the deck. I pushed it open and stepped out into sunshine so bright it momentarily blinded me.

"Meg, dear. Over here!"

I shaded my eyes and spotted Mother and Aunt Penelope. They were both waving at me, so I waved back and headed toward them, picking my way through rather a lot of white and cobalt-blue deck chairs and recliners.

Aunt Penelope was not as adept as Mother at the Royal Wave, a slight, graceful, minimalist motion of the wrist that most people associated with Queen Elizabeth II — a gesture designed to keep the waver from tiring, no matter how long she had to perform it to acknowledge her adoring minions. Then again, Mother had probably practiced it more, since she had a great many more adoring minions than Aunt Penelope, or for that matter, most people outside the British royal family.

They were both wearing elegant pastel dresses and wide-brimmed, flower-trimmed hats, and leaning against the rail at the very back of the ship. I stopped to take a picture of them with my phone.

"You look very nice," I said when I came close to where they were standing — or was it posing? "Trying on your outfits for some future tea at Buckingham Palace?"

"We're about to have afternoon tea in the main dining room," Mother said. "If you hurry, you can change in time to join us."

"There should be cucumber sandwiches." Aunt Penelope made this sound like a good thing. Perhaps to her it was.

"Thanks, but I'm feeling too grungy for anything as elegant as tea, and I don't think I can relax and enjoy myself until I make sure everyone in our party is safely aboard. With all their stuff." At least with their proper portion of the thirty-two suitcases. I reminded myself that it really wasn't my job to worry about the stuff people wanted to bring that was against the ship's rules. Last night I'd confiscated aromatherapy candles from my cousin Rose Noire, a portable travel iron from Mother, and fireworks from my brother, Rob. Pastime's packing guidelines prohibited just about anything that could accidentally set the ship on fire, which seemed quite sensible to me, but apparently the many recreational pyromaniacs in my family found it hard to grasp. I'd also vetoed the selection of dried or taxidermied specimens that Grandfather had been planning to use to illustrate his lectures, and wondered if he or one of his scientific colleagues had inspired Pastime's curiously specific prohibition on packing dead animals. On their heads be it if they had put any of the contraband back in their luggage. I'd done what I could. And surely it wouldn't be Gianpiero's job to search for contraband.

"I don't know what we'd do without you." Aunt Penelope beamed approval at me.

"Tomorrow, then, dear?" Mother asked. "They have tea every day. Isn't that civilized?"

"Very." Probably not the moment to explain that I was looking forward to getting away from civilization for a while. "Have fun."

I watched as they strolled down the deck and breathed a sigh of relief when they eventually disappeared into the doorway that led inside. I reached into my pocket and pulled out a document I expected to wear out in the next few days — a brochure containing a deck-by-deck map of the ship. I unfolded the brochure and glanced about to get my bearings.

I was leaning on the railing, looking down at the dock on the left side of the ship, which I should probably learn to call the port side for the duration. We were in the back of the ship — aft, or the stern. According to the deck plans, the main dining room was also aft, but on deck one, the level where I'd boarded — yes, I'd seen the sign. I recalled that there was at least one other less formal place to eat aboard ship — the Starlight Lounge, at the other end of deck four, offering a bar and casual dining. It was in the front of the ship. Forward, or possibly the bow. Just thinking the words made me feel deliciously nautical. I could go forward to the Starlight Lounge and have a cold drink.

But first I pulled out my cell phone and called Michael.

"How are you and the boys settling in?" I asked.

"Settling in? Not at all. I don't think we've spent more than fifteen minutes on the same deck since we got on board. The boys are still convinced there must be a pool hidden somewhere on the ship."

"Alas, they are doomed to disappointment."

"I think they'll live. I have reminded them that very soon they will be snorkeling in the crystal clear waters of Bermuda. Meanwhile they've discovered that there's at least one free snack area on every deck. And that they can summon a variety of frozen beverages by merely waving their Pastime cards at the bartender. Virgin frozen daiquiris, virgin frozen margaritas, virgin frozen mojitos. Right now we're at the miniature golf course on deck five."

"Deck five is big enough for a miniature golf course?"

"Only three holes," he said. "And they kind of overlap. Really more like a combination putting green and obstacle course. But the boys seem to be enjoying it."

"You need me to spell you?"

"No, I'm good. I know we all ran you ragged last night and this morning, and I don't just mean me and the boys. Go put your feet up, have a cool drink, and relax. We'll see you at dinner."

"Sounds like a plan."

"Oh, and don't forget what they told us," he said. "Pretty soon after we sail we'll be out of cell phone range — so get your phone connected to the ship's Wi-Fi now, or all of a sudden we won't be able to call or text each other, and we'll have to run around the ship looking for each other. Password's on your boarding pass."

"Roger." I dug out my boarding pass and made the Wi-Fi connection. Then I tucked my phone and the ship's map in my pocket and went back indoors. To my great relief, there were now suitcases outside our cabin doors — and the right suitcases. I pulled out my Pastime card and put it to use — it would serve as a combination room key, credit card, and ID badge for the duration of the voyage.

The cabin was brightly decorated in what

I'd begun to recognize as Pastime's signature colors — turquoise and white, with pastel accents. It was small, but not as cramped and claustrophobic as I'd expected. According to the brochure, it was three hundred square feet. Since measurements were not my strong point, I'd had no preconceived notion about whether that was large or small, although I'd assumed it must be a decent size as cruise staterooms went or they wouldn't be bragging. And the sliding glass doors that led out onto our private balcony brought in so much light and air that it didn't feel claustrophobic at all.

Of course, if we ran into rough weather and I had to watch waves crashing against those broad expanses of glass, maybe I'd rethink my approval. But for now, I was pleased. I'd stayed in smaller hotel rooms on land. Only in big, expensive cities like San Francisco or New York, but still — not so bad. In fact, to my astonishment, the room looked exactly as it had in the pictures I'd studied in the brochure and on Pastime's website.

The room Michael and I would occupy had two twin beds shoved together to form an ersatz king bed flanked by tiny bedside tables. Through the connecting door, I could see that the boys' room had the same two beds, but with the bedside tables placed between them. All the rest was exactly what you'd see in any hotel room — a small but efficient bathroom, a desk, a wall-mounted TV, a compact reading chair. The suitcases rather cluttered it up, but it would be fine once we unpacked — especially since only four of the suitcases contained our stuff. Three of the others belonged to Grandfather, who'd filled them with his scientific gear, and the fourth to Mother, who needed more than a measly two suitcases for her cruise wardrobe.

And why not get the unpacking over with now, so we'd be totally settled by the time the ship sailed? I put away our things, stored our four suitcases under the beds, and shoved the other four into a corner where they'd be as much out the way as possible until we could deliver them to their real owners.

I'd done all I could. So, still patting myself on the back for my own efficiency, I locked up and followed yet another arrow sign that pointed toward the Starlight Lounge, in the bow.

At the far end of the corridor I spotted a set of double doors painted midnight blue and spangled with silver stars. Silver glitter stars, I realized as I drew closer and saw the faint sparkling. Presumably the Starlight Lounge.

I paused in the doorway to look around. It was smaller than I'd expected. Of course, the brochure had described it as "cozy," or was it "snug"? Still, the windows running all around three sides of the room kept it from feeling claustrophobic. A uniformed crew member was standing behind the bar running a pair of blenders, one filled with a bright pink concoction and the other with something bright green.

And the lounge was rather crowded. Not a single empty table. I studied the occupants of the dozen or so tables, hoping to see someone I recognized. Surely one of my friends or family members would have ended up here. My cousin Rose Noire might have joined the tea party — requesting green tea and interrogating the waitstaff about whether the cucumber sandwiches were organic — but Dad would almost certainly find some way of weaseling out. My cousin Horace would certainly have volunteered to swab the decks if it would get him out of eating cucumber sandwiches. Grandfather was probably driving Trevor and Caroline crazy as he prepared for this evening's inaugural lecture, but his two-person film and recording crew should be here. And neither of them struck me as Earl Grey swillers.

Wait — was that them over in the corner? The occupants of a table were waving wildly at me.

No — I didn't know any of the three thirty-something men who were trying to get my attention. And after a quick glance, I decided I didn't much want to. Even from across the bar I could tell they were already well on their way to falling-down drunk, and their overfriendly smiles verged on leers.

Just then a small, birdlike fiftyish woman appeared at my elbow. "We're right over there in the corner," she said loudly. She went on in an undertone, "In case you're looking for a place to sit where you don't have to fend off the Three Stooges."

Relieved, I followed her to a table where three other women raised their drinks and welcomed me as if I were a long-lost cousin.

"Thanks for the rescue," I said. "If I'm intruding, just say so, and in a minute or two I'll pretend to remember something I need to rush off and do."

"No need," my rescuer said. "After all, isn't that one of the reasons to come on a cruise? To meet new people?"

"Just not *those* new people." An angular gray-haired woman nodded her head slightly in the direction of the three men.

"Nice new people," my rescuer said. "Sober new people."

"Speak for yourself." The third woman lifted up her martini glass. "I intend to consume quite a few of these over the course of the next week."

"And what's that going to do to your word count?" the first one asked.

"I'm not worrying about word count right now," the martini-drinking woman said. "I'm working on my synopsis."

"I could totally see killing one of those three off." The fourth woman, who hadn't yet spoken, was staring over her old-fashioned glass, studying the three men with narrowed eyes. "I need a new victim."

"Angie means killing one of them off in a book," my birdlike rescuer said. "She's a writer. We're all writers. But Angie's the only mystery writer, which means she's the only one who goes around looking for people to knock off."

"Only on paper," Angie said. "I'm very mild-mannered in real life."

"Yeah, right," the martini drinker said.

"I'm Kate." The birdlike woman pointed to herself. "Tish and I write romance." The gray-haired woman raised her glass, no doubt to indicate that she was Tish. "And

Janet writes fantasy." Janet was the martini drinker.

"Doorstopper fantasies," Janet said. "Big eight-hundred-page sagas. At the moment I'm doing a long-running series about a swordswoman adventuring her way through a pseudo-medieval world. Which means nothing that happens on this journey will ever make it into my books in recognizable form."

"Bookmarks, ladies," Tish said. All four writers reached into their purses and dropped brightly colored bookmarks on the table in front of me. "Our calling cards," she explained. "If anything we say makes you feel the sudden urge to learn more about our books, or better yet, buy them, we want you to be able to."

"Also some of us have our pictures on them, which will help you tell us apart," Angie added.

"I'd better pass out a lot of those suckers," Janet said. "So at least I'll get some good out of this trip."

"Janet's still vexed that we're not taking this cruise on a sailing ship," Kate explained.

"Too expensive, and the schedules weren't convenient." Tish's tone suggested this was a discussion they'd already had a few million times.

"And besides," Kate began. "I — Oh, my God! You won't believe who's here."

We all craned to see where she was looking.

The diva had just walked in.

CHAPTER 3

"Of all the gin joints in all the towns in all the world," Janet muttered.

"Do you know who she is?" I asked.

"Desiree St. Christophe," Kate said. From her expression, I could tell she expected me to recognize the name. "Not a romance reader, I deduce."

"Sorry, no," I said. "I gather if I was I'd recognize the name?"

"Maybe if you had a two-book-a-day romance habit," Tish said.

"And were fond of a particular flavor of romance that not many people write anymore," Kate added.

"Because there's almost no market for it," Janet pointed out.

"The kind with a heroine who's innocent and virginal," Kate said.

"And thick as a plank." Tish rolled her eyes.

"And gets ravished repeatedly by a series

41

of rogues and ne'er-do-wells," Kate continued. "Until one of them finally realizes he's actually in love with her and marries her to produce the obligatory happy ending. Desiree was big back in the seventies and early eighties, when there was more of a market for that kind of book."

"She has made something of a comeback with the new series," Angie said.

"A fluke." Tish waved her hand dismissively.

Desiree was scanning the room, just as I had, and having no more luck finding an empty table. In fact, even less luck — after glancing up when she entered, the Three Stooges had returned to their beer mugs. And my four newfound friends all had expressions that clearly said, "Please, God, don't let her sit here."

Desiree stood for a few more moments, looking around the room with a brittle smile on her face, as if annoyed that no one had noticed her plight and jumped up to offer her their table. My group were all studiously examining the contents of their glasses or carefully selecting just the right bits of pretzel from the bowl of bar chum on the table, so I followed their example. Then Desiree frowned and teetered over to the Three Stooges' table. Either she didn't often wear four- to five-inch heels or the ship was swaying more than I realized.

"Mind if I join you?" she asked the Stooges. She parked herself in the empty chair without waiting for an answer. "There don't seem to be any vacant tables."

"Oh, don't mind us." One of them leaped up. "We were just leaving."

"Yeah, we're about to be late for . . . um . . . ." The second one was following his friend's example.

"Karaoke," the third one exclaimed. "Can't miss the start of the karaoke contest."

They all three hurried out. I pulled out my Pastime brochure. I remembered seeing a photocopied insert that contained the day's schedule. Boarding time, safety drill, cast-off time, dinner service, Grandfather's lecture on the ecosystem of the Baltimore harbor. No karaoke contest.

Desiree didn't look as if she minded the Stooges' departure. She hoisted her purse into one of the now-vacant chairs. At least I assumed the enormous pink woven straw thing was a purse. Maybe she'd forgotten to check one of her suitcases. Then she looked around petulantly for the bartender, whose sense of self-preservation appeared to be highly developed, given the haste with

43

which he raced to her side. They began a lengthy conversation. The writers and I watched in silence.

At least they were watching Desiree and the bartender. I was surreptitiously studying them, matching the writers to the bookmarks.

Kate Trevanian — had fortune blessed her with an elegant name, or was that a pseudonym? She was fifty-something, petite, slightly plump, and definitely birdlike. She moved like a bird, with quick, darting motions, abrupt, yet not ungraceful. I was willing to bet her hair required outside assistance to maintain its medium-brown color, but the result was utterly natural looking. Her bookmark showed a handsome couple in Tudor dress with a modified version of Neuschwanstein in the background. Historical romances, evidently.

Tish, aka Patricia Gregory. She was about the same age as Kate or maybe a little older. Her tall frame was lean, elegant, and languid, rather like a greyhound at rest. Her salt-and-pepper hair was cut short and gave the impression that all she had to do was dunk it in water and run her fingers through it to achieve a carefree, tousled look. I tried not to hate her for this. Her bookmark showed only two sets of legs from the knees down — one male, clad in faded jeans and worn sneakers, the other female, in bright red high heels — and the way the legs were angled suggested that the two were closing in for a kiss. Contemporary romance, no doubt.

Janet and Angie were somewhat younger — late thirties, or possibly early forties. Janet Costello was a little shorter than me and about the same shape — well padded, but far from fat. Angie Weyburn was blond and barely over five feet, and while that probably made her much too short to be a model, she was definitely skinny enough, and had the cheekbones. I decided that if I wanted a relaxed conversation, Janet was the one to pick, but if it came to fending off the Three Stooges — verbally or even physically — I should opt for Angie. Janet's bookmark showed a cover with a woman wearing worn leather armor, holding a reasonably realistic sword, and eyeing something offstage that, from her expression, was about to test both armor and sword. Angie's bookmark showed a blond woman in a black FBI windbreaker holding a black gun two-handed and pointing both it and her steely gaze straight at me.

I looked up to see Angie scowling at Desiree and the bartender with much the same menacing expression.

"What could possibly be taking so long?" She began tapping her empty glass on the table. "I need another drink."

"And I haven't even had one yet," I said. "Maybe she's trying to order something they don't carry."

"It'd have to be something pretty exotic." Janet held up her empty glass. "They had at least a dozen different kinds of gin."

"Probably telling him all the things she's allergic to or disapproves of," Kate said.

"It could be worse," Tish said. "What if Nancy were here and had to watch it all?"

"Hell, yes," Angie muttered. "In that case, we'd have to kill Desiree. It would be justifiable homicide."

Just then the bartender hurried over to our table. His name tag identified him as Aarav Lal, from India.

"So sorry." He had what sounded like a rather posh English accent. "Sailing days are absolutely bonkers! Now what can I get you?"

I had to wait until the writers had ordered refills and I'd selected a frozen margarita before picking up the thread of the conversation.

"Who's Nancy? And why are you glad she's not here?" I was also curious about why they'd have to kill the diva if Nancy had been here, but with any luck they'd tell me anyway.

"Actually, we'd be delighted if Nancy were here," Kate said. "We'd much rather have her than Desiree."

"Not much of a contest," Janet agreed. "We'd rather have Attila the Hun than Desiree."

"Nancy Goreham — she was the fifth member of our writing group," Kate explained. "She always loved cruises."

Her tone — and her use of the past tense — sent a small shiver up my spine.

"Every year we take a trip together — a writing retreat to someplace beautiful and peaceful and above all warm," Kate continued. "We write, and we talk about writing, and we soak up whatever exotic scenery is around us to use in our upcoming books. Nancy always wanted us to do our retreat on a cruise, but we never managed to get it together. So since she's no longer with us, we finally decided to do it. In her memory."

"She'd be pleased," Angie murmured.

"To Nancy!" Janet raised her martini glass. The rest of us followed suit.

"She has a lot of nerve." Tish was staring over her reading glasses at Desiree. "Showing up for Nancy's memorial cruise."

"She probably didn't know." Kate, evidently the peacemaker.

"The hell she didn't." Tish scowled briefly, then looked up at Kate and winced. "Sorry. Not mad at you. But she had to know. It's been all over the discussion lists — how we were going to take the cruise in Nancy's memory, and have a small memorial service the last night out. So many people sent memories for us to share at the service. She knew."

"Maybe she has a vendetta against all of us for some reason," Kate suggested. "And now that she got rid of Nancy, she's going after the rest of us."

"I'd like to see her try," Angie said.

"Sorry — this must be pretty incomprehensible for you." Janet had noticed my puzzled expression. "You see, we blame Desiree for Nancy's death."

CHAPTER 4

I glanced over at Desiree, who seemed oblivious to all the hostile stares aimed at her. Did the writers actually suspect her of killing their friend?

"Nancy committed suicide," Kate said. "And no question, Desiree drove her to it. So as you can see, we're not exactly thrilled to be in the same galaxy with her, much less cooped up together on a relatively small boat."

"Ship," Tish corrected.

"Whatever." Kate rolled her eyes.

"And just look at her," Angie said. "The show-off."

Desiree was sitting sideways in her chair, with her right arm draped languidly across the back. Perhaps it was only an accident that she held her hand so that a shaft of sunlight glinted on the several large, sparkly rings that adorned her fingers. Her left hand toyed with the rim of her drink — something pink, graced with the requisite paper parasol. Her legs were crossed and one of her shoes was half off and dangling rather precariously from the toe. A highly impractical shoe if you asked me, with five-inch heels so thin they were almost invisible. The shoe itself was bright red suede with a lot of fussy scalloped detail around the edges, and the sole was either made of red patent leather or painted to look like it. And she was twitching her foot so madly that if I'd seen it in a movie I'd have suspected she was a secret agent using some sort of footwear-based semaphore signals to convey a message to her handler. This being real life, she was probably aiming either to flirt or to show off her fancy shoes.

"I wish my dad were here," I said aloud. "As a doctor, maybe he could tell us whether all that foot twitching is merely a nervous tic or the early warning sign of some profoundly serious neurological disorder."

This sent the writers into gales of laughter so loud and prolonged that soon nearly everyone on the lounge was staring at us. Even Desiree glanced in our direction briefly before looking away again and resuming the expression of someone bravely though ostentatiously ignoring a bad smell.

"Oh, God, I wish she'd heard that." Tish was wiping away tears.

"It's deliberate, you know," Kate said. "To show off the shoes."

"I suspected as much." I shrugged. "But her efforts are wasted on me. I know even less about fancy shoes than about romance novels."

"Christian Louboutin," Angie explained. "You can tell by the shiny red soles."

"I've heard of Christian Louboutin shoes," I said. "My mother often covets them noisily. I, on the other hand, couldn't tell them from a cheap knockoff."

"And probably aren't the least bit impressed." Janet raised her martini glass in salute. "I like your priorities."

We clinked glasses.

"How —" I began.

But just then the speakers strategically placed throughout the room crackled to life.

"Good afternoon, cruise family!" a perky voice exclaimed. "I'd like to invite you all to make your way to the main dining room for our mandatory safety drill."

"If it's mandatory, she's not really inviting us, is she?" Tish said. "She's telling us."

"Please make your way now to deck one," the voice continued. "There could be a wait for the elevators, so we recommend taking the stairs if possible. Start working off some of that delicious food you'll be eating this week!"

"I'll wait for an elevator, thanks." Janet was holding her martini under her nose and inhaling with a blissful expression on her face.

"Let's finish this round and then head down," Kate said.

"Remember," the perky voice added. "Everyone *must* attend the mandatory safety drill —"

"Or they'd call it the *optional* safety drill,"

Tish muttered. "And the ship cannot cast off until the safety drill is complete."

"Good grief." Janet took a healthy gulp of her martini. "They're escalating to threats already? I suppose we should wrap this up and get a move on. I most definitely do not want to be the last one to walk into the drill."

We weren't the last to arrive. Not by a long shot. My cousin Horace was probably the first one there, other than the crew, but being a Caerphilly County deputy as well as a crime scene investigator, he had an in-grained appreciation for following rules and orders. He also had a peculiar fondness for arriving first at a social event and studying his surroundings — I assumed so if by chance anything untoward happened, he'd have at least a general idea what the crime scene had looked like beforehand.

Michael and the boys had arrived with him, probably because the boys were under the erroneous belief that the safety drill would involve rowing away from the ship in the lifeboats, or at least jumping off the deck in a life jacket. Horace, Michael, Josh, and Jamie were the only other passengers there when the writers and I entered, although we were soon followed by an elderly couple who arrived on matching bright red rolling walkers, looking expectant at the mere idea of the mandatory safety drill, although I feared it might be as much excitement as they could handle for one day.

You'd have thought the crew would be delighted with the early arrivals, but instead they looked almost startled to see us. Obviously passengers who showed up early for the safety drill were a rarity. And it quickly became obvious that nothing would start until everyone was there, and someone would have to entertain the boys for a good long while.

Luckily Michael and Horace were up to the task. They'd helped the boys into a couple of life jackets the crew had brought in for the demonstration, and were pretending that the small stage at the stern end of the room was a life raft. Josh and Jamie took turns jumping off the stage into the dangerous waters represented by the dining room rug, while Michael and Horace, wearing dinner napkins folded over their faces as a sort of rudimentary great white shark costume, circled menacingly and occasionally pounced.

The elderly couple seemed to find this all charming. The crew seemed to find it rather startling. I wondered if perhaps the boys' game was a trifle insensitive to people for whom great white sharks were a genuine professional hazard. Although any resemblance between their game and real sharks was only coincidental — after all, real great whites probably didn't waste time tickling their prey before biting into it.

Satisfied that the boys were happy, I scanned our surroundings, since we'd be spending a lot of time here in the main dining room. It was filled with tables — mostly tables for four or six, with a few two-person tables tucked into corners. All of them had small brass stands in the center with the table number. Was there assigned seating? I didn't remember seeing anything about it in the pages and pages of information they'd sent us. And if there was, would it be a good thing or a bad thing? That might depend on who was assigned nearby. Or was it one of those situations where you chose your own table the first time and were then stuck with it, like in first grade, when thanks to being one of the last kids to arrive at school, I'd had to sit for the whole year between the class bully and the class clown?

"Just take any seat for the safety drill," one of the crew members said, so I settled down with the writers for the time being.

A few more people trickled in, but clearly the mandatory safety drill was pretty low on most passengers' lists of things they wanted to do while on board.

An officer strode in — at least I assumed he was an officer, since his uniform had more gold buttons and braid than those of any of the others in the room — although possibly less than First Officer Martin's. He shook his head at the scanty crowd, and spoke briefly to the crew. One of them went over to the wall, opened a small door, and pulled out a microphone.

"Attention, Pastime family!" The voice that came over the loudspeakers was the same perky one we'd heard before, which was curious, considering that it originated in a diminutive young woman whose fixed smile clearly showed that talking on the loudspeaker made her very nervous. "The mandatory safety drill will begin shortly in the main dining room. Please show up early — you don't want to miss the complimentary cocktails and smoothies!"

"Why don't they just say free?" Angie rolled her eyes. "Wouldn't 'free drinks' pull people in even faster?"

"Because technically the cocktails aren't free," Tish said. "We've already paid for them in those far-from-trivial ticket prices."

"Former English teacher," Kate said to me, pointing at Tish.

"What's with the former?" Tish said. "It's like being a Marine — once an English teacher, always an English teacher."

The latest announcement worked. People began showing up. Including two bartenders: Aarav from the Starlight Lounge and a tall blond woman. They began setting up a small bar along the port side of the room. Although it soon became apparent that the free cocktails would only become available when the safety drill was over.

Mother and Aunt Penelope showed up, still carrying fragile-looking flowered cups and saucers and holding cucumber sandwiches so tiny they'd have been perfect to set the table with if you were having a few Barbie dolls to tea. Caroline arrived, shooing Grandfather and the two photographers before her, and ignoring Grandfather's loud complaints that he already knew how to jump in a blasted lifeboat if he had to.

"You seen Trevor?" Grandfather asked as he passed by my table. "Doesn't answer his damned phone."

"If I see him I'll tell him you were looking for him." I repressed a brief spasm of irritation — at Trevor, for a change, instead of Grandfather. The whole idea of having Grandfather give lectures on board a ship had been Trevor's to start with. He was probably hoping that organizing Grandfather would be a lot easier on board a ship — so many fewer places to get lost in when he was supposed to be somewhere else, for example. Grandfather had immediately seized the idea and run with it, of course. But still — Trevor had started this all. He should be here to do his job.

My cousin Rose Noire arrived waving around a bundle of herbs — no doubt she'd been busy trudging from deck to deck, wafting sage and whatever else, improving the ship's chi as well as she could, given the ban on setting anything on fire. She'd joined the expedition largely because she was concerned about our foolhardy plan to venture into the dreaded Bermuda Triangle and believed that only her protective herbs and charms could protect us from the dire consequences of our foolhardiness. I'd eventually given up reminding her how many cruise ships sailed safely to and from Bermuda every year.

My brother, Rob, and Delaney, his fiancée, were among the last to arrive. Though not actually honeymooners yet, they were certainly acting the part. I didn't expect to see much of them during our voyage.

The room was getting crowded, and it was past the starting time, but evidently a few passengers were still AWOL from the safety drill. And clearly the crew members were getting more and more stressed and annoyed by the situation — although to give them credit, they were doing a decent job of disguising that fact with broad smiles and cheerful apologies to those of us who were waiting.

Finally, about twenty minutes past our scheduled start time, I saw a flood of relief wash over the crew members' faces. Presumably the last passenger had finally entered. I turned, and was not the least bit surprised to see Desiree the Diva entering the dining room, flanked by two male crew members who appeared to be half hustling her along and half holding her up. They plunked her down at a table near the door and one of them hovered right behind her as if he expected her to make a break for it.

"We're finally ready to start the safety drill," the perky-voiced young woman said. "Please turn off your cell phones." Meanwhile one of the other crew members was scanning Desiree's Pastime card and looking as if he'd gladly confiscate it and escort her back ashore while there was still time. Although he was still doggedly smiling at her.

The safety drill itself took all of ten minutes. A video showed happy passengers frolicking on a ship's deck. They all looked up with implausibly unpanicked expressions when a disembodied voice — presumably from the vessel's loudspeaker system — told them to collect their life jackets from their staterooms and report to their muster stations. Cut to a remarkably tidy stateroom so we could watch a cheerful young woman open her closet door and react with astonishment and delight to find a life jacket waiting therein. Cut to a close-up of the young woman very slowly putting on her life jacket with exaggerated care while another disembodied voice explained how to do it. Just in case the video wasn't clear enough, half a dozen crew members scattered at intervals throughout the audience put on a live demonstration — though none of them appeared to be anywhere near as enthralled with the process as the young woman on the video. The video then cut to a group of life jacket-clad passengers smiling like Stepford Wives as they waited in a line — presumably to board a lifeboat.

When the video ended a man stepped onto the stage — a tall, burly, distinguished-looking man with a lugubrious horsey face, a neat salt-and-pepper beard, a ruddy nose, and so much gold braid on his white uniform that I deduced he was either the ship's captain or a visiting admiral imported to add zest to the otherwise uninspiring safety drill.

"Good afternoon, ladies and gentlemen," he said. "I'm Captain Detweiler, your skipper for this cruise. I'd like to welcome you aboard the *Pastime Wanderer,* and wish you a very enjoyable voyage. Thank you."

He nodded pleasantly at us and strode down from the stage and toward the exit. He didn't particularly look as if he was hurrying, but his long stride covered ground, and he was out the door before anyone thought of any questions to ask him. I made a mental note not to expect an enthralling conversation if I were invited to sit at the captain's table for dinner some evening. Assuming they even still did that.

Another officer had hopped onto the little stage. The first officer.

"Good afternoon, Pastime family," he began. "I'm First Officer Martin. I'd like to echo Captain Detweiler's greetings and assure you that if there's anything I or anyone else in the crew can do for you, you have only to ask. And now if you'll just keep your seats, the crew will be taking your orders for those complimentary cocktails or smoothies!"

I bade the writers a temporary farewell and hopped over to the table where Michael and the boys were saving me a seat. Josh and Jamie were deep in a discussion of whether to repeat their favorite frozen concoctions or ask for something even more exotic.

"This is going to take forever," I heard Mother say at the next table. "They could at least have let us bring our teapot with us."

The half-dozen crew members in the room began circulating from table to table, taking drink orders.

"I wonder if there's any particular reason they want to keep us all here in the main dining room for what I suspect will be an unreasonably long time," I said to Michael.

"Maybe they're loading something they don't want us to see." His voice was slightly muffled by the dinner napkin he was still wearing over his face to maintain his shark disguise.

"Such as?"

"I don't know. Live whooping cranes and dodos and whatever other endangered species they intend to roast for our dinner. Kilos of cocaine. Caches of weapons for the Bermudian separatist movement."

"I think the cocaine gets smuggled into the U.S., not out, and is there even a Bermudian separatist movement?"

"Beats me," he said. "Probably they're just sick and tired of people trying to run back on land to buy something they forgot to pack. Lot of that going on when we were boarding. And the crew were all very nice about it, but it had to have been annoying."

As the crew members took drink orders, First Officer Martin circulated from table to table, schmoozing with the passengers. He was perfectly pleasant, but I decided a little of him went a long way. He was so . . . "perky" wasn't quite the word. Doggedly cheerful, perhaps. And yes, a little put-upon, as if once again he was stuck doing something that he thought should be someone else's job. I found myself hoping there wasn't such a thing as getting invited to the first officer's table at dinner. It would probably be a lot like dining with Trevor. Maybe the captain's table wouldn't be that bad — I could always bring a book.

Taking the drink orders went fairly quickly, and the half-dozen crew members who'd been doing it disappeared, probably to take care of urgent pre-sailing tasks that were easier to complete without passengers underfoot. And clearly it was going to take a while for the bartenders — there were three of them now — to make all the drinks. To distract us from watching their frantic efforts, the first officer hopped back up on stage. As he waited for us to quiet down, his smile looked strained, and I got the distinct impression that making speeches to the passengers was his least favorite part of his job. I began feeling just a little sorry for him.

"And now if you'll look on your table, you'll find a stack of game cards. We're going to play cruise ship bingo! Every square on your card has a short description like 'lives on the West Coast' or 'plays golf.' All the cards are slightly different. Your mission is to go around and meet your fellow passengers! Find out which ones fit the descriptions in the squares on your card, and get them to sign it. The first person to fill out his or her entire card wins a surprise gift!"

The room was instantly filled with murmurs that almost drowned out the sound of half a dozen blenders buzzing furiously. I felt a sudden twinge of guilt about ordering another frozen margarita — from the look of it, every single person in the room must have ordered a frozen concoction of some sort. Well, I had nothing else to do. I reminded myself to tip the long-suffering bartenders generously — if there wasn't a way to do that now, I could certainly find them later in the trip — and settled back in my seat to study my fellow passengers. And the few visible crew members. One of them was hovering over Desiree, and I noticed that she was already halfway through another bright pink drink with a parasol in it. As I was studying her with disapproving eyes, First Officer Martin, who'd been going from table to table exchanging pleasantries with the passengers, arrived at hers. I couldn't hear what he said to her, but I could have guessed from her thunderous reply.

"No, everything isn't satisfactory, dammit!" No one would ever accuse Desiree of not speaking up. I'd met opera singers who couldn't produce that much volume. "I had to wait forever for my last drink! And I don't want the same thing to happen with my next, so you tell them to bring it now."

The first officer said something inaudible — probably a reminder that there were other passengers who hadn't even received their first drink.

"Well, that's their problem, not mine." Desiree chugged the rest of her pink concoction and slammed her empty glass down on the table so hard that the paper parasol bounced out. Martin flinched as if she'd struck him.

While everyone else — me included — was merely watching openmouthed, Mother took action. She sailed over to the table.

"I just wanted to tell you how lovely your shoes look." Neither her voice nor her face revealed what I knew must be a struggle not to add "What a pity they're wasted on someone like you."

"They're Christian Louboutin," Desiree said. She lifted one leg rather suddenly, nearly skewering Mother, who had bent over to admire the red suede heels at closer range.

"Yes — the Pijonina model, isn't it?" Mother retreated ever so slightly — just out of kicking range. "I can never decide whether I like that or the Victorina Flame better."

They chatted briefly — although it was less of a conversation than a contest to see which of them could drop the most names of expensive shoe designers. After Manolo Blahnik, Jimmy Choo, and Ferragamo they lost me. Mother kept it up until Aarav, the bartender, carefully slid a frozen drink into place at Desiree's elbow. Then Mother gracefully extracted herself from the conversation. She stopped at our table on the way back to her own.

"What a . . . trying woman." She gave a sidelong glance at the boys, and I suspected she'd have used a less polite word in the absence of her grandsons.

"Did you find out if she wears your size?" I asked. "Because there's no use getting me to mug her for the shoes if they're the wrong size."

"Far too big for me, dear, but thank you anyway." And with a deceptively benign smile she returned to her own table.

"Mom! Aren't you playing?" Jamie looked puzzled.

"Why don't you fill my game card for me," I suggested. "And since you're doing all the work, you can keep the prize if you win."

"And here, Josh — you can do mine." Mi-

66

chael handed over his card.

The boys dashed off, overjoyed at having two chances to win the prize, and began showing their cards to Mother, Aunt Penelope, and the others at their table.

"Ah — there you are!" Grandfather had appeared at our table. "Trevor must have slipped out without waiting for a drink. Damn the man — Michael, any chance you could help Guillermo and Wim with something?"

Guillermo and Wim were Grandfather's cameramen and general tech experts.

"Sure. If Meg doesn't mind keeping an eye on the boys."

"No problem," I said. "But aren't any of you staying for the complimentary cocktail?"

"Hmph." Grandfather strode out as if mere cocktails were beneath his notice, with Guillermo in close pursuit.

"Caroline is going to bring them when they're ready," Wim said. "She can bring Michael's, too."

"Suits me," Michael said, and he and Wim strode out together.

Dad, who had been trailing after Grandfather, stayed behind briefly.

"If you see Trevor, tell him we've got it covered," he said. "And he should stay put, and use the anti-seasickness medicine I prescribed, and not worry about your grandfather until he's sure he's feeling all right."

"Oh, is that it?" I felt guilty over my harsh thoughts about Trevor. "Is he actually feeling seasick already? With the ship still docked?" That didn't bode well.

CHAPTER 5

"To tell the truth, I think what Trevor's feeling is anxiety over the possibility that he *might* get seasick," Dad explained. "Since he was starting to feel it while we were still on the pier."

"Or maybe just all-purpose anxiety," I suggested. "Getting Grandfather safely on board is no picnic."

"Also possible." Dad sighed. "But whatever the reason, he was definitely unwell. So I gave him a transdermal scopolamine patch and a couple of one-milligram Valium tablets. If he really is starting to feel any seasickness, the patch gives the best chance of stopping that, and if he's only stressing out, the Valium should help without making him so relaxed that he can't help your grandfather — one milligram's the pediatric dose."

"Good," I said. "A mildly Valiumed Trevor might be a lot less annoying to have around anyway."

"Unfortunately, I think Rose Noire overheard us," Dad added. "I think she's planning to take him some of her herbal tea."

"Yikes." Rose Noire's herbal teas were often effective, but unfortunately they almost always tasted vile. "Did you warn him?"

"I did, and if she drops by with tea he'll pretend to be napping. Please don't tell her that."

"Of course not."

"Well, I should go help your grandfather." He headed for the door, although I noticed that he was stopping to talk to people along the way. I hoped his presence wasn't mission-critical for whatever Grandfather was doing,

I glanced around. The boys had moved on to the writers' table. The first officer, still making the rounds of all the tables, was already there chatting with them. As I watched, a crew member delivered a tray of drinks. Kate and Tish grabbed their glasses and fled. First Officer Martin said something — probably another reminder to let him know if there was anything they needed — and moved on. The poor man looked exhausted — clearly socializing with several hundred strangers was grueling for him.

His departure left only tiny blond Angie, the mystery writer, and Janet, the fantasy writer. Janet had taken off a sweater, revealing that she was wearing a National Park Service t-shirt. A clue to her day job perhaps?

Mother and Aunt Penelope were discussing the ship's decor — and how they'd have improved it if given a chance. Sooner or later Mother would try to drag me into the debate over whether chintz would have been a better choice for covering the dining room chairs.

I decided to join the two remaining writers. They weren't likely to be discussing the carpet or the light fixtures — or if they were, at least they'd be figuring out how to describe them in a scene, or maybe how to kill someone with them, not what to replace them with. So I promised Mother I'd be back soon and headed for the writers' table.

"It's impossible," Angie was saying as I came near.

"For heaven's sake, snap out of it," Janet said. Now that I was closer, I could see that her t-shirt was from the Mordor National Park. So, not a day job. At least I hoped not.

"I should have stayed home to work on that synopsis," Angie said. "I can't do this."

"You'll figure it out. You always do. You've never yet missed a deadline."

"There's always a first time."

I had paused a couple of feet from their table, realizing I'd barged in on a conversation they might not want me to join. Angie glanced up, forced a slight smile, and gestured to an empty chair.

"Have a seat," she said. "Don't mind me." Turning back to Janet, she added, "I'm just going to pace the deck for a while and try to think of a way out."

A way out? Of what — the ship? Maybe Trevor wasn't the only passenger overcome with anxiety.

"Good grief." Janet shook her head, stood up, and looked at me. "See if you can cheer her up."

Janet headed for the exit. I sat. Angie made no move to go out to the deck for pacing. Maybe she was planning on finishing her drink first. Or just staring into it for a couple more hours.

"A way out of what?" I asked after a brief pause.

"Plot problems. I've created the perfect murder."

"Congratulations."

"It's not a good thing. I've painted myself into a corner. I have no idea how my detective is going to solve the case. I did it to myself with the last book, and the only way I could figure out to end it was to have my bad guy confess. Completely lame — I can't do that again."

"I'm sorry," I said.

"Normally I love our writers' retreats," she went on. "But normally we go in the winter, and I'm already working on the draft. We moved it up to fall to get more affordable rates, and it's turned out to be the worst possible time for me. I have to finish my synopsis this week so I can stay on schedule. I thought I could just hide in my cabin and research online while we were here, but when I tried it just now the ship's Wi-Fi was so slow it might as well not exist. I really hope that's just some glitch from being in port. But besides, the Internet is a poor substitute for what I really need — a doctor or a CSI, someone I can talk to for however long it takes to sort this out. It's hopeless."

Hmm.

"Hang on," I said. "I'll be back in a minute."

She nodded and went back to staring into her glass.

I'd already noticed that in spite of his enthusiasm for helping Grandfather, Dad had not yet made it out of the dining room. I crossed the room to where he was having a lively conversation with a couple of our fellow passengers. Although as I got closer I realized that the couple didn't seem to be enjoying the conversation nearly as much as Dad. When I came within earshot I realized why.

"Now the symptoms of Ebola are completely different," he was saying. "For a start —"

"Dad!" I grabbed his elbow and turned to the ashen-faced couple he was talking to. "Sorry to interrupt."

"Oh, that's fine," the wife murmured.

"Please don't feel you have to apologize," the husband said.

"I was just telling the Sandburgs about the differences between Ebola and dengue." Dad was beaming with enthusiasm. "Did you know —"

"Fascinating, I'm sure," I said. "But you're needed elsewhere — if that's okay with you," I added, turning to the Sandburgs.

"Don't worry about us," Mr. Sandburg said. They had both begun gently backing away.

"A medical emergency?" Dad perked up, as he always did at the prospect.

"No, but someone has need of your medical knowledge." I pulled him away from the Sandburgs and began to guide him across the room toward Angie.

"Amazing how little the average person knows about the more fascinating tropical diseases," Dad was saying. "Especially since, thanks to the explosion in travel, we're much more likely to encounter them these days. And —"

"Angie," I said, tugging Dad into place beside her table. "This is my dad, Dr. James Langslow."

Angie's frown eased a little.

"An M.D.?" She looked cheerful at the possibility.

"Not only an M.D., but a medical examiner," I said.

"How wonderful!" Angie exclaimed. "Do sit down."

"Angie writes mysteries," I added, turning to Dad.

"Angie Weyburn," Angie said, holding out her hand.

"Mysteries? Marvelous!" Dad shook her hand with genuine delight. "I'm a total mystery addict — but, um . . . what was your name again?"

"I write as A. J. Weyburn," she said. "Since —"

Blood Factor! Dad exclaimed, so loudly

75

that at least a dozen people nearby looked up, and one poor woman spilled her drink. "That was excellent! And *Dire Warning!*"

Angie was beaming.

"Thank you!" she said.

"I admit, I do have a bone to pick with you about the autopsy scene in *Deadly Reaction,*" Dad said. "When you had the medical examiner talking about petechial hemorrhaging —"

"Oh, God, I know," Angie said. "I didn't find out I got it wrong until after it was in print — the doctor who helps me with my research is a podiatrist, so he hasn't actually seen all that many autopsies."

"Dad can help with that," I said. "Nothing he likes better than talking about autopsies. Dad, Angie has figured out a particularly ingenious murder — and she needs help figuring out how her sleuth can solve it. Do you think —"

"What fun!" Dad sat down on the chair next to Angie. "Tell me all about it. And if I'm stumped, of course, we can call in Horace."

"Horace?" Angie echoed — clearly wondering what other treasures were in store for her.

"My cousin Horace Hollingsworth, who's a trained CSI," I said.

76

"He's here, too?" Angie asked. "On the cruise?"

"He's probably on deck five playing miniature golf." And, I suspected, wouldn't mind taking a break from that before long.

"Does he know anything about DNA?" Angie looked on the verge of fainting with delight.

"He's crazy about DNA!" Dad was almost bouncing in his seat. "And blood spatter — those are his favorites."

"This is amazing," Angie said. "Because I've got this scene —"

I left them to it. I strolled away a few paces and pulled out my phone. I texted Horace, saying, "Can you drop by the main dining room when you finish your next game? Dad could use your help with something." I caught Mother's eye and nodded in the direction of the boys, who were having their Pastime bingo cards signed by the still anxious-looking Sandburgs. Mother nodded back to say that she'd keep her eye on them. So I picked up my margarita, made my way back to the boarding lobby, and stood in front of the elevator. I pushed the up button. Which, since we were on deck one, was the only button available.

Of course, I hadn't yet decided where I was going. I suspected I'd have plenty of time to decide. I'd already noticed that the elevator — just the one, according to the map — was molasses slow. Impatient as I was, I'd probably end up racing up and down the stairs more often than not.

At the moment, though, I could use the time to plan my course.

As I was thinking, and watching for the elevator, I noticed something. Since this was deck one, the stairs ended here — at least I'd thought they did. There was a door under the stairway that I'd assumed was a closet built into the vacant space under the stairs. But now the door was open, revealing steps going down.

Down? Weren't we already on deck one?

I strolled over and peered downward. A half flight of steps went down to a landing, and then more stairs continued out of sight.

Unlike the stairs going up, these were narrow and utilitarian. I didn't need the CREW ONLY sign over the door to tell me passengers weren't welcome here.

"Sorry, but that's off-limits to passengers." The first officer had appeared behind me.

"I can read," I said. "I found the door hanging open. You might want to check to make sure none of the passengers have wandered down there by mistake."

"Um . . . thanks." His smile was a little

frayed, as if he was overdue for a break. He paused, obviously torn between going down to check for straying passengers and continuing on to wherever he'd been going when he spotted me. While he was hovering by the doorway, I decided to ask a question.

"By the way, just what do you call it down there?"

"I beg your pardon?" He looked puzzled — almost startled.

"Well, we're on deck one, right?"

He nodded.

"So what do you call that deck?" I pointed at the stairs leading downward.

"Deck zero, of course."

He finally made up his mind and went down the stairway toward deck zero, closing the door firmly behind him.

Leaving me with another question: Was there anything below deck zero? Other than the ship's hull and a whole lot of water, of course.

I made a mental note to ask if I ever ran into a crew member with more time to answer. Or maybe I could ask the first officer again, when he was looking less harried.

Just then the elevator arrived, which meant I had to decide where I was going.

The rest of my family were all happily occupied. Now would be a wonderful time to find a deck chair and read or just sit and think. And if I were out on deck, I could keep an eye out for when we set sail, which was supposed to happen in an hour or so. I could notify Michael and the boys when the time came, so they wouldn't miss it.

Having settled on my destination I punched the button for deck six, the top and smallest of the decks. It covered only about half the length of the ship, and contained nothing but two large awnings to provide shade in the daytime, a scattering of deck chairs, in both sun and shade, and — better still — a line of recliners. A peaceful place to watch and listen to the waves — especially with so many of the passengers down in the main dining room enjoying the complimentary beverages and playing cruise bingo

I stepped out onto deck six and took a deep breath. Heavenly. And almost deserted. At the aft end of the deck, a young couple I'd already pegged as honeymooners were lying in side-by-side recliners, holding hands. In the forward end, an older couple stood, taking turns inspecting the shore through a pair of binoculars.

I strolled over to the side of the ship and stood gazing out over the water.

"Amazing, isn't it," a voice said behind me.

I turned to see Janet lounging on one of the nearby recliners, martini in hand.

"Amazing is right," I said. "Great way to start the journey. We'll have a front row seat to watch the ship leaving the harbor."

"Which I'm hoping to do." She sighed. "I should be down there talking Angie through her anxiety. And I'll work on that — tomorrow. Maybe even later tonight. Right now I just want some peace and quiet."

"Don't worry about Angie," I said. "I introduced her to my dad, the medical examiner, and my cousin, the CSI. I left them trying to sort out her insoluble plot problem."

"Are you serious?"

I nodded.

"You're a lifesaver." She raised her glass in salute. I took this as an invitation to take the adjoining recliner.

"I was planning to do nothing at all until it was time to watch our ship leave the harbor," she said. "Now I can do it with a clear conscience."

I nodded, settled back, and sipped my margarita. We were on the left — correction, port — side, looking out over the busy Baltimore harbor. From below we could hear, faintly, shouts and thuds that probably indicated that some last supplies were being loaded onto the *Wanderer*. The harbor was full of vessels, everything from relatively tiny tugboats and modest Coast Guard cutters to huge cargo ships and tankers. I even spotted another cruise ship, this one a Carnival ship that dwarfed the *Wanderer*.

Watching everyone else working hard was strangely relaxing.

We sat in peaceful silence for a few minutes. Then curiosity overcame me.

"You can tell me to mind my own business if you'd like," I said. "But we're all going to be shipmates for the next week, and I'd like to avoid putting my foot in my mouth when I talk to you and your friends. Exactly what happened with your friend Nancy and Desiree the Diva?"

CHAPTER 6

"A fair question." She took another sip of her martini, leaned back in her recliner, and frowned slightly, as if trying to decide where to begin.

"Nancy was a very good writer," she said finally. "Versatile, too. She could write anything from Regencies to erotic paranormal romantic suspense — who knew that was a thing? But for all her talent, she never really had a very successful career. She wasn't good at asserting herself. Sticking up for herself."

Not, I suspected, a problem Desiree shared.

"And she had bad luck," Janet went on. "Once, she sold a book to an editor who loved it and was pushing to get a lot of promotion and marketing behind it. Then three weeks later the editor got hit by a car and was out on medical leave for months and months, and the book got reassigned to an editor who hated everything Nancy wrote. Made her rewrite it five or six times and finally rejected it. Things like that kept happening to Nancy. And probably as a result, she developed a classic case of writer's block. Lasted for . . . oh, six or seven years. We were all trying to encourage her, but it was as if she couldn't face ever showing her work to an editor again. Which was kind of a big problem, because after her divorce she was drowning in debt, and writing was the only thing she really knew how to do. She only just barely managed to keep her head above water by doing a lot of thankless freelance writing projects that ate up most of the time she wanted to spend on her fiction. But she finally had a breakthrough and finished a fabulous new manuscript, and her agent was getting offers from two or three different publishers — good offers, for serious money. Then it all fell apart." She fell silent and took another swallow of her drink.

"Fell apart how?" I asked.

"I'm not even sure I understand how it happened," Janet said. "But apparently Desiree accused Nancy of plagiarism — claimed she'd actually written the manuscript Nancy was trying to sell. Somehow the publishers all believed her. They withdrew their offers. Her agent dropped her. I guess she didn't want to go on. She killed herself." Janet just stared out over the waves for a while.

"This was recently?" I asked.

"Five months ago. Still pretty raw for all her friends."

I nodded. I wanted to ask how she'd killed herself, and how soon after the editor rejected her book, and whether she'd been going through any other personal difficulties at the time. And — apparently Dad had rubbed off on me — whether they were sure it was suicide. But I suppressed the questions. Not really any of my business, and what difference did it make anyway? They'd lost their friend. So I waited for Janet to break the silence.

"I'm not paranoid enough to think Desiree's after any of us," Janet said finally. "But do I think she took this cruise on purpose? Yes. Hell yes."

"But why? I mean, I can see why you'd dislike her, but not why she'd have it in for you. Does she have some kind of a grudge against your group?"

"She might. Kate and Tish haven't exactly made it a secret that they blame her for hounding Nancy to her death. And the romance writers' community is pretty close-knit. Everyone knows how they feel."

"Do you have any idea how Desiree convinced people that Nancy plagiarized her?" I asked.

"In other words, did Nancy really do it?"

"I wasn't thinking that."

"Why not?" Janet shook her head. "I've been thinking it. Not that it makes any sense that she would. She was a good writer — hell, she was a Rita winner once, and a finalist another time or two. That's kind of like the Oscars for romance writers. She was a damned fine writer, and Desiree was a hack. Nancy was depressed about being dropped, and depressed about her writer's block, and depressed because her husband dumped her once the kids went to college — which was nine years ago, but she was still depressed, probably because she was still in the resulting horrible financial situation. But I can't imagine her plagiarizing someone." She laughed hollowly. "Then again, I couldn't imagine her killing herself, either, and that definitely happened."

"So what's the plan?"

"Plan?" She looked startled. "Plan for what?"

"Coping with Desiree. Because no matter how much the crew may already want to put her back ashore, I think we're stuck with her."

"I don't know." She shrugged. "Not sure we really need a plan. Me, I just plan to pretend she's invisible."

"Sounds good to me," I said. "The best plans are always the simplest."

She nodded. Then she leaned back in her recliner and closed her eyes. I did the same.

I hoped she was able to forget Desiree and relax. And I felt slightly guilty that I was feeling so cheerful when clearly Desiree was blighting my newfound friends' enjoyment. I hoped they'd find a way to put her out of their minds and relax, as I was hoping to do once the trip started. I took some more of the relaxing deep breaths Rose Noire was so keen on, and they worked a lot better than they had on the dock. Getting everyone ready for the trip had been surprisingly hectic. But now we were safely aboard. Let the relaxation begin!

After about half an hour of mostly silent enjoyment of the harbor scenery, Janet got a text and went off to join her writer friends. Eventually Michael and the boys joined me in time to watch the ship cast off and leave the harbor. Apparently Josh and Jamie were under the impression that we were sailing out of New York's harbor, and were disappointed that Baltimore did not also boast a Statue of Liberty. But the Chesapeake Bay had plenty of interesting sights to amuse them — especially after Grandfather arrived, bringing several small telescopes for them to scan the shoreline with. The first two hours of our trip flew past.

"It's almost time for dinner," I said. "Although I'm not sure the boys will want to be dragged away from all this."

"And I suspect once we get out in the ocean there won't be nearly as much to see," Michael said. "Why don't you go down and get us a place? If the boys don't want to leave their telescopes, you can see if there's any way to get their dinners to go."

"Will do."

So I went down to the dining room by myself and looked around for a promising table.

I passed by the one where Dad and Horace were deep in discussion with Angie.

"They might look all the same at first," Horace was saying. "But the more you look, the more the differences jump out at you. Watch this."

He dipped his fingers into his glass of tomato juice and flicked some of the red liquid on the tablecloth.

"Notice the slightly oval shape. But if I

88

simply let the drops fall . . ."

He dipped his fingers again and held his hand over another clean area of the tablecloth.

"I see," Angie said. "But what if you see both?"

I left them to it.

Desiree the Diva was sitting by herself at a table for four, waggling her designer shoes at the world and glaring at anyone who even glanced hopefully at the empty chairs beside her. Grandfather, Caroline, and the photographers were eating at a table for six — I could have joined them, but I suspected they would be deep in plans for this evening's lecture.

"Join me, if you like." Janet waved to me from a nearby table. "I've got plenty of room."

"Room enough for four? My husband and twin sons might be joining me, if we can tear them away from the top deck."

"Plenty of room — they've all deserted me. Angie's happy as a clam, getting her plot problems solved. Kate and Tish got salads to go and went off with some ditzy but charming hippie lady to do yoga on the top deck."

"That would be my cousin Rose Noire," I said.

"Oops — sorry about the ditzy part."

"It's accurate," I said. "Her yoga classes are excellent, though. Just don't let her force you to drink any herbal tea."

"I'll keep that in mind."

"And I'm relieved she's only doing yoga," I said. "That's less likely to get her in trouble than holding a smudging ceremony to protect the ship. I have a feeling Pastime takes a dim view of passengers wandering around waving bundles of burning herbs."

"I have a feeling that might also be on the agenda," Janet said. "With Kate and Tish aiding and abetting her. For research purposes, of course. If your cousin's so anxious about sailing through the Bermuda Triangle, why in the world is she taking this cruise in the first place?"

"To save us poor skeptics from ourselves, I suppose." I couldn't quite suppress a sigh. "I'll say this much for her — she does quite a lot of smudging, and she almost never sets anything on fire."

"Well, that's a relief. Damn, but I'm envious. Of Angie, that is." She nodded her head toward the table at which Dad, Horace, and Angie were all three industriously dripping and flicking tomato juice at the tablecloth.

"I'm sure Dad and Horace would be happy to help you," I said. "Angie can't possibly keep them busy every minute of the trip."

"Thanks, but I've no need of modern medicine or forensics right now," she said. "What I really need to do is figure out how Rafaella — that's my series heroine — can plausibly fight off two pirates armed with cutlasses. I hate choreographing fight scenes — especially the sword fights. If I'd known how hard it was, I'd have made her a wizard. She could just wave her arms around dramatically, shout a little gibberish, and the pirates' swords would fly out of their hands."

"You're in luck," I said. "I can probably help you with your fight scene."

"Don't tell me you know how to fight with swords."

"Only a little," I said. "I mostly make them."

"You're a swordsmith?" She seemed to like the idea.

"A blacksmith," I said. "I've made swords, but there's really not much of a market for them unless you hit the Renaissance Faire and fantasy convention circuit, and I prefer actually seeing my family now and then. But my husband is pretty expert at sword fighting — he's a drama professor, and occasionally teaches a course in stage combat. I'll ask him if he can help."

"That would be awesome. And — oh, my God! You'll never guess who just walked in."

I turned to see who she was pointing at. I spotted Michael and the boys, and waved so they'd see our table. But I had no idea who Janet was gaping at.

"Who?" I asked.

"Don't laugh, but did you ever watch a TV show called *Porfiria, Queen of the Jungle*? A totally cheesy show, but a lot of fun, and the actor who played the conniving wizard Mephisto was incredible. I actually modeled one of my main characters after him. The guy who just walked in is either the actor who played Mephisto or a dead ringer."

I was having a hard time following her instructions not to laugh. Since it had been at least a decade since *Porfiria, Queen of the Jungle* had stopped filming, Michael no longer had to worry all that much about being recognized as Mephisto — and the fans who did recognize him tended to be grown-ups feeling nostalgic about their teenage obsessions. Which was fine by Michael — he'd happily settled into the quieter life of teaching drama at Caerphilly College.

"Oh, my God, he's coming this way." Janet's jaw dropped and she sat still, staring as Michael and the boys picked their way through the tables and joined us.

"Janet, this is my husband, Michael Waterston," I said. "And these are our sons — Josh and Jamie. Guys, this is Ms. Janet Costello. She writes books."

The boys were in a good mood and did us proud. Jamie waved cheerfully at Janet before sitting down. Josh gave a courtly bow before taking his seat.

"How do you do," Michael said. "You must be one of the writers Meg told me about."

Since Janet still seemed incapable of speech, I chimed in.

"Janet mentioned that she needs to choreograph a sword fight for the book she's writing, and I suggested that maybe we could help her."

"Great idea." Michael turned to the boys. "Hey, guys, want to show your mom's friend some sword fighting?"

"Awesome," Jamie said.

"I bet we don't get to use real swords, though, right?" Josh added.

"I doubt if there are any real swords on the ship," Michael said. "But we'll figure out something to use by tomorrow."

"You have the most amazing family," was the first thing Janet said when she found

93

her voice again.

We were still eating — and discussing swords — when Grandfather and his crew finished their meal and began setting up for the evening's lecture. Since quite a few people had come in late to dinner, thanks to staying on deck to watch our ship sail down the Chesapeake Bay, it looked as if many of them would still be eating when Grandfather started. Which shouldn't be a problem — after all, some of the other passengers might have come specifically because Grandfather was lecturing on board, and presumably if the rest hadn't actually sought out a cruise with an educational and environmental theme, they at least knew it would be happening around them.

Grandfather looked a little irritated. And he kept taking out his phone, calling someone, and then putting the phone away, looking even more irritated.

"I should go over and help," Michael said. "I assume Trevor must be still under the weather."

Kate and Tish were back. They had grabbed a table near the front and were looking attentive. Janet and I joined them

"Avid bird-watchers, I assume?" I asked.

For some reason, this sent Kate and Janet into gales of laughter.

"Kate and Janet are moderately enthusiastic bird-watchers," Tish said. "I just want to observe Dr. Blake in action."

"She's thinking of modeling one of her heroes after him," Kate explained.

"For a romance? Isn't he a little . . . um . . . long in the tooth?" I wondered if they'd gotten close enough to realize that Grandfather was in his nineties.

"Well, I was planning on making my character a little younger," Tish said. "But I want him to have Dr. Blake's irascible charm, and his stubborn determination to save the environment. And keep in mind that some of my books feature more mature heroes and heroines. There's an audience out there for books that show that romance isn't dead just because you've turned forty."

"Well, I can see that," I said. "Of course, it's been over half a century since Grandfather turned forty, so —"

"Grandfather?" Tish's eyes bugged. "Dr. Blake is your grandfather?"

"Didn't I tell you she had the most amazing family?" Janet said.

"I can introduce you after the presentation," I said. "Or just go up and introduce yourself if I fade early. And don't worry if he seems a little gruff at first — I'm sure he'll love the idea of having a literary character based on him.'

"Fabulous," Tish said, in the tone the boys tended to use while uttering their favorite adjective of "awesome."

I excused myself so I could find a place in the back. If the events of the day overcame me and I started yawning, at least Grandfather would be less likely to notice.

"Ladies and gentlemen," a crew member announced. "May I present our speaker, Dr. J. Montgomery Blake."

CHAPTER 7

Grandfather looked slightly annoyed — probably because he was used to being introduced by people who made a big deal about all his credentials and awards. He frowned as the crew member hurried away and disappeared into the kitchen. Then, thank goodness, he shook it off and began.

At first I almost panicked when I thought that in spite of all my efforts he'd managed to smuggle a stuffed gull on board. I was relieved when I figured out that it was actually a very lifelike statue of a gull, made of plastic or fiberglass or something. Not flesh and blood, anyway, and so not likely to give either the ship's crew or the Bermudian authorities a conniption fit. I breathed a sigh of relief and focused on his presentation.

His first PowerPoint slide read simply: THE SEAGULL.

"What's wrong with this slide?" he asked.

I considered suggesting "the fact that it's

completely boring," but I decided to let the rest of the audience have their chance to answer.

Not that anyone particularly wanted to. After what seemed like an eternity, but was probably only fifteen or twenty seconds, Grandfather nodded to Caroline, who was running the laptop with his presentation on it, and she clicked onto the next slide. Which showed the letters *S, E,* and *A* crossed out, so the slide now read: THE GULL.

"They're not *sea* gulls," Grandfather said. "Just gulls. Quite a lot of gull species live near the water — although not just the ocean. The Great Lakes boast quite a few species. And there are many species that live completely landlocked lives. Next slide."

The screen now showed a classic picture of a gull, with a white head, neck, and belly; gray wings; and a black-and-white tail. He was looking nobly off into the distance.

"So what's this?" Grandfather asked.

"A gull," called a couple of audience members.

"Very good. Specifically a ring-billed gull. *Larus delawarensis.* Next."

At first glance, the next slide seemed to show the same gull or possibly his brother, in a slightly different stance. Instead of looking nobly off into the distance, he appeared to be staring at the photographer with annoyance.

"What's this?"

"A gull!" At least half of the audience joined in this time.

"Good. A common gull. *Larus canus.* And next."

This bird looked as if one of the first two white gulls had slipped a black hood over its head.

"A gull?" About the same number of audience members, but sounding less certain.

"Yes. Very good. A laughing gull. *Leucophaeus atricilla.* And this?"

The fourth bird didn't have a full black hood like the third — more of a jaunty black cap, actually, and the rest of him was mostly gray and white. I had a feeling if I could see any of them side by side I'd see other, more subtle differences.

The audience had been well trained by now.

"A gull!" they shouted with great confidence and enthusiasm.

"Nope. This one's a tern. The common tern, *Sterna hirundo.*"

Grandfather looked very smug, and luckily the audience took it with good humor. Most of the audience. Two of the Three

Stooges, who'd been sitting near the back, got up and left, rather noisily. The third ordered another beer, slumped back in his seat, and began snoring. Desiree was frowning and looking at the bejeweled watch on her wrist. I predicted she'd be the next to flee.

"They all look so alike," someone called out. "How can you possibly tell them apart?"

"Very good! That's your first important lesson on gulls. Or to be more precise, gulls, terns, kittiwakes, noddies, skimmers, and to some extent, petrels. There are a whole lot of them, and they're really hard to tell apart. Gull identification is one of the hardest jobs an ornithologist can have. And what's more, in the northern hemisphere, a lot of these critters spend the summer in their breeding grounds in the arctic region, which means the only time they're around for birders to see them is — guess when?"

"Winter?" someone ventured rather timidly.

"Exactly! In the winter! Which isn't exactly a time when most sane people want to be spending long hours on boats or by the shore, getting snowed on or sleeted on and trying, in spite of their chattering teeth, to tell apart a couple of birds who look so much alike their own mothers would have a hard time."

He had the audience laughing now. I relaxed a little. And I saw, with relief, that the crew member who had introduced Grandfather had returned to awaken the snoring Stooge and escort him to the door. Desiree chose this moment to rise. Another crew member leaped to her side — quite possibly a crew member who'd been lurking nearby to refill her wineglass before she began bellowing complaints. I breathed a slight sigh of relief when the door closed behind them. Everyone else sitting in the room seemed at least moderately interested in Grandfather's lecture.

"But we birders are a hardy lot!" he was saying. "So for my fellow birders, I'll share a few tips on how to tell apart some of the gulls and other *Laridae.* And for the rest of you, I'll tell you a little bit about how strange and rather wonderful gulls and their relatives are."

I settled back to enjoy Grandfather's talk. Annoying as he could be at times, I had to admit that he was a great public speaker. You could tell the birders in the audience, because they were busily scribbling notes. The rest of us just sat back and enjoyed his enthusiasm, his jokes, and his admittedly

101

entertaining anecdotes. Interspersed with the side-by-side comparisons of the various easily confused gull species, he included funny photos of gulls: A gull standing on a post, with another gull standing on his back. A gull sitting on a car windshield, staring wistfully at a piece of toast lying on the dashboard inside. Gulls carrying various inedible objects, like brown plastic pill bottles or tennis balls. Gulls in the process of swallowing starfish, with one or more squirming starfish arms dangling from their bills — so many of these that I deduced starfish were a gourmet delight for gulls. Gulls swooping down to steal food from humans' plates. And any number of gulls caught in silly poses or with amusing expressions on their faces.

He also shared bits of gull and tern lore.

"Did you know that gulls are one of the few species of animals that can drink both fresh and salt water? They have a special set of glands right above their eyes that flush the salt out of their systems through openings in their bills."

Of course, part of the fun was when he acted out bits of bird behavior.

"They're also very sneaky. A bunch of them will get together and tap their feet rhythmically on the ground. This tricks the earthworms into thinking it's raining, the earthworms wriggle up to the surface, and bingo! The gulls get dinner." Grandfather's rendition of the gulls tapping on the earth, the earthworms — represented by his fingers — wriggling to the surface, and the gulls pouncing on their helpless prey were classic. With luck someone would be videoing on their cell phone.

Suddenly I had to stifle a yawn. Not a bored yawn — I'd been up since five in the morning. I looked at my watch. Technically, Grandfather's presentation would be over in about ten minutes. Which could mean a serious traffic jam at the ship's single elevator. I glanced around at the audience members. Most of them were listening intently. By now, anyone not fascinated by the topic of gulls, petrels, and terns had already departed, or maybe failed to show up to begin with. Grandfather showed no signs of tiring, which would mean he'd stay overtime and take questions. Maybe people would trickle out.

Still — maybe if I snuck out now, I could beat the crowd to the elevator. It had been a long day. Not a bad day, but definitely a long one. And tiring.

Then Grandfather uttered the magic words.

"So, I think we've got time for a few questions."

Hands shot up. Since the official presentation was over, I could sneak out with a clean conscience. After all, if I had any burning questions on gulls, terns, and petrels, I had plenty of access to Grandfather outside the cruise.

"I'm going to head upstairs and start getting the cabins ready for bedtime," I texted to Michael. Then I slipped out of my seat and made my way as unobtrusively as possible to the door.

Out in the long passageway, I took a deep breath, in preparation for a sigh of relief and contentment.

And then gagged, because I'd breathed in an amazingly foul odor.

I looked down at the passageway floor and saw a pool of vomit. Beer-infused vomit, by the smell of it.

"The Stooges," I muttered. Probably the third Stooge, the one who'd been so visibly drunk when the crew member had politely shown him to the door. I'd have bet anything he was responsible. Couldn't he at least have called a steward to clean this up?

Of course not. He'd probably disavow any knowledge of it if anyone tried to blame him.

Should I go back in and ask one of the crew members at the lecture to summon a cleanup crew? There were only two, the one who'd introduced Grandfather and another one who had been sitting in the audience, listening with rapt attention. The first one already had his hands full and the other was probably off duty.

I should just leap over the puddle and seek help on the other side.

It was a pretty big puddle. What if I missed?

As I was hovering with what I like to think was uncharacteristic indecisiveness, I heard a muffled shriek from somewhere farther down the passageway.

"No! Please! Leave me alone!" A woman's voice, with a faint foreign accent.

"Aw, c'mon, baby." A male voice, slurred.

I made my decision.

CHAPTER 8

I backed up as far as I could, to get a bit of a running start, and leaped. Luckily I cleared the puddle. I strode down the passageway. At the end of it was the boarding lobby, where we'd all entered the ship.

One of the Stooges was there, struggling with a petite young woman in a white crew uniform. His left hand was holding her wrist, and his right was groping her breast.

"No!" she said again, shoving at him.

"The lady told you to leave her alone," I said. "I suggest you do what she says."

He ignored me, and tried to pull the young woman closer to him.

My old martial arts teacher would have been proud of me. I punched the Stooge in the solar plexus. He let go of the young woman and staggered back, doubled over. While he was still off balance I grabbed one of his arms, twisted it behind his back, and forced him first to his knees and then flat on the floor. Then I sat on him.

"You might want to call someone," I said to the young woman, who, according to the name tag on her uniform, was Léonie Brunot, from France. She was standing openmouthed.

"Lemme go." The Stooge flailed his free arm uselessly.

"What's going on here?"

I looked up to see First Officer Martin a few feet away.

"This man tried to assault Léonie." I stood up and stepped away from the Stooge, figuring that if he tried to retaliate against me or resume harassing Léonie the first officer would have to intervene.

"I was jus' bein' friendly." The Stooge rolled over on his back and began staring at his wrist.

"He's drunk, and he was groping her, and he paid no attention when she told him very politely to stop."

The first officer studied the Stooge for a few moments, then glanced at Léonie. She was biting her lip and hunching her shoulders.

"Had a bit too much, have we, Mr. Evans?" The first officer's smile was definitely forced. I stepped aside and let him help the Stooge up. "I'll just make sure you

107

get to your cabin safe and sound. Léonie, I was looking for someone to do a cleanup just outside the dining door."

I was opening my mouth to protest, but I saw Léonie shake her head almost imperceptibly. So I held my tongue and watched as the first officer summoned the elevator and heaved Evans the Stooge inside.

"Thank you," she said when the elevator door had closed.

"He's not going to do anything, is he?" I asked.

"Against a passenger?" She gave a small snort of disbelief.

"But —"

"Léonie?" It was the off-duty crew member who'd come to Grandfather's lecture, and had apparently made his way past Lake Puke to the boarding lobby. *"Qu'est-ce qui se passe?"*

I knew enough French to be reasonably certain that he'd just asked what was going on.

"L'ivrogne m'attrapé encore," Léonie said. *"La dame m'a aidé."*

I wasn't sure what *ivrogne* and *attrapé* were, but I had a feeling she was telling the new guy what had happened. I was pretty sure *encore* meant again, which suggested this wasn't her first encounter with the

Stooge. And the last part meant that I'd helped her; I got that much.

The newcomer — Serge Charlier, from Belgium, according to his name tag — drew in a breath between his teeth and shook his head before turning to me.

"Thank you very much, *madame,*" he said. Like Léonie, he had only the faintest of accents. He opened his mouth as if to say more and then stopped himself. Clearly speaking ill of passengers, even a drunken one who'd attempted to molest a young woman, was frowned on. "Thank you," he said again. He turned to Léonie.

"Le capitaine?" he asked, softly.

"Encore bourré."

Whatever *bourré* was, it didn't seem to make Serge happy. He winced and inhaled through his teeth with a slight hissing noise. Léonie shrugged with Gallic eloquence. At least I think I'd have found it eloquent if I'd had the slightest idea what they were talking about.

"I will go and fetch a mop." She turned slightly.

"You are off duty, *chérie.*"

"As are you."

"But I, at least, have had some enjoyment from the evening. Permit me to deal with *cette bêtise.*"

He gave her a warm smile that made me wonder if they were more than mere shipmates. Léonie nodded, murmured thanks with a glance that included both of us, and departed through the door that led down to deck zero. Serge went back into the passageway. I peeked around the corner and saw him taking a mop and bucket out of a small closet and disappearing into the lavatory.

I pulled out my phone and texted Caroline.

"Keep everyone in the dining room for a few more minutes," I typed. "Cleanup in the hallway."

I waited until she'd texted back "OK," then made my own way to the elevator.

The elevator took forever. I contemplated taking the stairs. No. I'd start my staircase-based fitness regimen tomorrow. I leaned against the wall and closed my eyes instead.

"Meg? Are you all right?" Mother had appeared at my side.

"Just tired," I said. "Sneaking out on Grandfather's Q and A?"

"Beating the crowd." She nodded at the elevator.

An idea occurred to me.

"Mother, have you met a young crew member named Léonie?" I asked.

"Why yes," she said. "Very helpful — and so chic!"

I wasn't sure how Léonie managed to be chic while wearing the standard Pastime crew member's white gold-trimmed uniform, which looked rather like what an ambitious banana republic dictator with no fashion sense would invent for his palace guard to wear. But as Mother and I had long ago agreed, I had almost no appreciation for or awareness of chic. "You didn't get that from my side of the family," she was fond of remarking. Definitely not. Mother was not only effortlessly chic herself, but widely accepted as the ultimate arbiter thereof. Of course, now that she'd met Cordelia, my long-lost paternal grandmother, who was not shabby herself in the chic department, Mother had decided that Grandfather alone was to blame for my stubborn indifference to fashion.

"I think Léonie could use our help," I said aloud. "She had an unfortunate interaction with one of the Stooges." I brought Mother up to date on what I'd just witnessed outside the main dining room.

"Which of the Stooges?" she asked when I'd finished.

"His name is Evans."

"Since I haven't been introduced to any

of them — thank goodness — that doesn't really answer my question."

I thought for a moment.

"The one with the thinning reddish hair," I said. "As opposed to the one with the perpetual five o'clock shadow or the one who got slightly shortchanged in the chin department."

"I know the one you mean," she said. "I think we should make some effort to learn the other two young men's names. It will make a much better effect when we eventually have to report them to the proper authorities."

"I like the way you think," I said. "But if possible, I'd like to keep them from doing anything we'd need to report to the authorities. Because while the authorities, in the form of First Officer Martin, are almost certainly aware that at least one Stooge is no choirboy, I get the feeling they're encouraged to bend over backward to keep paying customers happy. So help me keep an eye out for Léonie, will you?"

"Of course. And I'll spread the word. And perhaps we should let her young man know."

"Her young man?"

"Serge, the sous chef. Such a nice young man."

"He already knows." I found myself wondering how Mother knew this. Less than a day on board and she was already au courant with the crew's love lives. "So if anything happens to the obnoxious Evans —"

"We will ensure that Serge has an alibi."

"By the way," I added. "Your French is better than mine. What does '*bourré*' mean? '*Encore bourré*,' to be precise."

" 'Drunk again.' "

I blinked.

"Are you sure?" I asked.

"Of course — why?"

"Isn't there anything that sounds like '*bourré*'?"

"There's '*beurré*,' " she said. "Which literally means 'buttered.' But it's also slang for 'drunk.' Who was using the word, and about whom?"

"Léonie applied it to the captain," I said. "And not just '*bourré*' — '*encore bourré*.' That's not encouraging."

"Agreed," she said. "Worrisome. Although that probably explains why poor Mr. Martin has been looking so stressed. If the captain is a tippler, so much more of the burden of running the ship falls on the first officer."

"Good point. I will think more charitably of Martin the next time I see him struggling to make polite small talk with passengers."

Mother had taken out her phone and was pressing a few numbers. "Penelope? We have a project."

I felt less worried about Léonie.

Back at the staterooms I laid out pajamas for the boys, and made sure the tooth-brushes and toothpaste were clearly visible. I picked up a few things, although luckily Josh and Jamie been so busy running around that they hadn't had much time to mess up anything. I turned down the beds. I was a little surprised that the crew hadn't already done that. And disappointed that they hadn't left behind any of the towels folded into monkeys or swans or elephants that I'd seen in all the pictures from friends who'd previously taken cruises. Maybe some other cruise line had dibs on that idea. Damn. I'd been looking forward to seeing how the boys would react to the towel origami.

I realized if I sat down, I'd fall asleep. I could open the sliding glass door onto our little balcony and see if the fresh air helped. More likely I'd end up falling asleep in the deck chair.

I locked up the cabins and headed for the sun deck. Which would be a moon deck by now, I supposed.

I found Janet standing at the stern, lean-ing over the rail, staring at the ship's wake.

"Evening," I said. "Mind if I join you?"

"Sure."

We both watched the wake for a while. I detected the lingering scent of herbs — sage, cedar, and possibly lavender. Either Janet had eccentric taste in perfume or Rose Noire had managed to do her smudging. I breathed deeply and imagined the smoke enveloping the ship in a fragrant protective cloud.

I was trying to decide why my imagination chose to tint the protective cloud purple when Janet suddenly shook herself, looked away from the wake — it was rather hypnotic — and spoke up.

"Is your dad . . . um . . . maybe a little too interested in murder?"

CHAPTER 9

"Murder?" I echoed.

"Sorry, that didn't come out right. I meant —"

"You're not saying anything my family hasn't said," I told her. "He reads a lot of mysteries — some would say too many — and as a result, he's probably just a little overeager to jump to the conclusion that a crime is being committed."

"Angie's like that." Janet grinned and shook her head. "The rest of us are all 'Oh, look, what a pretty garden!' and she's like 'What a great place to bury a body!' Of course, with her it's a professional hazard."

"Same with Dad, actually," I said. "Given that he's the local medical examiner, suspecting murder is a legitimate part of his job — or at least keeping his eye open for clues that will tell him the real manner and cause of death. And to do him justice, a couple of times he's alerted the police to a genuine homicide that a less careful medical examiner would have put down to accident, suicide, or natural causes."

"Yeah, that's a good thing." Janet paused, then blurted out, "But I'm a little worried that he's getting Angie riled up about the idea that Nancy's death might not have been suicide."

"Why? Were the circumstances suspicious in any way?"

"They seemed pretty cut and dried to me." She looked upset. "Nancy was over the moon for a few weeks because her agent had gotten offers from three different publishers. We had a champagne celebration. Hell, the rest of us were over the moon, too — the end of a seven-year publishing drought. And then the publishers withdrew their offers, one after another. Her agent finally got one of them to say why, and that was when Nancy found out Desiree had heard she was shopping the manuscript around and accused her of plagiarism. And for some reason the publishers believed it."

"How did Desiree even know she was shopping around a manuscript?" I asked. "Were they friends?"

"Not that I know of. They'd met — Nancy and Tish were on a committee with Desiree

117

eight or ten years ago, helping organize a local writing event. According to them, Desiree disappeared whenever there was any actual work to be done."

"Not the beginning of a beautiful friendship."

"Hardly. After that, I think they steered clear of her. Which wasn't that hard — Desiree drifted away from most of the local writing organizations when she figured out they weren't going to make her the boss of anything unless she did at least a moderate amount of work. So I have no idea how Desiree knew Nancy was submitting the book unless . . ."

She broke off and looked uncomfortable.

"Unless maybe one of the publishers told her," I said.

"And why would they do that?" Janet looked miserable. "The only reason I can think of is that Desiree had submitted a manuscript to one of the publishers that looked a lot like Nancy's. And that publisher cried foul and warned the others."

"You think maybe Nancy did plagiarize Desiree's manuscript? Or was it maybe Desiree doing the plagiarizing?"

"I can't see how either would be possible. They barely knew each other, and Nancy and Tish both disliked Desiree. Intensely."

"Understandably," I said.

"So I have no idea how Nancy could possibly have seen one of Desiree's manuscripts, much less stolen it. The only thing I can figure out is that maybe they both independently came up with the very same idea. And instead of realizing that it was a random coincidence, Desiree's publisher jumped to the conclusion that it was plagiarism."

"You think maybe Desiree helped them make that jump? Because from what you've said, it sounds like her style."

"Could be. But as far as I know, that was the only unsolved mystery related to Nancy's death. She was profoundly depressed — not only upset that the deal for this series fell through, but also worried that the plagiarism accusation would kill any future deals. Especially after her agent dropped her. She knew she'd have an uphill battle, getting another agent, and building a new career from scratch, and she'd probably have to do it under a whole new name, because her own would be poison. And then a couple of weeks later, she didn't answer the phone, and Kate went over to check on her and found she'd taken a whole bottle of pills."

"What kind of pills?" The doctor's daughter in me wanted specifics.

"I don't know. Kate would know, or Angie. Something that it's not a good idea to take a whole bottle of."

Which might explain Dad's interest in the case. He'd recently gone to a medical conference on suicide prevention and had, as usual, come home full of case studies and statistics. Fortunately, Mother repressed his attempts to share the case studies over dinner, but she let him have his head when it came to statistics. One that stuck in my mind was that less than 15 percent of people who attempt suicide with prescription or over-the-counter drugs succeed. "It used to be relatively easy to knock yourself off with barbiturates," he'd said. "Which is one reason they're no longer widely prescribed. The benzodiazepines that have replaced them won't usually kill you unless you combine them with alcohol or an opioid. But a lot of people don't know that."

So perhaps his suspicions were aroused by the fact that Nancy had been one of the 15 percent who were unlucky enough to succeed. I didn't see how he could make a leap from that to murder.

And perhaps I should have a word with him about stirring up someone who was probably still trying to get past the loss of a good friend.

"I'll talk to him," I said. "Maybe he was just doing what-ifs, and Angie misinterpreted them."

"Thanks." She closed her eyes and sighed. "This trip was supposed to help us heal. But thanks to Desiree it's ripping off the scabs all over again."

"And Dad's not helping."

"Actually, he might be helping Angie." Janet put her fingers to her temples and began massaging them as if trying to soothe a headache. "Angie has always been the one who wanted to find out more about what happened. I think the rest of us don't really want to think about it. How much pain Nancy must have been in to want to kill herself. How we didn't see it in time to stop her. To help her. But we all deal with grief differently. Maybe Angie needs to talk about it with someone, and maybe your dad's the right someone."

"I'll make sure he understands the situation," I said.

Just then I heard the ding of an arriving text and pulled out my phone.

"Michael and the boys are back at the cabin," I said. "I should go make sure Josh and Jamie don't stay up too much later."

"Yes, we want them well rested. They're

121

going to help me with my sword fighting right after lunch. Along with that very dashing husband of yours, on whom I freely admit I had a crush back in the day. You know, unless my memory is worse than I thought it was, it's been . . . well, a while since *Porfiria, Queen of the Jungle* was on."

"It was pre-twins," I said. "Except for the reunion specials. I think he had to do at least one of those when the boys were tiny."

"And he still looks good. Not totally unchanged, but very little changed, and possibly for the better. But you know what I like best about the present-day Michael?"

I shook my head. I wasn't sure I wanted to know.

"That he married you. An attractive but essentially normal woman. Not some anorexic, Botoxed blond starlet."

I had to laugh.

"Yeah, I have to admit, I've always found his preference for me one of his more endearing qualities."

As we wished each other a good night, she sounded less down than she had at first. I hoped venting to me had helped. Then I went back to the cabins to supervise the boys' bedtime. Which went surprisingly well. All the miniature golf and running up and down the stairs had a good effect. They were asleep almost as soon as their heads touched the pillows.

Michael followed their example. I found myself wakeful. Not unusual. Michael could almost always put aside anything and everything that was bothering him and fall asleep. I completely lacked this highly useful ability. I'd long ago learned that sometimes before I could fall asleep I had to figure out what was making my brain restless, and either deal with it or add it as an item in my notebook-that-tells-me-when-to-breathe, as I called the three-ring binder that held my voluminous to-do list. Most of the time just capturing things in my notebook allowed me to drift off, secure in the knowledge that I'd be tackling them in the morning.

So what was bothering me tonight?

The writers. I liked them. And I didn't like Desiree. I hated the fact that her presence was already casting a shadow on their retreat together. I hated still more the idea that she might have done it deliberately — might even be planning to cause them trouble. And why was Dad suggesting that their friend Nancy's death could be murder instead of suicide? Was he merely indulging his taste for detective drama, or had something about Angie's account raised his suspicions?

I rolled out of bed, opened up my laptop, and began composing an email to my nephew Kevin McReady. For years — ever since he turned fourteen or so — Kevin had been my go-to tech guru for everything from hardware problems and virus removal to complicated data searches. These days I could also call on Delaney — but Kevin wasn't on vacation with his significant other. And possibly just as important, he wasn't sharing a cruise with the people I was about to ask him to snoop on. And if he was someplace where he didn't have good Internet access, he could just leave for someplace that did.

I outlined the situation. Described Desiree. I had to rummage in my tote for my new collection of bookmarks to give him the other writers' last names. And Nancy . . . someone had said her last name . . . Goreham. Feeling very pleased with my memory, I finished up the email, tasking him with finding out as much as he could about all of them, especially Nancy's apparent suicide and the incidents that had led up to it.

And after all that, at first I didn't think I was going to be able to send it. Angie was right — the ship's Internet was lousy. It kept timing out while trying to send my email. Finally, after about fifteen tries, it went through. I felt a surge of satisfaction — task done!

And as I caught myself yawning a second or two later, I realized I'd done exactly the right thing. Just sending the email to Kevin was probably going to be enough to let me turn off my brain and go to sleep.

As I drifted off, I found myself looking forward to the next day. Friday would be spent entirely at sea — the ship wouldn't arrive in Bermuda until Saturday morning. But I was expecting our day at sea to be very pleasant. A hearty breakfast, followed by some miniature golf. Maybe a picnic lunch on the deck, followed by sword fighting with Janet. Maybe I'd go to afternoon tea with Mother and Aunt Penelope. And Grandfather had announced that he'd be lecturing about whales, dolphins, and sharks. He probably had tons of dramatically gory shark stories. The Sandburgs might not find it very reassuring, but the boys would be on cloud nine.

I fell asleep, my head filled with visions of dolphins gamboling in the ship's wake.

I woke up, and at first I didn't know why. It was still almost pitch dark. Of course, we had the curtains drawn, but I didn't think they were concealing sunlight. Michael was breathing softly, without even a hint of his occasional not-quite-snoring. I checked my phone, which was lying on the bedside table, hooked to its charger. 4:35 A.M.

I tiptoed over and peeked through the connecting door into the boys' cabin. They were both sprawled over their beds, as relaxed as rag dolls and sleeping soundly. I closed the door again, tiptoed over to the window, and pulled the curtain open just an inch or so. A lance of bright moonlight fell across the stateroom floor. I peered out. The moonlight reflected off a sea that was smooth as glass.

And we were motionless in it. Maybe that was what had awakened me. Suddenly it was obvious. Ever since we'd left port, the low, steady hum of the ship's engines had been in the background, so that by bedtime I'd stopped even noticing it. The low hum and an almost imperceptible sense of motion. Now, nothing.

Had we reached Bermuda? It didn't seem likely. Not at four-thirty. And I couldn't see land. Then again, our windows only showed the starboard side. Maybe on the port side . . .

I threw on my robe, donned my flip-flops, grabbed my phone and my Pastime card, and slipped out into the corridor.

Since our cabin was the last one along the

starboard side of the corridor, it only took a minute to reach the sun deck. Where no sun was presently available, but it did give me a panoramic view of the ocean. And that was all there was — ocean. No land visible in any direction. Unless there was a small rowboat-sized island hidden right in front of the ship's bow, the only place I couldn't see from my current vantage point. Not very likely.

And now that I was awake, I realized there was no chance we'd arrived at Bermuda. Today would be — okay, already was — Friday. The at-sea day. We weren't scheduled to arrive in Bermuda until Saturday morning. Traveling from Baltimore to Bermuda took a day and a half, not a mere twelve hours. Rose Noire had found that suspicious — evidence of some dangerous paranormal barrier that the ship could traverse only slowly and with great labor. I finally took out a map and showed her what a really long way it was — over eight hundred nautical miles — but I wasn't sure I'd convinced her.

And if she was awake, she'd probably be wondering why we'd stopped. Some peril in the seas ahead? Icebergs? Pirates? Probably not a storm, given the glassy stillness of the water.

They'd probably just stopped to make some minor repair. Engine trouble of some sort. I'd find someone to ask in the morning. In the meantime, probably time for me to go back to bed. A day at sea didn't mean a day of quiet for those of us accompanying lively eleven-year-old boys.

But the night was so pleasant that I stayed for a few minutes, leaning against the rail at the back of the sun deck.

I found myself imagining what I'd be feeling if I were aboard a sailing ship. Today, the dead calm meant smooth sailing and less chance of losing my balance and bumping into something as the ship coped with waves. A couple of centuries ago, maybe I'd be worrying about how long the calm would last and whether we were in any danger of running out of food or water.

But after a while the dead calm began to get on my nerves again. Engine trouble was the most logical explanation. But if we had engine trouble, why wasn't I hearing sounds of crew members scurrying around to fix it?

Possibly because the scurrying wouldn't be up here on deck four. After all, I'd figured out last night that deck one wasn't the lowest point on the ship. I knew deck zero existed — maybe that was where the engines were. Or maybe there was a deck minus one right below deck zero. It improved my mood to imagine that somewhere, far below, in the deepest depths of the ship, capable crew members were even now busy fixing whatever needed fixing. And if ship travel was regulated as closely as air travel, the problem could be something pretty minor. I'd once been on a flight that was delayed because the bathroom sink wouldn't stop dripping.

"No sense worrying about it now," I told myself. I'd see if I could find someone to ask about it in the morning. Later in the morning.

I returned to my cabin, made sure the curtain was pulled tightly closed again, in case our windows were facing east when the sun rose, and got back in bed. I lay there for what seemed like hours but was probably only fifteen or twenty minutes. I resisted the urge to pick up my iPhone to check, and eventually I fell asleep.

I woke up again to find the boys bouncing on our bed.

CHAPTER 10

Friday

"Mom! The ship has stopped."

"Mom! Why are we stopped in the middle of the ocean?"

"Are we going ashore?"

"In the middle of the ocean?"

"Maybe the land's on the other side. The port side."

"We're on the port side."

"No, we're on the stabbed side."

"That's starboard side." I finally got a chance to get a word in. "We're on the starboard side. But there's no land on the port side, either. We're stopped in the middle of the ocean and have been for several hours. I'm hoping we'll find out why soon."

As if in answer, someone knocked on our cabin door. When I opened it I found a crew member standing outside, holding a sheet of paper and looking anxious.

"Sorry to bother you, ma'am." He handed me one of those door hanger tags the ship provided for those who wanted to order breakfast in their rooms, then looked down at his paper and began reading in a mechanical tone. "As you have probably noticed the ship has stopped to make some minor but essential repairs. The power has been turned off to facilitate the repairs. A continental breakfast is now being served in the main dining room. If you prefer breakfast in your room please make your selections on this tag and hang it on the doorknob. The captain will give a briefing at seven-fifteen A.M. in the main dining room for those who would like more information on how this will impact your holiday. Attendance is optional. If you prefer to continue enjoying your holiday you are welcome to do so and we'll keep you posted." He looked up at me. I half expected him to ask if I had any questions, but then I realized from his expression that he was fervently hoping I didn't.

"Thank you," I said.

"You're welcome, ma'am." He looked immensely relieved. Then he steeled himself again, continued down the passageway, and knocked on the door of the boys' stateroom.

"You can skip that one," I called out. "They're with us."

"Yes, ma'am." He went on to 418.

"Well, that's not good news." Michael came in from the balcony.

I picked up my phone. Luckily it had finished charging by the time the power went out. I checked the time.

"It's already seven," I said. "They're not giving us much lead time on that briefing."

"You want to go?"

I was already grabbing some clothes.

"You guys want to go to the briefing?" Michael looked at the boys.

"A briefing means that one of the crew members will stand up on the stage and talk to us for a while," I put in.

"Yuck," Jamie said.

"I bet it's the first officer," Josh said. "The one who fake-smiles all the time."

"Josh!" I frowned at him. I was about to point out how much stress the first officer was under, but then I remembered that I hadn't even told Michael about the captain being *encore bourré.*

"Or would you like to get dressed and play some miniature golf and let your mom fill us in on what she learns at the briefing?" Michael picked up where I'd left off.

"If you do that, I can send someone up with breakfast," I suggested.

Not surprisingly, the boys opted for miniature golf and went back to their room to get ready. I threw on my clothes and hurried out the door.

I saw a small cluster of people standing beside the elevator.

"Seems to be out of order," one of them said.

"It's the power," another added. "No power in my room."

"Or mine."

"You'd think they'd have an emergency generator for, well, emergencies," one older lady said.

"Wait a minute," one of them said. "If the power's out, how are we going to get back into our rooms?"

"The card readers have a battery backup," someone else said. "I already tested it."

" 'Let's go with Pastime,' my husband says," grumbled another passenger. " 'So it's cheaper,' he says. 'How bad can it be?' "

I pulled out my phone to text Michael.

"Remember, elevator not working," I typed. It wasn't until after I hit SEND that I thought to wonder if the text would even go through. My phone hadn't had a cell signal since shortly after we'd left Baltimore, and with no power there'd be no more Wi-Fi connection.

Even before I got the "message not sent"

133

notification, I saw Michael and the boys exiting the cabin.

"Not even emergency power," I said, when they got close to the elevator.

"And that means no water," Michael added.

"Yikes," I said. "I hope this doesn't last long."

"Okay, guys," Michael said to the boys. "Last one to deck five is a rotten egg!"

They took off up the stairs. I could see that Michael was destined to be the rotten egg, but not by much.

"My toilet wouldn't flush," one of the passengers standing by the elevator said. "I was going to pour a bucket of water into it to make it flush, the way you do when the water's shut off, but there was no water."

"On a ship, all the water has to be pumped up to the staterooms," a more knowledgeable passenger said. "So there won't be water till the power's back. And pouring water into your toilet won't do anything. It's a vacuum toilet. Also requires power."

"Oh, dear," the first passenger said.

"We're going to have to take the stairs," a third passenger announced.

I took the stairs myself, heading downward. I saw a few other people on my way down. I was slightly surprised to find that forty or fifty people had shown up for the briefing — about a quarter of the passengers.

Or maybe they'd come for the buffet. For a continental breakfast buffet, the spread the harried-looking crew members were setting up wasn't bad, but neither was it anywhere near an adequate replacement for the hearty hot breakfast buffet promised in the brochures. I reminded myself that they were probably doing the best they could, and refrained from complaining. But others weren't being quite as philosophical. Had they not noticed the power outage yet? The resulting lack of running water? Or did they think the kitchen staff normally cooked over open fires?

Mother was presiding at a double table near the stage, where Dad, Horace, Rose Noire, Aunt Penelope, Rob, and Delaney were making serious inroads on a large supply of pastries and fruit. Actually, Rose Noire wasn't eating much. She was too busy worrying.

"I knew something like this would happen." She was actually wringing her hands. "I did what I could to ward it off, but I've failed you. And now we're marooned — marooned! In the Bermuda Triangle!"

I decided to find another table.

Nearby, Grandfather, Caroline, Wim, and Guillermo were eating while hunched over some papers. Planning for this evening's lecture, I suspected. I hoped it was a topic Grandfather could handle without his Power-Point. Although I also hoped the power wouldn't still be out by seven.

The four writers were sitting together at a table, all reading matching wads of paper, occasionally taking out a red pen and writing on their papers. Editing each other's work, perhaps?

I wasn't feeling sociable, so I merely waved at various friends and family before snagging a glass of cranberry juice and a croissant from the buffet. Then I took a seat at a table near the entrance, in case the briefing got boring and I wanted to sneak out.

A minute or so later, Captain Detweiler strode in, with a young officer and a crewman trailing behind him. As he stepped up onto the small stage, I studied him. His step seemed steady enough. He looked tired, but that was perfectly understandable. He'd probably been up in the middle of the night dealing with whatever had stopped the ship. Maybe I'd misheard Léonie. Maybe she hadn't said *"bourré"* or *"beurré"* but something that sounded similar and had a completely different meaning. Or perhaps what she'd said to Serge was merely the idle gossip of a disaffected crew member.

"Good morning, ladies and gentlemen." Detweiler's voice was good — no slurring. "As you already heard in the announcement, we've stopped to perform some minor repairs."

"Minor?" someone at the other side of room called out. "The whole ship's dark."

"And the toilets won't flush!"

"Unfortunately, we've had to shut down our electrical systems for the safety of the crew members performing the repair work. But I assure you we'll have everything up and running again as soon as possible."

"So what's broken?" someone else called out.

"I'd have to get our chief engineer to explain it to you — but we want him working on fixing the problem, don't we?" Captain Detweiler's smile was rather forced, and I decided he should have stuck to serious. "Our engineers are still diagnosing the precise nature of the problem, or were the last time I checked. But it shouldn't be much longer."

I ate my croissant and drank my juice while several other people asked variants on the same question, and received equally polite but uninformative answers. I wasn't impressed with the information content, but I had to admit that the captain seemed perfectly sober and of sound mind. Maybe Léonie had been exaggerating.

"They should just give it up."

I glanced over to see the speaker — a small bespectacled man eating a Danish, who was the only other person at my table.

"The people who keep asking questions, I mean," he went on. "Pastime corporate policy. Never tell the passengers anything negative. Always put a positive spin on it."

"So if sharks are circling the ship, it's a fabulous opportunity to get an up-close and personal view of marine life?" I suggested.

"More like 'sharks? Oh, you mean those dolphins over there? Note the unusually prominent dorsal fins.' It's the mushroom school of passenger relations. Keep them in the dark and dump . . . um, manure on them. I don't blame the crew — they can only do what they're told to do."

He finished his juice, rose, and left.

After a few more minutes, I decided to follow his example, having figured out that the captain had told us, if not everything he knew, certainly everything he had any intention of revealing. Out of habit, I pulled out my phone to brief Michael, and then stuck it back into my pocket. With no cell phone signal or Wi-Fi, I'd have to deliver the bad news in person.

And that would mean more stairs. And more miniature golf. Possibly a lot more. Not how I'd hoped to spend the day, but if it kept the boys entertained and prevented them from worrying about how long we'd be stranded here in the middle of the ocean, I could manage it.

"But surely you have some idea how long it's going to take to fix it," someone was asking the captain.

I slipped out of my seat and made my way to the door.

As I walked down the long passageway toward the elevator lobby, I decided to make a pit stop along the way — there was a lavatory near the boarding lobby end. And if the toilets really weren't flushing, the sooner I visited one the better.

I stepped inside, realized the lavatory had no windows and thus no light, and turned on my cell phone's flashlight feature. I was just locking the door when I heard running feet outside.

"Captain! Captain!"

Curious, I opened the door and peeked out.

A uniformed crew member was disappearing into the dining room.

"Captain! Come quick to deck four! The lady jump! The lady jump!"

CHAPTER 11

A clamor of voices arose in the dining room, and I wasn't surprised to see the captain and another officer hustling the hapless employee out into the corridor. I pulled the door almost closed, leaving enough of a crack that I could see and hear what was happening.

The officer had shut the dining room doors, muting the clamor inside.

"Vaclav, never do this again!" the captain snapped.

"But is emergency!"

"I don't care if the ship is on fire — you don't come running in and alarming the passengers. Now what's this about a lady jumping?"

"Off stern of deck four."

"You saw this?"

"No, I only find her things. Shoes and silk shawl. And note."

"What did the note say?"

"I do not know. Handwriting very bad."

"I don't think Vaclav's reading compre-hension is very strong," the officer said. "Not with English, anyway."

"What did you do with the things — the shoes and the shawl?" The captain was vis-ibly trying to keep his temper.

"I leave them there. Benigno guard them."

"You go back in and see if you can calm down the passengers," the captain said to the officer, "while Vaclav shows me what he found."

The officer disappeared into the dining room. I pulled the bathroom door all the way closed as the captain and Vaclav passed.

The stern of deck four. Not very far at all from the two cabins Michael, the boys, and I shared. Damn. Odds were they'd rope it off as a crime scene. Why couldn't our suicide have chosen some other deck? What if it freaked out the boys?

Then again, thanks to Dad and his habit of regaling us all with crime and autopsy stories, there was probably more danger that the boys would develop a slightly morbid fascination with the place. The boys and Dad.

And should I feel guilty that my first response to learning that someone had com-mitted suicide was to worry about what effect it would have on my sons?

And just who was the suicide? I did a quick inventory. Apart from Trevor, I'd seen everyone in our party this morning. And while Trevor was admittedly eccentric, and arguably the sort of tightly wound person that I could all too easily see committing suicide, if he took the leap I didn't think he'd leave behind a silk shawl and a pair of ladies' shoes. Then again, what did I know of Trevor's personal life?

On impulse, I strode to the elevator lobby. I dashed up the stairs, fumbling in my pocket as I went for my Pastime card so, if need be, I could pretend to be going to our cabin. But by the time I reached deck four no one was in the corridor, so I hurried out onto the stern deck.

There on the port side of the ship, and right beside the stern rail, was a small heap of things with a uniformed crew member standing guard over them. A pashmina shawl had been neatly folded and placed on the deck. On top of it were a small object that looked like a tuft of gray and white feathers tied up with a bit of string, and a note.

And beside the shawl, a pair of shoes. Red shoes with ridiculously high heels and fussy scalloped trim around the edges. One was standing up and the other had fallen over on its side to reveal the shiny red sole.

"Those are Desiree's shoes," I exclaimed.

The captain jumped, but to my relief he didn't try to chase me off.

"You know the owner of these?"

"Desiree St. Christophe," I said.

"A friend of yours?"

"No, only a passing acquaintance. I never met her before we came on board. But she's rather memorable — tall, with purple-red hair. Came on board wearing a long flowing orange caftan."

"I know the passenger you mean. Vaclav — ask Mr. Martin to join me."

Vaclav seemed happy to leave. The crew member who'd been standing guard — presumably Benigno — looked envious.

"How can you be sure these are Ms. St. Christophe's shoes?" the captain asked.

"They're Christian Louboutin shoes." I could see this rang no bells for him. "Hideously expensive designer shoes. I saw her wearing them in the Starlight Lounge yesterday, shortly after we boarded, and then again last night at dinner. And she wasn't just wearing them, she was waving them around so we could all see the red soles. That's how you know they're real

Christian Louboutin shoes — the shiny red soles."

The captain was looking at me as if he doubted my sanity.

"Look, I don't get it, either," I said. "I'd just as soon stick my toes in a blender as wear heels that high, but fashion-conscious women pay hundreds or even thousands of dollars for shoes like that. Ask any woman on the ship — most of them will have noticed. And besides —"

I leaned over so I could see the note — and since I was holding my cell phone in my hand, I sneaked in a picture.

"See — that's her name at the bottom of the note."

I didn't touch the note, but I pointed at the signature, scrawled in a loopy, feminine, but untidy hand. *Desiree St. Christophe.*

"Did she seem depressed last night?"

"I don't know." I shrugged. "I didn't talk to her."

"Do you know anyone who did?"

"Not really." I shrugged again. "I think she was traveling alone. Some of the other writers knew her, but not very well." I was about to add that none of them liked her very much, but decided not to. For one thing, they'd probably make that clear enough on their own. And there was also

145

the fact that suicide investigations had been known to mutate into murder investigations all too quickly. I had no desire to finger any of the writers for a murder.

The captain turned back to the small collection of possessions and stood for a moment, frowning down at it. I took the opportunity to take a couple more pictures from various angles. Probably a good thing for whoever would be investigating this, since it quickly became obvious that the captain had no understanding of how to preserve a crime scene.

As I watched, he leaned over, picked up the note with his bare hand, and read it.

Horace would probably have protested. I wanted to, but after all — this was the captain. Presumably he was the authority who'd be overseeing the investigation into Desiree's suicide.

The first officer stepped out onto the deck and joined us. Without a word, the captain handed him the note. The first officer read it — rather more quickly than the captain had — and shook his head.

"What a terrible tragedy." He handed the note back to the captain. "Vaclav told me what happened, so I checked her cabin and sent several crew members to do a quick check on all decks."

"No one reported hearing anything?"

"Not yet, sir."

"So we have no idea when it happened."

The first officer shook his head.

"It had to be sometime after four thirty-five A.M.," I said.

They both turned and frowned at me.

"How do you know this?" the first officer asked.

"We're in cabin 422 — that's just inside that door." I pointed at the door that led back into the ship. Not that I needed to tell them the location of cabin 422, of course. They could probably find any cabin on the ship in their sleep. "I woke up at four thirty-five and noticed the ship wasn't moving. I thought maybe we'd arrived at Hamilton."

"There would be no possibility of that," the captain said. "It takes —"

"A day and a half," I said. "I know. But remember, it was four thirty-five and I was half asleep. Anyway, all I could see from the cabin window was ocean so I came out here to find out if I could spot land from the starboard side. I still saw only ocean. And by that time I was awake enough to realize we couldn't possibly be in Bermuda already. So I stood here for a little while, wondering why the ship had stopped, and eventually I went back inside and fell asleep again. And that stuff wasn't there when I came out here." I pointed at the shoes and shawl.

"You're sure? It was nighttime."

"Yes, but it was also cloudless, and the moon was very bright. And I was standing almost exactly where Desiree left her belongings, leaning against the rail. Believe me — the stuff wasn't there then."

The captain frowned.

"The note is dated tomorrow," he said.

"Clearly she was not in a rational state of mind when she wrote it," the first officer replied.

They stood, frowning down at the note for a few more moments. I raised my phone, trying to be as offhand and unobtrusive as possible, and took a few more photos, of them and of the crime scene.

"Well, this seems to be pretty straightforward," the captain said. "Regrettable, but straightforward. Have one of the stewards collect these items and put them back in her cabin. Once we've got communications back, I'll notify the home office."

"And the note?" The first officer held it up.

"I'll take charge of that." The captain folded it up and put it in his uniform jacket pocket.

"Is that all you're going to do?" I asked.

They both turned my way again. They didn't look pleased.

"We've already scanned on all sides of the ship to see if her body is still floating nearby." The captain sounded annoyed. "If by some chance she changed her mind and wandered off rather than jumping, my crew will spot her soon. Would probably have spotted her by now, in fact. Is there something else you think we should be doing?"

"Search the whole ship!" I exclaimed. "Maybe she's playing a practical joke and hiding someplace."

"Not a lot of places to hide on a ship this size." The first officer's tone clearly showed that he thought he was humoring me. The captain's face just as clearly showed that he didn't think humoring anyone was necessary.

"What if she was about to jump, got cold feet, and ran back to her cabin, forgetting that she'd left her note and her shoes here?"

Okay, it did sound pretty far-fetched. At least they didn't actually roll their eyes.

"As I said, I inspected her cabin," Martin said. He turned back to the captain. "And will do so more thoroughly when I supervise the return of her belongings to it. And make sure it's locked so none of her things disappear."

"Good." Captain Detweiler strode off. I got the feeling he was deliberately not looking at me. The first officer pulled out his cell phone and punched a few buttons. After a moment he swore under his breath.

"Benigno," he said. "Gather up that stuff and take it to cabin 411." He pointed to the shawl and shoes.

Benigno didn't look as if he wanted to touch Desiree's belongings — maybe he thought it was bad luck — but he complied, draping the shawl over his left arm and holding both shoes by the long narrow heels in his right hand. The first officer led the way back inside. As he held the door open for Benigno, he gave me a brief smile before disappearing inside. A rather pained and morose smile.

"That's it?" I muttered.

I hadn't liked Desiree, and wasn't broken up about her demise, but still — this was cold.

Just then I noticed that they had left something behind. The little feathered thing. A faint breeze blew over the deck, picking it up and moving it a few inches. I went over and retrieved it before it could blow overboard.

It was mostly a little puff of feathers — white and gray ones. Gull feathers, probably. Or tern feathers, or petrel feathers — after seeing Grandfather's lecture last night, I'd accepted the fact that I'd probably never be able to identify most of them, not if they landed on the ship's rail beside me and obligingly turned in slow circles so I could identify all their markings. Figuring out which species these feathers had come from would probably be beyond even Grandfather's powers.

The feathers were tied up not with string, as I'd first thought, but with a narrow bit of ivory-colored satin ribbon. And stitched to the ribbon or threaded onto it were several tiny shells in tones of beige, white, and ivory.

I'd once held — very briefly — a tiny bundle of leaves, feathers, and oddments that was supposed to be the instrument of a voodoo curse. Not one aimed at me — and I wasn't sure I really believed in curses anyway — but still, it was a nasty little thing. I could almost feel the malice radiating out of it. Which didn't necessarily mean there was anything to the claim that the bundle was cursed. More likely it meant that one too many glasses of Rhum Barbancourt punch had made me more suggestible than usual. Whatever the reason, I couldn't put it down soon enough, and I found myself drawn to wash my hands rather more often than usual for the next day or so.

But this little thing — call it "the gull feather charm" for want of a better name — had rather the opposite effect. Looking at it made me think of gulls wheeling freely in bright skies over gentle seas. I lifted it to my nose and took a cautious sniff. It smelled only of sea salt. A good luck charm, maybe.

Although clearly it hadn't helped Desiree.

Still. I tucked it in my pocket. I could ask Grandfather what kind of feathers it contained. And I could show it to Rose Noire, who claimed to be able to read auras. I wasn't entirely sure I believed in auras — I tended to believe that Rose Noire was merely a good judge of character, and how could a little bundle of shells and feathers have character? But it would please her to be asked, and anything that would distract her from fretting about how we were marooned in the Bermuda Triangle would be a good thing.

Just then someone came out onto the deck. Léonie, carrying a mop and a pail of water. She nodded at me and smiled, then looked around, puzzled.

"I was sent to clean the deck," she said. "You did so already?"

"There's really nothing to clean," I said. "The captain wanted someone to swab the

152

part of the deck where Ms. St. Christophe jumped. I have no idea why. There's nothing to see." Just part of his attempt to pretend nothing had ever happened.

She started slightly, and clutched at her throat, murmuring something that sounded like *"mon dieu."*

"I'd say pour your bucket of water over in that corner, and be done with it." I pointed to the empty space where the shawl and shoes had rested.

Léonie nodded, and a matter-of-fact, practical look returned to her face. She poured a small amount of water by the rail, sopped it up with a few brisk swipes of the mop, and returned inside, bidding me *"bonjour"* as she passed.

I found myself all alone in what I couldn't help thinking of as a crime scene. Well, technically suicide was a crime, wasn't it? Back in Caerphilly, the whole area would be cordoned off with yellow crime scene tape, Horace would be hard at work doing his forensic thing, and Chief Burke would have long since chased me away — even if the chief was all but certain it was a suicide, and not a murder cleverly arranged to look like one. The captain hadn't even given a moment's thought to that possibility.

Then again, perhaps Dad, with his book-a-day mystery-reading habit and his passionate enthusiasm for detecting real-life crime, was having a little too much influence on my way of thinking.

Well, there were worse influences.

Although I wasn't looking forward to hearing what Dad had to say about the second suicide — alleged suicide — in the writers' circle.

I pulled out my phone and opened up the photos. It occurred to me that while I'd seen Desiree's signature on the bottom of the note, I hadn't taken the time to decipher the rest of it. Which wasn't that easy, especially on my phone's tiny little screen — her handwriting gave the first impression of being flowery and feminine, but it was actually surprisingly bad. After a great deal of peering and enlarging various parts of the note, I finally made it out:

Farewell! I can no longer bear the calumnies and unkindnesses of this all too cruel world! I want you to know that I have forgiven you — all of you — even those of you who have treated me so cruelly! When we meet again — as I hope we will — it will be in a better place!

"A little melodramatic, but otherwise

154

pretty generic," was my assessment. In fact, it was like something out of a bad movie. Or, perhaps more accurately, a bad novel. My new writer friends hadn't seemed to think she was a very good writer. Maybe I'd show them this note, too.

But first I'd go and see what the family was up to.

CHAPTER 12

I stopped by our cabin. Which was empty, but Michael had left a note.

"Power still out, so Horace is bringing breakfast up to the miniature golf course," it read. "Join us when you have a chance."

As I headed for the stairs, I wondered if news of Desiree's suicide had already made it to deck five.

"Mommy!" Jamie greeted me. "I'm ahead!"

"Quiet, everyone," Josh ordered. "I need to concentrate on my shot."

I held my tongue until Josh had finished, and then, while Horace was taking his shot, I pulled Michael aside and filled him in on what was happening.

"We should probably break the news to the boys before they hear it from someone else," he suggested. When I nodded, he called out, "Guys! We have something to tell you."

Josh and Jamie hurried over, trailed by Horace.

"Your mom heard that a lady went overboard sometime this morning," Michael said.

"You mean she fell?" Jamie asked.

"Maybe," Michael said. "But the ship's pretty safe, so it's more likely that she jumped."

"Maybe someone pushed her," Josh suggested. Clearly Dad's fondness for suspecting murder had rubbed off on him.

"It's possible," Michael said. "But we don't know."

"Is that why we're stopped?" Jamie asked. "To find her?"

"No, I think we're stopped to fix part of the ship," I said. "They don't yet know how long it will take. I don't think there's anything they can do to find her."

"So she's probably, like, dead?" Josh asked.

I nodded.

"Wow," Jamie said. Josh just nodded, and they both looked serious. Maybe even worried.

"So if you guys hear anyone talking about this, you'll know what's going on," Michael said. "And remember that I want you to always stick together and follow the ship's safety rules!"

They both nodded soberly.

"And when we find out more about what's going on — with the ship or the lady — we'll tell you," I said.

"So, I think it's Jamie's shot," Michael said. "Is the score still tied?"

The boys hurried back to the tiny miniature golf course.

"I should go see if there's anything I can do." Horace hurried off.

"He's in for a disappointment," I said as I watched Horace leave.

"You don't think the captain will let Horace help with his investigation?"

"I don't think he's going to do an investigation. He took the suicide note at face value. She's not in her cabin. If she chickened out at the last minute, I think we'll find her before long. Would have found her by now, if you ask me."

"How about if I stay here and either distract the boys or help them process this, whichever they seem to need," Michael suggested. "You see what you can find out."

"I'm going to start by finding the writers," I said. "They know more about Desiree than anyone else on the ship."

"Good idea."

I'd last seen the writers in the main dining room, where they'd been picking at fruit and pastries and listening to the captain with expressions that suggested they were not entirely satisfied with his non-explanations.

They were still there, sipping juice and nibbling pastries. Two of them had opened up laptops, and the other two had gone back to their stacks of paper. They greeted me with enthusiasm.

"So did someone really jump overboard?" Kate asked. "Or was the crew member over-reacting?"

"He did seem rather hysterical," Janet said.

"So would you be if you saw someone jump overboard and drown," Tish said.

"He didn't see anyone jump overboard," I said. "But he did find a few telltale objects by the ship's rail: a pashmina shawl, a pair of red Christian Louboutin shoes, and a suicide note."

I watched their faces to see how they'd react. It only took them a few seconds.

"Wait a minute — red Christian Loubou-tin shoes?"

"Are you serious?"

"Desiree?"

I nodded.

They were all silent for a few moments.

Kate put her hands over her mouth. Janet took a sip of her juice and then frowned at it, as if disappointed that it hadn't morphed into a martini in her hour of need.

"How do we even know it was a suicide?" Kate asked.

"There was a note," I said.

"Is that what the captain says?" Tish shook her head. "I wouldn't believe him if he told me the sky was blue. Has anyone actually seen the note?"

"I have," I said. "In fact, since I was already starting to worry about the quality of the captain's investigation by the time I saw it, I even took a picture of it."

"So you know what it says." Angie sat up straighter in her chair.

"Spill," Tish said.

"Here." I opened up my picture of the note and handed the phone to Janet, who was closest. She peered at it for a few moments and made what the boys, when younger, would have called a yuck face. Then, striking a dramatic pose, she read it aloud.

" 'Farewell! I can no longer bear the calumnies and unkindnesses of this all too cruel world! I want you to know that I have forgiven you — all of you — even those of you who have treated me so cruelly! When

160

we meet again — as I hope we will — it will be in a better place!' "

Maybe it was Janet's rendition, but it sounded even more melodramatic read aloud.

When she finished, they all sat silent, frowning for a few moments. Except for Angie, who had turned back to her laptop and was doing something with it. Taking notes for a book, perhaps?

"Well, it's got that . . . flowery style," Kate said slowly.

"By 'flowery,' you mean 'over the top,' " Tish said. "Queen of the purple prose."

"Way too grammatical." Janet was shaking her head. "And no way she would know the word 'calumnies.' Got to be a forgery."

"Now, now," Kate said. "I'm sure she could have found it in a thesaurus."

"God, yes," Tish closed her eyes as if in pain. "The things that woman could do to the English language with a thesaurus in her hand."

"Her characters never say anything," Janet said. "They divulge, expostulate, ejaculate, profess, enunciate, vocalize, interject, aver, adduce, give utterance to, spurt out, extoll, verbalize, vociferate — anything but say."

"We writers have a love/hate relationship with the word 'said,' " Kate explained, seeing my puzzled look. "Bad style to overuse it. Gets boring — said, said, said, said, said. But on the other hand, using overly pretentious synonyms for 'said' isn't good style, either. Desiree tended to err in that direction."

"So you think she wrote it?" I asked.

"You think she'd plagiarize her own suicide note?" Tish asked.

"I was wondering if someone else might have written it," I explained. "Someone who wanted to make murder look like suicide."

"What a bloodthirsty imagination you have." Janet sounded impressed.

"When you have a medical examiner for a father and a cousin who does crime scene analysis, you're maybe a little too ready to see homicide wherever you go."

"You know, it does sound like something out of a book," Janet said.

"It *is* out of a book." Angie had been totally focused on whatever she was doing with her laptop, but now she looked up. "But it's okay — it was one of her own books. I guess you're allowed to plagiarize yourself."

"Which book?" Kate asked.

"*Sweet Savage Suitor.* The one with the bad Fabio clone in the leopard-print loincloth on the cover."

"And you know this . . . how?" Janet seemed amused.

"Yes," Kate said. "I have to admit, I'm surprised you recognized it. And even knew which book."

"I didn't completely recognize it," Angie said. "It sounded vaguely familiar. So, I searched through all her books for 'calumnies and unkindnesses,' which I thought would be a pretty unique text string, and there it was."

"Wait — there's no Internet at the moment. So you happen to have all her books on your laptop because . . . ?" Janet was grinning. In fact they all were.

"You actually read her?" Tish asked.

"I had this vague idea that maybe I could find a way to analyze her style and prove that Nancy hadn't plagiarized her," Angie said. "But before I could make much headway — well, Nancy was dead."

That cast a pall over the conversation.

"Of course," Janet said eventually, "if you were going to knock her off and make it look like a suicide, why not steal a suicide note from one of her own books? Anyone who knows her would find the highfalutin style plausible. Anyone who reads her and recognizes it figures words failed her at the end and she fell back on something she remembered writing."

"I'm so glad you're not saying that to the captain," Kate murmured. "Although more likely it will be the long-suffering first officer who conducts the investigation, don't you think?"

"I doubt if they'll do much of an investigation," I said.

"Oh, I hope you're wrong," Kate said. "Even Desiree deserves . . . I don't know. Closure for her family, or whatever."

"Does she have family?" Janet seemed to find this implausible.

"Several exes and a grown kid or two," Angie said. "Maybe she's different with family."

"Well, we can't do anything about Desiree." Tish stood up. "Or about the ship. I vote we find a quiet place and all get some work done."

"Before the first officer shows up again." Angie glanced at me. "You missed the part where he tried to organize a Trivial Pursuit tournament after breakfast."

"He means well, but he doesn't seem to understand that some of us have things to do." Janet glanced down at her notebook.

"Your mother dealt with him quite nicely," Tish added.

"But now that she's gone, I bet he'll be

164

back." Janet picked up her notebook and stood, staring anxiously at the door to the kitchen.

"The library lounge," Angie suggested.

"Might as well," Kate murmured. "We'll see you later."

"Are we still on for swordplay this afternoon?" Janet asked me.

"Deck six at two o'clock, if that still works for you," I said.

"Fabulous."

They hurried out. There were still several dozen people occupying the main dining room, conversing or reading. Were they exhibiting the very human tendency to cling together in times of crisis? Or merely trying to avoid having to go up the stairs to their cabins and then back down again at lunchtime?

"So, who's up for charades?"

First Officer Martin had returned, looking haggard and trying his best to smile cheerfully. I slipped out before he could assign me to a team.

I decided to drop by my cabin for the book I was reading — a paper book luckily, rather than an e-book — and take it up to deck six. The book was my reading group's latest selection — not what I would have chosen for shipboard reading, but I needed to finish it by the time we returned. I wasn't sure I'd be able to concentrate on it — I might give in to the temptation to fret over the highly unsatisfactory events of the morning. But at least having it would give me a good excuse for chasing away anyone who tried to interrupt my fretting.

I made for the part of the deck where there was a row of six blue-and-white recliners, all wonderfully shady, thanks to being tucked under a canvas awning. The honeymooning couple occupied the first two, lying with their eyes closed, holding hands. An iPhone lay on the husband's stomach, and they were sharing a pair of earbuds, each taking one.

At the far end was a small, bespectacled man in shorts and the most subdued Hawaiian shirt I'd ever seen, all in black and white and gray. I recognized him as the man I'd briefly shared a table with at breakfast — the one who had been so disparaging of how Pastime was handling our current problems. He appeared to be reading a book — an oversized coffee table book about tall ships. When he saw me, he hugged the book tighter to his chest. I nodded politely and took the middle recliner, leaving one empty recliner between me and him and one between me and the honeymooning couple.

I hoped the first officer didn't show up. I didn't think anyone here was in the mood for one of his ice-breaking games. If his methods were typical, cruises must be hell for introverts. Or people, like the honeymooning couple, who only wanted to spend time with each other.

Or people like me, who wanted some peace and quiet to think.

And instead of browbeating innocent passengers into forced merriment, why didn't he concentrate on whatever administrative details had to be done to deal with Desiree's suicide? Even if they weren't going to investigate, surely they had to write up at least a rudimentary report. If nothing else they'd need to pack her things and figure out who to hand them over to when we got back to Baltimore.

Not my problem. And even if I wanted to make it my problem, not much I could do.

I pulled out my book, and while I was at it, my notebook-that-tells-me-when-to-breathe. I opened the notebook to a fresh page, in case I had any useful thoughts. Then I opened my book and tried to focus on the words. None of which made sense. I tried rereading the last few pages, to help me get back into the plot. It didn't help much. Then I let it fall flat on my stomach as I leaned back in my recliner to think.

I didn't actually close my eyes, but since I had my sunglasses on, it probably looked as if I were napping.

The small, bespectacled man glanced my way a few times. Eventually, he seemed to relax and stopped hugging his book so tightly to his chest.

Behind the book, he was hiding a thick sheaf of legal-sized papers. He was slowly reading through them, occasionally picking up a pen to make a notation.

Okay, I was mildly curious why he was being so secretive about his papers. Maybe later I'd figure out a way to get a glance at them. But for now . . .

"Meg, we have to do something."

CHAPTER 13

I started, and opened my eyes to see Dad and Horace standing at the foot of my recliner. Evidently I had dozed off while thinking.

"Do something about what?" I asked.

"The sheer incompetence of it all!" Horace fumed.

I noticed that the small, bespectacled man two recliners down had looked up at their arrival and then gone back to his book — but I had the feeling he was eavesdropping.

"Any specific examples of incompetence you'd like to share with me?" I asked.

"They don't seem very interested in taking advantage of our expertise." Dad sounded hurt. "I offered our services to the first officer — my medical and Horace's forensic services. He didn't seem interested."

"He all but said 'don't call us, we'll call you.' " Horace didn't look hurt. He looked irritated.

"Maybe they have a doctor on board," I suggested.

"No, they don't," Dad said. "I found that out yesterday. I spotted the location of the ship's hospital on the map, and I dropped by. I thought I'd inspect the facilities, pay my respects to a colleague. But there was no one there, and when I asked where the doctor was, they looked as if I were crazy."

"If there's no doctor on board, who staffs the hospital?" I asked.

"Two crew members with EMT training." Dad shook his head. "And some hospital — a hospital bed and a first aid kit, that's about it."

"Besides, even if they did have a doctor on board, I doubt if they'd have their own forensic expert." Horace didn't look irritated anymore. He looked mad. "So who's working the crime scene?"

"Not much of a crime scene to work," I said.

"Well, of course not, to the untrained eye," Horace said. "But who knows what I could find if they gave me a chance? Fingerprints! DNA! Trace elements of all kinds! And —"

"I get it," I said. "And if I were the captain, I'd have been overjoyed to find out that I had trained professionals to help me deal properly with this morning's suicide."

"Alleged suicide," Dad and Horace said, almost in unison.

"But there isn't a crime scene anymore. After the captain inspected it, he told the first officer to take her belongings back to her cabin and have a steward clean the deck."

Horace and Dad stared back at me for a few moments in stunned silence.

"Unbelievable," Dad finally murmured.

"Are they idiots?" Horace exclaimed.

The man two recliners down had definitely been eavesdropping. He hadn't turned a page — either in his book or his hidden document — since Dad and Horace had arrived, and now he burst out laughing.

"Yes, they're complete idiots," he said. "Sorry — I know it's rude to eavesdrop. But there you have it in a nutshell. They're idiots."

"I'd be interested in hearing why you say that, Mr . . . ?"

"Lambert." He slid off his recliner and onto the one next to me. "Ted Lambert."

He held out his hand and we all three shook it in turn.

"The thing is — you're absolutely right." He sat very erect on the edge of the recliner and pushed his wire-rimmed spectacles farther up his nose. "It's idiotic. But it's not really their idiocy — it's company policy."

"Company policy to destroy a crime scene?" Horace sounded incredulous. "Instead of preserving it until the proper authorities come on the scene?"

"Ah, but who are the proper authorities? And what is the likelihood that they will come on the scene?" Mr. Lambert's round owlish face radiated the same passionate enthusiasm Dad often displayed when he had found a new subject to obsess on. "The ship's registered in the Bahamas, you know — that's actually the most common registry these days."

"I thought that was Panama," I said.

"Oh, very good!" Lambert looked pleased. "Used to be Panama, yes; and Panama's still number two. But Bahamian registration's almost double Panama's now."

"So the ship's owned by someone in the Bahamas?" Horace looked puzzled.

"No, it's American owned," Lambert said. "But registered in the Bahamas. It's what's called a flag of convenience. The practice started out a century ago when the U.S. passed some fairly forward-thinking laws to improve vessel safety and working conditions for sailors. And of course, as soon as the laws were passed, the ship-owning companies started trying to figure out how to get around them. So they started registering ships in other countries."

"Thereby avoiding any laws they didn't like?" I asked.

"Yes." Lambert was favoring me with the sort of smile teachers save for their star pupils. "Shipping lines tend to prefer countries whose laws are pro-business, of course."

"Meaning the countries that have the most lax safety, labor, environmental, and consumer protection laws," I said.

"Very good! You must have studied up on this."

"No," I said. "I'm just good at making logical deductions. But you appear to have studied up on it. Any particular reason why?"

"Because I'm a glutton for punishment." Lambert sighed, and his enthusiasm dimmed a little. "I'm an attorney, you see. And I'm completely incapable of getting into something without studying up on the legal aspects of it."

"So who investigates a shipboard crime?" Horace asked. "Specifically, this crime. The Bahamian authorities?"

"The Bahamians?" Lambert gave a barklike laugh. "You must be kidding. They're a thousand miles away. They're not going to do anything. If we were in the territorial waters of a country, or better yet in a port, that country's laws would apply. At least probably. But here at sea, in international waters, we're covered under admiralty law. Which basically means the captain's in charge."

"Oh, great." I could see from their expressions that neither Dad nor Horace had much confidence in Captain Detweiler's detective abilities. And they didn't yet know about his allegedly being *encore bourré* last night.

"The captain or his security officer," Lambert added.

"Well, that's something," Dad said. "Maybe we need to talk to the security officer."

"Since that would be First Officer Martin . . . well, good luck with that." Lambert grimaced. "I can't imagine that he'd do anything other than what the captain tells him to do."

"This is crazy," Horace muttered.

"Technically, the FBI has jurisdiction if the perpetrator or victim of a crime is a U.S. citizen," Lambert went on.

"So maybe they're waiting for the FBI to

do their investigation?" Horace looked hopeful. He'd enjoyed the several times he'd worked cases with colleagues from the FBI.

"Don't hold your breath," Lambert said. "In practice, what that usually means is that the ship files a report with the FBI and the FBI does however much investigation they feel it's worth. And that almost certainly won't happen until the ship gets to port — even the FBI doesn't have the resources to fly agents out to every ship where a crime's reported. And the FBI's investigation is only as good as the evidence they have to work with, and there's nothing to make the ship do more than a token job on that."

He shook his head and the three of them fell silent for a while — contemplating Pastime's highly unsatisfactory investigatory procedures, I assumed. I was ruminating on something else.

"Look, I don't mean to pry," I said to Lambert finally. "But you know all this about how little real law enforcement there is on board a ship — and you came anyway?"

"The wife," he said. "Always wanted to take a cruise. I tried to convince her to fly to some tropical island and just hang out on the beach — but no. She wanted a cruise. I figured, how bad could it be? Then this happens. And to top it all off, she picked a week when I have to work on a brief for one of my biggest clients." He held up the sheaf of papers he'd been hiding behind his book. "Due Monday. I only hope we get to someplace with working Internet by Monday, or I'm totally screwed."

"We should let you get back to it," I said.

"That's okay." He picked up a beach bag and tucked both book and brief in it. "I've spent two hours on the damned thing already today, and I need to rest my eyes. So do you know the dead woman?"

"No," I said. "I know who she is, that's all. Why?"

"I gather she came on this trip alone," he said.

I nodded.

"Wish there was some way of getting in touch with her next of kin, whoever that is."

"Let me guess — you want to help her next of kin sue the cruise line."

"Me? No." He laughed softly. "I do corporate law. Contracts. I wouldn't know the first thing about suing Pastime. No, it's just that . . . she probably did jump. But what if she didn't? What if someone pushed her, or if she fell overboard because of a broken railing or something that would constitute negligence on the part of the cruise line —

176

just how hard do you think they're going to look if there's no one putting pressure on them? No friends or family. Anyway — I've got to run. The wife's expecting me."

He smiled at us and trotted away.

"He has a point," Dad said. "Ms. St. Christophe has no friends or family here. So it's up to us to speak for them. And her."

He lifted his chin as if bravely, though recklessly, taking on a dangerous mission. Horace echoed his pose.

I decided not to point out that both of them would probably still be trying to investigate even if the entire ship were full of Desiree's friends or family. And for that matter, even if Desiree's friends and family were dead set against an investigation and the captain were investigating vigorously and capably anyway.

"Let me know what you come up with." I leaned back into my recliner.

"Aren't you going to help us?"

"I think the most useful thing I can do now is think." I tapped my forehead. "Remember Poirot's little gray cells."

"Excellent!" Dad beamed at me, and then the two of them nodded vigorously at each other. I was expecting them to stride off to investigate, leaving me to think in peace. Instead they both leaned on the ship's rail, looking thoughtful. Clearly they weren't entirely sure how to begin their investigation.

I remembered something. I pulled out the little feather charm.

"By the way," I said. "What do you make of this?"

I held it up. They both stared at it for a moment and then exchanged a puzzled look.

"I found it at the crime scene." I should have mentioned that right off the bat. Suddenly they were interested. I handed it to Dad and they both peered intently at it.

"I don't like the look of this," Dad said. "Considering our destination . . . do you think it could be some kind of sinister voodoo thing?"

"We're heading to Bermuda, not Haiti, remember," I said. "I don't think voodoo's much of a thing in Bermuda."

"We don't know that for sure." Dad was clearly reluctant to give up a dramatic theory. "Rose Noire seems to be quite agitated about our being becalmed in such a dangerous place. And she's berating herself for not doing enough research on the local supernatural perils."

"I'm not a big believer in the supernatural," Horace said.

"But what about the nocebo effect?" Dad exclaimed.

"There is that," Horace said. "Opposite of placebo," he added, looking at me. "If you believe something will hurt you, sometimes it will. Psychosomatically."

"What if Desiree was superstitious?" Dad suggested. "And someone, knowing that, left this in her cabin, knowing it would drive her over the edge."

"It's a theory." I realized from Dad's expression that he was a little hurt that I wasn't taking his theory more seriously. "I can ask the writers if she was known to be unusually superstitious. And I'll turn that feather charm over to the authorities, once we're finally in contact with some authorities. Authorities other than the captain and the first officer, who would probably say it's nothing and toss it overboard."

"In the meantime, perhaps you should hide that horrible thing somewhere — what if it does its evil work on someone else? Psychosomatically," he added, seeing Horace's expression.

"You're the first people to see it," I said. "Apart from the captain and crew members who were at the crime scene — and I don't think they were particularly shocked or horrified by it. They didn't even bother picking it up."

"Still — don't carry it around," Dad said.

"I'll find a safe place to hide it," I said. "Just as soon as I show it to Rose Noire and get her take on its aura."

"Good." Dad seemed much relieved.

"Meanwhile, don't you two have some work to do?"

"She's right, you know," Horace said. "Although before we begin investigating, we need to do some serious planning."

"Yes." Dad didn't sound thrilled. Clearly he wanted to be doing, not planning. "And for that we need sustenance!" he said, more happily. "Let's do our planning over a bowl of soft-serve ice cream."

"It's only an hour till lunch," Horace pointed out.

"A small bowl, then. What with the alleged suicide and the power outage and whatever it is they're having to repair, who knows if they'll be serving meals on schedule. We should eat while we can."

"And if they don't get the power back soon, all the ice cream will have melted," Horace added. "Better get some before that happens."

With that they finally did stride off and disappear inside.

The deck was so quiet I could hear the occasional wave slapping against the hull, and occasionally a faint hint of sound from one of the newlyweds' earbuds.

I went back to staring at my book and trying to think, or at least stay awake.

Until Dad reappeared.

CHAPTER 14

"I forgot to ask — do you want any ice cream?"

"No thanks." I went back to my book. After a minute or so I realized he was still standing over me. I glanced up.

Dad looked troubled.

"Something wrong?"

"It's about the writers," Dad said.

Oh, dear. Was he tiring of his role as medical consultant to Angie? That seemed unlikely — unless he felt helping her was going to keep her from spending as much time as he wanted on investigating Desiree's disappearance.

"What about the writers?" I asked aloud.

A pause.

"I hate to say it, because they're all very nice, and Angie has to be one of the best new mystery writers to come along in a while — I should lend you one of her books — but . . . well . . ."

"Are you trying to suggest that if Desiree didn't leave the ship under her own steam, they're the most likely suspects to have helped her along?"

He nodded, evidently relieved that I'd had the same thought.

"Of course, you've spent more time with the other three than I have," he said. "Maybe I've gotten the wrong impression."

"If you've gotten the impression that they all hated Desiree's guts, then you're right," I said. "I also think it would be safe to say that none of them have been cast into the depths of despair at her untimely death."

"But they haven't broken out the champagne, either, right?"

"Not that I've noticed." Come to think of it, how would I describe their reaction? I mulled it over, with Dad waiting patiently, as if he guessed what I was doing. "If I had to describe their collective reaction, I think stunned would be the most accurate term," I said finally. "I also think they're a little relieved — Desiree made life hell for their friend. From something Janet, the fantasy writer, told me, I think maybe they were worried that she'd go after one of them next. It must be a relief to know that can't happen. And they wouldn't be human if they didn't feel just a twinge of satisfaction."

"Oh, yes." Dad nodded vigorously. "They believe Desiree's responsible for their friend's death."

"And karma's already gotten her. And yet, they're women, raised in a society that tries to drum into us the importance of always being nice, so I bet they feel terribly guilty about even that little twinge of satisfaction."

"Yes." Dad sounded thoughtful. "So imagine how wracked with guilt one of them would be if she had pushed Desiree over the side. Does one of them seem more stressed and anxious than the rest?"

"Up until I introduced her to you and Horace, I'd have said Angie. But she was already stressed and anxious before Desiree jumped or was pushed, and for all I know, stressed and anxious is her normal state of mind. I don't know them that well."

"But now is the perfect opportunity to change that." Dad beamed at me. "Get to know them. Find out which ones are rooming together, and whether any of them are heavy sleepers and —"

"I get it, Dad. I read the occasional mystery book, too. I'll find out as much as I can about them, their relationship with Desiree, their whereabouts last night, and anything else that seems useful."

"But be careful." Dad looked suddenly

184

stricken. "After all, this could be a murder investigation."

"And one of them could be the murderer. I'll be careful."

"Worse, what if they're all murderers?" Dad's expression was a curious mix of anxiety over the dangers I might be facing and excitement at what would be, in one of his mysteries, an elegant plot twist. "They all have motive — the same motive."

"You're thinking a real-life *Murder on the Orient Express.*" I tried not to let him hear my skepticism. "I'm sure Agatha Christie would approve, but *Murder on the Pastime Wanderer* doesn't quite have the same ring."

He chuckled slightly. I went back to my book.

"You're not going to just sit there reading, are you?" Dad sounded very disappointed.

"Of course not." I didn't look up from my book.

A pause.

"That certainly looks like what you're doing."

I lowered my book.

"Yes," I said. "But what you fail to take into account is that before picking up this book, I reviewed all the evidence we've found —"

"That wouldn't take long."

"And all the suspects, and everything they've said about their relationship with Desiree. Having loaded all that into my brain, I'm now going to do something else completely different with the top level of my brain so my subconscious can work undisturbed."

"Do you find it works?"

"At home, it works very well. Of course, if I were at home, I'd do the laundry, or run errands, or best of all, spend some quality time at my anvil. Blacksmithing's always good at giving the old subconscious the peace and quiet it needs to do its work." I hoped he'd notice the not-even-very-subtle bit about peace and quiet.

"So you're hoping to close your book in a little while and have the solution?"

"Unlikely," I said. "About the most I'm hoping for is that eventually I'll think of something useful we can do to get us closer to a solution."

"Even that would be a good thing." Dad looked disappointed that I wasn't promising miracles.

"And just between you and me," I added, "I'm also going to test a theory. If I go around asking people questions in the wake of a suspicious event, they're bound to be on their guard and clam up. But if I just lounge here with my book, looking like someone minding her own business, people with something they want to get off their chests are much more likely to sidle up and confide in me."

"Now that sounds more like it. Carry on!" Dad hurried off with a satisfied expression.

I focused back on my book. What I'd told him wasn't a complete fabrication. I often had some of my best ideas while doing something else. And I sometimes deliberately did something else in the hope of jump-starting my brain. But I wasn't sure my subconscious had enough information to come up with anything brilliant. Especially since what I was sure Dad wanted me to come up with was proof that Desiree had been murdered. And by whom.

I wasn't expecting success. But at least I could finish the book my book club was supposed to be discussing right after I got back. I planned to give some of my fellow members the third degree about why they'd insisted on choosing it, an operation that would be much more successful if I'd actually finished the wretched thing.

I heard someone settling into the recliner to my left. I glanced over. One of the Three Stooges. Not Evans of the thinning red hair, the one I'd knocked down the night before.

This was the five o'clock shadow one. I wondered, briefly, if he knew what his buddy had been up to. Probably not, or at least he had no idea that I was the one who had thwarted his buddy. If he'd known that, he'd probably steer clear of me. But instead he took the recliner right beside me, rather than politely leaving at least one empty recliner between himself and a stranger. I deduced that he was planning to attempt conversation. I stayed focused on my book. If I'd known my plan to let suspects come to me and reveal themselves would involve interacting with the Stooges —

"I'm going to kill my travel agent if I ever get back to Baltimore," he announced.

I lowered my book slightly and looked at him over my sunglasses.

"If that's intended as a pickup line, you need to work on your technique," I told him. "Starting with your ability to identify single women to try your lines on." I waved my left hand slightly so my wedding ring caught the light.

"Pretty sure there aren't any single women on this tub," he said. "At least none under sixty."

He was wrong about that, but if Rose Noire had managed to avoid encountering him so far, I wasn't going to ruin her day.

And maybe his buddy hadn't told him about Léonie.

"There's not even a casino." From his tone, you'd think gambling facilities were up there with electricity and running water as basic requirements for civilization.

I shrugged and returned to my book.

"And that old dude who took over the main dining room after dinner and kept droning on about birds and stuff — how come they let him get away with that?"

"Actually, they're paying Grandfather to do that." I'd have gone back to my book but I wanted to see his expression when the word "Grandfather" sank in.

He winced.

"Sorry. I'm sure he's great if you're into all that educational stuff. Me, I'm not an egghead. I just wanted to have some fun."

He looked so forlorn that I felt just a little bit sorry for him.

"Your travel agent didn't tell you this was supposed to be a quiet, environmentally oriented, educational cruise?" I asked.

"Nope." He shook his head. "She told us Pastime was cheaper than most cruise lines to begin with, on account of it being new and trying to build market share. And that this cruise was dirt cheap because it was the last minute and they still had two double

189

staterooms that hadn't sold. We've done it before, you know. Gotten a bargain on a last-minute cruise out of Baltimore or even New York. There are almost always a few unsold rooms, and we don't much care about the destination — the journey, not the arrival, matters, am I right?"

I suspected what mattered for him was the party, not the journey.

"I'd have a talk with my travel agent," I said. "She definitely didn't do you any favors this time." And she hadn't done the rest of the passengers any favors, either. I was almost positive he or one of his buddies was responsible for the puddle of beery vomit I'd found outside the main dining room after Grandfather's lecture. It had definitely been one of the Stooges who'd badgered Léonie. And I wasn't optimistic that either transgression was a one-time thing. If he wanted help killing his travel agent, I might just volunteer.

"And what's with the crew, anyway?" he said. "Have you ever been on a cruise where the crew all ran away when you asked them something?"

"This is my first cruise," I said. "So I have no basis for comparison." And maybe he hadn't heard that at least one crew member had every reason to avoid him and his

190

friends. Although he was right — the crew didn't hover. I wasn't sure this was such a bad thing. I'd once read an online review that complained that a store's sales clerks had left the shopper completely alone the whole time she'd been there. To me, that sounded like a selling point, not a shortcoming.

"It wasn't so bad last night," he went on. "But this morning it's like they've ordered them not to talk to us any more than they have to."

He did have a point. I hadn't seen the captain since his token appearance at the briefing. And I hadn't seen another crew member since I'd left what I still thought of as the crime scene.

"Maybe a lot of them don't speak English all that well," I suggested. Like poor Vaclav, who'd come to report Desiree's suicide. Although Léonie and Serge were pretty fluent. Maybe they were the exceptions. "It's a pretty international bunch, from what I've seen of the name tags."

"That's typical — the international part. Every cruise I've been on, it's like the United Nations or the Olympics or something. Crew members from all over the world, and most of them really young. I guess working cruises gets old after a while.

But they all spoke English just fine. Better than me sometimes. Never had them hide from me before."

I nodded. It was on the tip of my tongue to ask if it was all the Pastime crew members who were avoiding him or just the women.

"Whatever's going on with the ship is probably causing them a lot of extra work," I said.

"I guess." He didn't sound convinced.

Another question occurred to me.

"You said you and your friends snagged two unsold double staterooms," I said. "But I've only ever seen three of you. Is there a fourth?"

"Yeah, our buddy Barry." He shook his head. "I wouldn't hold my breath waiting to see him. He's never taken a cruise before and it turns out he gets seasick."

"Really? In this weather?" I waved my hand to indicate the cloudless blue sky and glassy smooth water.

"I know," he said. "Doesn't make sense to me, either. We've tried Dramamine and Bonine and Benadryl and ginger and green apples and an acupressure wristband and every other seasickness remedy we know of. He just lies there moaning and pu— Um, you know. Driving the porcelain bus."

I nodded and returned to my book. Curiously, when I'd started reading, I'd had trouble focusing on it, but at the moment, I found myself looking forward to getting back into it.

"Hal," he said. "Hal Burkhart."

I glanced up to see that he was holding out his hand.

"Meg," I said. I ignored the hand, and I didn't see any reason why he needed to know my last name.

"Say, would you like to — never mind." He got up so quickly that he half stumbled over the recliner. "I can see you're really interested in that book of yours."

He fled.

Apparently I was getting very good at giving people what my brother called "the Mother look." I hadn't even been trying.

But when he was talking about his friend Barry, I found myself wondering how Trevor was getting along. Dad would probably know. Out of habit I pulled out my cell phone.

Which had no signal. Of course.

I heaved myself out of the recliner and headed for the stairs.

As I descended, I made a mental list of the most likely places to find Dad. I got no answer at 501, the cabin he was sharing with Mother, or down the hall at 508, which was

Grandfather's cabin. I went down to deck four and lucked out — he was in the Starlight Lounge, conferring with Grandfather, Caroline, Wim, and Guillermo.

Then again maybe lucking out was the wrong expression.

CHAPTER 15

"There you are!" Grandfather sounded as if I'd forgotten to show up for some important appointment. "We could use your help. We have a problem."

"Only one?" It probably came out a little more sarcastic than I'd intended. "So far there's the ship being stopped in the middle of nowhere, all power and communications being out, the crew not telling us the first thing about what's happening and when it will be fixed, the captain not doing even a token investigation of a passenger suicide —"

"Alleged suicide," Dad corrected.

"Alleged suicide, if it makes you happy." I turned back to Grandfather. "Were you talking about any of that, or is there more?"

"I can't find Trevor," he said. "I'm beginning to wonder if the blasted man's fallen overboard, too."

"Okay, that's also a problem." If no one in

this room had seen him . . . I shoved down a twinge of anxiety. More than a twinge. "When did you last see him?"

Grandfather pondered.

"When I sent him to fetch my ginger beer."

"That's a why, not a when. Was this sometime today?"

"Yesterday. Before the ship set sail. I told him to find out if the ship stocked ginger beer and, if it didn't, to go and get a couple of cases pronto."

"Ginger beer?"

He obviously sensed the mix of puzzlement and disapproval in my tone.

"I need it for my throat! I'm going to be doing a hell of a lot of talking with all these nightly lectures. Ginger beer's how I keep my voice in shape."

Or was it Grandfather's equivalent of Van Halen's legendary "no brown M&Ms" clause? Although I'd read that Van Halen's clause was actually intended to reveal whether a venue had actually read and complied with all the complicated technical requirements in their contract. Maybe when Grandfather was out of earshot I'd ask Dad if ginger beer really was good for a speaker's voice — because I suspected either the effect was psychosomatic, or maybe Grandfather just liked ginger beer.

But that could wait.

"This was after boarding began?" I asked.

"Yes, but quite a while before we sailed," Grandfather said. "He'd have had plenty of time to find the ginger beer and get back on board."

Plenty of time? I'd handed over luggage duty to him less than half an hour before boarding ended. Then again, it was Trevor's job to be a miracle worker, and he was very good at it. Or maybe he'd already completed the ginger beer errand before taking charge of our luggage.

"Perhaps you underestimated the difficulty of finding ginger beer on the Baltimore docks," I said aloud. "And if ginger beer is so essential to the success of the expedition, why isn't it on your supply list?"

"It will be next time." Grandfather scowled, as if planning a few harsh words with whoever had imperiled the strategic ginger beer supply.

"Remind me, who's Trevor rooming with?" I asked.

"We got him a single room, remember?" Dad said. "We thought it would be better for the efficiency of the expedition."

Yes, I remembered now. And it was not so much for the efficiency of the expedition as the sanity of whoever got stuck with him as a roommate. Horace, who'd been originally tapped to share with him, had flat-out refused. The same persistence, attention to detail and, well, persnicketiness that made him such a natural for the role of Grandfather's assistant made him less than popular as a roommate. Then there were his allergies, his sensitivities, his hypochondria . . .

"Has anyone seen him since the ship sailed?" I asked.

They all looked briefly at one another and then shook their heads.

"I asked who could tell us if he'd gotten on board," Caroline said. "And they told us the first officer."

"Oh, great," I muttered. "I think the first officer has a few other things to occupy him."

"Well, he seemed to be sorry he couldn't help us, but all the data is in the computer. If Trevor left the ship in search of ginger beer, he'd have been marked as on shore, and if he returned they'd have marked him as on board."

"And if he wasn't back by sailing time — well, they did warn us that the ship waits for no one," I said. "But until the computers are back up, they can tell us nothing."

She nodded.

"I didn't see him at the mandatory safety session," I said. "Which might suggest that he wasn't in their computer as having boarded."

"But it could just mean that they checked his cabin, found he was prostrate with seasickness, and gave him a rain check." Caroline looked annoyed. "I asked several crew members if that's possible and got a different answer every time."

"I'm impressed that you've actually found crew members to ask," I said. "They've been thin on the ground this morning. Let me see what I can find out."

"I knew she was the one to tackle it," Grandfather said. "Let's go see what we can figure out for tonight's lecture."

He strode out, followed by Caroline and the photographers.

I sat back, took a deep breath, and shook my head briskly. Sometimes that helped clear the cobwebs.

"Can I help you with something?" I looked up to see Aarav, the bartender, hovering, with an easy smile on his face. "Margarita? I can't do frozen at the moment, and it won't be all that cold, but it will taste good anyway."

"I see you have me pegged. Maybe later.

But tell me — do you have any idea how I could get in touch with a crew member named Gianpiero Mulder?"

"Don't think we have anyone by that name." He looked puzzled. "I think I'd have noticed."

"He's one of the porters."

"Ah, the porters." Aarav's puzzled look vanished. "They don't come on board. They're not part of the crew."

"You mean they don't work for Pastime?"

"They work for Pastime, but they're not part of the crew. Shoreside employees. Plus they're Teamsters."

He said the word "Teamsters" with a faint shudder and an expression that was a curious mix of distaste and envy.

"The crew belongs to a different union? Or do you just not like the Teamsters?"

"I'm fine with the Teamsters," he said. "I'd love to join them. Theoretically all crew members have the right to join a union, but it isn't hard to figure out that they're happier with you if you don't. Which is why they discourage fraternizing with the porters. So I can't say I've ever met this Mulder fellow."

"Damn," I said. "We're looking for one of the passengers — my grandfather's assistant. Guy named Trevor. We haven't seen

200

him since the ship sailed, and we're beginning to worry that Grandfather sent him on an errand that took him so long that he didn't get back in time for our departure."

"You didn't notice him missing until today?"

"We thought he was locked in his cabin suffering from either seasickness or hypochondria. But he's still not answering his door, and we're getting concerned. The worry-warts are even fretting that maybe he fell overboard. The last time I saw him he was going on board with our party's luggage, so I thought maybe Gianpiero the Teamster might have more of an idea where he went. Wait — what about the young woman who checked people on board — I don't know her name, but she'd have had to check him out if he'd gone back off the ship, right?"

"Yes." The bartender nodded. "And she'd have logged him out on the system, so normally you could just have the first officer check the system to see if he'd come back on board. Only with the systems offline . . ."

"I know. But maybe the crew member who logged him out would remember — because it must have been annoying, having someone either cut it so close to the sailing time or miss it entirely."

"She probably would, because there's always a bit of a fuss if someone misses a departure. But she's not crew, either. Shore-side employee, and so not on board."

"Damn."

"Sorry. I wish there was something I could help you with."

"Maybe there is." I had to laugh. "It's not important but — well, you're a crew member."

"Just don't ask me to splice the main mizzen or anything nautical like that."

"No, you're doing just fine here with the margaritas," I said. "But I have a weird question I've been wanting to ask a crew member."

"Yes, ma'am?" The look on his face suggested that I'd have a hard time coming up with a question so weird that Aarav hadn't heard it before.

"What's below deck zero?"

"Below deck zero?" He frowned. "Um . . . mostly water. After you get past the ship's hull, of course."

"So it's the lowest deck — no deck minus one or zero two or anything like that."

"No, ma'am. Deck zero is it."

"And getting back to our missing party member — would I be correct in assuming

202

there are not a lot of possible hiding places down there on deck zero?" I went on. "I mean, if Trevor got into a snit about Grandfather taking him for granted and decided to hide to make us all worry —"

"He'd stand out like a sore thumb on deck zero." He grinned ruefully and shook his head. "Most of the crew's packed four to a small cabin when the ship's fully crewed. Not quite as bad when they're under full strength like this trip, though the cabins are still pretty tiny. Two to a cabin for a few of us who are senior — I bunk with the head chef. And every corner's packed with storage bins and lockers and supplies. Pretty much zero chance he could hide on deck zero. And not a whole lot of opportunity for hiding anywhere else, for that matter. Have you checked his stateroom?"

"We don't have a card key for it."

"Ask one of the stewards who service that deck," he said. "Or the first officer. If there's a genuine reason to be concerned about his well-being . . ."

"Thanks. I'll try that." Assuming I could talk a crew member into realizing I had a valid reason for snooping in Trevor's room. I stood. Time to go looking for a gullible steward. "Oh, one more thing —"

I paused, trying to figure out a way to ask

him about the curious invisibility of most of the crew, when the door slammed open.

"I have no idea what you're talking about!" First Officer Martin strode in, looking cross and harried. "You're the engineer, not me. Just fix it."

"Easy for you to say." A burly crew member had followed him into the Starlight Lounge. "But if —"

He spotted me and stopped. The first officer had regained his composure and was smiling at me. Or trying to. I could tell he was both busy and in a bad mood. Understandable, actually.

"May we help you?"

"I was trying to find out how to get into a cabin someone's locked out of." I was about to reel off the explanation of Trevor's seasickness, but he cut me off.

"Any of the stewards can let them in," he said.

Clearly not the moment to bother him. And the employee who'd entered with him was dressed not in a Pastime uniform but a grease-stained coverall. Not a steward, obviously.

"Thanks." I got the definite feeling that he was waiting for me to leave to continue his somewhat heated discussion with coverall guy, so I made my exit.

I headed back to our cabin. Caroline and I each had a file with all the paperwork for all the members of the combined Blake Foundation/Langslow family contingent. Trevor's room was on our manifest. With luck I could use that to talk a crew member into letting me in. I could even say I was doing what the first officer had told me to.

Back in the room, I pulled out the file. Trevor was in — well, supposed to be in — room 210, which was right next to the elevator lobby on deck two. I headed for the stairs.

And on my way down, I lucked out. I ran into Léonie on the landing between deck four and deck three.

"Bonjour," she said, with a smile that was a lot more genuine than I could remember seeing from anyone else on the crew today. Well, apart from Aarav, the bartender, for whom smiling was almost a job requirement.

"Bonjour," I said. "Is there any chance you could tell me who to ask about getting something done?" I explained about Trevor's cabin.

"Pas de problème," she said. "I have access to the staterooms on that floor. If you would follow me, please?"

When the door to 210 swung open, we

saw two bags in the center of the floor. I had the fleeting, irrational impression that they felt abandoned and were huddling together for comfort. The bed was perfectly made.

"It does not appear that he has been here," Léonie said. "If this were one of the singles cruises, I would not concern myself — passengers on those sometimes spend very little time in their own staterooms. But on this cruise . . . I think you are right to be worried. Let us hope that *monsieur* merely missed our sailing."

"Because if he went overboard, the captain's not going to do much."

"*Eh bien,* to do him justice, there is not much he can do. If a passenger falls overboard, we can throw him a life preserver and lower a boat to rescue him. If we see him, of course. If we do not see him until he is underwater, what can we do? We do not carry a diving team. There is also the fact that company policy discourages anything that makes the news or upsets the passengers or interrupts the ship's schedule. But even so, believe me, if there was anything the captain could do to find Madame St. Christophe or your friend, he would do it. Losing even one passenger does not look well on his record. Losing two on one voyage — *mon Dieu!* Even leaving one behind would be a black mark."

"So Captain Detweiler is probably sweating bullets right now. Very worried, that is," I added, seeing her puzzled look.

"I like sweating bullets." She seemed to be filing the idiom away for future use. "Yes. Between the loss of a passenger and the increasing delay, he is very much worried."

"He's not telling the passengers much about the delay," I said.

"A problem with the navigation system. The engineers say they can fix it, but it will take hours and hours, and requires the power to be off, because they do not particularly wish to electrocute themselves. And the captain does not seem to realize that to stand right behind them and ask every five minutes how much longer they will take does nothing to speed them up."

"In fact, I bet it slows them down."

"It is possible." She nodded.

"I can tell you another thing the captain doesn't seem to realize," I said. "That the less he tells his passengers about what's going on, the more worried they get, and the more likely they are to complain and write negative reviews when they finally get back to land."

"It is unfortunate," she said. "And also

unfortunate that First Officer Martin *does* understand this. He will use that as he can."

"He wants the captain's job?"

"Oui." She nodded. "He has wanted it for a long time now. Pastime is only a small cruise line, and the job of captain does not present itself very often. He may have to wait until Captain Detweiler leaves."

"And Captain Detweiler doesn't look old enough to be anywhere near retirement." It was the perfect opening for her to spill the beans about the captain being *encore bourré,* but she said nothing. I actually liked her for that. "So Martin's in limbo unless Detweiler gets a job elsewhere —"

"Unlikely. Most cruise lines prefer to promote from within."

"So Detweiler's probably planning to stay put until retirement, and Martin's only hope is for the captain to screw up — in which case, Martin gets the job?"

"Probably," she said. "Pastime, too, likes to promote from within. For most of the crew, that would be the only reason for regret if Captain Detweiler's career were to suffer as a result of what currently happens aboard the ship. Should the first officer replace him — well, fortunately my contract is up soon. I do not think I will sign again with Pastime. But it would be better if that were not widely known," she added, looking worried, as if suddenly realizing she had said too much.

"Of course." Perhaps I should take what she had to say about Martin with a grain of salt, given that she obviously didn't like him.

I'd been scanning the cabin as we talked, looking for some signs of occupancy. And not finding anything. Although something odd did catch my eye. One of the zippered outside pockets of Trevor's suitcase was half-unzipped, and the top of a paperback was sticking out of it. Which wouldn't have seemed the least bit odd — Trevor was an avid reader — but what I could see of the book's cover bore the name "Desiree" in large, flowery, bright red letters. I pulled the book out of the pocket, revealing "St. Christophe" in the same overblown script. The title appeared to be *The Sharp Claw of Love* — although the script typeface was hard to decipher. The cover illustration showed a woman in a disheveled red gown, who appeared to have fainted on top of a sleek black panther.

"*Monsieur* is a reader of romance?" Léonie sounded amused.

"Not that I know of," I said. "I'd have expected either one of Patrick O'Brian's seafaring novels or something earnest and self-improving."

I flipped the book open and saw an inscription: "To my adorable Trevor, with grateful thanks for everything you have done for me!!!!"

"To my adorable Trevor?" I read aloud.

"Your friend knew Ms. St. Christophe?"

"News to me." I didn't like the past tense. Of course, it was obviously applicable to Desiree. But not, I hoped, to Trevor. "Maybe he doesn't know her. Maybe he met her during boarding and did something useful for her and she gave him the book to thank him."

"She thanks him for everything he did for her," Léonie pointed out. "And besides — this is not a new book — it has been read."

She had a point. Definitely not a brand-new book. Was Trevor a covert reader of romance? Had he, perhaps, learned that one of his favorite authors was coming on the cruise and brought this well-thumbed paperback to get it autographed?

Stranger things had happened. But on the whole, I preferred the idea that he'd done her some small service on the pier and been rewarded with a book. A battered one, because it was the only one she had in her pink straw suitcase. And maybe the gushing inscription was just her style.

"I think I'll hang on to this," I said. "Nothing else I can do here — but thank you for letting me in."

"You are most welcome." She followed me out of Trevor's cabin. "And not just because I know who to thank for the many guardian angels who seem to be watching over me on this voyage. It is good of you to concern yourself for your friend."

"I only wish I had concerned myself about Trevor last night."

"When the power eventually comes back, we can check with our staff at the Baltimore pier," she said. "If he missed the ship, they will offer to help him arrange a flight to Hamilton — perhaps even in time for him to greet you when we sail in."

"Let's hope so."

She smiled, wished me *bonjour,* and left. I stood for a few moments thinking. Okay, thinking and dreading climbing all the way back up to deck five. Especially since there was more than an even chance Grandfather and the rest had gone elsewhere. Like down to the main dining room to figure out whatever adjustments they needed to make to their setup in case the power wasn't back on by seven and they had to do the session with no slides and no microphone. And that was assuming anyone would even want to attend a lecture if the power was still out by evening.

And why even go looking for them? My search to find out what had happened to Trevor seemed to have reached a temporary dead end. When we got communications back, I could find the first officer and get him to contact Baltimore to see if Trevor was there. And if he was, maybe I could get him on the line to ask about his connection to Desiree. But until then . . .

"When I said I wanted to get away from civilization, this was not what I had in mind," I grumbled.

CHAPTER 16

As I was hovering by the stairwell, I spotted Rob and Delaney coming up.

"Morning," I said. "Did you happen to notice if Grandfather and Caroline and the rest were in the main dining room?"

"Wim and Guillermo were a little while ago," Rob said. "But they were just fetching some sandwiches and sodas to take up to deck six."

"Rats," I said. "As far away as they can possibly get without climbing a mast — not that a ship with no sails needs masts, of course."

"It has mast-like things on top of the roof," Rob said. "Although they probably have a more nautical word for roof. They could climb those."

"The mast-like things are masts," Delaney said. "They don't need them for sails, but they still use them for hanging things that need to be high up — like signal flags and radio antennas."

"Then they're definitely not being used for anything right now. Good time to climb them." Rob almost sounded eager to do it himself.

"We're going up to deck six," Delaney said. "Want us to give Caroline and Grand-father a message?"

"Please," I said. "Tell them I got someone to let me into Trevor's room and there's no sign he was ever there. We're hoping he just missed the sailing time and will fly out to Bermuda and meet us there," I added, see-ing the alarm on their faces.

"Of course, if we had power, we could just call him," Rob said.

"I think that's what I miss most in a power outage nowadays," I said. "I could live without electric light, and do just fine on cold food. But the ability to call someone, and to look something up the minute I start wondering about it — that's what I miss. Communications."

"I know," Delaney said. "I keep taking out my phone and trying to do stuff with it. And I'm kicking myself for not bringing a satel-lite phone. Or a shortwave radio."

"She's going into Internet withdrawal," Rob teased.

"At least the phone's still good for taking

pictures and telling the time," I said. "Although maybe I should ration that. Who knows how long the power will be out?"

"Oh, charging things isn't a problem." Delaney held up what looked at first like a cell phone, until I realized that instead of a screen with brightly colored icons on it I could see only a sort of gray grid pattern. "Solar charger." She held up another similar object. "I'm field testing several different models — I figured the ship would be the perfect place for it."

"We're going up to deck six because it's got the most open deck space," Rob explained. "Find a nice sunny spot to arrange all the solar chargers and then sit in the shade and watch them work. Drop by later if you need a recharge."

"I'll hold you to that."

They resumed their climb. I decided the idea of a soda sounded nice. A ginger ale, maybe. Even if it would probably turn out to be lukewarm. So I headed down and took the well-traveled passageway to the main dining room.

I found three of the writers — Tish, Kate, and Janet — sitting around a table, looking a little glum. They looked up warily when I came in and then relaxed when they saw it was me.

"Have a seat." Tish gestured toward an empty chair.

"We can use her as a fourth." Janet shoved a stack of cards over toward where I was about to sit.

"Oh, don't worry," Kate said, seeing my expression. "You don't actually have to play bridge with us. I don't even know how."

"But if that wretched first officer comes in and tries to force us to have some kind of fun, pick up your cards and pretend to be fascinated," Tish said.

"I know he means well," Kate grumbled. "But he is seriously getting on my nerves."

"We did tell Angie and your father to let us know if there was anything we could do to help them with their investigation," Janet said. "But I got the definite impression they were relieved not to be saddled with us. After all, it's not as if we have any expertise in criminology."

"Speak for yourself," Kate said. "I'm pretty knowledgeable about Judge Henry Fielding and the Bow Street Runners."

"I think police work has progressed a little since the 1700s," Tish remarked.

"No doubt, but the offer stands." Kate lifted her chin and assumed a determined expression. So did the others. Were they perhaps a little put out at not being asked to join the investigation? Or relieved to be left to get on with their work?

"Oh, and in case you're interested, lunch is served." Janet waved over at the buffet tables. I'd assumed they were occupied by the remains of breakfast, for the convenience of late risers. The fruit, pastries, and cereal were still there, but they'd been joined by bread, butter, mustard, mayonnaise, and a selection of sliced cheeses and cold cuts.

"Better help yourself while it's still fresh." Tish didn't sound very thrilled at the prospect. "There hasn't been time for most of that to spoil —"

"I wouldn't risk the mayonnaise," Kate said.

"— but I doubt if they've got any way of keeping it fresh," Tish continued.

"Surely it's early for —" I was glancing at my phone and stopped. "Okay, it's noon. Not too early for lunch. Maybe I'll take your advice. You know, I get the distinct feeling that none of you are particularly enjoying this unscheduled break from the hectic pace of the modern world."

Their expressions changed from merely glum to downright annoyed.

"Well, apart from the lack of a morning shower," Tish said, "and the fact that if this continues the toilets are going to be pretty . . . um . . ."

"I think we can all fill in the blank," Kate said. "And also, we made a bit too merry in the bar after your grandfather's talk and didn't do a good job of plugging in our electronic devices."

"I did plug stuff in," Tish said. "But it was nearly two when I did, and I guess they didn't have much time to charge."

"My laptop's completely out of power." Janet held up a spiral notebook. "I was supposed to write a synopsis while I was on this trip and turn it in to my agent when I got back. I'm trying to do it with pen and paper, and remembering just why I do it on the computer."

"And I'm feeling guilty because my laptop still has power." Tish gestured to the Mac-Book on the table in front of her. "But only twenty percent, and who knows how long the ship's electricity will be out, and I have to make my word count every day or I'll be in trouble when I get back."

"Not your fault," Janet said. "And anyway, your laptop wouldn't help. All my notes and my draft are in *my* laptop, and besides, you're Mac and I'm PC."

"Come over from the dark side," Tish whispered.

"I seem to be the only one who planned

to take a real break on this trip," Kate said. "But my e-reader's down to ten percent. And I didn't bring any paper books because of the weight. So instead of lying in a deck chair, losing myself in a book, I'm saving what little power I have left for bedtime. I have a hard time falling asleep without reading."

"Surely they'll fix whatever it is by bedtime," Tish said.

"I'm not betting on it."

I couldn't help it. I burst out laughing. Not so much because it was funny — although it was — but because I was so relieved to find that they weren't, like Dad, obsessing about Desiree's suicide or murder.

"Come with me," I said. "And bring your dying devices. There may be hope."

I led them up to deck six. Rob and Delaney had settled in under the starboard sun shade, happily watching the patch of sunny deck at their feet where Delaney's solar chargers were doing their thing to three phones, two iPads, and a laptop. And even better, Grandfather's contingent had set up their industrial-sized solar chargers in a sunny spot on the other side of the deck, and were sitting under the port sun shade having, to my surprise, what sounded like a poetry appreciation session. Grandfather, in his best orator's pose, was declaiming:

Day after day, day after day,
We stuck, nor breath nor motion;
As idle as a painted ship
Upon a painted ocean.

"It'll only depress them," Caroline said.

"Don't you mean 'impress them'?" I said. "I had no idea Grandfather ever read poetry, much less memorized bits of it. *The Rime of the Ancient Mariner* — right?"

"He only recites it because he considers it an early, prescient expression of environmental awareness," Caroline said.

"I'm impressed that he knows it at all," I said. "But if he's planning for tonight's talk, don't you think you might want to avoid the next verse?"

I echoed Grandfather's dramatic pose and recited:

Water, water, every where,
And all the boards did shrink;
Water, water, every where,
Nor any drop to drink.

"Oh, very good," Tish said. "Most people mangle that last line."

"English teacher." Kate nodded in Tish's direction.

"On a more mundane note," I said to Caroline. "Can you spare a few volts for the writers? All their infernal devices are running low."

"Be our guests."

Caroline, Wim, and Guillermo got busy setting up the various cables required to charge everyone's phones and laptops and e-readers. Delaney came over to contribute a few cables from her collection. The writers settled into chairs and recliners and seemed to be enjoying just watching their devices being refueled.

"This is fabulous," Janet said. "I don't know how to thank you."

"By the way, Delaney," I said. "Remember that project you were telling me about — Project Bacon?"

"You know, that's a great idea," Kate said. "You probably could cook bacon if you put a sheet of metal out in this sun."

"This Project Bacon's a lot less practical," Delaney said, with a chuckle. "It's called Project Bacon because a bunch of us geeks started off to see if we could add anything useful to the old debate about whether Sir Francis Bacon actually wrote Shakespeare's plays. Which he probably didn't according to our programs."

"You use computer programs to analyze the text, then," Tish said. "I've heard of that."

"These days there are a lot of programs out there to do it," Delaney said. "Ours is a bit different because it's an open-source project — anyone with something to contribute can join in, and even more important, anyone can see how we're doing the analysis."

"Do you also use it to detect plagiarism?" Janet asked.

I could see that Tish and Kate were paying close attention. By now they'd probably guessed why I'd brought up Project Bacon.

"That's one of the main practical applications," Delaney said. "The other being what you might call forensic use."

"Forensic?" I echoed.

"Say you have a case — and this is from real life, by the way — where a woman is getting sexually harassing emails from someone in her company. The cyber techs do their thing and figure out the emails were sent from some guy's computer — only he claims he didn't do it. They have a fairly open office plan, so anyone could have gotten access to his computer and sent them. And what's more, she has it in for him, he

222

claims, and could have written the emails herself and sent them to herself from his computer, to make trouble for him. That's where our software comes in. We feed fifty to a hundred pieces of writing from each of them into our program, until we get a profile of how each one writes. And then we feed in the harassing emails and our program tells us which one wrote them."

"How accurately?" Tish asked.

"Up in the high nineties," Delaney said. "Ninety-seven, ninety-eight percent accuracy in our latest testing. Which means, yeah, there's room for error, but if you're in court facing charges that you wrote threatening emails — or tried to frame someone else for writing threatening emails — and the prosecution has a witness ready to testify that there's a ninety-seven percent certainty that you wrote the emails — odds are you'll settle."

"So if you have a manuscript, you could compare it with books by two different people and see which one wrote it?" Tish asked.

"Sure," Delaney said. "You wouldn't even need books — if you had a bunch of letters or emails from each person, that would work just as well."

"So it's not just word choice?" Tish looked

excited. They all did.

"No, it's subtle neuro-linguistic stuff. Which is not my expertise, but I've gotten pretty good at working with the neuro-linguists so the program finds what they need to find."

"Is there any chance you could do some testing for us?" Kate asked. "When we get back to land, of course."

"Sure — that would be fun." From her expression, she really meant it. "But why not now — I mean, if it's stuff you have in your laptops or tablets or phones."

Tish, Kate, and Janet exchanged glances.

"Pretty sure I've got Nancy's last manuscript in my laptop," Kate said. "From when she asked us to critique it before she sent it to her agent."

"I've got all her old regencies in my e-reader," Tish said.

"Me, too," Janet said. "And I might have something of Desiree's. And we know Angie does."

"I'd kind of like to see how well this works first," Tish said. "Not that I'm doubting you —"

"Hey, seeing's believing," Delaney said. "I have an idea. You've probably all got a lot of emails in your laptops. Save a bunch of those — at least fifty, a hundred if possible.

224

I'll analyze those. And then you can give me a bunch of your manuscripts, and I'll tell you which manuscripts match which emails."

"You can do that?"

"No, but our program can." Delaney clearly thought it sounded like fun.

"What if someone were deliberately trying to avoid her usual word choices and turns of phrase? Like writing in a different genre or trying to imitate someone's style?" Kate asked.

"Wouldn't stump the program. It's the neuro-linguistic stuff. Don't ask me to explain it, because I'm not a neuro-linguist."

"Just the best damned programmer you'll ever meet," Rob said.

I could see the writers pause for a moment to smile at that. Sometimes I was very proud of Rob. The fact that Delaney was an acknowledged genius in something he barely understood didn't seem to bother him one bit. He was proud of her. I found myself wondering if little bits of Rob might make it into some of the writers' future books.

"So, got any files for me?" Delaney asked.

The writers claimed their laptops — still tethered to various chargers — and set to work. Delaney rummaged in her tote and came up with flash drives and cables. I decided to leave them to it. True, analyzing Nancy's and Desiree's manuscripts was something of a distraction from their writing — but if Delaney's program turned up anything interesting, it could have a bearing on the suicide. Alleged suicide. They'd found a way to help Dad's investigation.

I strolled over to where Caroline was sitting.

"Want some iced tea?" she asked, pointing to a pitcher.

"Is it really iced?" The pitcher didn't seem to be sweating.

"No, with luck it's finally down to the ambient temperature. But it's wet. The lemon makes it seem refreshing."

She had a point. I let her pour me a glass. "How did you make it, anyway?"

"Plugged my little hot plate into one of the solar batteries and boiled the water on it." She sounded pleased with her own ingenuity.

"I thought hot plates were against Pastime's rules."

"Probably. Aren't you glad I pay no attention to rules?"

"Good point. Where is Dad, anyway?"

"Off with that mystery writer. See for yourself — they're probably still trying to fall off the deck four sun deck."

226

Fall off the ship? That didn't sound like a very good idea. Given how hard it had become since the breakdown to find a crew member when you needed one, anyone who fell overboard had better be able to tread water for a good long time.

I went to the stern and peered over the rail. Deck four ran the length of the ship. Deck five stopped about twenty-five feet short of the stern, and deck six another twenty feet short of that. So from where I stood, I could see both the deck four and deck five sun decks.

On deck five I saw several familiar parasols gathered around a small table that contained a tray of tea paraphernalia — cups, saucers, spoons, napkins, lump sugar, lemon slices, and a couple of glass containers in which tea bags were slowly steeping.

"When they get tired of making sun tea, I'll lend them my hot plate," Caroline said, obviously following my gaze.

Dad and Angie were at the back of deck four, peering over the rail.

"Interesting," I murmured.

"You think they've found something?" Caroline asked. "Or were you using 'interesting' the way your mother does, because you can't think of anything polite to say?"

"I have no idea if they've found anything," I said. "But I just realized something. I'd assumed that Desiree chose the deck four sun deck to jump from because it was the closest one to her room. She's only a few cabins down from us. Room 411."

"Seems pretty obvious," Caroline said. "Although it does beg the question of why she didn't just jump off her private balcony. If I were hell-bent on self-destruction, that's what I'd do. More convenient, and less chance of interference."

"But she was a diva," I pointed out. "A drama queen. That little still life she left behind — the designer shoes, the expensive shawl — that was meant to be seen. Photographed. She wouldn't want it hidden away in her cabin."

"Point taken." Caroline frowned. "And I just realized something else — what if she wanted to be found? Not just her fancy red shoes and her shawl, but her. Maybe she wanted someone to grab her as she was going over the rail, or dive in to save her once she hit the water. What if she expected to be saved?"

I nodded. It sounded all too plausible to me. I pulled out the pamphlet with the floor plans of all the decks — well, all the passenger decks — and studied it.

"There's no place you can jump from in the bow except for that open stretch of deck two. And you can only get there through the Moonbeam Lounge, which the map says is locked up at midnight."

"Probably to keep people from raiding the bar."

"And the navigation bridge is at the front of deck three," I added. "It looks straight down on that part of deck two. I'm pretty sure they have to have someone in there all the time."

"Even when the ship is stopped?"

"Probably."

"So the front of deck two would be a good place to jump if you wanted to be seen," Caroline said. "But there'd be a danger of them stopping you before you actually went over the rail, and it would be hard to get to. And there's no way she could have jumped from the stern up here or on deck five.

She'd just land on the next deck down."

"It would have been perfectly feasible to jump from the stern of deck one, two, or three," I said.

"They're all covered over," she said. "Maybe she wanted to end it all under the open sky."

"Maybe," I said. "Or maybe she thought jumping from four would make the biggest splash. Give her the biggest chance of rescue."

Caroline winced at that.

"She could always go over the side," she pointed out. "From any deck she pleased. Most of the sides are taken up with private balconies, but I think there's at least one public one on each deck."

We moved to the starboard rail and peered over.

"All the balcony rails." I shook my head. "You'd have to leap pretty far out, because if you bounced against the side of the ship going down, you could get caught on one of the balcony rails. And whether she really was trying to kill herself or just hoping for a dramatic rescue, I think the whole idea would be to land in the water, not have her limp body found half on and half off someone's balcony."

"That makes sense," she said. "In a morbid way."

"It's a morbid subject."

Dad and Angie had given up staring over the rail and were inspecting the deck. They'd found a magnifying glass somewhere — although it didn't look like a very powerful one — and they were now examining the spot where Desiree had left behind her shawl and shoes.

And the tiny feathered object. I'd almost forgotten about that. I checked, and saw that it was still tucked in my pocket. I should show it to someone eventually. Then I focused back on Dad and Angie. They were back at the rail, leaning over, peering down at the water.

"Any idea what they're doing now?"

"They're trying to figure out if Desiree really could have jumped from there." Caroline shook her head. "Since, as you and I have just established, it's one of the few places where it looks possible. But if you look closely at the outside of the ship, there are a lot of various . . . I don't know. Sticking-out bits. I'm sure they all perform some useful nautical purpose, but don't ask me what. If you wanted to jump —"

"Which I don't."

"You'd have to pick a stretch of the rail where there weren't any of those sticking-out bits. Or at least none big enough that they'd stop you. Some of them would merely snag your clothes, of course, which is why they're having Horace check everyplace he can reach on the stern of deck four and below, in the hope of finding a torn bit of cloth. They might yet come up with some trace evidence."

"And the crew are letting them do that?"

"The crew." She snorted. "If the crew try to stop you from doing anything, just ask them what's wrong with the ship and when we're going to get back underway and how much of a refund you can get for the inconvenience. They disappear like songbirds who've spotted a hawk."

"Useful," I said. "I'll keep that in mind. Listen, are you and Grandfather planning to do any of your remote broadcasts from Bermuda?"

"Yes," she said. "Assuming we ever get to Bermuda. At this point, it wouldn't surprise me if they turned around and went back to port once they finish this repair, whatever it is. Wouldn't surprise me and wouldn't exactly upset me, either."

"But you've got the equipment — the fancy radio gear and the solar-powered batteries."

"We have. At least I think we have. Solar

batteries right over there. All the transmitting gear is supposed to be in Trevor's baggage. Of course we have no idea if Trevor's here, much less his baggage."

"His baggage is here — I checked. I'll see if I can get someone to let me in again and bring it to you."

"That would be nice," she said. "And is there something you want me to do with it when I get it?"

"You think that stuff might let you contact someone? Like maybe the Coast Guard or the U.S. Navy?"

She cocked her head to one side.

"We should be able to. You don't think the ship has already done that?"

"I wouldn't want to bet on it."

"Meaning you don't want to bet our lives on it."

"Precisely." I nodded. "Even if they've been in contact, I bet they're not saying 'Help! We're stuck in the middle of the Bermuda Triangle with no power and no water and we have no idea what's wrong with our ship, much less how to fix it.' Because I think if they'd said that we'd have seen results by now. The Coast Guard takes that kind of thing pretty seriously."

"I agree." Caroline frowned. "They're probably handing out the party line. 'Don't worry about us; we're just stopped for minor repairs.' "

"Exactly."

"You get me the equipment and I'll get Guillermo and Wim working on making contact with the outside world."

"And then once you make contact, see if you can raise Trevor. I'd feel better, knowing he's just been left behind."

She nodded. Then she bustled over to the other side of the ship, where Guillermo and Wim had evidently found something worth photographing. Something very far away, presumably. I couldn't see anything in any direction but calm water and cloudless blue skies. But both of their cameras sported zoom lenses so large that I'd have worried that it would unbalance me and send me tumbling over the rail. I glanced down again at Dad and Angie. Maybe I should drop by and suggest that they shouldn't both lean over the rail at the same time. What if a sudden wave hit and they both toppled over into the ocean? Dad might not listen, but Angie struck me as having some shreds of common sense.

Janet appeared.

"So it's a little early for our fencing session," she said. "But communications being what they are, I figure it could take a while to find your husband and sons."

"They're probably on the miniature golf course in the bow of deck five," I said.

"I can go get my digital camera and meet you there."

It occurred to me that it would keep Dad happier if I found out where the writers' rooms were.

"What deck are you on?" I asked. "Because if another deck's more convenient for you —"

"Deck three," she said. "Our posse's in 313 and 315, if you ever want to find us. And there aren't any big public spaces on our deck, so deck five's fine with me." She dashed off.

Connecting rooms, I noted, on my trusty ship's map. Dad would probably decide that this made it less likely that one of them could be up to something sinister without the other three being involved, or at least aware. Which was a good thing, since I suspected he was wasting any time he spent suspecting them. Of course, he might also wonder if it was significant that their rooms were almost directly beneath Desiree's. I would probably have to calm him down by pointing out that it was a small ship, and suggesting that perhaps the writers, like Desiree on deck four and Grandfather on deck five, had opted for staterooms as close to the elevator and stairs as possible.

I found Michael and the boys on deck five as I'd expected — although the boys had ceded the course to a couple of senior citizens and were doing yoga under Rose Noire's direction. Michael was watching from a nearby deck chair.

"Oh, to be that flexible again," I said, as I took the chair beside him.

"And to have that endurance," he said. "I'll have you know that I kept up with them for the first forty-five minutes of that, but there are limits. Have you finished your book club book?"

"I read maybe two pages," I said. "I kept getting interrupted."

"Sorry."

"Don't be. If it hadn't been for the interruptions, I'd have fallen asleep over it. Unfortunately, this month is earnest, depressing, socially relevant month in the book club."

"Seriously?"

"Well, they don't call it that," I said. "But every few months, a couple of the members insist that we read something more meaningful, as they put it. Apparently I missed getting the gene for appreciating meaningfulness. I may just pretend to have a conflict again on meeting night. And I won't be the only one."

"You know, we may laugh sometimes at your father's bloodthirsty taste in books," Michael said. "But when he lends me a book it damn well doesn't put me to sleep. So what have you been doing while turning your back on social relevance?"

I succinctly filled him in on what I'd been doing — not forgetting the puzzling presence of the autographed book in Trevor's luggage. And, to the extent I knew, what the rest of the family had been up to, including the solar festival happening on deck six and my plan to claim the equipment that was in Trevor's cabin so Caroline could call for rescue.

"You think they'll give you any hassle about claiming Trevor's luggage?"

"I don't plan to give them a chance to," I said. "I'm going to find Léonie again. I trust her. Or maybe the first officer, if I can't find Léonie, though he's pretty swamped. Not sure about anyone else."

"Now? Or after our fencing session?"

"Right after our fencing session," I said. "And maybe I'll send Rose Noire to look for her in the meantime."

"Good idea. Get her mind off the dire peril she thinks we're in, thanks to being

237

stranded here in the Bermuda Triangle."

The yoga lesson broke up when Janet arrived, rather breathless. I managed to convince Rose Noire that finding Léonie would go a long way toward returning us to civilization, and she hurried off with great enthusiasm. Michael and I began helping Janet with her sword fight.

Michael had found half a dozen long, semi-rigid foam rods — part of the packing materials for some of Grandfather's equipment. Armed with these, I took on the role of Rafaella, Janet's heroine, while Michael and the boys played the two — sometimes three — pirates who were trying to capture her. Michael called out directions and corrections to the boys and me, and Janet hovered, taking photos by the score and pelting us with questions.

After an hour and a half, Michael was satisfied that we'd properly choreographed her fight scene, and Janet felt confident that she could actually write it. Only the boys were dissatisfied when we finally called a halt, and they could only be persuaded to sheathe their foam swords by Janet's promise that she'd think of another fight scene we could work on tomorrow.

I made a mental note to see if we could postpone the second fight scene if the power and water weren't on by tomorrow. Because while doing it had been fun, I really wanted to follow it with a long soapy shower and a spell of sipping a cold beverage in an air-conditioned room, none of which was possible at the moment.

Not something I could fix.

"Since Rose Noire hasn't returned, I'm going in search of Léonie myself," I said.

"I plan to see if I can arrange something like a seawater bath for the boys and me," Michael said. "If I can find a bucket and a really long rope, we can put on our swim-suits, go down to deck one, and take turns soaking each other."

"Good plan. I might join you later."

"If I see Léonie, I'll try to keep her from leaving and call you," he said. "By which I mean the low-tech version of calling — I'll stick my head over the side of the ship and yell your name, and if that doesn't work I'll send the boys to look for you."

We were really going to appreciate our cell phones when we got back on land.

Before leaving the front of deck five, I peered over all the railings to see who or what was there to be seen. Nothing much except for Horace, searching the open deck area in the bow of deck two. On the back deck, Mother and Aunt Penelope were sip-

239

ping their tea. They appeared to be thumbing through a stack of decorating magazines, occasionally showing each other something of interest. I fled before they could try to suck me in. No sign of Léonie.

She wasn't in the Starlight Lounge on the fourth floor, either. Or in the small library lounge, also on the fourth floor, which turned out to be an actual library, complete with books, just a few doors down from our staterooms. The writers were there — at least the three of them who weren't out snooping with Dad. They looked rather downcast — even Janet, who had been over the moon a few minutes before when we'd finished the fight scene. And they seemed to be without their various electronic devices, which was odd. Or maybe not — perhaps they'd left them up on deck six to charge and come down here to get some work done. They were all huddled around a table, each holding a sheaf of papers.

Before I could say anything, Angie bounced in.

"Hey, you guys," Angie said. "You'd never guess what — what's wrong? You all look as if someone died. Someone else that we actually care about," she added.

I suddenly had an idea what might be wrong.

"Does this mood of gloom have anything to do with the neuro-linguistic text identification project?" I asked. "Or is Delaney still working on that?"

"The what?" Angie asked.

"Delaney, Meg's brother's fiancée has a program that's supposed to tell you who wrote something," Tish explained. "You feed in stuff you know various people have written and then you feed in an unidentified manuscript and it tells you which of those people, if any, wrote it."

"That sounds interesting." Angie looked puzzled.

"The preliminary results weren't quite what we hoped they'd be," Tish said.

"Rather unsettling," Kate said.

"Downright depressing," Tish said,

"Actually, the preliminary results were fabulous," Kate said. "We fed in a whole bunch of emails we had in our computers, and then we started giving Delaney manuscripts without telling her who'd written them, and she pegged us every time. She even spotted that Tish and I had collaborated on that time-travel novella, the one that had a Regency story and a modern-day one."

"But then we gave her Nancy's last manuscript, and according to the program, Desi-

241

ree wrote it." Tish looked grim. "It was a near-perfect match for Desiree's last ten books."

CHAPTER 18

Yikes. I didn't envy Delaney, having to break the news to the writers that their dead friend had been a plagiarist.

"Maybe her program isn't as good as she thinks it is," Janet said. "No offense, Meg, but I don't believe Nancy was a plagiarist."

"I'm not surprised at her results," Angie said.

"You're not?" Tish exclaimed.

"I'm flabbergasted," Kate said.

Janet just shook her head. And they were all staring at Angie as if she'd committed high treason. I suppose from the group's point of view she had.

"Do you really think Nancy —"

"Let me explain." Angie held up her hand. "I know something you don't. Nancy swore me to secrecy. And maybe I should have told the rest of you about this a long time ago, but . . . well, she made me promise not to. And after she died, it seemed kind of academic. And besides, I thought it could still cause problems. Legal problems for her estate. Or maybe even problems for me — Desiree was always pretty litigious. But now . . ." She hesitated, as if still uncertain whether to break her promise to her dead friend.

"It's all right." Kate's tone was soothing.

"Just spill it." Tish's tone was anything but soothing, but it seemed to help Angie make up her mind.

"Nancy was ghostwriting for Desiree." Angie's gaze darted back and forth as she tried to judge the effects of her words.

The writers were speechless. Well, only for thirty seconds or so, but that's a long time to be speechless, and I got the impression that being speechless wasn't something that happened to writers very often.

"So she wasn't blocked after all," Kate exclaimed.

"Or at least only blocked on her own work," Tish suggested.

"She wasn't the least bit blocked," Angie said. "Desiree had her on a six-book-a-year treadmill."

From the way they reacted, with groans and grimaces and eye rolls, I assumed this was a punishing schedule.

"Wait — Nancy was the one writing the

Fiefdoms of the Were-Knights series?" Janet asked.

"Fiefdoms of the Were-Knights?" I echoed.

"I always said Desiree didn't think of that series idea herself," Tish said to Kate.

"Was I arguing with you?" Kate said.

"Of course, I assumed her publisher had thought it up," Tish went on.

"No, the whole series was Nancy's idea," Angie said. "And she did all the writing. I'm not even sure Desiree bothered reading them after the first few. If you read all the interviews she's done about the series, you'll notice she doesn't give a whole lot of concrete details."

"I can't tell you how relieved I am," Janet said. "I've been secretly devouring the Were-Knight series ever since it started. I picked up the first one so I could make fun of it, and I was hooked."

"Are we having confession time now?" Tish asked. "Because yeah, those books have become one of my major guilty pleasures, too."

"I wanted to hate them," Kate said. "I really did. I wanted them to be as awful as Desiree was, so I could blame her comeback on slick marketing and gullible readers."

"I think everyone in the romance world

felt the same way," Angie said.

"Okay, this is an interesting question," Janet said. "Which is worse — when someone you really like writes awful books, or when the author of a fabulous book turns out to be a horrible human being?"

"Oooh, good question," Tish said. "I think —"

"Let's stick to the subject for the moment," Kate said. "Why didn't Nancy tell us she was ghostwriting for Desiree?"

"She wanted to." Angie looked sad. "But Desiree had her under such a draconian non-disclosure agreement that she was terrified to."

"We'd have kept her secret," Tish said.

"You'd have tried," Angie said. "But would you have been able to keep from snickering or rolling your eyes when Desiree strutted around taking all the credit? I know I couldn't have. But I never go to romance conventions — the rest of you do."

They all fell silent. Digesting what they'd just learned, no doubt. I was doing the same thing. Apparently Desiree wasn't the utter has-been they'd made her seem. She was a former has-been with a booming second career, thanks to a hot new series. A series they all enjoyed. Maybe a series whose success they all envied. Would it make them happier to know that the books they admired were written by a friend rather than an enemy? Or would they beat themselves up about not realizing Nancy had written the Were-Knight books, and not doing anything more to help her escape the trap she was in? And perhaps more important, what light did this revelation shed on Desiree's suicide — or murder? Angie knew that Desiree had abused and exploited their friend, which made her a much more plausible suspect in my book. In spite of their obvious dislike of Desiree, the other writers didn't seem to have the same compelling motive. It might be maddening to know that someone you considered a horrible human being was writing books you enjoyed, but I didn't quite see that as a motive for murder. But maybe writers' minds worked differently. And for that matter what if one — or several — of them had been feigning surprise at Angie's revelation? We only had their word for it that Nancy hadn't confided in them, too.

Probably a good idea to get them talking again. See what else I could learn.

"I didn't know romance writers wrote series," I said aloud. "Or should that be serieses? Anyway, I thought the whole point of a romance was that the hero and the heroine got together in the last chapter and lived happily ever after, making every book a one of a kind."

"The term is stand-alone," Tish said. "That used to be the case, but then we romance writers noticed how great the series concept was for mystery and speculative-fiction authors. Look what a big deal it was every time a new Harry Potter book came out, or the latest Sue Grafton — everyone preordered it or ran out to buy it the first day it was released. Doesn't work quite as spectacularly for less well-known authors, but still — it helps."

"It's the reason TV networks like a series," Janet said. "If people like it they keep coming back for more."

"So you drag the romance out over several books?" I was still puzzled.

"No, it's more like in the first book of a series, the heroine meets her Mr. Right, and then in the second book her next youngest sister meets *her* Mr. Right. Given a sufficiently large family, you can keep it going for quite a while."

"Or the Mr. Rights are all brothers, or all the characters live in the same small town, or work for the same company, or someone who's an interesting secondary character in book one is the main character in book two."

"So this is the new thing in romance?" I asked.

"Not really," Tish said.

"Nora Roberts has been doing it for years," Janet said.

"Decades," Tish corrected. "You don't read much romance, do you?"

Tish was smiling, so I didn't think I needed to lie.

"My dad's always shoving mysteries at me," I said. "I can't even begin to keep up with *his* must-reads. With two kids in middle school . . ."

"We'll give you a reading list so you can catch up later," Kate said. "If, as I suspect, you haven't touched a romance since you were a teenager you'll be surprised at how they've changed. It's not just about boy meets girl — it's about women having agency, in their lives and their relationships. And —"

"Getting back to Desiree's series," Tish interrupted.

"Which was really Nancy's series," Angie pointed out.

"The series we now know Nancy was ghostwriting for Desiree." Tish nodded to Angie. "It revolved around a kingdom with a sort of brotherhood of knights, unabashedly modeled after the Knights of the

Round Table. Only they were all were-creatures of one kind or another."

"Not just werewolves?" I asked.

"No, an amazing variety of were-creatures. The first one was a werewolf. After that she had a weretiger, I think. Or maybe it was a werelion. And a werebear."

"Nancy actually thought it was a really silly idea and couldn't possibly run all that long," Angie said. "She said she was expecting three, maybe four books. By the time she had done six or seven books the were-creatures were getting a little far-fetched."

"The werepanther wasn't bad," Janet put in. "Or the werehorse."

"The wereshark was actually pretty cool," Kate said.

"But after more than twenty books, Nancy was running out of animals that she could have her knights change into and still maintain some plausibility as dashing alpha male protagonists." Angie shook her head. "I kept telling her to come up with a killer idea that would only work using one of the animals she'd already used and get Desiree to talk the publisher into letting her start repeating."

"To tell the truth, I couldn't believe how long she'd kept it going," Tish said. "Makes a lot more sense now that I know it was

Nancy who made readers swoon over heroes who turned into badgers and rhinoceroses and coyotes when the going got tough."

"Okay, now it makes more sense," I said, half to myself.

"What makes more sense?" Kate asked.

"If Desiree and Nancy hardly knew each other, then there would be almost no way for one of them to plagiarize the other's manuscript," I said. "But if Nancy was ghostwriting for Desiree, I can think of all sorts of ways. I mean, manuscripts had to go back and forth somehow. They could have gone to each other's houses. One of them could have given the other a flash drive, not realizing that she'd accidentally left a draft on it. Or sent an email with a file attached to the wrong address."

"Nancy wouldn't plagiarize." Janet shook her head, but her expression was anxious, as if she was beginning to wonder if her faith in Nancy was misplaced.

"Maybe Nancy didn't," I said. "Maybe Desiree did."

"Stole Nancy's manuscript?" I could see they were starting to like the idea.

"What if Nancy had told Desiree she wanted to stop ghostwriting," I said, "and Desiree didn't want to let her go?"

"No 'what if' needed," Angie said. "That

251

happened."

"So while that was happening, what if Desiree got her hands on a copy of Nancy's manuscript and sent it to her agent and her publisher before Nancy submitted it?"

"That I can believe." Tish looked grim.

"And maybe it gets worse," I said. "What if the publisher had access to a program like the one Delaney was running? They'd get the same results we did — the new manuscript and the Were-Knights series were written by the same person."

"Only they'd think that person is Desiree," Kate murmured.

"Desiree killed her," Janet exclaimed.

"Not outright, surely," Kate murmured.

"Drove her to suicide," Janet insisted.

"I doubt if she meant to," Tish said. "Why would she kill the goose that was laying all those golden eggs for her? She probably thought once she torpedoed the new series, Nancy would go back to ghostwriting."

"Maybe she didn't mean to drive Nancy to suicide, but she did," Janet said.

"Or maybe she did mean to," Kate said.

"Or maybe it wasn't really suicide," Angie said quietly. "What if Nancy found out what Desiree had done and threatened to make it public? Threatened to say the hell with the non-disclosure and tell the world that Desiree had stolen her manuscript. Desiree wouldn't kill the goose that laid the golden eggs — unless the goose made it plain that from now on she was keeping the eggs for herself. Maybe we should talk to the police. Tell them everything we know and get them to reopen the case."

"What's the use?" Kate asked. "Desiree's dead, too."

"But if she killed Nancy . . ." Janet protested.

"First things first," I said. "Let's test this new theory. You mentioned feeding some of your emails into Delaney's system. Did you feed in any of Nancy's or Desiree's?"

"We didn't do any of Nancy's," Janet said. "We only did Desiree's recent books. And I don't think any of us would have any emails from Desiree."

"No, not enough to be useful," Kate said,

"Wait — what about the discussion lists?" Angie said. "Doesn't she post on some of them?"

"Yes, and we might have some in our mailboxes," Kate said.

"I don't," Tish grumbled. "I read and delete."

"Fortunately I'm not nearly so organized," Kate said, "I need to take my computer up to Delaney anyway. I was going to wait until

253

I was a little less depressed over the results she gave us. But now that we know we just didn't dig deep enough — I'll go get it and take it up to her."

"And we didn't do any of Nancy's old books," Janet said. "From before the so-called block."

"Or Desiree's old books," Tish added. "Ones she wrote herself. Or had ghostwritten by somebody other than Nancy."

"Of course, I'm not sure any of us would have any of Desiree's old books," Kate said. "Not one of the subgenres I usually read."

"I've got some of her old books in my e-reader," Tish announced. "From when I was doing that column for the newsletter on really awful sentences that had actually appeared in published books. Desiree was a gold mine for that. Let's go get your computer and my e-reader."

The two of them hurried out.

"Perhaps we should warn Delaney that we're descending upon her for round two," Janet suggested.

"She won't mind," I said. "She revels in this kind of stuff."

"We might need to apologize a bit for doubting her," Janet said.

So Janet, Angie, and I headed toward the stairway and trudged up to deck six.

CHAPTER 19

Delaney and Rob were still there, surrounded by a small delta of Delaney's equipment. Grandfather and Caroline were drinking pseudo iced tea, tending their own chargers, and watching Wim and Guillermo photographing things. Or maybe the two photographers were just scanning their surroundings with the giant mutant zoom lenses in the vain hope of finding something worth photographing. All I could see in any direction was the far-off horizon. Janet went over to begin looking through her laptop for items that might be of use. Angie and I joined Rob and Delaney.

Delaney looked a little down. More than a little, actually. Rob had the anxious expression of a devoted dog who can't figure out what to do to cheer up his depressed owner, but isn't planning to give up anytime soon. I hoped Delaney's mood wasn't due to the writers' disappointment with her first round of results.

"Morning," I said. "Although not a very good one, I see. What's wrong?"

"You mean apart from being marooned in the middle of the ocean with no Internet?" Delaney said. "What could be wrong?"

"Delaney's kind of bummed out," Rob said. "You know the lady who jumped overboard?"

Angie and I both nodded.

"She wrote this series of books that I loved." Delaney shook her head sadly.

"Would that be the Fiefdoms of the Were-Knights series?" I asked.

"You too?" Her eyes lit up. "Aren't they great?"

"I'll have to take your word for it," I said. "I haven't read them — I only just heard of their existence today."

"But yeah, they were — are — great," Angie said.

"I just love the weresquid." Delaney chuckled slightly as she spoke

"Weresquid?" I turned to Angie for enlightenment. "I know you said she was scraping the bottom of the barrel for were-creatures to be the romantic heroes, but a weresquid? Seriously?"

"Oh, he wasn't one of the romantic heroes." Delaney was now giggling. "He was the king's chief counselor and also the spy-master. A recurring character, and one of the best sources of comic relief."

"Yes." Angie smiled. "There was a lot of comic relief in those books. That should have been everyone's first clue."

"First clue to what?" Delaney asked.

"Desiree St. Christophe didn't write the Were-Knights," Angie said. "A friend of ours did. She always had a great sense of humor."

"And Desiree had no sense of humor?" I asked.

"She had a negative sense of humor," Angie said. "Hilarious jokes fell flat just from being told in the same room with her."

"That's a relief," Delaney said. "When I saw the name on the passenger list I got all excited, thinking how great it would be to meet the mind that invented with Sir Architeuthis. And then she turned out to be this . . ."

"Diva?" I suggested

"Witch, maybe?" Angie said.

"I was just going to say bitch," Delaney said. "Totally bummed me out, because I've really liked those books, and I was afraid after meeting her I wouldn't be able to enjoy them anymore."

"Don't take it out on the books," Angie

257

said. "Desiree had nothing to do with them. My friend Nancy wrote them, every word. And you'd have adored Nancy."

"Past tense," Delaney said. "So she's gone, too? Damn. I was hoping there for a moment that if Desiree hadn't written them, maybe that meant there would still be more."

"Nancy died five months ago," Angie said.

"Oh." Delaney frowned. "Well, that kind of explains it."

"Explains what?" I asked.

"All the fan groups have been puzzled, and starting to get a little worried, because there didn't seem to be any new books in the pipeline for a while," Delaney explained. "And then finally there were, but just titles — no information. Not even what the were-beast was going to be. When either Desiree or the publisher said anything, it was always something really generic about looking forward to the adventures of another dashing knight."

"Maybe they were frantically trying to find someone to take Nancy's place," I suggested, turning to Angie. "And having a hard time of it."

"It would be Desiree doing the looking," Angie said. "And yeah, she'd have a hard time of it. Nancy was an amazing writer.

Incredible range. She could write a comic scene that would have you in stitches, then turn around and write a romantic encounter that would make you want to elope with a werekoala. Or a sex scene so hot you'd be wanting a cold shower. She'd be a hard act to follow. We should ask Tish and Kate and Janet if they've heard any rumors in their writing communities."

"You haven't in yours?"

"She wouldn't really be looking for a mystery writer." Angie shook her head. "She'd need someone with a toehold in both romance and fantasy. Damn! I should have told the rest of the group before. Maybe they'd have been able to get the word out to be very careful — what if someone else got trapped in a horrible contract with Desiree?"

"Then the someone else just got a very lucky break," I said. "You say Desiree would be the one doing the looking — I gather Nancy's contract was with Desiree then, not her publisher."

"Oh, yes." Angie nodded. "Nancy was pretty sure the publisher had no idea who was doing the writing. Desiree wasn't very self-aware, if you ask me, but she was totally paranoid. She was probably afraid that if the publisher found out someone else was

259

doing the writing, they'd try to cut her out."

"And would they?"

"Would they try to dump a demanding high-maintenance diva for a pleasant, hard-working writer who can actually do the work? I would."

"Then Desiree wasn't really paranoid, was she?" I countered. "I mean, does it count as paranoid if they really are out to get you?"

"Good point," Angie said through giggles. Then her face fell. "You know what this means, of course."

"Anyone on board this ship who's a writer is a suspect," Delaney said. "That stinks."

"Yes." Angie nodded and slumped back in her chair. "And the four of us are the only writers on the ship."

"That we know of," I said. "I'll be blunt: Do you know for certain that it's not one of you? Taking over for Nancy, that is, not bumping off Desiree."

"But doesn't that amount to the same thing?" Angie said.

"She has a point," Rob said.

"It would give you motive," I said. "It wouldn't prove you did it."

Angie frowned and thought for a few moments.

"Nancy's been dead five months, and was trying to break her contract with the diva for about four months before that," she finally said.

"So Desiree had plenty of time to recruit a replacement." If she didn't want to answer my question about her friends, I wasn't going to push it.

"And if she found someone, I know she'd have had them get to work immediately. She was a hard taskmaster. And she must have found someone if they announced new titles. And whoever it was . . ."

Her voice trailed off and she sat thinking.

"We're close," Angie said finally. "The four of us — used to be the five of us. We meet weekly to critique each other's work. A lot of other days we're having lunch or breakfast or dinner or coffee in pairs or groups to share news or word counts or maybe brainstorm. A couple of years ago we had to ban calling each other before three in the afternoon because we spent so much time on the phone that it was interfering with our productivity."

"Her death left a big hole in all your lives," I said.

"Yes." She blinked a couple of times before forging ahead. "And before that, for the last seven years, Nancy's life had — well, a big hole would be a good way to describe that, too. A big fat hole in the middle of her life and, by extension, our lives together. She still did the meetings and the meals and the phone calls, but it was about our work, not hers. She almost never brought anything. The few times she did, you could tell her heart wasn't in it. She finally told me what was going on about two years ago, because she had to tell someone. And after that, I could see that the big fat hole wasn't her being blocked. It was her hiding the fact that she was working all the hours God gave on books for Desiree and only finding scraps of time for her own work. And didn't feel she could turn to us for support because of Desiree constantly harping on the non-disclosure agreement."

I nodded.

"But even though we didn't know what she was doing, we knew something was up. She had to lie to hide it and say she was blocked and supporting herself with boring freelance jobs. So if one of the others was working on a secret project, I'd know something was up. I know what projects they're all working on and how hard they're working on them and what long hours it takes. There aren't any big fat holes in their lives — or mine. So I'm as sure as can be that none of them were ghostwriting for Desiree. But how could I explain that to the police, or the FBI, or whoever ends up investigating this?"

"If anyone ever does," I said.

"That idea isn't very comforting, either." Angie closed her eyes for a moment as if in pain. "We could have this hanging over us, unresolved, forever. 'Oh, look, it's those friends of Nancy Goreham's. The ones who blamed Desiree St. Christophe for her suicide and managed to throw her overboard on that cruise.' Not something I want to hear whispered behind my back for the rest of my life."

"Well, then you've got a mission. You and the rest of your group."

Angie cocked her head as if asking what.

"Your mission, should you choose to accept it, is to see if there are any other writers aboard. Writers so hungry to get published that they'd be willing to accept the very unfavorable terms of a contract with Desiree."

"I get it." Angie nodded. "Because maybe the new ghostwriter has had time enough to figure out what a pickle she's in, and that would make her the most likely suspect if Desiree had help going overboard."

"She or he, I assume," I replied. "Or aren't there men who write romance?"

"Yes, but it's more likely to be a woman.

Not only because we outnumber men in the romance world, but also because I think Desiree was better at bossing women around."

"But it could be a he, so don't overlook the male crew and passengers as you do your sleuthing."

"Right." She pulled out her phone, looked at it for a second, and then stuck it back in her pocket. "Life will be so much easier when we get power back," she said. "If we had power, I could just text Tish and Kate and tell them to meet me back in the library lounge ASAP instead of running all over the ship looking for them. Janet?"

"I'll be there," she said. "Just let me give Delaney the files I have."

"Tish and Kate are coming up with some more files," I told Delaney. "So you can prove that Desiree didn't write the Were-Knight series."

"Cool," Delaney said.

"Tell them to meet me back in the library lounge," Angie said. "Laters!"

She bounced away looking revived by having something to do.

"So what happens next?" Delaney said.

"Not much," I said. "The captain considers the investigation closed, so unless someone comes up with some reason to think

Desiree's death wasn't suicide — someone like Dad or Horace or the writers — and manages to convince the captain —"

"I meant with the Fiefdoms of the Were-Knights," she said. "What happens to the series now that both the ghostwriter and the writer who was claiming the credit are dead?"

"I don't know," I said. "You should ask one of the writers."

"I hope they get someone to continue it," she said. "Someone good. I'd hate to think of never seeing Sir Architeuthis again."

"The weresquid?"

She nodded.

"You seem to be fixated on the were-squid."

"Not really," she said. "It's just that he's by far the funniest character. Like one time — I should explain that the way being a werewhatever works in the Fiefdoms world is that you turn into your alter ego at the full moon, but you're also in danger of changing whenever you're experiencing strong emotion, good or bad."

"That must be awkward if you're doing a boy-meets-girl story," I said. "One would think strong emotion would be pretty pre-dictable there."

"And she uses it brilliantly! Like the scene

where Sir Tigris, the weretiger, is alone with Princess Catlyn for the first time, and when they're talking his words sound like purring. Not sure what it is, maybe a lot of r's, something about the rhythm of the sentences — it's really subtle but it's awesome. And Sir Architeuthis, the weresquid — the king is always yelling at him, "Get a backbone, man!" and sometimes that stresses him out so much it makes him start to change, and of course a squid doesn't even have a backbone — I'm not doing it justice; the way she does it, it's great. And then a couple of times in really tense scenes when Sir Architeuthis realizes he's in serious danger, he'll fart a little black ink."

This sent her off into gales of laughter.

"Maybe I should read these books." Rob guffawed along with her.

I chuckled a little, to be polite. Clearly you had to have read the books.

And maybe I should read the books. I'd have plenty of time now if I had a copy. Actually I probably did have a copy — I was pretty sure *The Sharp Claw of Love* was part of the series. But reading it wasn't a good idea — if it turned out to be evidence of some kind, my reading it could destroy whatever clues it contained. No, I should tuck it safely away and find myself another way to read the Were-Knights. If we had power and an Internet connection, I'd just go online with my iPad, download an e-book of the first one in the series, and find a quiet corner.

Of course, while I didn't have the Internet, I did still have Delaney.

"Do you have any of these weresquid books on one of your devices?" I asked Delaney.

"All of them — you want to try one?" She sounded eager.

"If you're not using whatever device they're on," I said. "And if you're okay with me borrowing it."

"Not a problem," Delaney said. "Or if you like, I could use one of my cables to transfer the first one onto your phone — you've got an e-reading program on it, right? And I'll charge it up for you while I have it."

"Have at it." I handed her my phone. She reached into her tote bag, produced a white cable, and attached my phone to one of her solar chargers.

I felt very comforted, seeing my phone being recharged. Totally silly, since there wasn't a whole lot I could do with it right now other than take pictures and check the time. The feeling of being partly naked without it was also silly. Clearly I was too addicted to the wretched thing.

I glanced around. Down on deck five, Mother and Aunt Penelope had pulled out their sketchbooks and were hard at work, no doubt coming up with a complete redesign for the main dining room, or possibly the boarding lobby. Dad and Horace were down on deck four heaving some sort of weight over the railings and then hauling it back again with the attached rope. Probably a gallon milk jug or some similar container from the ship's kitchen.

Time to get back to my search for Léonie.

CHAPTER 20

I stood up to leave.

"Meg!" Grandfather waved me over to where he and Caroline were sitting.

"This business of stopping in mid-ocean," Grandfather said. "I don't like it."

Caroline rolled her eyes and pulled her sun hat over her face. I deduced that whatever Grandfather was on about had worn out her patience.

"I don't think any of us likes it," I said. "But it's not as if the crew are doing it deliberately."

"How do we know they're not?" Grandfather was frowning with suspicion as he scanned the horizon.

"What possible reason could they have for stopping the ship in the middle of the ocean?" I wondered if he was trying to crack a joke and failing more dramatically than usual.

"I think that's what we need to find out."

He abandoned his study of the horizon and fixed his gaze on me, from which I deduced that he was actually expecting me to do the finding out.

"Maybe they're in league with pirates," Rob called out from his recliner on the other side of the deck. "And they've stopped the ship here so the pirates can ambush us."

"Now there's an alarming thought!" Grandfather didn't look particularly alarmed. He looked as if he was under the delusion that a pirate attack might be entertaining.

"Unlikely," I said.

"How do you know?" Grandfather asked. "You read all the time about modern piracy being on the rise."

"Off the coast of Africa, definitely, and in southeast Asia," I said. "But there's not a lot of it in the Western Hemisphere, and most of that is in waters off the coast of South or Central America, and aimed at cargo ships carrying valuable stuff. And they don't attack out in the middle of the ocean, where they'd be sitting ducks if anybody's navy came along. If you look at the map of where modern pirate attacks take place, it's always off the coast of some country that doesn't really make a whole lot of effort to catch them."

"There's a map?" Rob, who had strolled over to join the conversation, sounded interested.

"It's called the Live Piracy Map." I might regret telling him this. Then again, he'd probably forget all about it in an hour or so. "The International Chamber of Commerce maintains it. Look it up when we get Internet back."

Rob was pulling out his phone and making a note.

"And you know this because . . . ?" Grandfather seemed suspicious.

"About a week ago Aunt Penelope saw one of the Pirates of the Caribbean movies and had a panic attack about whether pirates could attack the cruise," I explained.

"Not a big Johnny Depp fan, then?" Rob suggested.

"Evidently not," I said. "Mother told me to figure out a way to calm her down and keep her from canceling. So I did a little research."

"Doesn't completely rule out piracy," Grandfather said.

"It was enough to convince Aunt Penelope," I countered.

"Stranger things have happened." Grandfather didn't give up easily.

"Yes, much stranger things, I'm sure. For

example, maybe they're out here waiting to rendezvous with an alien spaceship." Probably not a suggestion I should make in front of Aunt Penelope. Or Rose Noire.

"Cool." Rob was grinning. "So when they say 'take me to your leader,' do we lead them to the captain or to Gramps?"

"You keep thinking," Grandfather said. "There's bound to be a logical explanation."

With that he stomped off.

"A logical explanation." I closed my eyes and took a deep breath. "If you ask me, 'our ship broke down and we're trying to fix it' is pretty damned logical."

"He's just annoyed because he can't figure out an environmental reason for it."

"An environmental reason?

"Like someone trying to smuggle some endangered species out of Bermuda and stopping here to hand off the loot to their henchmen. He liked that theory at first."

"Well, I can see the flaw in it."

"You can?" Rob sounded surprised. "He had to tell me."

"And just what did he tell you?"

"Well, there are a fair number of endangered species in Bermuda — including some that live only in Bermuda. But most of them are crustaceans and marine worms, and none of them have any commercial value. So that theory's a no-go."

"Very true." I nodded with approval. "There's also the fact that we're on our way *to* Bermuda, so even if any of the worms and crustaceans had some commercial value, we're still hundreds of miles away from them, and rendezvousing with the henchmen would be premature. Did he really say 'henchmen'?"

"He did." Rob grinned. "Maybe he was being ironic."

"Grandfather doesn't do ironic. It's always possible that someone is trying to smuggle something into Bermuda — I'm sure that happens all the time — but I'm not sure why that would require stopping in the middle of the Atlantic for hours." At least I hoped it would only be hours. "Because the idea of rendezvousing with the henchmen out here in mid-ocean is pretty improbable."

"Why?" Rob looked put out. Maybe the mid-ocean rendezvous had been his contribution to the theory.

"I'm pretty sure smugglers try to be as unobtrusive as possible," I said. "Handing off the merchandise in port, under cover of all the passengers coming and going from the ship — that's what I'd aim for if I were an international smuggler. Not sitting in the middle of the ocean where the passengers, on top of already being anxious and suspicious, have nothing else to do but watch every little thing that's happening on board."

"I guess Gramps and I wouldn't make very good smugglers. So you think that's all that's happening — the ship broke down and they're trying to fix it?"

I nodded.

"Bo-ring." Rob rolled his eyes to emphasize his disappointment.

"Yes, I hope it will be."

I headed down to deck five and back to the bow, where the miniature golf course was. Michael and the boys were gone — presumably to lunch — but Rose Noire was sitting cross-legged at the front of the sun deck, meditating. Or maybe only trying to meditate. Her face didn't wear its usual serene post-yoga expression. She opened her eyes and smiled at me.

"You're too late for yoga," she said.

I tried to hide my shock. Normally Rose Noire had an apparently endless capacity for yoga. Had the boys actually tired her out?

"But we're going to smudge the ship later," she said, "as soon as I figure out a good blend of herbs and essential oils. And then I'll go looking for Léonie again — unless you've found her?"

"Not yet."

"I'd have kept looking, but I realized that I needed to do something to improve the ship's energy. A lot of people have been spiraling down into a very dark mood — and that's very dangerous in a place like this. Do you know how many ships and planes have been lost here? And we've already lost one passenger — I would not be at all surprised to find that the insidious miasma of the Bermuda Triangle was what drove Desiree St. Christophe to suicide."

"Alleged suicide," I corrected. "Dad's suspicious that she might have been pushed."

"A murder's even worse! So I rounded up as many people as I could for a couple of hours of yoga and meditation."

"That's nice." At least I hoped it had been nice — that she hadn't drafted too many unwilling participants and hadn't talked any of the senior citizens into attempting headstands. Unfortunately her yoga and meditation hadn't seemed to lighten her mood.

I sat beside her, though not cross-legged, since I wasn't feeling all that limber today. "Right now, if you've got a moment, I've been meaning to ask you something." I reached into my pocket and fished out the little feather charm. "What do you make of this?"

"What is it?" She took it and began turning it over in her fingers.

"You tell me. Give me a read on what you think of it, and then I'll tell you what I know."

Rose Noire didn't shrink from the challenge. She held the feather charm up to the light and turned it this way and that. Then she held it so close to her eyes that she went cross-eyed while studying it. She lifted it to her nose, inhaled deeply, and held her breath for a few seconds. Finally she enclosed it in both cupped hands, shut her eyes, and sat motionless. If I asked her what she was doing, she would probably look offended at the interruption and explain that she was assessing its aura. I try not to ask questions when I can already guess the answer.

And I knew better than to rush her. "Assembly of Japanese bicycle require great peace of mind," I reminded myself — one of Michael's favorite quotes, from *Zen and the Art of Motorcycle Maintenance*. Since I was pretty sure Rose Noire sometimes tested us, to prove that she had the greater mastery of patience and fortitude, I liked to out-zen her as often as possible.

So I closed my own eyes and tried to think of something useful. Aha! My book club book. Maybe I should come up with a few deep insights about it to share if I couldn't weasel out of attending the meeting. Although deep insights would come more easily if I could actually stay awake while reading it.

I found myself feeling sorry for the writers of meaningful, socially relevant fiction. They didn't really seem to have a lot of fun. They didn't dare have their heroines end up with anything like an attractive hero at the end of the book, or they'd be accused of writing romantic twaddle. I doubted that they were allowed the vicarious pleasure of having their heroines take up sword fighting and highway robbery like Janet's Rafaella, and I was certain they weren't permitted dragons. They could probably get away with a modest number of dead bodies, but only if the deaths gave their main characters the opportunity for some profound spiritual awakening. Maybe, if the few earnest members of the book club continued to insist on foisting their choices on us, I should suggest —

"Meg?"

I opened my eyes. Apparently Rose Noire had finished her examination of the little feather charm's aura.

"Sorry," I said. "A lot going on. So what do you think of it?"

"I don't know what to think of it."

"Dad came up with a theory that it might be a sinister voodoo fetish that's causing all of the problems on board the ship, and if we don't throw it overboard the ship's systems will never be fixed and people will keep jumping overboard until there's no one left."

"He can't possibly believe that."

"No, I don't think he believes in voodoo to begin with. But that doesn't stop him from thinking it's a neat theory."

"A misguided theory. I sense no evil in this. There are hints of some kind of pain and suffering in the background, but they're definitely in the past and have been completely healed. There's nothing but good energy in it now. So what do you know about it?"

"I found it lying right by the shoes and shawl Desiree St. Christophe left behind when she jumped overboard," I said. "And I'm pretty sure the feathers are from a tern. Or a gull."

"Well, it certainly didn't make her jump overboard," she said. "Maybe it was just left there by someone completely unconnected with her suicide."

I nodded.

"Then again . . ." Her eyes went distant, and she sat holding the feather charm. I waited patiently. I trusted Rose Noire's insights. I didn't necessarily buy that she had the ability to read auras or whatever she was doing at the moment. If you asked me, her insights came from a keen if sometimes overly optimistic knowledge of human nature. But sometimes they were uncanny.

"It feels to me like a protective charm," she said. "So perhaps whoever left it at the site of Desiree's suicide did so to help counteract the pain and negative energy left behind by her act."

"And didn't bother to report her suicide?"

"Perhaps they knew how much pain the news would cause." She smiled and handed the tiny bundle of feathers back to me. "All I know is that there's nothing evil in this."

I hoped she was right.

"Which is more than I can say for this place." She shuddered slightly, as she swept the horizon with her gaze. Then she shut her eyes and returned to breathing slowly, with a determined expression on her face.

I went back to searching the ship's public spaces for Léonie.

She wasn't on the fifth-floor stern sun

deck, where Mother and Aunt Penelope, still occupied with their sketches, had been joined by a half-dozen elderly people, fanning themselves with room service menus and copies of yesterday's activities schedule, and fretting about how much warmer it was going to get. Maybe it was a good thing we didn't have Internet, so I couldn't check the weather and give them what I suspected would be an unwelcome forecast. And none of them had seen Léonie.

She wasn't in the Starlight Lounge, and there wasn't even anyone tending the bar — only a small bottled water collection, neatly arranged on one of the tables like a silent apology. I snagged one.

She wasn't in the equally empty library lounge.

She wasn't kibitzing on Dad's and Horace's experiments in throwing weights over the side of the deck four stern sun deck.

She wasn't in any of the public spaces on any of the decks. Nor did I see a single crew member anywhere. On the second floor, I actually went out on the bow sun deck and looked up to make sure all the lifeboats were still hanging in place. I'd begun to wonder if the entire crew had sailed away and left us behind.

Then again, what if those weren't the only

lifeboats? What if there had been a fleet of inflatable lifeboats, hidden down on deck zero, that the crew had taken to —

"You're getting a little paranoid," I told myself.

I loitered for a while in the boarding lobby, near the door that led to deck zero, waiting for someone to come out. I finally tried the door, only to find it locked. I slid my Pastime card through the nearby slot, but the card-reader's light remained stubbornly red.

On my way up, I tried a few doors. Trevor's room was locked and my Pastime card wouldn't work on it, either. The door to the navigation bridge was locked, and I didn't even bother knocking.

Frustrating. If the cabins had ordinary door locks I'd have had a go at picking the one to Trevor's cabin. Some years ago, after rereading too many Dortmunder and Bernie Rhodenbarr books, Dad decided to learn how to pick locks. To his great dismay, he proved to be an almost comically incompetent lock picker, but he'd taken some consolation in the fact that I'd become reasonably proficient. But even if I'd brought along his burglar's kit, it would do nothing against a card key lock.

But Delaney might have some idea how

to deal with it.

I trudged back up to the sixth floor.

Delaney had disappeared. Though clearly she was intending to come back — she'd left Rob half dozing in his recliner, with all her little solar devices arranged in a delta at his feet. Caroline, performing a similar function for Grandfather's collection of solar devices, looked less thrilled by her enforced idleness.

I took a nearby chair and settled in to wait for Delaney. If Dad showed up, I'd claim to be doing some deep thinking. More like deep worrying. Something really peculiar was going on aboard the ship. At least one person had gone overboard — maybe two, if Trevor had made it back on board in time to sail with the ship — and the crew was becoming almost as invisible as Desiree and Trevor.

Desiree and Trevor. I didn't like putting them in the same sentence, given that Desiree was definitely fish food by now, and I hoped Trevor was merely back in Baltimore, sulking over being left behind.

And wasn't it more than a little weird, Trevor getting left behind? Trevor, who didn't even need to look at his well-worn leather planner to know exactly where Grandfather needed to be at any given moment? Who always checked on traffic, road closures, and weather conditions before setting out to drive Grandfather anywhere? Who could always find anything Grandfather needed, whether it was the power adapter required to plug in a laptop in Botswana or an authentic Macanese restaurant within driving distance of Caerphilly?

Okay, maybe I could see Trevor getting left behind because of bad information from the Pastime staff. If they told him he had plenty of time to go in search of ginger beer. But what if he'd *wanted* to be left behind?

I pondered that for a while.

Even if Trevor had deliberately engineered being left behind, there could be an innocent reason. Maybe, given how badly he suffered from seasickness, he'd chickened out at the last minute. Decided that with so many people there to ride herd on Grandfather — Caroline, Wim, Guillermo, Dad, even me — he could stand down this time.

Still. Not like Trevor. So unlike Trevor that I found myself trying to think of some less innocent reason for his absence. What if he'd done his research on Pastime and foreseen that our trip was likely to fall afoul with the sort of problems we were experiencing? No, he'd have told Grandfather, surely, and tried to talk him out of it.

Maybe he had told Grandfather. And maybe Grandfather had ridiculed his misgivings and gone ahead with the trip anyway.

Or maybe over the year and a half he'd been working for Grandfather he'd gradually built up a pathological hatred of his employer, and had deliberately helped steer Grandfather into signing with Pastime instead of one of the more well-known cruise lines. And bribed the captain and crew into arranging our being marooned in the middle of the Bermuda Triangle, and then, while we were all helpless and unsuspecting —

I shook myself. Maybe I should leave plotting to Dad and the writers.

Still, I'd feel a lot better when I'd had a chance to talk to Trevor and find out just what had happened.

"Oh, look," Caroline exclaimed, pointing at something behind me. "It's your turn!"

"My turn for what?" I swiveled to look in the direction she was pointing, but didn't see anything unusual. Unless she was pointing at the unusually sleek and elegant-looking gull perched on the deck rail. Wait — was it a gull?

"Oh, you mean tern with an *E*," I said. "I get it. But what makes it *my* tern?"

CHAPTER 21

"I think she was pointing out the tern to me," Grandfather said. "And yes — that's it. Wim! Guillermo! Grab your cameras!"

"Is it a rare sort of tern?" I asked. "An endangered tern species?" If so, it was rather nicer than some of Grandfather's endangered species, which were all too often rather drab or slimy invertebrates. The tern was mostly white and pale gray, though its bright orange-red legs and bill added a nice note of color to what would otherwise be a pretty monochromatic look. And it had a sharply defined black cap of feathers that covered the top of its head, including the eyes, and continued on down the back of its neck, giving it the rather jaunty look of a winged Zorro.

"No. It's a South American tern, *Sterna hirundinacea.*" Grandfather didn't take his eyes off the bird. "It's fairly common in South America, as the name would suggest.

Rather unusual to see one in the northern hemisphere, though. And yes, definitely *Sterna hirundinacea.* Too large to be *Sterna hirundo,* and notice the curve of the bill."

"I'll take your word for it." I looked around to see what was taking Wim and Guillermo so long to appear with their cameras, and found that they'd already started photographing the visiting tern. Apparently the tern had appeared at a moment when their cameras were still equipped with the giant zoom lenses that I was so worried would drag them overboard if they weren't careful. In order to get a picture of the whole bird, instead of a close-up of one of its eyeballs, they had backed up so far that they were now more in danger of falling off the deck six sun deck onto the miniature golf course on deck five.

"Also rather peculiar to find *Sterna hirundinacea* this far out in the ocean." Grandfather was studying the tern with an enthusiasm that probably owed more to boredom than anything else.

"Too far for them to fly?" I studied the tern to see if it was showing signs of relief at having found our ship just as it was sinking into exhaustion. It didn't look particularly relieved. It looked rather sly and pleased with itself. Maybe it had spotted something it planned to purloin for its dinner.

"No, they can fly just fine, but they tend to stay around the coastal regions. They feed on fish, crustaceans, and shellfish — easier to find those in coastal waters."

"Although I assume terns are like gulls and we should cover up any food we don't want him to steal," I said.

"No, that's one nice thing about terns," Caroline said. "Gulls will eat anything, but by and large terns stick to a seafood diet. So unless anyone's been eating sardines, our lunches are probably safe."

"I'm going to go get some of my reference books." Grandfather turned, paused briefly to nod with approval at what Wim and Guillermo were doing, and strode off toward the stairs.

"At least it's not a Desolate tern," Caroline murmured.

"Would that be some kind of bad omen?" I was puzzled, since I hadn't ever noticed Caroline to be especially superstitious. Of course, I hadn't ever been becalmed with her in the Bermuda Triangle before.

"Not so much a bad omen as a really unfortunate coincidence if we want Monty to be easy to live with. Relatively easy to live with," she added, seeing my expression.

"Okay, not a complete pain in the neck."

"So just what is a Desolate tern?" I asked.

"Newly discovered species," she said. "Inhabits the Kerguelen Islands, also known as the Desolation Islands, since they're about two thousand miles southeast of Madagascar. Possibly a bit closer to Antarctica, which doesn't much help with the isolation. One of the most remote and godforsaken places on earth, that's the point. A former student of Monty's is out there studying the wildlife and discovered a new, previously undiscovered species of tern."

"And Grandfather's jealous?"

"A little," she admitted. "I'm not sure how much it's because he would have liked to discover it and how much because he hates being reminded that he's past his days of camping out in a tent for months on end in below-freezing temperatures. But he'd have gotten over that and moved on to basking in the kid's reflected glory and reminding us at regular intervals that he taught him all he knows except for the name."

"Let me guess: He thinks it should be called Blake's tern."

"Bingo!" She rolled her eyes. "Or at least to be acknowledged in the scientific name. *Sterna blakeii.* But we got word that the kid might be calling it *Sterna maturinii.*"

"Naming it after himself, I suppose." I shrugged. "After all, he was the one who spent the months in the tent."

"Oh, no," Caroline said. "He couldn't very well name it after himself — that just isn't done. The scientific equivalent of belching loudly at the table. But you can name it after anyone else you please. Your spouse. Your kid. Your parent. Your mentor — that's rather what Monty was expecting. Or anyone else you happen to like or admire. Even a fictional character. For example, there are quite a lot of Paleocene and Pliocene animals and modern wasps named after Tolkien characters, thanks to some energetic scientists with a Middle Earth jones. And Star Trek references like *Conus tribblei* and *Ladella spocki.* And Harry Potter references, like *Ampulex dementor* and Star Wars, like *Agathidium vaderi* and *Trigonopterus chewbacca.*"

"I never knew scientists had so much fun," I said. "So what was it again that grandfather's former student is naming his terns?"

"Sterna maturinii," Caroline said. "After Stephen Maturin, the physician/naturalist from Patrick O'Brian's nautical novels. Apparently he's quite the rabid O'Brian fan."

"Well, Grandfather does already have a

few species named after him," I pointed out.

"So does Maturin," Caroline countered. "A Central American weevil and a Kenyan waterweed. Which wouldn't annoy Monty quite so much if Maturin were a real naturalist."

"How many does Grandfather have?"

Caroline frowned in concentration for a few moments.

"Eight, I think. He'd know for sure. But asking him would only set him off again."

"Asking me what would set me off again?"

Oops. Neither of us had noticed Grandfather coming up behind us, with Rose Noire trailing behind him carrying half of the dozen or so thick books he'd brought back.

Caroline rolled her eyes. I decided to come clean. Well, partially.

"Caroline was telling me that if this tern had turned out to be a completely new and previously unknown species, it would be considered crass of any of us to name it after ourselves."

"That's true," Grandfather said. "The discoverer gets to name it, but no self-promotion allowed."

"Not exactly fair for people like you who have discovered so many new species," I said. "You don't get much credit. But I supposed it would get boring if everything were *blakeii.*"

"That's true." Grandfather raised his chin and assumed a look of noble self-sacrifice.

"Still, think how exciting it must be to have a species named after you," Rose Noire said with great enthusiasm. "After all, how often do scientists discover a completely new and unknown species?"

"All the time," Grandfather said. "Mostly invertebrates, of course."

"Which is not surprising," Caroline said. "Since an estimated ninety-seven percent of all animal species are invertebrate."

"Invertebrates are also an important part of nature," Rose Noire said. "And it's still an honor."

"Hmph." Grandfather shook his head. "Some honor. You'd be surprised at some of the people who have species named after them. Adolf Hitler has a beetle. *Anophthalmus hitleri.*"

"How horrible!" Rose Noire exclaimed.

"It's a blind cave beetle," Caroline said. "Found only in half a dozen particularly damp, nasty caves in Slovenia. The jury's out on whether it was intended to honor Hitler or make fun of him. The thing's of no interest whatsoever unless you're either a beetle freak or a collector of Nazi memorabilia, and beetle poaching by the latter could very well drive the species into extinction."

"The poor thing." Rose Noire shuddered. "Can't they just rename it?"

"There's a longstanding scientific tradition of never doing that," Caroline said. "Once the name is approved, the world is stuck with it. Although some people are arguing that it's foolish to insist on observing a tradition that endangers an entire species."

"So who decides the name?" Rose Noire asked

"Whoever discovers the species," Caroline said. "It has to follow a set of rules, of course. And as I said, it's not always an honor. Some researchers at Cornell recently named three slime-mold beetles after a bunch of politicians. Not sure that was intended as an honor."

"David Attenborough has a dozen species named after him." Grandfather sounded curiously testy. "Including a dragonfly and two spiders."

"How many —" I began. I was intending to ask Grandfather how many species were named after him, but suddenly remembered that this was a sensitive issue. "How many things were named after Hitler?" I asked instead.

"Just the blind cave beetle and a very primitive Paleozoic fly that was already extinct when they named it," Caroline said.

"I would rather like a spider," Grandfather mused. "Quite the most extraordinary people have spiders. Buddy Holly. Johnny Cash. Bono. Angelina Jolie . . ."

"Nelson Mandela and Terry Pratchett have spiders," Caroline pointed out. "And Edward Abbey."

"Penn Jillette," Grandfather continued. "Harrison Ford."

"That should have been a snake," Caroline suggested. "Given how much Indiana Jones hated them."

"Alan Alda." Grandfather went on. "Pancho Villa. Lou Reed. David Bowie. John Lennon. Bob Marley. Neil Young. Orson Welles. Elvis Presley. Pink Floyd. Frank Zappa, for heaven's sake."

"The people who are discovering spiders seem very interested in rock and roll," I said to Grandfather. "Perhaps you should form a band."

"There are even spiders named after fictional characters," Grandfather said. *"Pimoa cthulhu."*

"John Cleese has a lemur," Caroline said.

"Avahi cleesei."

"Hmph." Clearly in the throes of acute lemur envy, Grandfather snorted and strode off to stand near Wim and Guillermo. Rose Noire set her load of books near him, and he settled down to alternate between looking over his photographers' shoulders to second-guess them and leafing through one or another of his books.

Luckily, the tern remained oblivious to the excitement around it. It seemed perfectly content to sit on the railing, gazing out over the glass-smooth ocean. I felt envious. I'd have loved to sit and gaze over the ocean if I didn't know that before long Dad would appear, demanding that I do something to prove that Desiree had been murdered. Or had murdered Nancy Goreham. And how was I supposed to do either of those things, stuck here with no power, no communications, no —

"Mom!" Josh and Jamie burst onto the deck. "Dad says —"

"Ssshhh!"

The boys were momentarily nonplussed at having so many grown-ups shushing them. Grandfather wasn't among the shushers, though.

"Now that's interesting," he said.

"What is?" Caroline asked.

"The tern didn't flee when the boys clattered in." Grandfather pointed his finger at the bird. "Inch a little closer to him."

Caroline inched closer. The tern shuffled sideways and finally took to the air to avoid her. But only briefly. One of his wings didn't open all the way, and instead of taking flight he merely used his wings to make an airborne hop and land a little farther down the rail.

"He's been injured," Grandfather said. "Appears to be a broken wing that didn't heal properly. Clearly he can't fly all that well. That might explain how he ended up here, so far out of his normal range."

"You think he hopped aboard the ship when it was in South America and is still here?" Caroline asked.

"Yes," Grandfather said. "Might not even be this ship. He could have ridden one ship up from South America to Baltimore, and then jumped ship to join our vessel."

"How do you suppose he catches his food?" Caroline asked.

"Good question. Wim, why don't you go down to the kitchen and see if you can get any kind of seafood for him. We can toss some of it around where he can get it."

Maybe Grandfather had just answered the question of how the tern caught his food.

Maybe he hung around the ship until some-one, crew or passenger, took pity on him and fed him.

"Sardines would be nice," Grandfather called after Wim. "Or any kind of seafood that's not too far gone. Unlike humans, he's probably got enough sense not to eat any-thing that will make him sick," he added, turning back to me. "I wouldn't be surprised to find that someone on board's been feed-ing him. Or maybe he's a general ship's mascot."

As if commenting on Grandfather's sur-mise, the tern hopped a little closer to him and festooned the railing with a long streak of white poop. The railing, and the cuff of Grandfather's trousers.

"Not, perhaps, a universally beloved mascot," I suggested.

"It's all Trevor's fault." Grandfather scowled at his cuff.

"I'm not sure why you're blaming Trevor for something you could have avoided by standing a little farther off from the poor bird," Caroline remarked.

"Not the bird — this!" He flung his arms wide. "Our being here on this wretched boat in the first place."

"And in the middle of the dreaded Ber-muda Triangle," Rose Noire murmured.

"Nonsense," Caroline shot back. "You've been talking about doing shipboard lectures for years — long before Trevor came to work for you. Or are you going to blame him for following your orders and making it happen?"

"No, but it's his fault we're here on Pastime. We could have hooked up with National Geographic or Smithsonian or Cunard or —"

"Clearly you must be talking about some other person named Trevor." Caroline was staring at him in disbelief. "Because the Trevor I know did his damnedest to talk you *out* of Pastime. Or don't you remember when he came right out and said it was a badly run second-rate wannabe company?"

"Well, yes," Grandfather said. "But I thought he was just trying to manage me."

"Manage you?"

"You and Meg do it all the time. You know I'm a very strong-minded and determined person —"

"Actually, 'stubborn as a jackass' is the phrase I generally use," Caroline said. "But go on."

"So you deliberately tell me the opposite of what you want me to do, because you think I'll dig in my heels and end up doing what you want."

Caroline and I exchanged a glance. He was right — we did often use that tactic. News to both of us that he'd figured it out.

"I thought Trevor was doing the same thing," he went on.

"Trevor's not sneaky like us," I said. "And he's very good at research. So if he told you sailing with Pastime was a bad idea, I'm pretty sure it was because he thought sailing with Pastime was a bad idea."

"Well, how was I supposed to know that?" Grandfather stomped away to the other end of the sun deck and pretended to be fascinated by the horizon. The horizon, and what Rose Noire was doing. She'd lit a smudge stick and was beginning to make a slow clockwise circle around the outer railing of the deck, all the while casting anxious glances over her shoulder at the sky as if expecting something ghastly to descend at any moment.

"He can blame Trevor if he wants," Caroline muttered. "I know better."

"Just why did he pick Pastime, anyway?" I asked. "Or was it a case that Pastime was the only one that wanted to hire him?"

"Oh, no," she said. "He was in quite serious negotiations with National Geographic. And Smithsonian. And I think he also had some genuine interest from the Audubon

Society and Cunard — the lot, in fact. But they all wanted some kind of input into what his lectures would be about. Pastime gave him carte blanche. You know how much he likes having his own way. I expect that's what did the trick. Ridiculous, blaming this all on Trevor."

"Maybe — but in that case, what do you make of this?" I fished *The Sharp Claw of Love* out of my tote bag and handed it to her.

"One of those books Delaney loves so much?" she asked, frowning slightly at the rather lurid cover.

"Check the title page." I flipped the book open to it and pointed.

" 'To my adorable Trevor'?" she read aloud. "Is this some kind of practical joke?"

"You tell me — you've seen more of Trevor than I have."

"Yes, and 'adorable' isn't the first word I'd use to describe him. Or the hundred and first. Where did you get this?"

"Tucked into an outside pocket of his suitcase."

"Looks well read."

"Or maybe just battered." I shook my head. "Maybe Trevor — or someone — has been carrying it around for quite a while. Like that wretched book I've been trying to read for my book club. I've been carrying it everywhere for nearly a month now, and it's beginning to look as if I've been playing kickball with it."

"Let me see." She held out her hand, and I gave her *The Sharp Claw of Love.* She let it fall open, apparently at random, and began reading the resulting page. I waited as patiently as I could manage.

"My, my." Her eyebrows rose. "A little . . . warm for my tastes, but I'd say she was a pretty good writer."

"Actually, she wasn't," I said. "She just knew how to hire a good ghostwriter."

"Either way, this book's been read." Caroline was letting the book fall open at random again. "Well read. Yes, here's another one. Random wear and tear doesn't make a book fall open at what Monty Python would call the naughty bits. Someone's been reading this."

She handed the book back to me with a flourish.

"You could be right." I was testing her methodology and getting the same results. "The question is, who was doing the reading? And when?"

"It's Trevor's book."

"It is now."

"And the evidence suggests it has been

300

for a while."

"All the evidence suggests is that someone has read it," I countered.

"More than once. At least in part." Caroline was grinning.

"But we don't know that the reader was Trevor. He could have picked up a used copy and gotten her to sign it when he happened to see her. Or he could have done something nice for Desiree, and she rewarded him with a battered book because it was the only one of her books she had with her."

"But why did she have a battered book with her?" Caroline asked. "And not just battered but well read. Do you really think she was reading her own book?"

"It wasn't her own book," I protested. "Not in the sense that she'd written it. Maybe she had to read it to find out what was in it. Maybe she was being interviewed about it. Or maybe she was boning up so she could crack the whip over her new ghostwriter."

"It's possible." Caroline didn't sound as if she believed it. "But if you ask me, it's a lot more probable that Trevor brought along his own well-read copy. And got it signed. Or maybe it was already signed."

"So maybe Trevor knew her," I said.

301

"Or knew *of* her."

"And in either case, does it have anything to do with her death? Or with how we ended up marooned in the Bermuda Triangle?"

"Oh, please don't mention the Bermuda Triangle to me." Caroline glanced over her shoulder at where Rose Noire was vigorously wafting smoke over the starboard railing. "I've already spent an hour this morning waving maps at Rose Noire, trying to convince her that we're not actually in it."

"We're not?" I was surprised. "That's good to know. Not that I'm all that superstitious, but still . . ."

"What gives the Bermuda Triangle its name is that it's a roughly triangular-shaped area." Caroline was holding her exasperation in check, but only just. "With Bermuda as the top point of the triangle and Miami and Puerto Rico as the other two points — which means that the whole thing is pretty much south of Bermuda. I don't know precisely where we are, but draw an imaginary line between Baltimore and Bermuda. We're somewhere on or near that line, and the whole line is considerably north of the Bermuda Triangle, the way I see it."

"But I bet Rose Noire sees it differently."

"She seems to think it covers most of the North Atlantic." Caroline shook her head.

"And she seems to believe every tall tale about it that's ever appeared in the *National Enquirer.* I may just talk your grandfather into giving a lecture to debunk it all. Might cheer people up."

"Good idea," I said. "But wait until we're underway again. Better yet, once we've docked in Bermuda. I don't think his lecture would have the intended effect if he gives it while we're still marooned."

"You're probably right. Here comes one of your writers." She pointed to where Janet had just emerged from the stairway. "Maybe you should ask her about Trevor's book."

"Hey, Meg!" Janet arrived at our side, puffing a little.

"Did you run up from deck one?" I asked.

"Only from deck four. It's getting old."

"Think how fit we'll be when we finally get to Bermuda."

"And how skinny, if the meals get any skimpier. What do you think of this?"

She held up a small handmade poster that advertised "How to get your book published!" The text promised that four best-selling authors would share the secrets of how to break into the publishing industry, followed by the writers' names and several book titles apiece, and ended by inviting people to attend at 6:00 P.M. in the main dining room.

"A ploy to flush out Desiree's new ghost-writer?"

"Any aspiring writer would be crazy not to attend," she said. "Especially since they can pretend they only came because it's dinnertime. But if we have a few keen-eyed people there to help us figure out who's interested in what we're saying and who's only there to stave off starvation . . ."

"I'll be there," I said. "You'll only have an hour, you know. Grandfather will be doing his lecture at seven."

"That's why we chose six," she said. "If anyone gets really into it and wants to talk our ears off, we can always say 'wonderful, but it's time to listen to Dr. Blake now.' Look good to you?"

"Looks great."

"Then we'll make a few more copies and post them in strategic locations. Later!"

She dashed off, waving the poster like a banner.

"Weren't you going to ask her about the book?" Caroline asked.

"Plenty of time for that," I said.

"Meaning you suspect her?"

"I suspect everybody," I said. "And I just thought of another possible explanation for the book. What if someone planted it in

Trevor's luggage? And left it partly sticking out of an unzipped suitcase pocket to make sure we'd find it. The more I think of it, the more suspicious that was — Trevor would never leave a suitcase pocket unzipped, much less have something hanging out of one."

"But why? To frame Trevor, I assume, but of what?"

"What if Desiree's apparent suicide wasn't suicide but murder?" I suggested.

"And the killer planted the book so if we figured out it wasn't suicide we'd suspect Trevor? Nice plan, but it'll backfire if Trevor's still back in Baltimore. He'll have a fabulous alibi."

But what if he had joined Desiree at the bottom of the Atlantic? Or had even preceded her there. Not something I wanted to say out loud at this point.

"Maybe someone planted it to create confusion," I said with a sigh. "In which case, they've succeeded beyond their wildest dreams."

"Good point." Caroline frowned slightly. "Do you even know if that's really Desiree's signature?"

"Looked genuine to me," I said. "Of course, the only thing I have to compare it with is her suicide note." I pulled out my phone, opened up the picture I'd taken of the suicide note, and handed both phone and book to Caroline. She spent several minutes peering back and forth between the two.

"Looks genuine to me." She sounded disappointed. "Of course, I'm not a handwriting expert. And I should think her handwriting might be easier to fake than most. The way she makes some of her letters is . . ."

"Unusual?" I suggested.

"I'd have said downright peculiar. If you got those right, someone might not notice the more subtle things you got wrong."

"So either it is Desiree's handwriting or it's a forgery by someone who has reason to know what her handwriting looks like." I tucked my phone back in my pocket and the book in my tote. "Keep your ears open — if we find out one of our fellow passengers is a vacationing graphologist, we might get a better read on the inscription. I'm going to have another go at finding Léonie. And not just so we can use the equipment that's packed away in Trevor's suitcases. Once we get our hands on them, I'm going to turn them both inside out."

"Good plan."

I headed for the stairway and met Delaney coming up. I drew her a little away from the tern-watching crowd.

"You don't happen to have a handwriting analysis program in your computer, do you?" I asked.

"Sorry. I bet I can find one if we get Internet back."

"Might come in useful. And is there any way you could figure out how to open one of the card key locks?" I explained about Trevor's luggage, my difficulty in finding Léonie, and my reluctance to let any other crew members know I wanted to collect it.

"If we were at home, no problem," she said. "Not sure I have the right equipment here. Let me play with it a while."

"I'll let you know if I ever find Léonie and don't need it anymore."

"Cool," she said. "Although given how weird things are going around here, even after you bag Trevor's stuff it might be nice to have a little more access."

I had to agree.

She returned to the recliner beside Rob. I noticed that she'd pulled out her own card key and was staring at it, visibly lost in thought.

Just then Wim returned with a plate of something fishy-smelling. Probably just what Grandfather needed, assuming the way to the tern's heart would be through his stomach. But the mere smell made my stomach turn. Time to have another go at finding Léonie.

CHAPTER 22

The afternoon dragged on. Léonie remained unfindable. The temperature rose. As I traveled through the ship I could see more and more passengers leaving their doorways and their balcony doors open to get cross-ventilation, so as you walked down the passageways you could wave at people who were fanning themselves while sitting on their balconies or lying on their beds. Every time I passed one of the doors leading into the crew's portion of the ship I'd try it, only to find it locked.

I checked my phone occasionally to see if by some lucky chance it had found a stray signal and downloaded my email. But every time I checked, I found nothing. No cheerful notes from friends. No announcements of sales from the several thousand companies that had me on their mailing lists. No excited requests for donations from politicians. And more to the point, no scoop on

Desiree and the other writers from Kevin.

At one point I ran into Rose Noire on the deck two sun deck, fretting aloud to two other passengers about all the dire perils that could befall us here in the Bermuda Triangle. And not just any passengers, but the Sandburgs, the elderly couple who were probably still recovering from Dad's monologue on disgusting tropical diseases. We'd be lucky if they didn't sue the entire family for emotional distress when we got back to civilization.

"Good news!" I trilled, barging into the middle of the conversation. "Caroline has discovered that we're not in the Bermuda Triangle after all!"

"But Meg —" Rose Noire began.

"Let me tell you about it — you don't mind, do you?" I added to the already retreating Sandburgs, who shook their heads and smiled gratefully at me.

Turning back to Rose Noire I put my forefinger to my lips and shook my head slightly.

To my relief, she stayed quiet until the Sandburgs had scuttled inside.

"But Meg," she protested. "I think they need to know what's going on."

"No, they don't," I said. "They really don't. I take it you don't agree with Caroline's map that shows we're not in the Bermuda Triangle after all."

"The Bermuda Triangle isn't a place that has precise physical boundaries," she began. "It's much more amorphous. Intangible."

"More a state of mind than anything else," I suggested.

"Precisely!" She beamed at me. "So that's why it's so important —"

"To keep as many passengers as possible in the sort of positive, optimistic mood that is the best antidote to any kind of negativity. Especially people like the Sandburgs — a lovely couple, but do you really think they have the kind of psychic armor needed to withstand something like the Bermuda Triangle? Especially if you go around forcing them to think about it all the time."

I expected her to protest that I had no idea what I was talking about. Instead she looked at me with a small puzzled frown on her face.

"I know you think you're humoring me," she said finally. "But I rather think you have a very valid idea here. Quite possibly a brilliant one. I'm going to have to think about this."

She wandered off looking very pensive.

"That's me," I said under my breath. "Brilliant, if only by accident."

The next time I saw her, she was leading a small group of passengers through a guided meditation, exhorting them to breath out negativity and breath in strength and calm. And extolling the benefits of doing so in the open air, in the middle of an ocean that was pumping out healthy ions, and far away from all the mechanical and electronic contraptions that could befoul the chi.

The passengers would never know what I spared them.

Grandfather remained on deck six, alternately napping and observing the tern, even after Wim and Guillermo had grown tired of photographing the bird and gone back to searching the horizon for more interesting photographic subjects. At one point Rose Noire showed up — taking a break between meditation sessions, I assumed — and studied the bird with even more interest than Grandfather.

"Perhaps he's been sent to us as a spirit guide," she said. "Sent to help us in our present peril — to lead us out of the Bermuda Triangle."

"Then we're doubly out of luck," I said. "Until the ship's fixed, we can't exactly follow anyone anywhere, and even if we could, he's certainly not going anywhere with a broken wing. Some spirit guide."

"I didn't mean literally follow him." She let a faint note of exasperation creep into her voice. "Follow his example."

"If you mean we should all hover around Grandfather and let him toss sardines at us, I'll pass, thanks."

"The tern is not panicking or even fretting." Rose Noire's tone conveyed that she was graciously ignoring my sarcasm. "It remains calm, accepting that regardless of whether the ship is steaming toward its destination or becalmed here, the universe remains the same beneficent and wonderful place."

"Of course the tern's calm," I said. "Not only is he home, but he has more suckers than usual to fetch fish for him. We'll see how calm he is when the sardine supply runs out."

Rose Noire rolled her eyes and disappeared. A few minutes later I heard soft chanting from the deck below.

I resumed my search.

Once, while trudging down the fourth deck passageway, I stopped and tried the door to Desiree's cabin. Which, not surprisingly, didn't open. I decided that if I ever did find Léonie again, and if she agreed to let me borrow her key card, I wouldn't just fetch Trevor's luggage. I'd search Desiree's room. I wasn't quite sure what I'd find — I doubted that she'd have left behind a signed confession that she'd killed the writers' friend Nancy, or stolen her manuscript. But if she had a laptop with her — and from what I'd seen, laptops seemed to be almost required equipment for traveling writers — I could borrow it and see what Delaney could uncover.

At six, the writers' presentation on how to get published was well attended — and well received. I had no idea how many of the audience really had literary ambitions and how many were just overjoyed to have some form of entertainment after a long, power-less day — and for that matter, some form of distraction from an uninspiring meal of fruit, power bars, cheese and crackers, cans of fruit cocktail, and tins of sardines.

Dad and I made a list of everyone who took notes, everyone who went up afterward to get business cards from the writers, and everyone who even seemed more than casually interested. Tomorrow I'd work on figuring out their names, and where their cabins were, and how we could manage to engage them in conversation that might reveal if they secretly harbored an ambition to ghostwrite for Desiree. For tonight, I was content to sit back and enjoy Grandfather's lecture on sharks.

It wasn't until near the end of the lecture that I finally spotted Léonie. She slipped through the door at the back of the room and seemed to be scanning the crowd for . . . what? Then she slipped out again. Should I follow her? Probably a good idea to let at least a few minutes pass before — No, I should follow her.

"Back in a few minutes," I whispered to Michael.

When I left the main dining room for the long passageway, I saw her at the far end, entering the boarding lobby. I walked as fast as I could and found her talking to the first officer. Actually, more like being told off by the first officer.

"Our priority should be the passengers," he was saying as I drew near.

"Sorry," I said. "Didn't mean to interrupt."

"Did you find your key card?" Léonie asked.

I was opening my mouth to say that I'd never lost it when I realized what she was doing.

"No — sorry. Pretty sure I must have left it in the room."

"I should go and assist madame," Léonie said to the first officer.

He nodded, then turned and stumbled off, looking exhausted. He slid his key card through the slot beside the CREW ONLY door and disappeared into the forbidden realms of deck zero.

"If madame will follow me?"

She led the way up the stairs. I waited until we were outside Michael's and my room, with no one visible around, before saying, quietly, "Sorry — I hope I didn't get you in trouble."

"No — in fact you gave me a good way to escape yet another lecture. I am not in the running for employee of the month, you see." She looked up and down the corridor to see if anyone was passing. No one was, but just in case, she took out her key card and swiped it through the door. "You were looking for me?"

"Yes. I want to ask a favor."

She raised one eyebrow.

"Can you lend me your key card for a few hours?" I asked. "I want to collect our friend Trevor's luggage — one of his suitcases actually contains stuff for my grandfather anyway, and as for the other one — well, with everything so disorganized we'd like to have it where we can keep an eye on it."

She studied my face for a long moment, and then nodded.

"I will pretend that I lost it and have been looking for it," she said, handing me her card. "I can get by without it for a while. But it would be better if we could find a place for you to leave it, instead of handing it back to me."

I liked the fact that she hadn't asked why I wanted to borrow the key card this time, instead of just getting her to let me in again.

"I assume you don't want to be seen aiding and abetting one of the passengers," I said aloud. "I know — I could hide it in one of the books." I led the way into the library lounge, which was only a few doors down from our cabin — and fortunately empty for the moment. I studied the shelves around us. During a moment of boredom earlier in the day I'd given them a reasonably thorough inspection and I was fairly certain we could pick out a book that would remain unmolested for years on end. In fact, any number of them. The volumes lining the walls were a mixture of fancy-looking books, probably bought by the yard for their covers, and unloved books left behind by passengers of previous voyages.

We settled on a faded leather-bound copy of Edward Bulwer-Lytton's *Paul Clifford*. I'd heard of it before, largely because of its infamous first line: "It was a dark and stormy night." But I doubted there were more than a couple of people on board who would have known about this — Dad and Caroline came to mind — and it was the sort of book whose appearance suggested that it was more likely to provide an allergy attack than a good read. I didn't explain the significance of the book to Léonie, but she wrinkled her nose and agreed that yes, it was a book no sensible person would even touch. And to make it even better, it was ex-library, and still had an old-fashioned card pocket glued to the inside back cover.

"A perfect hiding place," Léonie said with satisfaction. "You can just slip the card in there."

"And I'll have it there by midnight."

We found ourselves grinning at each other.

"In spite of all this, I am having fun," she said. "I should have become a mutineer long ago."

"Up the rebels," I said. "Which is how the Irish say *vive les rebelles.*"

"Then up the rebels. And *à bientôt.*" She hurried off.

Back downstairs in the main dining room, Grandfather's question-and-answer session was coming to a close. I drew Michael aside.

"Can you keep the boys busy for a little while?"

"I can," he said. "Actually, we were all planning to go up on deck six and watch *Raiders of the Lost Ark* on Delaney's laptop. And then as many of the sequels as they can stay awake for. The boys swear they've never seen any of Indiana Jones — not sure how we missed sharing that with them — and Rob and Delaney seem to consider this a form of child neglect. So since she just happens to have digital copies somewhere in the vast collection of electronic doohickeys she brought along . . . don't you want to watch with us?"

"I'll catch up with you when I can." I explained about my plan to retrieve Trevor's suitcases and search Desiree's room.

"You sure you don't need help with that?"

"I was going to enlist Dad," I said. "Not that you wouldn't be a lot more help, frankly, but it isn't a tough mission, and I think he'd be hurt if I didn't ask him."

Dad, of course, was delighted by the opportunity to begin his life of crime on the high seas. My only problem was keeping him from dashing off to begin our burgling expedition while people were still slowly making their way up to their cabins by the light of their flashlights and phones.

"Go put on your burgling clothes and come to Michael's and my cabin at nine," I said. "And by burgling clothes, I mean comfortable clothes and sneakers. I am not going to walk down the passageway with you if you're dressed like a ninja. Casual wear."

"Roger!"

At nine on the dot, I heard a knock on the cabin door, the familiar "shave and a haircut, two bits" knock.

"Hi, Dad." I didn't even have to look to see it was him.

He slipped in and stood, bright-eyed with excitement. For a moment I wondered if maybe I should have asked Dad to watch the boys and invited Michael to join me.

No, Dad would enjoy this more. And if we got caught burgling Desiree's cabin, at least the boys would have one parent who wasn't behind bars.

"Here's the plan," I said. "First we go down to Trevor's cabin and collect one of his suitcases."

"Why only one? We can carry both."

"Maybe not a bad idea," I said. "If we can carry both. But the one we really need is whichever one isn't full of clothes. The one that contains Grandfather's fancy radio equipment."

"We can use that to radio for help! Excellent!"

320

"And it could be heavy, so if we can't handle both, we leave his clothes and take the bag with the hardware."

"But what if he put some bits of radio equipment in his own suitcase? Load balancing, or whatever."

Yes, unfortunately, I could see Trevor doing that. Caroline or Wim or Guillermo or the three of them together would have packed the case containing the radio equipment with maximum efficiency and enough padding to ensure its safe arrival. But Trevor never trusted that anything was properly done unless he did it himself. Most of the time that was a good thing.

"You have a point," I said. "So we'll take both suitcases. Even if it takes two trips."

And maybe that would be useful. Maybe people wouldn't pay us much mind if they got used to the sight of us hauling suitcases up three flights of stairs.

No, make that two. We'd bring the suitcases to Michael's and my cabin on the fourth floor. Once we'd secured them there, we'd search Desiree's cabin. And we could get Wim and Guillermo to collect Trevor's suitcases later. After I'd searched them. Not that searching would do much good — what evidence could I possibly find to support my paranoid suspicion that he'd deliberately missed our sailing? A note gloating that he'd arranged to have us stranded in the Bermuda Triangle, and asking us to give our regards to the pirates he'd hired to slaughter us? And unless his suitcase held a collection of Desiree's books with increasingly affectionate, personal dedications, my search wasn't likely to clear up the question of whether he had any prior connection to Desiree. I pushed my wild imaginings aside.

On a more practical note, it occurred to me that Desiree's cabin occupied precisely the same spot on the fourth floor as Grandfather's did on the fifth, right beside the elevator. If anyone spotted us going into or coming out of her cabin, we could claim that we had mistaken it for Grandfather's, noticed the door hanging open, and gone in to check on him. Or we could pretend we'd intended to go into the library lounge, which had the same position to the left of the stairs that Desiree's room occupied on the right. Or —

"Meg? Are we going soon?"

"We're going now," I said. "Let's keep it casual."

I hoped no one ran into us on our way down to deck two. Dad wasn't trying to be furtive, thank goodness, but his whole body language shouted "Look at me! I know something you don't know!" And creeping around with no light other than the flashlight beams from our phones felt pretty furtive to begin with, even though everybody had been doing it all day in the windowless corridors.

Luckily we made it to cabin 210 without encountering anyone who might have remarked on his jaunty demeanor. Léonie's card key worked just fine, and the two suitcases looked exactly as I'd remembered them. Which didn't mean they hadn't been tampered with, but if they had, at least it had been by someone making a reasonable effort at subtlety.

I tested them both and grabbed the heavy hard-sided case, which I assumed would contain the radio equipment. Dad took the other one.

"Hang on a sec," I said, when we were about to leave. "I want to see if there's any ginger beer here."

"You want to stop in the middle of a burglary to have a soft drink?" Dad asked.

"If there are cases of ginger beer anywhere in this room, then they'd probably have come on board with Trevor." I was checking the closet, the drawers, under the bed, and in the bathroom. "The fact that I'm not finding any is a good thing."

"Your grandfather would probably feel differently."

"I'm sure even Grandfather would rather find out that Trevor was left standing on the pier in Baltimore with a couple of cases of ginger beer than that he'd come on board and disappeared somewhere between Baltimore and here," I said.

"Oh, I see. Yes, definitely."

I grabbed the big suitcase and, after first listening out the door and then peeking out in the hope of leaving unseen, we scurried down the passageway.

As we reached the stairs we heard someone coming up.

"Pant a little," I whispered. "We're resting."

Two of the Stooges appeared. Hal, he of the five o'clock shadow, and the chin-deficient one we didn't yet have a name for.

"Evening," I said.

"You're out late," Hal said.

"Hauling some of Grandfather's stuff back up to him," I said. "Don't worry, Dad. Only two more decks. We'll stop at every landing."

"Why not let us do that?" Hal said. "Come on, Victor — let's not let this lady and her dad wear themselves out."

I didn't protest too hard. Hal and Victor

were visibly a little the worse for drink, and if it was possible to get a contact high from beer fumes, Dad and I would be in trouble. But they were undoubtedly strong, and made quick work of hauling the suitcases up from deck two to deck four.

"Thanks a lot," I said, shaking each Stooge's hand. "Dad, do you want to come in for a minute and say good night to your grandsons if they're still awake?"

"Love to," Dad said. "Thanks again," he added as he, too, shook both Stooges' hands.

"No problem," Victor said.

"Glad to," Hal added.

It occurred to me that if they continued showing signs of common decency I'd have to find a new nickname for them.

I'd worry about that tomorrow. The Stooges left. Dad breathed a sigh of relief, but at least he waited until the door was closed.

"That was close," he said. "Wait — the boys aren't actually here, are they?"

"No," I said. "Michael took them up to deck six to watch *Raiders of the Lost Ark* on Delaney's laptop. We think they're a little young to find out that both their mother and their grandfather are daring cruise ship burglars."

"So now what?"

"We give the Stoo— We give Hal and Victor time to go back downstairs again."

Dad stood by the door, staring at it. I bled off some of my nervous energy by tidying up the two rooms, checking my watch from time to time.

When ten minutes had passed, I returned to the door.

"Okay," I said. "Part two of our mission."

CHAPTER 23

I opened the door and peered out.

"The coast is clear," I said.

We slipped out of the cabin and scanned up and down the corridor with our phone flashlight beams. No one in sight.

"Try not to look quite so furtive this time," I told Dad. "Her cabin is right by the stairwell. Pretend we're just heading to deck six to join Michael and the boys."

"And if someone sees us lurking there?"

"We're resting before tackling the last two flights."

Dad nodded and continued down the hallway looking a lot more natural. When we came to 411, I whipped out the pass key and quickly slid it through the slot. The door clicked open, and Dad and I hurried inside.

I closed the door behind us. Once inside, I held out my phone and slowly ran the light around the circumference of the room. Dad was still fussing with the door for some reason.

"I never noticed it before, but these cabins don't have any kind of inside security lock." He was aiming his phone's light at the door and frowning. "You know, the kind of lock that can't be opened from the outside. Don't hotels usually have that?"

"Yes, but what good would that do us right now? If someone tried to get in and found the door locked from the inside, I think they'd figure out something was up."

"So what do we do if anyone comes along?" Dad asked.

"We hide in . . ." I looked around. There weren't many options in the tiny room. "In the bathroom or out on the balcony. Whichever one we can get to first."

"Right."

"So where do we look?" I said. Rhetorical question. There weren't all that many options. I knew people whose closets were bigger than this room.

"I'm going to start with the bathroom," Dad said. "You can learn a lot about someone by studying their medications."

"I have a lot more confidence in my ability to learn about someone from what's in her purse." I ran my flashlight beam around the room. The giant pink woven straw purse

I remembered Desiree carrying wasn't visible. "So let me know if you find that."

Dad nodded and disappeared into the bathroom. I started right outside the bathroom, with a small two-drawer side table. Nothing in either drawer. Nothing on the armchair next to it. I kept moving clockwise. Nothing on the balcony except the gleaming white table and chairs. Nothing in or on the nightstand to the left of the bed. Nothing on the neatly made bed apart from the perfectly arranged pillows. Although it did seem a bit odd that the bed was made.

"I'm not finding any medicines." Dad appeared in the bathroom doorway. "Not many toiletries, for that matter. She travels light for, um . . ."

"For a woman of, shall we say, late middle age who did not appear to be a devotee of the natural look?"

Dad nodded.

"She also didn't exactly settle into her room," I said. "Michael and I aren't over-packers, and we only had one suitcase each, but we still used every single drawer available for our stuff." I was checking the drawers of the nightstand to the right of the bed. Nothing. A small travel alarm sat on top.

"The bed's made," Dad said. "Do you

suppose she never went to bed Thursday night?"

"Or maybe whichever crew member is assigned to clean the room cleaned it sometime today."

"Before she was found?" Dad frowned. "Or after?"

I shrugged exaggeratedly.

"But — if it was after, they tampered with evidence —"

"I don't think the captain gets that her room could be evidence," I said. "I think for him it's pretty cut-and-dried. 'We have the note. What more do you want?' That's what he'd say."

"Idiots," Dad muttered. "Unless she made the bed herself before she jumped."

"Why would she do that?" I asked.

"I don't know." Dad shrugged. "Not wanting to leave behind anything untidy."

"Doesn't sound like her," I said. "Not sure I can see anyone doing that just before taking their own life."

"Neither can I," Dad said. "But then I also have a hard time figuring out the taking-your-own-life part."

I was examining the bed.

"Pretty neatly done," I said. "But that doesn't rule out the possibility that she made the bed herself. Being a diva and knowing how to make a tight hospital corner aren't mutually exclusive. You say there's not much in the bathroom?"

"See for yourself."

I followed Dad into the bathroom.

A plastic hairbrush and a half-empty tube of toothpaste sat on the tiny vanity counter. The complimentary soap bar had been unwrapped, though it hadn't seen much use.

"Maybe she never really unpacked?" Dad suggested. "Have you checked her suitcase?" He pointed to where it stood against the wall beside the closet.

"I was working my way methodically around the room," I said. "Clockwise. I was going to check the desk next, then the closet."

"I'll be unmethodical then and skip right to the suitcase." He flipped the suitcase on its side, knelt down, and unzipped it

The desk was also empty apart from the various papers supplied by Pastime — a TV channel guide, a map of the ship, a booklet marked GUEST SERVICES.

"It's maybe half full." Dad was staring down into the suitcase, occasionally poking gently at its contents. "She must have unpacked partway. But no toiletries."

"Let's see what the closet has to offer us."

I pulled open the door, which made a

slight creaking noise. I looked inside and, in spite of knowing we needed to stay quiet, I couldn't help uttering a small yelp.

"What's wrong?" Dad looked up.

"There's a body in the closet."

CHAPTER 24

I was momentarily frozen. Dad jumped up from his post beside the suitcase and hurried over. I wasn't sorry to back away from the closet to make room for him.

Wedged into the closet — in the right side, where much of the already limited space was taken up with the life jacket — was a body. A man's body. And not a small man, which was probably why he'd been shoved into something like a fetal position, with the life jacket pulled back in place to obscure his face.

We both just stared for a few moments. Eventually Dad reached out and touched the dead man's wrist.

"Cold," he said. "And no pulse." He grabbed the fingers and tried to flex them. "Rigor mortis."

"So he's probably been dead at least a few hours but less than a day." One of those bits of information I'd picked up from Dad, though I preferred never to have any use for it in real life.

"More or less." Dad nodded absently. "We need to see who he is."

Curious. Under normal circumstances Dad wasn't the least bit squeamish. He did autopsies, for heaven's sake. Why didn't he just pull the life jacket aside to see?

Then I remembered something.

"No one's seen Trevor since yesterday afternoon. Are you thinking it could be . . ."

Dad nodded almost imperceptibly. I felt a sudden twinge of guilt at the suspicions I'd been aiming at Trevor.

I studied the body more closely. He looked bulkier than Trevor. Or did he just look that way because of the way he'd been doubled up to fit into the closet?

"I assumed he was in his cabin, working through his seasickness." Dad shook his head. "I should have checked on him. Should have forced one of the staff to open his door when he didn't answer."

"Don't move the life jacket just yet." I pulled out my phone and took some pictures of the body from a variety of distances and angles.

Dad nodded approvingly. And my picture taking seemed to give him time to regain his usual imperturbable manner.

"Good job," he said. "Now let's take a closer look." He reached out and carefully pulled the life jacket aside.

It wasn't Trevor. We both let out the breaths we'd been holding.

"He looks familiar," I said. "I've seen him before somewhere."

The dead man's head was bent in what would be an uncomfortable position if he were still alive, with the face almost horizontal. Dad was tilting his head slightly so he could see the man's face right side up.

I tilted mine in much the same way. Yes, I'd definitely seen him before.

"He's a crew member," I said. "I saw him arguing with First Officer Martin this afternoon in the Starlight Lounge."

"Arguing about what?"

"Something about the ship repairs." I shook my head. "Martin said something like 'you're the engineer, not me — just fix it.' Then they shut up when they realized I was nearby."

"If he's someone who's mission critical for fixing the ship, we're in trouble," Dad observed.

I reached into the closet and pulled at something — a Pastime ID card in a plastic holder that hung from a cord around the dead man's neck. I couldn't easily pull the cord over the man's head so I slipped the card out of its holder. Unlike our short-term passenger cards, it had a picture of its owner on it — yes, that was him — and his name: Anton Bjelica, from Serbia.

"His name is Anton," I said. "Don't ask me to pronounce the last name."

"We're interfering with a crime scene, you know," Dad said.

"A crime scene Captain Detweiler will do a whole lot more interfering with as soon as he sees it. As in completely destroying it." I tucked the card in my pocket and used my phone to take several shots of the dead man's face.

Dad stretched out the hand holding his iPhone, shone the flashlight beam on the man's neck, and slowly ran it along the darker line encircling it.

"I expect the cause of death will turn out to be ligature strangulation," he said. "Note the ligature mark."

I noted and, more usefully, while noting I took a series of pictures of it with my phone.

"What do — ?" Dad began. Then he froze as we heard the slight clicking noise the door lock made when you slid a card through it.

I shoved the closet door shut. We were closer to the bathroom, so we both dashed into it. I pulled the bathroom door most of the way closed, and we plastered ourselves against the wall on either side of the doorway and flicked off our phones' flashlight beams.

A light appeared. Dad and I froze and stared at the thin shaft of light that fell across the bathroom floor between us. Apparently our visitor had a powerful flashlight. More powerful than our phone flashlights, at least.

At first we heard nothing, and I silently cursed the carpets. Then more light appeared — moonlight. The intruder had opened the curtains. A familiar noise followed — the sound of the sliding glass door to the balcony being opened. Maybe it was a good thing we'd hidden in the bathroom.

Another noise — softer, but nearer by. A soft creaking. The closet door opening.

Some rustling and thumping followed, and a few muted clicking and clanging noises.

Then a few moments of silence, followed by a distant splash.

More sliding glass door noises.

More silence, and then the light went out and the cabin door opened and closed.

Dad took a step. I put my hand on his shoulder as a silent signal to stop. What if the intruder came back?

After what seemed like several centuries, Dad and I exchanged a glance. I nodded. I slowly pushed open the bathroom door. We both flicked on our phone flashlights to take a better look. Yes, the room was empty.

So was the closet.

"He took our body," Dad muttered.

"And threw it overboard."

Dad stared at my phone.

"Those pictures you took," he said. "They're the only record of that poor man's fate."

"Well, that and his Pastime key card."

I slid open the balcony door as quietly as I could, went out, and stared down at the water. Dad followed.

"Wouldn't the body float?" I asked softly.

"He must have weighted it down."

I stepped back inside and looked around. I couldn't see anything missing, and certainly not anything that could have weighted a body. Dad followed me in, and from the way he was studying the room, I suspected he was coming to similar conclusions.

"Let's get out of here," I said. "Whoever just did that would not like to find out that anyone witnessed him throwing the body overboard. Him or her. Murder's an equal opportunity crime. We have no idea who was in here."

I closed the sliding glass doors. I took a quick glance in the side of the closet that hadn't contained the body. A couple of dresses hung there, and one pair of shoes rested on the floor.

"What did they do with the Christian Louboutin shoes?" I asked. "I could have sworn the captain told the crew member who collected them to take them back to her cabin."

"Maybe he changed his mind and took possession of them himself."

"Or maybe someone stole them." I took a quick glance around. "I don't see her as a minimalist traveler. Some of her stuff's missing. Quite possibly a whole lot of her stuff. Maybe she didn't have a laptop — I was hoping she did, so I could get Delaney to search it. But no cosmetics? No way."

And also no copies of any of her books. Maybe she had given Trevor her only copy.

I made a quick circuit of the room, taking pictures of everything — the stuff and the empty spaces alike. Dad was shifting from foot to foot, clearly torn between his approval of my efforts to document the crime scene and his intense desire to leave it.

Then I opened the door and stuck my head out. No one in the corridor.

"Let's make it fast," I whispered.

We hurried out and pulled the door shut behind us. I could tell Dad's first impulse was to run back to Michael's and my room, but I grabbed his elbow and slowed him down to a casual saunter. As long as we hadn't been spotted actually leaving the room, anyone who saw us would merely assume we were coming back from the stairs or the Starlight Lounge.

"We need to figure out who we can tell about this," Dad said quietly. "I don't know about you, but I'm feeling a lot less suspicious of the writers all of a sudden."

"I take it you won't argue with my suggestion that we not tell the captain," I said. "Or any of the crew."

He nodded.

"Hang on a sec," I said as we reached the door of Michael's and my room. "I want to check something."

I reached into my pocket, took out the key card I'd retrieved from Anton Bjelica's body, and swiped it through the lock. The door clicked open.

We hurried inside.

"The good news is that we can give Léonie back her card and still have access to anything the dead guy had access to," I said.

"How will that help?" Dad asked. "Unless, of course, Stefan was assigned to this deck."

"Anton," I corrected. "Léonie isn't assigned to this deck, or deck two, for that matter, but we had no trouble getting into Trevor's and Desiree's rooms. I bet they just give the crew access to everyplace they might need to go while working with the passengers."

"That's good," Dad said. "But what are we going to do with it?"

Good question.

"I'll figure that out tomorrow," I said "But it makes me feel better to know we have access — without anyone knowing about it."

"Not even Léonie?" Dad asked. "Your mother rather likes Léonie."

"So do I," I said. "But we don't really know her that well. She's definitely not a Pastime loyalist — we know that much. What if she is secretly happy about our being marooned because it hurts Pastime? And besides, if this was one of your mystery books, wouldn't the one crew member who's actually been kind and helpful and sympathetic turn out to be the killer?"

"Good point." He looked a little blue — clearly our adventure wasn't turning out to be as much fun as his books.

"You go up to deck six," I said. "Let Michael know everything went smoothly and the two of us will not be spending the night in the ship's brig."

"Do you suppose it has a brig?" Dad asked. "I'd like to see that."

"If I run across one, I'll let you know."

"And where are you going?"

"To return the key to Léonie. Or at least to the clever hiding place where I'm going to leave it so no one will see us together and suspect that she's been aiding and abetting us. Now hurry — you might still get to see the scene where they open the Ark."

He brightened — that was one of his favorite scenes — and hurried off.

I waited until he'd disappeared up the stairway. Then I locked the door behind me and headed for the library lounge.

It was unoccupied. Rather than dash in, hastily stuff the card in *Paul Clifford*'s card pocket, and rush out, I decided to dawdle for a little while to lend plausibility to the notion that I was in search of non-electronic reading material.

I started browsing a little to the left of where *Paul Clifford* was shelved, pulling out a book here and there. When I came to the book itself, I plucked it out and tucked the key card inside the card pocket.

And then instead of putting it back on the

shelf, I gave way to the impulse to do something Dad had taught Rob and me to do as children. Stitchomancy, he had called it — telling our fortune by means of a book. I closed my eyes, opened the book at random, and read the first sentence my eyes fell on:

So ended the conference of the robbers.

"I was looking for a fortune, not a recap of recent events," I told the book sternly. "And technically Dad and I were burglars, not robbers. Let's try again."

Of course, the game usually worked a lot better if you asked a specific question. But what to ask? "Was Desiree murdered?" might be a good one, although books rarely ran to yes or no questions. "Who killed Anton Bjelica?" might be nice, but asking for proper names was always a silly idea, especially when such a large number of the crew — and for that matter, the passengers — bore names that wouldn't be in common usage in the England of 1830, when Bulwer-Lytton was writing. "When will we resume our voyage?" was what I really wanted to know, but I wasn't sure I wanted to hear the answer. I settled on "What's really going wrong on board the ship?"

The second answer didn't seem a whole lot more fortune-like:

Meanwhile let us glance over the destinies of our more subordinate acquaintances.

"Subordinate acquaintances." Did that mean the crew? Did the real answer lie with them? Should I try to expand my acquaintance past the helpful Léonie? Or did it just mean people I didn't know all that well?

One more time. "What's really going on?"

O time, thou hast played strange tricks with us; and we bless the stars that made us a novelist, and permit us now to retaliate.

"That's a little ominous," I said. Novelists retaliating — was the book trying to warn me that one of the writers was behind — behind what? Desiree's apparent suicide? The breakdown of the ship? Bjelica's death?

"This is silly," I told myself. "You're asking for wisdom from a book whose opening lines have become synonymous with purple prose."

I snapped the book closed, left the library lounge, and went back to our cabin. Time to search Trevor's luggage. I was tired, and still a little shaken by our discovery of the body, and I almost wanted to leave it locked up in our cabin and worry about searching it in the morning. But as Dad and I had just demonstrated, anything locked in a cabin was fair game to anyone with crew access on their Pastime card. If he and I

344

hadn't decided to burgle Desiree's cabin tonight, Anton Bjelica would have gone to his watery grave without anyone other than his killer being the wiser.

"Get it over with," I muttered, stifling a yawn.

The larger, hard-sided suitcase was entirely filled with electronic equipment. None of the items even resembled a laptop, and most of it was stenciled with PROPERTY OF THE BLAKE FOUNDATION.

The smaller suitcase contained Trevor's belongings. No laptop, and no papers of any kind. But he'd probably have kept those in the black leather messenger bag that never left his side — his equivalent of my trusty tote bag. Or if he had left any papers in the suitcase, someone had beat us to the search.

Only one book — a paperback copy of *Master and Commander,* the first of O'Brian's nautical series. I attempted to reproduce what Caroline had done with *The Sharp Claw of Love,* letting the book fall open where it would, but the results weren't nearly as dramatic. If anything, the book had a slight tendency to fall open at naval battles, but I wasn't sure that signified anything. I'd read the book myself, and while it had been a while, I seemed to remember that there were rather a lot of naval battles.

But was there something sinister about Trevor's choice of books? Given Grandfather's current state of indignation that his former student had named a newly discovered tern after one of O'Brian's characters instead of Grandfather, I'd have assumed that everyone who knew him would go to almost any length to avoid reminding him of the whole thing. Bringing along a copy of *Master and Commander* seemed like a deliberate provocation. Especially since, from what I'd seen, Trevor did most of his reading on one or another of his electronic devices. He could read all twenty of O'Brian's Aubrey and Maturin series right under Grandfather's nose without anyone being the wiser. But if he pulled out this seemingly innocuous paperback, all hell would break loose.

"Sorry, Trevor," I said aloud. "I'm confiscating this." After all, while I'd flipped through it enough to confirm that there weren't any interesting bits of paper stuck between its pages, it would take a lot more time and concentration than I had right now. Trevor could have scrawled faint notes in the margins, or used pinpricks or underlining to spell out cryptic messages. Maybe —

Maybe Dad's fascination with mystery was having a little more influence on me than I'd realized. I stifled another yawn. I could enlist Dad to study the book for clues — he'd probably enjoy it. The important thing was to keep the book hidden from Grandfather — which meant not leaving it in Trevor's suitcase. I could just imagine Grandfather, already irritated by Trevor's absence, pawing through the suitcase in search of some item Trevor normally found for him and finding O'Brian.

I tucked the book away in one of the drawers — beneath my underwear.

The book had been a good find. But apart from that, searching his luggage had been pretty useless. I had learned nothing. Well, nothing useful. I couldn't imagine when I'd need to know that Trevor preferred boxers to briefs. The sheer size of his collection of over-the-counter medicines was impressive, but hardly relevant to anything.

So I packed up the contents of the suitcases again and left them in the middle of the cabin. With luck, I could get Wim or Guillermo to collect them before bedtime. Then I headed for the stairs. I arrived on deck six in time to catch most of *Indiana Jones and the Temple of Doom.* Although Michael and I missed a few of the high points while I brought him up to speed on what Dad and I had found.

At my suggestion, Michael and Guillermo slipped out toward the end of the movie, when the boys — and for that matter, everyone else — were glued to the laptop screen, to relocate Trevor's luggage from our cabin to the one Guillermo shared with Wim.

At bedtime — a rather late bedtime — I expected to have trouble getting to sleep, between the visions of Anton Bjelica that kept appearing whenever I closed my eyes and my impatience to hear how Caroline, Wim, and Guillermo were doing with the equipment in Trevor's bag. And the heat didn't help. At one in the morning it was still stiflingly hot, which didn't bode well for tomorrow. If the crew didn't get the power going again, and we had to cope without air-conditioning . . . .

CHAPTER 25

Saturday

It was hot when I woke up, at around 6:00 A.M. Hot and sticky. The fact that the boys had crawled into bed with us in the middle of the night didn't help.

"I really need a shower," Josh said, when he woke up.

"Yeah, you do," Jamie said, adding, more kindly, "We all do."

"I'll haul up a few more buckets of seawater for a rough shower later," Michael suggested. "First, let's go downstairs and see what's for breakfast."

"Cereal, probably." Josh rolled his eyes.

"That's okay — I like cereal." Jamie, ever the optimist.

"If they haven't run out of cereal." And Josh, reliably the pessimist.

So we trooped down to the main dining room. A few people were there already, picking over the offerings on the buffet tables. It looked a lot like a rerun of last night's buffet dinner — cheese, cold cuts, fruit, and crackers. Although this time the crew had mostly set out boxes. A carton full of individual cereal boxes. A wooden crate containing oranges. A case of granola bars. No crew members were visible — they must have stolen out in the middle of the night to restock the tables. This was getting creepy.

I was relieved to see that Josh and Jamie were frowning suspiciously at the cold cuts and cheese.

"This looks kind of yucky." Josh wrinkled his nose.

"Smells yucky, too," Jamie added.

"Try the cereal," I said. "It should be fine. But no milk. It could have spoiled."

I noticed that Wim had piled a plate with the ham the boys had just turned up their noses at.

"Don't eat that," I told him. "It may have gone bad."

"So soon?" Wim said.

"It's been over twenty-four hours now," I pointed out.

"And it smells funny," Jamie said.

"If you are careful not to open the refrigerator or freezer too often, food will keep there for a couple of days," Wim said.

"In the freezer, maybe," I said. "The rule

of thumb we use is forty-eight hours if the freezer is fully packed and twenty-four for a half-full one. A refrigerator will only stay reasonably cold for four hours or so, and that's if you keep the door closed. After that everything starts spoiling. You want to bet your life that everyone on the kitchen staff was really careful about closing doors? Or that none of the food they loaded on for the journey was getting a little too close to its sell-by date to begin with?"

Wim looked at his plate and leaned down to take a delicate sniff. Then he sighed and took it over to empty its contents into a trash can.

"Stick to cereal," I advised. "And no milk unless it comes from a can that you see opened."

"Right." Wim sounded glum.

"How are you doing with the equipment from Trevor's luggage?" I asked.

"Do you want the technical explanation or the easy one?"

"Do you really need to ask?"

"An important part is broken," he said. "But Guillermo and Delaney are fixing it. We should be ready to test it out in an hour or so."

"Excellent."

Wim went back to the buffet table and

began searching for unspoiled items. Josh and Jamie grabbed two single serving boxes of cereal apiece and followed Michael to a table. I spotted Mother, who was standing to one side, surveying the scene with a look of profound disapproval. Sympathy and more than a little concern swept over me. Things on board weren't too bad yet for those of us who were fond of camping. But Mother's idea of camping was staying in a hotel that didn't have a four-star restaurant. This must be difficult for her. I felt a slight twinge of guilt — which made no sense. It was Grandfather's fault she was here, not mine. I didn't see anyone within earshot of her, so I went over.

I didn't want to add to her stress, but I needed her help. And maybe helping would prove a distraction.

"Mother," I said, keeping my voice low. "Did Dad tell you what he and I found last night?"

She nodded. Her mouth was compressed into a tight line.

"Michael and I don't want the boys left alone for a minute." I glanced over my shoulder to make sure they weren't listening. "I could use your help with that."

"I agree," she said. "Let's brief some of the others. Horace, Rose Noire, Rob and

352

Delaney, Caroline . . ."

"Not Grandfather," I said.

"No," she agreed. "He'd only go racing up to the bridge to provoke a confrontation. But I think Wim and Guillermo can be trusted. Yes, we should definitely protect the boys. But . . ."

She frowned and fell silent for a few long moments, clearly lost in thought. Then she visibly straightened her already erect spine — how did she manage that effect? — lifted her chin, and assumed what I thought of as her Joan of Arc expression.

"Meg," Mother said. "This has gone far enough. We must Do Something."

I cringed slightly. When Mother said that, I usually ended up being the one who did whatever she thought needed doing. She was very good at enlisting people in general to accomplish whatever projects she wanted to push forward, but in addition to being the handiest potential lieutenant at the moment, I was also, in her view, the most capable of them all. I reminded myself that some people would see this as a compliment.

"I can think of a lot of things I'd like to do," I said. "Things that would definitely improve living conditions on board, and maybe even get us on our way again. Not that I see any chance of the captain either doing them or letting any of us do them."

"Precisely," Mother said. "We will need to take over the ship."

"I think that's technically known as mutiny," I pointed out.

"No," Mother said. "If the crew did it, it would be mutiny. What I have in mind is more of a revolt against a tyrannical and incompetent dictatorship."

"I think calling it a consumer protest might be less fraught," I suggested. "We, the Pastime customers, protesting unsafe and unsanitary conditions and treatment by the ship's management that amounts to outright abuse."

"That's the ticket." She looked at her watch. "It's a quarter of seven. We need to convene a meeting. Do you think an hour will be sufficient time to notify all the passengers?"

"Some people might still be asleep."

"In this heat? I doubt it. We'll need to send messengers, of course."

"I can recruit some," I said. "But a meeting about what? What do you want the messengers to say?"

"That if they're dissatisfied with what's happening on board the ship they should come here to the main dining room at eight o'clock for a discussion of what we, the passengers, can do."

That didn't sound unreasonable. If nothing else, people might feel better after airing their grievances. And maybe there were a few things we could do, if Mother was serious.

"I'll find some messengers," I said aloud.

I glanced around the dining room. Normally I'd have sent the boys, but now — not unless I teamed them with at least one adult.

I spotted the writers at a nearby table, stoically munching on dry cereal, and went over to join them.

"May I enlist you for a project when you're finished eating?" I asked.

"Won't take long." Kate swallowed hard. "What do you need?"

I explained Mother's idea for an all-passenger meeting, and they responded with enthusiasm. They wrote down our official invitation text on four sheets of paper torn from Janet's spiral-bound notebook and then took off. Since there were four decks with passenger cabins — decks two through five — they were planning to take one floor each.

"We're going to run into people with mobility issues," Janet said over her shoulder from the doorway.

"Note the cabin numbers," I said. "I'll see if I can recruit some burly guys to carry down anyone who wants to come but can't make it under their own steam."

Wim and Guillermo readily agreed to serve as human porters and hurried off to start at the top, on deck five. I scanned the rest of the people in the dining room. Most were middle-aged or even elderly, and looked as if they'd already completed their day's exercise getting down to the dining room in the first place. Then again, the passenger list did skew rather older.

The Stooges. Two of them were sitting at a table, glumly chewing cornflakes — Bart Evans, of the thinning reddish hair, and Hal Burkhart, of the five o'clock shadow. I strode over to their table. They looked alarmed when they noticed my approach, and Bart choked slightly on his cornflakes. I didn't waste time on formalities.

"How would you like to do something useful?" I omitted "for a change" but they probably heard it in my voice. I explained about the proposed meeting.

"Lots of little old people on board," Bart said. "Some of them couldn't do the stairs even if they wanted to."

"We've been taking meals up to these two

little old ladies across the hall from us," Hal said. "Both of them on walkers. The crew ought to be doing something for them. And I'm not looking forward to breaking the news that this is breakfast." He waved at a small stash of cereal boxes on the table beside them.

Okay, so maybe the Stooges weren't completely unredeemable.

"That's excellent," I said. "We all need to do a lot more of that kind of looking out for each other. Right now, I need a few burly guys to help or even carry anyone who can't make it down here on their own."

They both perked up slightly at the word "burly."

"Go up to deck four," I went on. "You'll find a lady there going from door to door, inviting people to the meeting. Introduce yourselves to her and let her know you're the muscle for anyone who needs help. When you finish with deck four, see if they need help on two or three. Oh, without power we'll have no microphone; if you notice anyone has hearing aids, try to get them to sit near the front."

"Can do," Hal said.

"Okay if I drop off breakfast with our ladies on the way up?" Bart asked.

"Not only okay but excellent," I said.

"And if they're in the mood to be carried down, bring them first."

Bart strode off, probably glad I didn't seem bent on using him for a punching bag again. Hal lingered.

"Um . . . I heard that there's a doctor on board. Do you know who he is? Or she," he added quickly.

"My dad," I said. "What's wrong?"

"Any chance he could do something for our buddy Barry? He's still sick as a dog. We didn't want to leave him alone so we're taking turns sitting with him."

Ah. I'd wondered where Victor was.

"I'll see if Dad can drop by and check him out," I said. "What cabin number?"

"He's in 208. Thanks!"

He hurried off to catch up with Evans.

At this rate, I would definitely need to find something other than Stooges to call them.

I decided to make myself useful. I grabbed a trash can, started at one end of the buffet, and began throwing away anything that looked or smelled suspect.

People begin streaming into the dining room. Wim, Guillermo, Rob, Horace, and the three no-longer-Stooges appeared from time to time carrying an older passenger, pushing someone in a wheelchair, or hovering in mother-hen fashion behind a passenger on a walker.

Dad showed up, and I dispatched him to room 208 to check on the ailing Barry. Janet and Kate reappeared — evidently they were doing decks four and five, which had fewer cabins and more public deck areas. They settled down at a table together with their laptops. I peeked over their shoulders and discovered that they were creating a central list of who was in each cabin, with notes on which ones had needed assistance.

"Great idea," I said. "We can expand on that later. Add any useful skills they might have."

Aunt Penelope and Rose Noire had raided the cleaning supply closet off the passageway and joined my efforts to clean up the buffet area, not only trash-bagging the suspect food, but also stacking the dirty dishes and attacking the tables with spray cleaner — one that contained bleach, I noted with approval.

Occasionally one or the other of the two doors separating the dining room from the kitchen would open a foot or so and a crew member would peer out. Then they'd pop back inside the kitchen and slam the door shut again, as if they feared we'd begin using them for a game of live Whac-A-Mole.

Not that some passengers weren't

tempted.

"You think they've noticed that we're doing their job?" Aunt Penelope asked, glaring toward the kitchen door.

"I'm getting very bad vibes from the kitchen right now," Rose Noire intoned.

"We'll deal with the kitchen later," I said.

"Have to get in there first."

"Leave that to me," I said.

"Ooh — I can't wait to see that." Aunt Penelope was probably expecting to see me batter the door in with a fire axe. She'd probably be disappointed when I pulled out Anton's Pastime card.

Then again, maybe the fire axe wasn't such a bad idea. Maybe I should keep the card a secret. Because once we finished doing whatever Mother had in mind, I planned to use the card to invade the crew-only spaces and poke around. Even if I didn't learn anything relevant to Desiree's alleged suicide, Trevor's apparent disappearance, or why someone had murdered Anton Bjelica, at least I could satisfy my curiosity about what all the crew were up to down there.

Mother was circulating among the arriving passengers, greeting the ones she'd already met, introducing herself to the ones she hadn't yet, and visibly charming and cheering everyone.

Pretty soon, nearly every chair was taken, and the crowd seemed . . . remarkably cheerful, as if the mere idea of having a meeting to figure out what we could possibly do had restored their good spirits.

Eventually, Wim and Bart the former Stooge appeared in the back of the room with yet another senior citizen. They gave me a thumbs-up sign. I went over to see what that meant.

"Everyone who's coming is here," Wim said.

"And that's pretty close to every passenger on the ship," Bart added. "Cranky little old lady in 512 doesn't want to come, and we have two down with seasickness, 232 and 208."

"Excellent. Have a seat, and I'll tell Mother we can get started."

I returned to the end of the room where Mother was sitting and gave her a thumbs-up.

"Your public awaits," I said.

CHAPTER 26

Mother stepped up onto the small stage and beamed at the assembled passengers. An expectant murmur rose from the crowd.

"Ladies and gentlemen. Fellow passengers." She knew how to project, so even without a microphone most of the passengers would be able to hear her, and with luck I'd have managed to steer the hard of hearing to the front row. "Thank you for coming. I think we're all concerned that this cruise is not turning out the way any of us expected."

People nodded, and a few chuckles rippled through the crowd.

"I would like to suggest —"

"What's this then?" First Officer Martin burst through the door behind Mother — the one leading in from the back deck — and strode toward the small stage. "We can't have this. I suggest all of you —"

"Mr. Martin," Mother said. "This is a

meeting of the passengers. We'll let you know if we have any questions you can answer."

Martin had reached the stage and put his foot on the lower of the two steps leading up to it. At least half a dozen of the men seated nearby — Dad, Michael, Rob, Horace, Wim, and the provisional non-Stooge Hal — leaped to their feet and took a step or two toward him. Martin probably didn't even see them. For once he wasn't smiling, though he didn't look threatening. He had the sick, despairing look of someone suddenly realizing things are far worse than he imagined. Mother had turned toward him, hands on her hips, looking like the most immovable object imaginable. Martin flinched slightly, pulled his foot back, and turned to the audience.

"Now, folks," he said. "I know everyone's a little upset about the delay, but —"

"Mr. Martin." Mother didn't shout or increase her volume at all — just hit him with the Voice, accompanied by a gimlet stare and the tight-lipped expression that suggested she, like Queen Victoria, was not in the least amused.

He shut up in mid-sentence and stared at her.

"If we feel an irresistible urge to play

363

another game of charades, we'll let you know." Mother articulated each word with icy precision. "For now — isn't there something useful you could be doing to help get this ill-fated vessel back on course?"

Martin looked around at the hostile faces turned toward him. He attempted a rather ghastly version of his usual smile and then fled through the nearest door, back onto the tiny rear deck. He didn't reappear, so either he was lurking out there, working on a comeback line, or he'd chosen to take the outside stairs to wherever he was going.

Or maybe he was spying. He was welcome to.

Once the door shut behind him, Mother bestowed another gracious smile on her audience and went on.

"I know many of us are dissatisfied with the current state of affairs on board the ship."

Murmurs of agreement.

"The captain and his officers have not been forthcoming about why we are stranded here, far too close for comfort to the Bermuda Triangle." She glanced over at where Caroline and Rose Noire were standing. I suspected Caroline had briefed her on Rose Noire's fixation and the need to avoid setting her off. "Nor have they given us any idea of what they are doing to remedy the situation or how long it will take. Many of us are also dissatisfied with the quality of the service we are receiving. Obviously we cannot expect to enjoy the same level of comfort we were promised when we contracted with Pastime for this cruise. But increasingly, many of us are suffering discomfort, even hardship, because no one is even attempting to ensure that our basic wants are met. I don't blame the crew —"

Some dissenting murmurs arose at this.

"No, I don't blame them. While obviously there are some crew members who are more diligent and helpful than others, it has become clear to those of us who have begun to investigate the situation that the ship has been deliberately understaffed — to a degree that may not even be legal."

"Shame on them!" someone called out, and there was a smattering of applause.

"While things were going well, the crew, by means of exhaustingly long shifts, were for the most part able to keep the inadequate staffing level from affecting our comfort. But they were already at the breaking point when the current crisis happened."

A man raised his hand. I recognized him as Ted Lambert, the attorney who'd done so much research on cruise law before embarking. Mother nodded at him.

"Do we know exactly what's wrong with the ship? And do we have any idea whether the ship's inadequate staffing levels contributed to the problem?"

"To answer your first question: we have been informed that the ship's navigation system has broken down, and they have turned the power off for the safety of the workers who are repairing it. Having been given the same excuse for over twenty-four hours, we now plan to take steps to determine whether there's any truth to it. As for the second question — we don't yet know that understaffing contributed to this disaster, but I consider it highly likely."

This set off a round of exclamations and side conversations. Mother waited for thirty seconds or so, and then raised her hand for silence.

"We have already had one tragedy aboard this ship." She paused for a moment, with an expression of stoic sorrow on her face, and I could hear scattered sniffles from the audience. "We cannot do anything about poor Ms. St. Christophe — but I, for one, think it's time we took action for our own safety. In fact, to take over some of the ship's functions that are being done badly or not at all."

Back to murmurs of agreement, and scattered applause.

"And for that purpose, I'd like to turn this meeting over to my daughter, Meg Langslow, who has been developing plans for dealing with our situation."

Loud applause as Mother gestured for me to come to the stage.

I'd have to wait till later to kill her. Or at least give her a piece of my mind. Or mention that I could think of a few things we might want to be doing did not constitute a plan.

But something needed doing, and if I didn't want Mother's efforts to fire up the rest of the passengers to go to waste . . .

"Thank you, Mother." I opened up my notebook-that-tells-me-when-to-breathe to a blank page and set it on the podium so I could pretend I had a plan written in it. I took out my pencil, too, to write down whatever I was about to pretend I was reading.

"First of all, I want volunteers to help create a detailed list of everyone on the ship," I said. "Obviously, Pastime has this — or would have it if they could access their computer systems. But neither we nor they have access to that information now. We need to know who's in each cabin. We need to know who has mobility issues that make it difficult for them to get meals with the elevators not running. We need to know who has medical issues that could cause them problems. We need to know who has skills that might help us deal with this crisis." And while I wasn't going to say it aloud, we needed to know if anyone else had disappeared since we'd set sail. "If you'd like to volunteer to help with the census, please see Caroline Willner after the meeting — Caroline, would you raise your hand?"

Caroline not only raised her hand, she waved it vigorously, no doubt to assure me that she didn't mind being drafted.

"If there's anyone here who has medical skills, please identify yourself after the meeting to my father, Dr. James Langslow."

Dad leaped up and did a sort of Rocky-style two-fisted victory arm pump, to the applause of the crowd.

"Anyone who's got skills in engineering or computers or any other area of technology that might be useful in restoring the power and helping the crew get this tub moving again, please see Delaney McKenna after this meeting." Delaney jumped up and waved her arm with enthusiasm.

"And last — for now, at least. The

kitchen." A mixture of groans and cheers. "Maybe I'm fussy," I went on. "But the last couple of buffets they've thrown out on the tables haven't exactly been gourmet spreads, and I suspect I'm not the only one who's begun to worry about food poisoning. We need volunteers to take over the kitchen, clean it up, throw away anything that could have gone bad through lack of refrigeration, and come up with the most appetizing meals we can manage with whatever un-spoiled food remains. But first, cleaning — no skill needed, just elbow grease. If you're game, see Mother after the meeting."

I pointed in her direction, and Mother responded with the Royal Wave.

"That's it for now, folks. If anyone has questions that need answering or sugges-tions about what else we could be doing, come up and see me after the meeting."

Caroline, Dad, Delaney, and Mother each moved to one corner of the room, and I was delighted to see that at least half of the people in the room were flocking to one of the corners.

Of course, the other half were crowding around me.

Within fifteen minutes I'd filled another whole page in my notebook. Fortunately, most of the notes were about either people volunteering skills I hadn't asked about or problems I could easily refer to one of the four lieutenants I'd just drafted.

I put Horace in charge of finding out who had devices that needed recharging — not just phones, tablets, and laptops but everything from battery-powered toothbrushes, shavers, and hair dryers to wheelchairs, oxygen compressors, and mobility scooters — and setting up a procedure to ensure that the more mission-critical devices got top priority.

I also realized that we needed some way to get news and announcements to people. I closed my eyes and listened to the voices around me for a few moments. Then I opened my eyes again and cut a passenger out of the crowd around Mother. Hal, one of the former Stooges. One of his buddies had joined Dad's crew and the other was in Delaney's orbit.

Being singled out seemed to make him nervous.

"I work in sales," he said. "Bart and Victor have useful skills, but me —"

"You have a loud voice," I said.

"Sorry," he said. "It's just that —"

"It's okay." I held up my hand in a "stop" sign. "That wasn't a complaint. Sometimes loud is useful. Do you also have a reasonably good memory?"

He nodded.

"Good. You are now officially our town crier. When we have announcements to make to all the passengers, we'll send you up and down the decks, shouting them at the top of your lungs."

He grinned as if it sounded like fun. I wondered if he'd realized how many trips up and down the stairs he'd be making.

"You're also our . . . I don't know what to call it. Person in charge of noticing things and keeping track of things and reporting things. Checking in on the people who are confined to their cabins to make sure they're okay and arranging to get them anything they need. Noticing where people are, so, for example, if someone needs a doctor, you'll have some idea where to find Dad. Stuff like that."

"Town crier and chief busybody," he said. "And maybe also the Town Watch. Can do."

"Great." I handed him a page from my notebook. "Here's the current list of seasick and otherwise cabin-bound people and empty cabins. Start wherever you like. Work your way through all the decks, checking on the cabin-bound folks and adding anyone else in need of help. Note whatever's going on throughout the ship. Report back if

371

there's anything you think we need to know. Then do it all over again. And —"

I paused. Had I decided to declare the ex-Stooges trustworthy?

Maybe. He'd been one of the men who'd stepped forward to defend Mother. He got points for that in my book.

I pulled out my phone and called up the picture I'd taken of Desiree's shoes and shawl.

"If you happen to see either of these objects anywhere on your rounds —"

"Confiscate them?" He sounded as if he thought that would be fun.

"No. Be subtle. Pretend you don't even notice them. But find me or my dad immediately and tell us where they are and who has them. And don't tell anyone — not even your buddies."

"Gotcha." He winked and tapped the side of his nose. "Mum's the word."

With that he set off.

I returned to my list. Were there any EpiPens on board? Could we launch the lifeboats without power if we needed to? Was there any gluten-free cereal in the kitchen? Did we have any way of making coffee? Was there any air freshener that could be used to mask the smell from the toilets?

Just for a moment I felt sorry for Captain Detweiler. And even more for First Officer Martin, who'd at least had the gumption to talk to the passengers — even if his ideas of what we should be doing differed from ours.

Another head peered into the dining room from the door to the kitchen. And this time it didn't disappear immediately.

Léonie. I hurried over to the door.

"First Officer Martin is not a happy man at the moment." She didn't sound as if his unhappiness distressed her unduly. Annoying that the only two crew members who hadn't disappeared seemed at odds with each other. Was their antagonism typical of the *Wanderer*'s crew? And if so, had it contributed to our being marooned?

I'd worry about that later. Unlike the other crew members who'd peeked out, Léonie opened the door far enough for me to see into the kitchen, which was a mess. Even worse than my kitchen usually looked on those occasions when the boys decided to surprise Michael and me with breakfast in bed.

"I don't want to get you in trouble," I said. "But I could use some information."

She cocked her head, rather like a bird, as if to say, "yes?"

"I've found some passengers with skills

373

that might let them help repair whatever's wrong with the ship. Where should I send them?"

She blinked and looked startled for a moment. Then she smiled rather mischievously.

"Fixing the ship would be excellent," she said. "The place where most of the engineers have been working is the small mechanical room next to the navigation bridge. In the bow of deck three. As you approach the bridge, the last two cabins on the right — 302 and 304 — belong to the captain and the first officer. The last door on the left, which would be 301 if it were a cabin, is the small mechanical room. There is also the engine room on deck zero, which is where the useless emergency generator can be found, but the small mechanical room is where most of the distress has been."

Excellent. And the probable whereabouts of the captain and the first officer would have been my second question.

"The remaining crew members bunk on deck zero, right? Including the other officers?"

She nodded. Her face clouded and she bit her lip as if trying to decide whether or not to say something.

"One hears that your father is doctor," she said finally. "This is true?"

I nodded.

"They have been trying hard to hide it from the passengers — but there is sickness on deck zero. I think it is time something was done about this. Do you think perhaps — ?"

"I'm sure Dad would be glad to help." I tried not to show the sudden anxiety her words had provoked. "What kind of sickness?"

"People . . ." She spread her hands as if unable to find the word, and then made a graceful gesture, arcing her hand out from her mouth.

"They vomit?" I asked.

"And spend a great deal of time in the lavatory. I do not know if it is a sickness or if perhaps some were not so wise about what they have eaten since the power goes."

Oh, great. Which was worse — food poisoning or norovirus?

I'd leave that to Dad.

"I'll tell him," I said. "And I didn't hear it from you. Oh, and can you prop this door open? I have a volunteer cleanup crew that wants to come in.

"That would be most excellent."

She popped out of sight and returned with a broom, whose handle she stuck in the door opening. Then she flashed me a quick smile and disappeared.

Delaney and her crew were closer, so I dashed over to talk to her first.

CHAPTER 27

"My sources suggest that the repair action is going on in the small mechanical room by the bridge," I said. "If you don't find everything you need there, try the engine room, which I suspect is downstairs on deck zero. If you have any trouble getting in, come and find me."

"Awesome," Delaney said, and she and her motley tech crew rushed off. I grabbed Guillermo before he left.

"Call me paranoid," I said. "But when we get back on land, Pastime is going to try to claim things weren't nearly as bad as we know they are."

"Yeah." He grimaced. "Afraid we'll sue, I bet."

"And they're right to be afraid. We have a lot of lawyers in my family. So while fixing whatever's wrong with the ship is important, so's documenting what we're going through. Don't leave your video camera behind."

"Outstanding." He grinned and gave me a thumbs-up. "I'll tell Wim."

Then I hurried over to where Dad was conferring with his new medical team. An older man with a cane. A middle-aged woman in the sort of comfortable-looking yet sturdy shoes that would make Mother wince and inspire me to ask what brand they were. Rose Noire. And one of the no-longer Stooges — the one whose chin was only a little weak, now that I studied him with less jaundiced eyes.

Dad made the introductions. Bob, the older man, was a pediatric oncologist — I hoped we wouldn't need his specialty and was a little dubious about how useful he'd be until Dad mentioned that he went on annual volunteer missions to Haiti. Since conditions on board were rapidly beginning to resemble those in a third-world country, no doubt Bob would prove useful and feel right at home. Heidi, the middle-aged woman, was a seasoned ER nurse — just hearing that lifted my spirits. Victor, the former Stooge, was a paramedic. And while Rose Noire mainly dabbled in new-age remedies, because of the increasing amount of time she spent wandering about in various woods looking for unusual herbs, she'd wisely taken rafts of courses not just on first aid, but on wilderness survival first aid.

"And, of course, Caroline is a retired nurse," Dad added. "So I think we have a good team, should any medical problems arise."

"One has arisen." I relayed what Léonie had revealed about the crew's plight.

"Oh, dear," Dad said. "Whether it's food poisoning or norovirus —"

"We need to get down there right away," Heidi said. She stood up. They all did.

"Not much we can do except rehydrate," Bob said. "But if we're lucky that will be enough."

"Heidi — can you do a quick check of the ship's hospital?" Dad said.

"The so-called hospital," Heidi muttered.

"See if there's anything there that we'd find useful and then meet us on deck zero as soon as possible. Everyone else, follow me to deck zero! Including you, Meg — we could use your help to assess the situation."

He accompanied my invitation with an exaggerated wink, from which I deduced that our new mutiny project hadn't completely driven sleuthing out of his mind. I nodded back — I had to admit that however worried I was about the crew, I was eager to see what could be learned on deck zero.

I led the way to the boarding lobby and

used Anton's card to open the door to reveal the stairway to deck zero.

Was it just my imagination or did opening the door also reveal a rather unpleasant smell?

Not my imagination. Dad frowned. Bob grimaced. Victor gagged and had to stop and brace himself before continuing down. Rose Noire plucked a sachet out of her pocket and clapped it in front of her nose and mouth.

Maybe it was a good thing none of us had eaten a big breakfast.

The smell grew stronger as I descended the stairs. By the time I set foot on deck zero, I'd have called it a stench.

We arrived in a lobby that was smaller than the boarding lobby on the deck above and windowless, with doors on all sides. To our right, a door hanging halfway open led to the crew's quarters. The lobby and what we could see of the corridor through the open door were covered with a cheap though functional-looking beige industrial carpeting that probably hadn't looked particularly clean when it was brand new. Now it was marred with patches of what I suspected was vomit.

"We need to get a cleaning crew down here," Rose Noire muttered.

Dad nodded and headed into the narrow corridor. Things got worse there. More spots of probable vomit, and an odor that suggested, as one of my techie nephews was fond of saying, that the crew's gastrointestinal woes had been bidirectional.

We began peering into cabins on either side of the corridor — cabins that would have given a hermit crab claustrophobia. Most of the rooms had two sets of bunk beds, one on either side of a foot-wide strip of floor, and the bunks themselves seemed narrower than most cribs. And nearly half of the bunks were occupied by miserable-looking crew members. Crew members clutching their stomachs and moaning. Crew members vomiting. Crew members hunched over the toilets in bathrooms too small to make a decent shower stall. Crew members sprawled unconscious on their tiny bunks.

At least I hoped they were all merely unconscious.

The medical crew dived in. Dad darted into the first cabin and began checking vitals on its occupant. The rest of the crew followed his example.

I decided I could be more useful elsewhere. Fetching that cleaning crew, for example. I headed back down the corridor.

If my grasp of the ship's layout was correct, there should be a stairway leading up directly into the kitchen.

Which already looked like a completely different place. At least twenty passengers were busily scrubbing everything in sight — floor, walls, cabinets, counters, appliances, even windows. Mother was actually holding a cleaning rag, although she was doing more gesturing than cleaning with it. And I was especially pleased to note that the cleaning crew was about evenly balanced between men and women — at least if you counted the men who were going to and fro with buckets of water.

And Wim was there with a small video camera, documenting the squalor before it disappeared.

"Should we really be using up quite so much water on cleaning?" I asked Mother. "I mean, what if —"

"Yes, we should definitely ration the water, dear," Mother said. "So until we have some idea how soon we'll either get under way again or be rescued, we thought it might be prudent to use seawater for the initial rather . . . unpleasant round of cleaning. Michael and the boys have organized a bucket brigade on the stern deck."

"Any chance you could spare a few volunteers to help out on deck zero?" I asked. "Volunteers with strong stomachs. And strong immune systems."

I gave her and the other listening volunteers a rundown on what the medical crew had found, doing my best to hint at the squalor below rather than describing it too accurately. Mother called for volunteers, and before long half of the passengers who had been working in the kitchen were trooping down the stairway with rags, sponges, mops, and buckets of salt water.

Followed by Wim with his camera.

I left the kitchen for the dining room. Caroline was sitting in one corner with her laptop. She beckoned me over.

"As soon as Kate gets back I'm going to let her take over the passenger inventory so I can go down and help with the patients."

I nodded.

She glanced around to see if anyone was close enough to overhear and dropped her voice.

"I got through to the Coast Guard this morning," she said softly.

"That's great!" I only just managed to keep my voice down. A wave of relief washed over me. There was still a world out there, and now they knew we were here.

"And I think I've convinced them to come

and rescue us."

"You think?"

"They were a little skeptical at first, because someone claiming to be our captain has been in regular communication with them, saying that we're merely stopped for minor repairs and everything is fine aboard ship."

"That jerk! And what if they don't believe you?"

"Then I keep calling. One of the passengers who's an attorney has made a study of these situations —"

"Ted Lambert?"

"That's the one. He seems to think that what usually happens is that the cruise line sends parts and technicians to fix the situation."

"And who's going to make them? Besides, I don't want technicians from Pastime — I want the Coast Guard!"

"I quite agree," she said. "But I don't know what else we can do."

"So we sit here and wait for Pastime?"

"All we can do."

"I don't think so. Look, the whole reason you've got the equipment that lets you contact the Coast Guard is that you were going to do webcasts from Bermuda, right?"

She nodded.

"Any reason we can't webcast from the ship? Show them how bad things are?"

Her face lit up.

"No reason at all," she said. "I'll get Wim and Guillermo right on it."

"I already told them to film whatever they can. Meanwhile I'm going to see if I can get a list of crew members. Make sure there's no one else missing." I turned to go, and then thought of one more thing. "Did you reach Trevor?"

"Not yet. I'll keep trying."

She dashed off — presumably in search of Wim and Guillermo. I went back down into deck zero and peeked into cabins until I found Léonie, standing in the hall, holding two buckets, and watching what was going on inside the cabin.

I peered over her shoulder — Dad was doing vitals on a pale, sweaty crewman. I stepped back to give the poor man some privacy.

"How's it going?" I asked Léonie.

"Your father believes the problem is food poisoning," she said. "Which relieves the mind very much, since it is not contagious. And we have narrowed it down — it appears to have come from the beef stew. As far as we can tell, all the crew members who are suffering from the sickness ate the beef stew that was the main entree the first night out. It is quite robust, and popular with the male crew members. For those of us who are vegetarians or who are seeking to eat less red meat, there was a vegetarian lasagna. None of us who ate that are unwell."

"That's a relief," I said. "I guess we're lucky the captain and the first officer didn't eat the stew, so there's still someone in charge."

"Lucky!" She rolled her eyes. "They do not stoop to eat *les déchets* . . . the garbage they have served to the crew." I nodded. Then I realized something.

"Wait a sec— the first night out? That was before the power went out."

"And the beef should not have had time to spoil," she said. *"Oui.* It was left over from our last cruise, and they knew the passengers would turn up their noses at it. I suppose they hoped it was merely unpleasantly odorous, not actually dangerous. It would be interesting to know who gave the order to serve the beef instead of disposing of it, *n'est-ce pas?"*

"It would indeed. Make sure Caroline Willner knows this."

"Mrs. Willner already knows," Léonie said. "She thinks we should sue the company. Of course, this requires a lawyer, and for that one would need money, which we do not have."

"I bet if she tried, Caroline could find a lawyer who would do it pro bono. And if she can't, I might have a try myself."

" 'Pro bono' means 'cheap'?" Léonie sounded hopeful.

" 'Pro bono' means 'for free,' " I explained. "Short for *pro bono publico,*' which in Latin means 'for the public good.' Because I think it would be very much for the public good if Pastime were made to pay for poisoning its employees and stranding its customers in the middle of the Bermuda Triangle."

"Oh, yes." From Léonie's sudden fierce expression I suspected the noxious beef stew was only the tip of an iceberg. "At least one good thing comes from having too few crew members," she went on. "We have enough space to move people about while we clean the cabins."

"While we're moving people about, we should take an inventory, or census, or whatever," I said. "Make sure every crew member who's supposed to be here really is."

"You think the lady with the purple hair is not the only one to go overboard?" she asked.

Her words reminded me of hearing Anton Bjelica's body splash into the ocean, and I wasn't sure I could keep a poker face. So I exaggerated my reaction.

"Oh, good heavens, I hope not," I said. "No, I was worrying about the possibility that one of the crew could have become ill while in some remote part of the ship and be lying there sick, with no one to help him."

"True," she said. "Those of us who are not unwell have not had much time for searching. One could make a list — see, each cabin has two or four slots outside, with little cards to say who is supposed to be in it. Once we have a list, then we can search to see where each one is."

From the way she phrased it, I deduced that she was not volunteering for the task. That was okay. I was hoping to avoid doing much nursing.

"I'll make the list," I said. "And then perhaps you could help me figure out where everyone is."

"*Bien.* For now, I will fetch more water." She hefted the bucket and headed for the stairs.

I went up and down the corridor, jotting down names. Then Léonie and I made a quick trip up and down the passageway, matching names and faces. Apart from the captain and the first officer, whose quarters were on the third floor by the bridge, only three crew members were not here on deck zero, either among the stricken or among those caring for them.

One of them, of course, was Anton Bjelica. So although I couldn't say so to Léonie, it was really only two missing crew members.

According to Léonie, Bjelica was a member of the ship's engineering crew, as was the other crew member whose continued existence we hadn't yet confirmed. The rest of the engineers were among our patients. No wonder repairs were going so slowly.

"An unfortunate coincidence," Léonie said. She had switched from cleaning to nursing, and was patiently spooning water into the mouth of one of the patients.

Simply a coincidence? Or an ominous sign? If someone had wanted to sabotage the ship and keep it marooned for some period of time, they'd probably want to put the engineers out of commission. Maybe Anton Bjelica had turned up his nose at the beef stew and had to be dealt with some other way. What about the other one we hadn't found yet — Third Engineer Gerard Hoffman. Had he gone overboard, too?

"Have you seen Gerard Hoffman lately?" I asked.

"He should be up on the bridge," she said. "He was the only one really trying to fix the ship."

"He's not sick then? Or at least not as sick as the rest?"

"Just as sick, if you ask me. But more stubborn."

I decided to go up to the small mechanical room and see if the missing Hoffman was there — helping, hindering, or just observing what Delaney and her volunteer tech force were up to.

But before I went . . .

"If you're not using them, may I use your cleaning supplies? I might as well help out for a little while, as long as I'm here. With some cleaning," I added. "I didn't inherit any of Dad's medical abilities."

"Cleaning is also important." Léonie smiled, and then returned to spooning water into her patient's mouth.

I picked up the nearby bucket and sponge and went down the hall to an empty room. Not just any old empty room — one I'd already scouted out as a target.

CHAPTER 28

The room I wanted to search was a four-person room, but occupied on this journey by only two crew members. If Gerard Hoffman came back while I was here, I'd pretend I'd picked this room to clean on purpose, to thank him for his heroic efforts to fix the ship in spite of his illness. Anton Bjelica wasn't going to show up to complain that I was invading his privacy. And I suspected no one else would much care if I searched the things Bjelica had left behind while I was cleaning up the room he'd never see again.

Although there wasn't that much to search. Beside each set of bunk beds were two narrow lockers — you couldn't really call them closets — and beneath each set were two built-in drawers. Probably one locker and one drawer per crewman. Since I didn't know which bunk was Bjelica's, I started with one of the drawers on the right and quickly figured out it belonged to Hoffman. Presumably Bjelica's bunk, drawer, and locker were on the left.

Not a tidy person, Anton. The drawer was mostly full of t-shirts and underwear, jumbled together in a way that probably made it difficult to get dressed in a hurry. I did find a few interesting items. I took a picture of his Slovenian passport. And of the scattered papers that were obviously a part of his personnel file. Half a dozen disciplinary actions in as many months — was Bjelica a marginal crew member? Or was Captain Detweiler a stern martinet? My money was on the latter. And yes, it was Detweiler's signature on all six of the reports.

I shoved them back where I'd found them and went on to the closets. Nothing in either Hoffman's or Bjelica's closets except several sets of Pastime uniforms. White shirts with gold epaulettes, white trousers with stripes of gold braid, white belts with gold buckle — between the dazzling white fabric and the overabundance of polished gold-colored hardware, I felt the momentary impulse to put on sunglasses.

And just out of curiosity, I checked the sizes on some of Bjelica's clothes. His t-shirts were XXL. His uniform didn't have sizes, but I eyeballed both the pants and jacket and compared them to Michael's clothes. He was definitely shorter than Michael's six foot four, but not by that much. And he was wider. Barrel-chested, and not slim. A big guy. Not someone who'd be easy to throw overboard.

Just then I heard someone coming down the hallway, so I hurriedly pushed the drawer shut and focused on cleaning. Hoffman's bunk wasn't too bad — obviously he'd spent most of his sick time up in the small mechanical room. Bjelica's bed didn't look as if he'd been sick in it at all. It didn't even really look slept in — more as if he'd pulled back the sheet and then been called away before he actually got into bed.

"This is better." I looked up to see Léonie standing in the doorway, rubbing her back as if to ease it.

"It wasn't all that bad to begin with," I said. "But I'm assuming Gerard Hoffman's up there trying to help with the repairs, in spite of being so sick, so I thought he deserved a clean room to come back to. What about his bunkmate — Anton . . . er . . ."

"Be-*yell*-it-sa," she said. "That's as close as I can come, anyway. You can ask him when we find him."

"Have you seen him lately?"

"No." She shook her head. "Not since all this began. And that is odd, because he should be either in the engine room or the small mechanical room."

"Could he have fallen overboard?"

"Unlikely. They do not want to be sued all the time, so they make it hard to fall overboard, even for a passenger who has been drinking. And for an experienced crew member, in such calm weather?" She shrugged as if to say stranger things had happened but not by much.

"So if he went overboard it was no accident."

"You think perhaps he, too, jumped overboard?"

"That, or maybe someone had it in for him. I mean, there aren't a lot of places for him to hide."

"If he has enemies, I don't know who they are. And I would not expect him to kill himself — but then I did not know him well. He speaks no French, and his English is very bad, and I do not speak Slovene. On duty, he stays in the engine room, and he spends most of his off-duty time by himself, listening to heavy metal music." She shuddered slightly. "I am not sure I would recognize him without his earbuds on. So who knows? Perhaps he was an unhappy soul, and the example of Madame St. Christophe drove him over the edge. They do say that suicide can be contagious, no?"

"Yes." Of course, so could murder. I was tempted to confide what Dad and I had seen to Léonie — but no. I trusted Léonie more than the rest of the crew, but still.

"Or perhaps he is somewhere else on the ship," she was saying. "Some people, like dogs, prefer to be solitary when they are sick."

"I'll spread the word to keep an eye out for him."

"Well — to work." She straightened up, picked up a bucket, and headed down the passageway toward the stern. I wondered how many times today she'd gone up and down the stairs between deck zero and the kitchen. She was going slowly so she could glance into each cabin as she passed. We'd propped all the doors open, partly so we could do this and partly in the hope that it would keep the cabins a little cooler. Unfortunately, deck zero didn't have windows that could be opened, only sealed portholes. Probably a safety issue, this close to the surface of the ocean — or were we below the surface? I hadn't actually noticed — but in either case, tough on the occupants with the air-conditioning not working.

I headed the other way, toward the central stairs, and tried to do the same thing — glancing left and right. I spotted several of Dad's team sitting with patients.

Near the end of the passageway, I glanced inside a cabin and then stopped in the doorway. The man inside was moaning something. Moaning and clutching his abdomen. I took a step into the cabin and realized it was one of the few crew members I actually knew: Serge, who'd attended Grandfather's lecture and cleaned up after Evans so Léonie wouldn't have to do it. Serge who, according to Mother, was Léonie's young man. I couldn't remember his last name. I glanced up at the sign outside his door. Charlier. Was that it? I couldn't remember. And given the way we'd been moving people around to empty the cabins for cleaning who knew if this was his own cabin or just where we'd parked him while we cleaned his out.

Irrelevant anyway. I stepped to his bedside to see if I could do anything to help him.

"Serge? What's wrong? What do you need?"

He opened his eyes — half opened them, actually, and they were so glazed with pain that I wasn't sure he really saw me.

"My turn," he muttered. "My turn."

His turn for what?

"His turn to die," was the first thing that came to mind.

"Don't be melodramatic," I told myself. He was half unconscious and probably hallucinating something completely unrelated to anything happening on board. He could be flashing back to some childhood memory. His turn to bat. His turn to ride the pony. Or maybe, given his expression, something less pleasant. Although offhand I couldn't think of any childhood traumas that involved turn taking.

Not a puzzle I could solve now. I grabbed the plastic tumbler sitting on a narrow shelf behind the head of his bed and filled it from a nearby bottle of water. I also dampened a washcloth. Dad had recommended cool compresses. Room temperature was the best we could manage at the moment, but at least it was usually a little cooler than the patients' fevered brows.

I returned to Serge and tried to get him to drink a little of the water — with no success, but I took a corner of the washcloth and managed to drip a little into his mouth. He seemed to like that, swallowing convulsively each trickle I squeezed in and then opening his mouth in a way that reminded me of a clutch of orphaned baby birds I'd helped Grandfather raise, so young at first that their eyes weren't yet open, and yet their mouths were always open wide for food.

It was a slow process, and my eyes began to roam around the tiny room. And then suddenly froze. Hanging over Serge, attached to the bottom of the top bunk, was a little charm made of shells and feathers. I still had the charm I'd found with Desiree's shoes, shawl, and note, but I didn't have to pull it out to realize that it was nearly identical to the one dangling over Serge.

"Help."

I realized that I'd frozen in place, staring at the charm, and Serge had grown restless. His eyes were half open again.

"My turn."

I kept dripping bits of water into his mouth until he finally subsided into sleep. Then I put the not-very-cold compress on his forehead and stared for a few more moments at the feather charm. Stared at it, and then took out my phone and snapped a picture of it.

Then I backed out of the cabin and pulled out my list of crew members. Yes, Serge Charlier — he was in his own cabin. And as far as I could tell, his own bunk. So the feather charm must belong to him.

I went looking for Léonie. I found her spooning drops of water into the mouth of a pale young woman with circles under her eyes so dark they looked like bruises.

"Has Dad been here to check on his patients recently?" I asked.

"Just an hour ago. Is there a problem?"

"I'm a little concerned about Serge. He seems agitated."

"Yes." She frowned and shook her head. "He seems so much worse than the others. Perhaps it was because he tried to keep going after he began to sicken. Although your father says it's more likely that his immune system was already a little weakened, so the poisons in the stew had more effect. But he will be fine, your father says." She sounded understandably anxious.

"If Dad thought he was in any danger, he'd be with him." I made my tone as reassuring as possible. "He's in his own cabin, right? Serge, I mean, not Dad."

"Yes." She looked puzzled.

"That's good," I said. "I think people who are sick do better in familiar surroundings."

"Yes." She smiled slightly. "Even such surroundings as these."

"I'm going to look in on everybody and

then go up to see how the repairs are coming."

She nodded and returned to her patient.

I did look in on everybody. I took a good, long, hard look to see if anyone else had any little feathered charms in their cabins. No one had.

Did that mean that Serge had something to do with Desiree's suicide? Alleged suicide, as Dad and Horace would insist.

I decided I'd done my bit for nursing the sick crew members. I needed to find a quiet corner where I could digest what I'd found here on deck zero.

And for that matter, where I could take a closer look at the papers I'd photographed in Anton Bjelica's cabin.

I trudged up to deck one and made sure the wedge that was keeping the door open was wedged in tightly. That wouldn't prevent someone — I suspected the captain or the first officer — from periodically slamming it closed.

Hmm. . . . maybe if we detached the card reader for the time being? Or maybe just disassembled the lock. If I could find some tools, I could do that myself. I took out my notebook and added it to my task list.

I peered into the main dining room. Things looked a lot less frantic there than they had when I'd left. Mother spotted me and hurried over. Oops! Chances were she'd have new work for me.

"Come inspect the kitchen, dear," she said. "You wouldn't recognize the place."

She was right. For one thing, the place was spotless — I was willing to bet it hadn't been that clean when the ship sailed. And for another, the swarm of cleaners had been replaced by a much smaller crew who appeared to be cooking lunch.

"We'll be having canned chicken noodle soup, tossed salad, and several kinds of canned vegetables," Mother said, noting where my gaze had gone.

"That's great. Delaney got the power going, then? Or is it just the emergency power?"

"The stoves are propane-fueled," she said. "So no electricity needed."

"Still a fabulous improvement."

"We could have had hot food all day yesterday if there had been anyone well enough to cook it. And I'm sure everyone's looking forward to hot coffee in the morning."

Actually, I was hoping the ship would be back to normal by morning, but I didn't want to jinx it, so I just praised her efforts to the skies.

Michael and the boys were still hauling up buckets of water, but now most of their buckets were being poured over swimsuit-clad passengers. And according to Mother, the cleaning crew was moving on to cleaning cabins and latrines on the upper decks.

"And it's not even noon yet," Mother said, with understandable satisfaction.

I pulled out my phone and checked. Only eleven-thirty.

"Great work," I said. "I'm going up to check on Delaney."

As I strolled down the passageway, I pulled out my phone again and opened up the weather app. The forecast wouldn't have updated since the ship's Internet went out, but at least I could see what the National Weather Service had been predicting back then.

And it wasn't good news. Apparently, we were still within range of the heat wave that had been baking the entire Eastern Seaboard. A high in the low nineties today. The mid-nineties tomorrow. And while the two tropical systems forming in the Atlantic had seemed very far off indeed when we'd set sail, I'd feel a lot better if I knew where they were now. And whether they were moving in our direction, and if so, how rapidly.

Not problems I could do anything about.

So I continued up to deck two. If I stayed in the main dining room, I'd be sucked into solving someone's problems. Or I'd feel guilty about other people working and pitch in to clean something or haul more buckets of water. But on deck two there was a small lounge area. If there was no one there — and yay! There wasn't — I could examine the photos I'd taken in peace and quiet and still hear if anything was happening.

In fact, I could even open the sliding glass doors and step out on one of the few balconies that wasn't private.

And there was a breeze — not much of one, but still, any breeze was welcome. I lifted my face and breathed a few calming breaths.

Then I pulled out my phone. I opened up my pictures of the official reprimands Anton Bjelica had received. Which would have been a lot easier to do with the papers themselves instead of the tiny pictures on my phone's screen. Still —

"Found something interesting?"

CHAPTER 29

I jumped before I realized it was only Dad sneaking up behind me.

"Possibly," I said. "Remember Anton Bjelica?"

"Of course." Dad shuddered slightly. "So that's how you pronounce it?"

"According to Léonie. I searched his cabin."

"Oh, well, done! What did you find?"

"Not much," I said. "The only interesting thing was a bunch of papers that suggested he wasn't exactly in the running for employee of the year."

"Oh, dear." Dad's face showed that he wasn't entirely sure I should be speaking ill of the dead.

"Which still doesn't give anyone the right to toss him overboard."

"Agreed. So where are the papers?"

I held up my phone.

"I decided not to steal the actual papers,"

I said. "I think mutiny on the high seas is enough of a crime for today. So I took pictures instead."

Dad peered at the screen and shook his head.

"Too small," he said. "Maybe we need to get Delaney to transfer that onto a computer."

"Give me a few minutes." I pulled the phone back to the optimal position for reading it myself and used my fingers to enlarge the first photo. "I know what they are, more or less, from seeing them while I took the pictures — six official notices reprimanding Bjelica for disciplinary infractions."

"What kind of disciplinary infractions?"

"That's what I'm trying to figure out. Okay, this first one is for being five minutes late for duty. They docked him an hour's pay for that."

"A good thing I'm not on the crew." Dad chuckled softly. "I'd never break even."

"The second one is for not being in proper uniform. Another hour's pay docked. Now this is interesting. This second one has an addendum from First Officer Martin. 'The missing button has been replaced and Mr. Bjelica's uniform is now acceptable. Penalty reduced by half.' "

"Very interesting," Dad said. "So the

405

captain is a stern disciplinarian and the first officer takes a more humane approach?"

"Or maybe they're just running good cop/bad cop on the crew," I said. "Here's another uniform infraction — this time the captain's dinging him two hours' pay for having a dirty uniform and the first officer cancels the fine entirely. Apparently Bjelica was in the middle of performing regular maintenance on the backup generator when he was called to go to the navigation bridge immediately. And this next one — good grief; shades of Captain Queeg in *The Caine Mutiny*. Apparently Bjelica raided the kitchen and ate food designated for consumption by the passengers. Detweiler docked him a whole day's pay for that."

"I don't like the sound of that," Dad said. "It reminds me of Oliver Twist asking for more gruel while Bumble the Beadle dines on roast beef. Or am I imagining that scene?"

"It's probably in one of the movie versions. And since you and Léonie figured out it was feeding the crew beef considered too far gone for the passengers that caused the food poisoning epidemic, maybe Bjelica had good reason for raiding the passengers' food. First Officer Martin all but erased Bjelica's punishment for that, too."

"Good for him."

"I hate it when I have to completely re-arrange my view of the world," I said. "Here I've been thinking of Captain Detweiler as sort of a distant, benign authority figure, the nautical equivalent of an absentminded professor — too focused on navigation and whatever other lofty things a captain has to worry about to pay much attention to the passengers who happen to be cluttering up his ship, but essentially good and noble. Who delegates dealing with the passengers to his first officer, who isn't all that good at it but at least tries. Now it begins to look as if Detweiler is a petty vindictive tyrant crushing the souls of his crew. It's going to take a while to get my head around that."

"Yes." Dad nodded and looked thoughtful. "I suppose we'll have to try to think more kindly of poor Mr. Martin. Especially since . . . well, remember that bit of French you asked your mother to translate? Any more news on that front?"

"You mean, have I found out if the captain's a secret tippler?" I shook my head. "No idea. Of course I haven't seen the captain since yesterday morning, so who knows? Although I think we should probably take anything Léonie says about the officers with several grains of salt. I get she's

407

definitely a disgruntled employee, and while I completely understand why, it means she might not be the most reliable source when it comes to Detweiler and Martin."

"If only Martin would stop trying so hard." Dad sighed and shook his head.

"Yeah, his manner's a little smarmy," I said. "Maybe that's understandable, if Detweiler's a martinet and Martin has a vested interest in making sure no one complains about anything. Still — he's trying too hard. Someone should do him a favor and tell him to tone it down a bit. Someone other than me," I said, before Dad could volunteer me for the job.

"I'll suggest it to your mother," he said. "None of this exactly gives anyone a clear motive for murdering . . . um . . . Anton."

"No. Now if it had been the captain's body we found, Anton would be top of my suspect list right now. But I'd still want to check out everyone else's personnel files before arresting him."

"Yes." Dad looked thoughtful. "There could be other crew members with equally good reason to resent the captain."

"In fact, for all we know, Anton's the captain's golden boy," I mused. "Everyone else could have an inch-thick collection of nastygrams instead of only six. But since the captain's not our victim, all that's irrelevant."

"And what does Anton's murder have to do with Desiree's alleged suicide?" Dad went on. "Because it's a little hard to imagine that two suspicious deaths happening so close together in such a small community aren't related somehow."

"Also a good point."

"Perhaps Desiree was pushed — and Anton witnessed it! Forcing the killer to do away with him!"

"Could be." In one of Dad's beloved mysteries, that would almost certainly be the case, but real life was rarely that neat. "I like that idea better than the possibility that someone knocked off Anton to keep us stranded here as long as possible. Maybe we should figure out who the rest of the engineering staff are and put a guard on them."

"I wish we could definitively prove that none of the writers are involved." Dad's tone was rather wistful. "Angie's got an excellent head for plotting — she could be very useful in solving this."

"I'm definitely keeping my eyes open for anything that would prove their innocence." Of course, I was doing it because I liked the writers, doubted that they'd done in Desiree, and didn't want whoever eventually investigated this to give them a hard time. I suspected Angie's plotting expertise was in inventing intricately convoluted plots that would baffle her FBI agent sleuth — and her readers — until the last chapter. That didn't necessarily translate into being good at unraveling a real-life puzzle.

"I don't think the writers are high on my suspect list for throwing Bjelica overboard," I said aloud. "I'm pretty sure only one person entered Desiree's cabin while we were hiding in the bathroom. Does that match your recollection?"

Dad nodded.

"I checked the sizes on his clothes, and Anton was a big guy. Not that much shorter than Michael, and definitely a bit wider."

"The writers aren't that big. Or that young. For that matter, I don't think the first officer's as tall as I am. The captain, now . . ."

"Don't underestimate what a fit person can do, especially a fit person who's trying to cover up evidence of a murder."

"Good point."

He looked so glum.

"Hey!" I said. "There's a set of free weights on the fifth-floor sun deck, right beside the miniature golf course. Shall we have a weightlifting competition and narrow down our pool of suspects?"

I meant it as a joke. Dad seemed to be seriously considering.

"Maybe later," he said. "For now, I should go back and check on my patients."

"How are they doing?" I asked. "And there's only us here — don't sugarcoat it."

"They should all make it." He looked grim. "But no thanks to the captain. Food poisoning isn't usually fatal — although sometimes the sufferer may wish it was. But severe dehydration can be fatal, and I don't think the healthy crew members were really aware of the danger."

"Not to mention the fact that even if they'd known what to do, there might have been too few of them to cope with so many patients. Look in on Serge Charlier, will you? He seemed a little worse off than the others."

He nodded and dashed away.

I decided to drop by the bridge, on deck three, to see how the repairs were going.

I found Delaney sitting on the floor reading a technical manual of some kind. Nearby, a rumpled crew member slept on the floor. She held her finger to her lips and motioned me to step outside.

"Gerard finally stopped puking and fell

asleep," she said. "I hope that means he's over the worst of it. And given how hard he's been trying to help while still feeling horrible, I say let him sleep."

"Gerard Hoffman." I pulled out my crew inventory and put a check mark beside his name. All of the crew names now bore check marks except for Bjelica and Arav Lav, the bartender. Most of the passengers probably knew Arav — I'd ask if anyone had seen him. For now, I planned to keep pretending to most of the world that I didn't know where Bjelica was. "So how's it going?"

"You want the good news or the bad news?"

"Let's start with the good news," I suggested. "Because I have the sinking feeling that you're about to deliver a pinch of good news and a pound or two of bad."

"Something like that." She grinned, though, so I was encouraged to hope that even the bad news would be something we could handle together. "The good news is that there is a backup generator. It didn't kick in when the main power went off because for some reason no one can quite explain, it was lying in a million pieces on the engine room floor. But we should be able to reassemble it and get it going."

"How soon?"

"Not sure," she said. "I've got most of my team focused on that right now, but none of them's exactly a generator expert. They can do it, but it will take longer."

"Does the ship have a generator expert?" I asked. "Wait — don't tell me. He's on the sick list."

"No, we already checked, and the generator guru's not down in the sick ward. Maybe we could get Hal to add a message to his announcements for him to report to the engine room. It's a guy named Anton something-or-other."

"Anton Bjelica," I said.

"That sounds right."

"But we can fix the backup generator without him, right?"

"Eventually." She frowned. "What do you know that you're not telling?"

I suppressed a wayward impulse to say that Anton Bjelica was now sleeping with the fishes.

"Dad and I were doing some skulking about last night," I said instead. "I'll tell you the long version when we have more time. The short version is that Anton Bjelica is dead, and someone tossed his dead body overboard last night."

"Oh." She blinked and looked momentarily stricken. "That's awful. Did you report it? To the captain or whoever?"

"We didn't see who did the tossing," I said. "And we assume whoever did that was either the person who garroted him or an ally. So no, we didn't report this, because for all we know we'd be reporting it to whoever did it."

"Good point." She thought for a moment. "Well, if you need me, I'll be down in the engine room helping with the generator. The backup generator won't run the whole ship, but it will get us emergency lights and the water-pumping system."

"Running water? Sounds like heaven."

"And with luck, working toilets. If they were stupid enough not to put the toilets on the emergency circuit, I'll rewire a few myself. And while running water and working toilets won't get us to Bermuda any faster, they'll sure make being stranded here a lot less painful. So I think we should make that our priority."

"Make it so," I said.

"Aye-aye, Captain." Delaney giggled and turned to leave.

"Wait," I said. "That was the good news, right? What about the bad news?"

"Main navigation system's hosed." She grimaced. "And if you ask me, it was sabotage. I could explain why if you really want to know."

"Would the explanation be technical?" I asked. "Because if it is, I'm not sure you should waste time explaining it to me."

"Don't sell yourself short," she said. "But yeah, I should save the explanations for whatever law enforcement agency investigates the sabotage. The point is, whoever did this broke stuff. We need parts. Now that we have at least some contact with the outside world, they can fly in the parts — and experts to install them. But that'll take time."

"What kind of time?" I asked. "Hours or days?"

"I guess that depends on how organized Pastime is." She shrugged. "So in the meantime, let's see what we can do with the backup generator."

She hurried off.

Two days ago, I might have been reassured to know that Pastime was aware of our plight. I'd probably have trusted that they'd do their best to end our ordeal as soon as possible. But after what I'd seen on board the ship . . .

"We need to talk to the Coast Guard," I muttered.

Just then I heard a thud on the ceiling.

Or, since there was nothing anywhere near the ceiling, maybe it was a thud on the floor of the deck above us.

Another thud. And another. Followed by three quick thuds close together.

Someone was pounding out SOS.

I raced for the stairs.

CHAPTER 30

What was above the bridge? I didn't have time to pull out my map of the ship's decks, but I was pretty sure I knew — the Starlight Lounge.

When I reached deck four, I looked around. No one in sight. I hoped the SOS was a genuine call for help, not a trap.

I opened the door to the Starlight Lounge carefully and peered in. It was dark — all the curtains were drawn. The pounding had stopped.

"Anyone here?" I called.

No answer. I pulled out my phone and turned on the flashlight feature. I played it over the room. The light reflected on glass tea light holders on the tables and on the crystal of the chandeliers.

The pounding started up again, somewhere to my left. I moved toward it, carefully and quietly.

It was coming from behind the bar. From

what appeared to be a locked closet behind the bar.

"Is anyone there?" I called.

Rapid, though rather feeble pounding.

I tested the door. Locked.

Just then I heard Hal, the town crier, out in the corridor.

"Lunch is being served in the dining room!" he was bellowing.

I ran to the door.

"Hal! In here!" I called.

He came running, bringing a giant flashlight with him. Was it having more company or more light that made the room suddenly seem much less creepy?

"What's wrong?" he asked.

"Someone's trapped in there," I said. "I want backup in case it's someone who got locked in for a good reason."

He seemed to find that amusing.

While I felt a lot more confident, now that I had backup, it would have helped if my backup was someone who might have a useful idea of how to open the closet door. Hal tried running at it in the hope of breaking it open with his shoulder.

"Owww!" He sat down hard on a nearby chair. "Maybe that wasn't such a good idea."

"It's a fairly sturdy door," I said. "And I suspect it opens out. Let me try something."

418

The light from Hal's flashlight had revealed that there was a card key reader beside the door. I still had Anton Bjelica's card in my pocket. I slid it through the slot.

The lock clicked open.

I opened the door to find a walk-in wine closet lined with racks and coolers, and an unconscious figure slumped just inside the door. Aarav the bartender. He was clutching a bottle — a magnum of Dom Pérignon, I noticed. Apparently, that was what he'd been pounding with. He'd been sick, rather neatly, in the far corner of the closet, and I could see the fragments of at least one broken wine bottle on the floor. And some rather frayed and bloodstained cords.

"Poor beggar." Hal seemed to forget about his shoulder. "Wonder how he managed to get locked in here. I'll take him down to deck one." He stooped down to pick up Aarav.

"Hang on a sec," I said. "He's not wearing his Pastime card around his neck on a cord like most of the crew."

"He's a crew member, though," Hal said. "The bartender."

"Yes — Aarav Lal." I was searching Aarav's pockets. "But what happened to his card?"

"Definitely not on him," Hal said. "Hey, it

looks as if he tried to cut his wrists. You think he tried to off himself, then changed his mind and signaled for help?"

"No, I think someone tied him up." I pointed to the tangle of cord in the corner. "And he managed to break a bottle and saw through the cord to free himself." On a hunch, I checked Aarav's head. Hidden by the glossy black curls was a nasty lump. "And I'm pretty sure whoever tied him up knocked him out first."

"Damn."

"Take him down to deck zero," I said. "And tell Dad to check for concussion."

"Roger." Hal gently lifted Aarav's long but slender body and strode out.

I grabbed the door before it could close all the way and picked up something to prop it open with. Curious. The object I'd picked up was the push bar, the one that let you escape from the storage closet if you got locked in. Whoever had tied up Aarav did his best to make sure he didn't escape.

And why had Aarav become ill so much later than the other crew members? Side effect of being hit on the head, maybe?

And why attack Aarav? Did this have anything to do with Desiree's or Anton's deaths?

We'd have to ask Aarav when he came

around. At least I hoped he'd come around.

I threw the push bar inside the closet, shoved the door closed, and hurried after Hal. I'd come back later to clean up the wine storage closet. With backup.

Time to see what Caroline was doing. I returned to the stairs and found Janet standing just outside the entrance to the library lounge with her hands cupped over her eyes.

"Headache? I've got aspirin and acetaminophen, and my cabin's just down the hall."

"Thanks, but I've already taken some," she said. "What I really need to do is escape the source of my headache, but that doesn't seem very likely. We've been checking out some of the aspiring writers who surfaced after our lecture on getting published."

"Any good suspects?"

"Not really." She closed her eyes and shuddered. "I can't imagine Desiree hiring any of these people to replace Nancy. On the other hand, if you're looking for someone guilty of murdering the English language, we've got a hot prospect in there. Speaking of which, I shouldn't leave Kate to deal with her solo for much longer. I just had to take a break."

"Courage!" I said, and began climbing again.

I found Caroline and Grandfather on deck

six. Caroline was sitting under the sun shade, tending all the solar devices — Delaney's along with the ones she and Grandfather had brought. Grandfather was leaning against the stern rail with the resident tern sitting on his shoulder. Occasionally he'd fish something out of his pocket and feed it to the bird — presumably dried fish of some sort. Both Grandfather and the tern looked curiously pleased with themselves. A few other people, including Angie and Tish and a small flock of elderly ladies, were seated nearby, either using electronic devices that were tethered to solar chargers or watching devices that were charging.

"How are things going down below?" Caroline asked when I joined them. "Your dad ordered me to come up and take a rest — says it's mainly a cleanup job now."

"The kitchen is clean, the rest of the ship will be soon; the stoves are propane, which means we'll be having a hot lunch; and Dad's reasonably sure none of the crew are going to die."

"So when's the cavalry coming?" Grandfather asked.

"If you mean the Coast Guard, I don't know," Caroline said. "Call me paranoid, but I get the distinct feeling that the captain or the first officer has already been in contact with them and poisoned the well."

"Poisoned the well?" Grandfather echoed.

"Convinced them that we passengers are uppity and entitled and making a big thing out of a small delay," I explained.

Caroline nodded.

"Well, that's complete bull— er, bull manure." Grandfather had glanced around and hastily changed course upon seeing the nearby gray-haired ladies. "How can they possibly think that?"

"They're probably inclined to take the captain's word," Caroline said. "I mean, he is the captain. Eventually they'll figure out he was, shall we say, shading the truth?"

"But eventually is not good enough," I said. "We need to do something now."

"I've talked till I'm blue in the face, and all I get is that they're aware of the situation," Caroline said.

"A picture's worth a thousand words," I said. "And we don't just have pictures — we have video. So we've decided to make a documentary."

"An excellent idea!" Grandfather said. "But won't that take some time?"

"Not if Wim and Guillermo have been doing as I asked at the beginning of the day and documenting what's going on here," I said. "By now they should have plenty of video of how horrible conditions had become before we stepped in to take care of things. And we can ask a couple of the writers to help us with a script."

"Excellent," Grandfather boomed.

"Do we know where Wim and Guillermo are?" I asked.

"No, but given how long they've been gone, they'll be showing up to recharge their camera battery packs anytime now." Caroline was glancing at her watch.

"I think we need to confront the captain," Grandfather said. "Ask him some hard questions about what he's doing to resolve the crisis."

That figured. Grandfather was fond of confronting people he believed were responsible for the environmental and animal welfare problems he battled. Any number of his documentaries featured such confrontations — with poachers, dogfight organizers, CEOs of polluting corporations, and officials of regulatory agencies he deemed too lax. Angie and Tish were occupying recliners near the stern — although instead of lying down they were both sitting up and tapping away busily on their laptops. And staying close to the sources of solar power. I strolled over to them.

"I have a project for you, if you're willing," I said.

"Will it help us get out of the Bermuda Triangle?" Tish asked.

"We hope so. We're going to make a short documentary about what's happening here on the ship, which Delaney will then try to send to the outside world in the hope of stirring up sympathy."

"The hell with sympathy — we want action!" Angie said.

"If we get enough sympathy, the action will come," I said. "We need someone to write a script for Grandfather's voice-over that will fire people up."

"Ooh, like in all those nature specials. 'Here we see the alpha male defending his territory.' " Angie did a pretty good imitation of the typical whispered voice-over.

"Grandfather will purr like a kitten if you can manage to call him an alpha male," I said. "But I think it's more likely to be a description of the reeking toilets and the puking crew. Depends on what kind of footage Wim and Guillermo have captured."

"Count me in," Tish said.

"I'll go find Kate and Janet." Angie jumped up and headed for the stairway.

"They're in the library lounge interviewing aspiring writers," I said. "So they will probably love being rescued. And if you see

Wim and Guillermo, send them up."

Within minutes, Caroline and the writers were all hard at work with laptops and the hard drives on which Wim and Guillermo stored their video footage. Hal, the town crier, came by, announcing that lunch was served and taking orders from those unable to make it to the dining room. I volunteered to fetch lunch for the production team. By the time I returned, Guillermo and Wim were back, doing something with the video. Assembling into a whole the segments Caroline and the writers liked, I gathered from the bits of conversation I overheard.

Only Grandfather was unoccupied, and thus restless. He bolted his soup and salad with a distracted air while looking over Wim's and Guillermo's shoulders.

"Shaping up nicely," he said. "But I think it's time we tackled the captain. He's the missing piece. Who's with me?"

Wim and Guillermo exchanged a look.

"You keep on with the edits," Wim said. "I'll do this."

Wim hefted his shoebox-sized camera and followed Grandfather to the stairs, filming all the way. Caroline and I fell in behind him. I suspected she was going along to keep him in line if necessary and figured she might need some help.

We trooped down to the third floor and marched along the corridor toward the bow of the ship. Grandfather was striding at the head of our procession — to my relief he seemed to be handling all the stairs reasonably well and was only slightly short of breath.

At the far end of the passageway, I could see Bart Evans, part of Delaney's tech crew, standing in the open door to the navigation bridge. He waved, and turned to say something to someone behind him. When we arrived at the end of the corridor, Delaney met us.

"Looking for me?" she said.

"No, actually, we are looking for Captain Detweiler," Grandfather boomed.

"Good luck." Delaney gestured at the door of 302. "As far as we know, he's in there."

"Start filming, Wim," Grandfather said.

I took a few steps back to make sure I'd be off camera, but I stayed around to watch. Grandfather, obviously an old hand at this kind of thing, stepped aside so Wim could focus on the door, with the nameplate front and center. Then Grandfather stepped into the picture and knocked on the door.

"Captain Detweiler! We need to speak with you."

No response.

"Captain Detweiler! It's Dr. Blake! I need a word with you!"

Grandfather stood by the door with his arms crossed, glowering at it, making his impatience visible. I had to hand it to him — he was a ham. His body language made the wait seem twice as long. Then he turned to the camera.

"Unfortunately, I'm afraid this will turn out like most of our efforts to get answers from the captain — or his crew. In fact —"

Just then the door swung open and Captain Detweiler appeared in the doorway.

"Wha's the prollem?"

CHAPTER 31

Captain Detweiler stood in the doorway, swaying slightly. I almost didn't recognize him. He was hatless — I'd never seen him without several pounds of white canvas and gold braid on his head — and his graying brown hair was uncombed and sticking out in all directions. He was still wearing his uniform trousers, but they were badly wrinkled, and he'd shed his jacket, revealing a stained white sleeveless undershirt. One foot was bare, the other bore a white sock with several holes in it. He didn't seem to have shaved for a day or so, and his eyes were bloodshot.

Grandfather allowed his surprise to show, but didn't say a word for quite a few seconds — he just let the camera take in the captain's disreputable appearance.

A pity the camera couldn't also capture the pungent reek of alcohol the captain gave off.

"Captain, we need to speak to you about the state of affairs aboard the *Pastime Wanderer*!" Grandfather boomed, causing the captain to wince visibly.

"S'all unner controw," the captain mumbled. "Go 'way."

He tried to shut the door, but Grandfather's foot prevented him.

"Captain!" Grandfather exclaimed. "You appear to be in a state of intoxication."

"Go 'way." The captain batted feebly and uselessly in Grandfather's direction.

Sensing, no doubt, that Wim had the footage they needed, Grandfather withdrew his foot. The captain shoved the door shut. We heard a few crashing and clinking noises.

Grandfather turned to face Wim's camera. He stared at the camera for a few seconds, shaking his head.

"We are beginning to understand the real reasons for the dire plight of the *Pastime Wanderer*'s passengers and crew," he said, in his most sepulchral and disapproving voice. He held his pose for a few seconds. "Or words to that effect," he added, in a more normal tone. "If those writers come up with something snappier, we can splice it in. Let's head back up to deck six."

They trooped away, already absorbed in a conversation about how to work in the

Detweiler footage. I stood in the corridor, watching them go, and musing. I was starting to wonder if the captain's failure to investigate Desiree's suicide was really standard cruise ship operating procedure, as Ted Lambert seemed to think. Maybe another captain would have investigated — a captain whose hold on sobriety wasn't already threatened by the difficulties of the journey, setting sail with fewer crew members than he really needed, and then seeing those crew members begin dropping like flies.

And First Officer Martin must have been trying to do both his job and the captain's for a while now. I glanced over at his door. I heard — or imagined I heard — a noise inside.

On impulse, I knocked on his door. Maybe it was time to talk to Martin. Tell him we know what he'd been dealing with. Try to enlist his help. He must know things that could help us deal with this crisis, if we could only gain his trust.

He didn't answer the door. I knocked again, waited a little while longer, then gave up. The noise I'd heard probably came from the captain's cabin anyway. So I left and headed for Michael's and my cabin.

When I stepped out into the fourth-floor

corridor, I spotted Martin at the other end. His back was to me. I instinctively ducked back into the stairwell, and then wondered why. A few minutes ago I'd been eager to talk to him. Why had I changed my mind so quickly?

Maybe because I was curious about where he was going and what he was doing. The only other time I'd seen him on deck four was when he and the captain had inspected the scene of Desiree's suicide. I peered out and saw him disappearing through the door at the end of the corridor, the one that led out onto the stern sun deck. Interesting. Maybe the suicide was still on his mind, too. Of course he could have some other reason for visiting the deck. Still — interesting. So instead of going into our cabin, I continued to the end of the corridor and peered out through a window that gave me a view of the deck.

He was just standing there, leaning against the rail right outside the door. He held his hat in one hand, and without all that gold braid and starched fabric he looked not only less official but a lot younger. And smaller. And not nearly as self-confident. In fact, he looked pretty awful — he had deep bags under his eyes, and his jaw was clenched in a way that suggested pain more than tension. As I watched, he took out a handkerchief and mopped his face and forehead. Then he held the heel of his hand to his forehead. Looked as if he was also nursing a headache.

Okay, he was annoying, but clearly the trip was taking a toll on him. And now we knew at least one reason why. I felt a twinge of guilt — I'd probably added to his stress. Then I reminded myself that however stressed he was, he'd at least partly brought it on himself. He probably thought we were treating him very badly. Maybe we had, but we wouldn't have if he hadn't been behaving like such an officious twit.

Maybe I'd apologize to him later.

He eventually took his hand away and glanced down at his watch. He frowned and shook his head. Was there somewhere he wanted to be right now — someplace on Bermuda, perhaps? If not for the breakdown, we'd be in the middle of our first day on shore. Or maybe he was just shaking his head in dismay that we'd been stranded so long.

Should I go out and talk to him?

Maybe later. Right now, he didn't look like someone who wanted company. He leaned his elbows on the rail again and put his face in his hands. I got the impression he wasn't going anywhere anytime soon.

For that matter, he was stuck on the ship like the rest of us, and thanks to Anton Bjelica's card key, he couldn't hide on deck zero anymore. I'd have a much better chance of hunting him down when I was ready to talk to him. Once I'd had a chance to plan what I'd say.

I headed back to deck six.

I found the whole video team huddled over Caroline's monitor.

"Good!" Caroline said. "You're just in time. Roll it, Wim."

"Of course it's still rough," Wim said.

"And it can stay rough," Caroline said. "We want it a little rough, to underscore the authenticity."

The video began with a short clip of Grandfather on the Baltimore pier, holding forth on the purpose of our journey, followed by a short montage of happy shipboard life. Passengers waving to whoever was on shore when we sailed. Passengers in the prow of the ship smiling as the breeze whipped their hair about, in a deliberate echo of the famous scene from *Titanic*. Mother and Aunt Penelope sipping tea together. The boys playing miniature golf. Passengers clinking wineglasses over dinner.

"All that changed the following morning,"

Grandfather's voice-over intoned, as the camera slowly moved in a complete circle, showing nothing but the flat, calm, empty ocean in all directions. "The ship was motionless . . . and a passenger was missing." A montage of my shots of Desiree's shoes and shawl, ending with a shot I must have taken — although I didn't remember it — of the captain as he turned his back on the scene of Desiree's suicide and walked back into the ship. "Did well-known romance writer Desiree St. Christophe actually commit suicide?" Grandfather asked, as the camera appeared to close in on the shoes and shawl. "Or was it murder? So far, Pastime has not even begun an investigation, and it may be too late to ever learn the truth." My picture of the shoes and shawl gradually faded into a video of the same spot of deck, empty except for a tiny little bit of down that rippled slightly in the almost nonexistent breeze.

"Awesome!" "Much better!" "Now *that* works!" various other people exclaimed.

Shots from yesterday — passengers gazing balefully at the meager buffet . . . passengers sniffing the food suspiciously . . . elderly passengers fanning their sweat-sheened faces . . . passengers creeping around in the dark by the light of their phone screens . . .

and a close-up of a toilet or two. Hints of outrage crept into Grandfather's tone.

And then shots from today — the passengers cleaning the kitchen, complete with close-ups of rotting food. Passengers nursing sick crew members — thank goodness they hadn't shown any actual retching. Michael and the boys hauling up bucket after bucket of water. Delaney and her crew hard at work on something mechanical — the backup generator, I assumed — that looked to have about a hundred thousand pieces, all of them spread out individually on the floor.

"Who is to blame for the disaster aboard the *Pastime Wanderer*?" Grandfather asked. "Management has been unresponsive." Somehow Wim and Guillermo had managed to capture half a dozen short clips of the captain or the first officer rapidly exiting whatever room they were in. They followed that up with the footage of the inebriated Captain Detweiler. And then the video cut to Grandfather, standing here on deck six, leaning against the stern rail.

"We've been told help is on the way, but it's been over twenty-four hours since our journey was interrupted, and we've heard nothing from the outside world. Conditions are difficult; elderly passengers and those with medical conditions are at increasing risk. Why hasn't Pastime done anything? What are they trying to cover up? How much longer will this ordeal last for the passengers of the ill-fated *Wanderer*? This is Dr. Montgomery Blake, somewhere . . . in the Bermuda Triangle."

"Excellent," Grandfather said.

"It'll do," Wim said.

"At least the fade finally works," Guillermo added.

"I think it's awesome," I said. "How soon can we get it to the outside world?"

"I can upload it to the Blake Foundation website," Wim said.

"And then we can send out a link to all our mailing lists," Caroline said.

"And —"

Suddenly we all heard a noise behind us. It appeared to be coming from the elevator shaft. Then the elevator doors burst open and Delaney stepped out.

"Let there be light!" she exclaimed.

Cheers erupted all over the deck.

"Only emergency lights," she added, as she strolled over to join us. "But that's better than nothing. And the elevator and the water pumping system are also on the emergency circuit — so flush toilets!"

"But not the air-conditioning?" Caroline asked.

"Big power hog, so no," Delaney replied.

"Then I think we need to see about moving some of the crew members up on deck where they can cool off," Caroline suggested. "It's already steamy, and I suspect it's going to get worse before it's better. The passenger cabins are bad, but at least they all have windows that can be opened. The crew cabins are like ovens."

"Let's go move them," Grandfather said. "To the rescue!"

Guillermo and Wim hoisted their cameras.

"Not you, Monty," Caroline said. "I need you to look over some more of this video footage. See if you can think of any way we can salvage a video out of it if this tub ends up being sent back to Baltimore instead of on to Bermuda. Or if there isn't, figure out what, if anything, the boys can shoot to fill in."

Grumbling, Grandfather sat down in front of her laptop, put on his reading glasses, and began pressing keys on her laptop.

"We don't want him overdoing it and keeling over down on deck zero," Caroline muttered as soon as the elevator doors closed.

"Is it safe, giving him access to the video footage?" I asked.

"Don't worry — we never let him any-where near the original files," Guillermo said.

"We don't even want me near the original files," Caroline added. "So anything on my laptop's a copy."

Down on deck zero, things were looking better than they had even a few hours ago. Maybe because the worst of the befouled cabins had been cleaned and it smelled better. None of the sick crew members looked totally recovered, but most of them were either sleeping or lying quietly. They all looked pale and drawn, but definitely alive and for the most part happy to be so.

Dad heartily approved the idea of moving the patients to cooler quarters on deck. So we filled the sun deck in the bow of deck two with recliners, rigged some canvas covers so they'd have shade, and helped the recovering crew members out there — or simply carried them if necessary. Dad turned the Moonbeam Lounge into an impromptu hospital for a few of the critical cases — including Aarav, who was still un-conscious.

"If he comes to —"

"If he comes to, it could be a while before he's strong enough to be questioned." Dad frowned at me and shook his head as if disappointed by my lack of consideration for Aarav's well-being. "He's almost certainly got some degree of concussion."

"I'll let you decide when he's ready for questioning," I said. "Just keep in mind that it could be rather useful to find out who gave him that concussion. Because that might be someone we don't want helping out with the nursing."

Dad returned to watching over Aarav with a more troubled face.

The afternoon wore on. The fresh air seemed to revive the outdoor patients. Some of them merely slept peacefully, while others were sitting up and seemed to be enjoying the novel sensation of being waited on by passengers.

I prowled through the ship, checking on things. Delaney and her tech crew were back in the small mechanical room, doing something that might possibly let them fix the navigation system. Michael and the boys were having another fencing session with Janet. Grandfather was pecking away with two fingers on his laptop — no doubt writing up a scathing indictment of Pastime. Or maybe he was still planning to give a lecture tonight. Preparations for dinner — and much-anticipated after-dinner coffee — were under way in the kitchen. Most people still had their cabin doors open, for cross-ventilation, but I saw fewer people just sitting miserably. An informal backgammon tournament had broken out in the dining room. Nearly every hall had a few bridge foursomes playing. People were coping.

I hoped some rescuers arrived before the current mellow mood evaporated.

On one of my trips to the bridge, I ran into Léonie carrying a tray of food and knocking on the captain's door, with a worried look on her face.

"Perhaps your father should check on the captain?" she asked when she saw me.

"He does, at regular intervals," I said. "And after the captain passed out, we searched his cabin and confiscated all the alcohol. Does he do this often?"

"Never!" She looked shocked. "Well, almost never. He is not a bad man, merely . . ."

"Weak?" I suggested.

"Perhaps," she said. "He takes the safe path, always. So now, when so many things have gone wrong that there is no safe path, he does not know what to do." She stared at the captain's door for a little longer. Then she seemed to rouse herself, shrugged, and strode off, still carrying the tray.

At one point, I spotted Wim racing down

the stairs with his camera. Maybe he'd just spotted a rare bird perched on the ship's rail, but still — I followed to see what was up.

I arrived on deck two, where all the sick crew members were recovering, to find a demonstration getting started. Half a dozen of the crew members were waving picket signs. Not very traditional picket signs — evidently sticks and cardboard had been hard to find aboard ship, so the discontented crew members had made their signs using Sharpies on white plastic garbage bags. More like picket banners. PASTIME UNFAIR TO WORKERS! one banner read. NO MORE 20-HOUR WORK DAYS! read another. But the other four all read simply UNION NOW! And, of course, Wim and Guillermo were busily filming from various angles.

Caroline was standing nearby, nodding her approval. I had no doubt she'd egged them on. She was fond of mentioning that her grandmother had been a suffragette. She regularly marched for a variety of progressive causes. And she was always the first to show up when Grandfather organized a demonstration to protest some environmental issue. One of her pet peeves was that she rarely got arrested anymore. "They deliberately ignore me," she had been known to say, "because they know how bad they'll look arresting a tiny little gray-haired grandmother."

I went over to stand by her.

"Just out of curiosity, in what way is Pastime unfair to workers?" I asked. "Not that I have any doubt that they are, mind you — by now I'm quite willing to believe the worst of them. But I was wondering what particular injustice sent the crew over the edge at this already complicated moment in time?"

"What you really want to know is why they're protesting at a time when you'd rather have them doing everything they can to get the ship back in action and keep the passengers as comfortable as possible in the meantime," Caroline said.

"Well, not really," I replied. "Since I recognize all six of them as either kitchen staff or housekeeping staff who wouldn't be able to make much of a contribution to getting the ship back in action. They've all been working like dogs alongside the passengers all day; if they want to use their scant leisure time to protest Pastime's heinous labor practices, more power to them."

"And would it surprise you to learn that their heinous labor practices may have helped cause the pickle we're currently in?"

"I'm all ears," I said.

"The ship's understaffed," she said. "Seriously understaffed in just about every department."

"We knew that," I said. "Including engineering, I assume?"

"Especially engineering. Which means that they were already behind the eight ball when the navigation system broke down, and things got even worse when most of the crew members with any technical expertise succumbed to the food poisoning. So, any chance you could get more of an audience for this shindig?"

"You mean the demonstration?"

Caroline nodded. I considered pointing out that it wasn't that much of a demonstration — six crew members marching up and down the deck, looking rather anxious as they waved their banners and chanted their slogans

"Preferably witnesses with cell phone cameras," she added.

I found Hal, our town crier, and tasked him with circulating through the ship to advertise the protest. By the time I got back to deck two, the protest was sounding a lot more confident.

And had gotten a lot bigger. It was up to nearly two dozen picketers now. All the new recruits were passengers — including Rob and Caroline. Although most of the crew members still recovering in recliners seemed to be cheering them on.

Before long, Hal's announcements bore fruit. I glanced up to see that the front rails of decks four, five, and six were lined with passengers looking down on the protest. Many of them were holding cameras or cell phones.

"What is the meaning of this?"

Damn. First Officer Martin had appeared.

"How is Captain Detweiler feeling today?" I asked him, more in the hope of distracting him than anything.

"I want every one of you to stop this ridiculous nonsense right now!" he bellowed. "Do you realize how bad this looks?"

I could see some of the crew members cringe — and for that matter, one or two of the passengers. But they kept marching. Martin snorted slightly, reminding me of a bull about to charge a matador.

But just as he took a step toward the protesters, Caroline stepped out of the picket line and into his path.

"These crew members are all off duty," she said. "And they are exercising their first amendment rights to —"

"They can go exercise their first amendment rights someplace else." Martin looked rather smug. "This deck is private property — Pastime Cruise's property — and they do not have permission to demonstrate here."

He probably had a point. Not a point I wanted to spend time arguing — I had a few other things to get done. But I was curious, so I hung around and watched as he and Caroline went back and forth for several minutes.

"Fine," Caroline said finally. "We won't picket on Pastime's deck."

The first officer smiled in triumph — no doubt thinking that he'd nipped the crew's rebellion in the bud.

"Attention, everyone!" Caroline called out. "We move to plan B."

One of the crew members began passing out life jackets and life preservers. The protesters, crew and passenger alike, quickly strapped themselves in. Then Rob and one of the kitchen crew climbed up on the rail and jumped off the ship.

CHAPTER 32

"Wait! What are you — You can't —"

But no one was paying attention to the first officer's sputtering. Some of the protesters leaped off the ship, whether gracefully or awkwardly. The majority donned their lifesaving gear, trotted toward the stairs, and eventually reappeared at the stern of deck one, which made for a lot shorter jump.

I was relieved to see that Caroline had opted to stay on board. Not that I had any doubt of her ability to stay afloat, but she'd be much more useful here on deck to foil the first officer's attempts to squelch the protest.

He lifted his gaze to the upper decks, and his scowl faded a little. Perhaps he was taking momentary comfort at seeing that the cheering passengers with their cameras and cell phones had disappeared. No doubt his annoyance would return when he realized that they'd dispersed to vantage points along the port and stern sides of the deck, the better to see and film the new phase of the demonstration.

Meanwhile a new chant was floating up from the ocean's surface.

"One, two! One, two!
"Pastime is unfair to crew!"

I recognized Rob's voice.

"Three, four! Three, four!
"Show those Pastime crooks the door!"

Glancing over the side, I realized that the counting served a purpose other than providing convenient rhymes for insults to the cruise line management. Rob was leading the floating protesters in a primitive form of synchronized swimming. On the first "one, two!" they would all reach out with their right arms and roll over on their backs. On the second "one, two!" they'd reach out with their left arms and return to their original position. And on "Pastime is unfair to crew!" all those who were trailing banners behind them would wave them furiously in the air. And then with "three, four!' they'd start the whole thing again. Occasionally four or five of them would gather in a circle with their feet in the center and wave their legs in something that might approach unison if they kept practicing for another century or two.

"Five, six! Five, six!
"No more Pastime dirty tricks!
"Seven, eight! Seven, eight!
"Fire the captain and first mate!"

I glanced over at First Officer Martin. He was just staring at the swimmers with a mournful expression. He lifted his hand to his face and then pulled it down again, as if he really wanted to rub his temples to ease a headache, but was determined not to show weakness in public.

Eventually he turned around and went back inside.

Probably not the optimal moment to try enlisting his cooperation.

The protesters kept it up for a while. Michael and the boys came down and joined in, although not until Mother had interrogated Grandfather and satisfied herself that there were unlikely to be great white sharks in the vicinity. Of course, for Grandfather there was no such thing as a short and simple answer to such a question, and long after the boys had joined the swimmers he was still holding forth on sharks.

"*Carcharodon carcharias* is most commonly found in an epipelagic habitat," he was saying. "And traditionally —"

"Ship ahoy!" Wim shouted. He and Guillermo both had the enormous zoom lenses on their cameras and were leaning off the starboard side.

"Well, that's good news." Grandfather picked up his binoculars and ambled over to join the two photographers. "Which way?"

"Astern," Wim said.

"We'll get a better view from deck six," Guillermo said. The two of them dashed inside.

"What kind of ship?" I asked. And then immediately wondered why it mattered. Because from the clenching of my stomach, clearly my subconscious thought it mattered. Maybe I'd been listening too much to various family members' wild speculations about smugglers and pirates and voodoo curses. The odds were overwhelming that the ship, still invisible for those of us peering astern with only our naked eyes, would be perfectly harmless. Another cruise ship, changing course to assist us. Or a cargo ship playing Good Samaritan. Maybe even a Navy or Coast Guard ship. Why did its arrival fill me with such anxiety?

Because as soon as possible, Dad and I had to find someone trustworthy to tell about Desiree's alleged suicide and Anton Bjelica's very definite murder. Right now, whoever had killed Bjelica probably thought he'd gotten away with it. He or she. Probably he, but if I had to, I could have hefted Bjelica, and I wasn't the only strong woman on board. We had no idea who had thrown the body overboard, but the odds were pretty high that it was a crew member, since he'd been able to get in, both to hide and eventually to dispose of the body. And it also seemed logical that the killer was the one doing the body disposal — unless there was some kind of sinister conspiracy on board. I wasn't sure I even wanted to think too much about that. And was it just my imagination, or did Bjelica's murder give us all a good reason to look more closely at whether Desiree had really gone overboard under her own steam?

So while everyone else was hoping the ship would bring fresh provisions and whatever help Delaney's crew needed to finish repairing our ship, I was really hoping there would be someone on board who could take charge of investigating all this. And the food poisoning that had felled the crew — was it really an accident? Was it really food poisoning?

Someone to take charge of investigating all of this, yes — but someone discreet enough not to put Dad and me in danger. Because right now, whoever had thrown Anton Bjelica's body overboard had no idea there were ear witnesses to his crime. He might worry that we'd overheard something that would let the authorities identify him. He might wonder if we were lying about not having seen him and decide to get rid of us as possible eye witnesses.

And I was afraid that the longer we waited to tell someone in authority about Bjelica's murder, the more people would be inclined to doubt us, no matter how hard we tried to explain the wisdom of not reporting it to someone who could be a suspect.

The swimmers all scrambled aboard and nearly everyone made a dash for one of the stern decks — even a few of the recovering crew members. Most of them made for higher decks, which gave a better view.

I went out through the main dining room to the small stern area on deck one. I leaned on the rail and tried to look as happy as the rest of the passengers as the Coast Guard ship slowly drew near. It pulled up a little way from our starboard side and promptly lowered a boat — a rather curious boat that looked like a cross between a sleek speedboat and an inflatable raft. The boat, carrying an officer and four crew members, pulled up beside where I was standing. They seemed a little surprised to see me. The officer stood up in the boat and peered at me.

"Where are the crew?" he called out.

"Incapacitated," I shouted back. "Food poisoning."

He blinked for a second.

"Can you throw down the ladder?"

Michael appeared, and between the two of us we figured out how to unfurl the ladder in question. Just as the officer was climbing up, Mother emerged from the dining room door. When he climbed over the railing, she stretched out her hand.

"Welcome!" she exclaimed. "You can't imagine how glad we are to see you."

"Er . . . yes, ma'am. Who's in command of this ship?"

"Technically, that would be Captain Detweiler," Mother said. I was relieved that she hadn't pointed to herself. Or for that matter, to me.

"Captain Detweiler is in his cabin," I said. "But I think you'll find that he's incapacitated. Most of the officers are incapacitated — except for First Officer Martin, who doesn't show his face much — and most of the crew as well. Food poisoning. We've managed to restore emergency power — and by *we* I mean a group of passengers with tech and engineering skills — but according to the one member of the engineering crew who's been conscious enough to help out, we'll need parts to repair the several other things that still need fixing."

The officer blinked at us for a few moments. He was young — surprisingly young — with clean-cut features and close-cropped hair so blond it was almost white.

"I'm Lieutenant Tracy," he said.

"Meg Langslow." I offered my hand, and introduced Mother and Michael. The lieutenant didn't seem all that happy to meet us.

"Maybe you should show me just what's going on here, ma'am," he said, when the introductions were complete.

"Glad to," I said.

He snapped a command down at his boat, and three of the four crew members in it scrambled up the ladder. Then he ordered another crew member to stay at the ladder.

"Lead me to the bridge, please, ma'am," he said.

When we stepped into the dining room, we found at least half of the passengers there. The crowd cheered enthusiastically but, thanks to Mother's and Michael's efforts, they didn't mob the Coast Guard party. In fact, they left a path clear through the middle of the dining room.

I led them up to the bridge. Captain Detweiler didn't answer his door, but apparently he'd left it unlocked before passing out on the floor of his cabin. Lieutenant Tracy almost managed to conceal the distaste he felt at the sight. First Officer Martin didn't answer his door, either, and it was locked. On the bridge, Gerard Hoffman, the recovering member of the engineering crew, was delighted to see the Coast Guard party and gave the lieutenant a voluble account of the several things that had gone wrong with the ship. I almost understood parts of it. To my delight, he also waxed eloquent about the great work Delaney and her crew had done.

By the time he finished, the lieutenant was looking a little stunned.

"Do you have any idea where to find your first officer?"

Hoffman and I shook our heads.

"Any of your officers?"

I stepped over to the windows at the front of the bridge and pointed. The lieutenant joined me and we looked down on the sun deck where some of the ailing crew members were still recovering. You could sort of tell they were crew members because most of them wore at least some part of their uniform. Some of them — no doubt the ones who were still feverish — had cold compresses over their foreheads. Bob was taking the pulse of one. Dad had his stethoscope to the chest of another. Rose Noire was handing around cups of something. Not, I hoped, one of her herbal teas. Léonie was refilling water glasses.

"We brought the sick crew members out on deck because of the heat," I said. "Dad — that's him with the stethoscope — says we were lucky. Severe dehydration can be fatal. But we didn't lose anyone, and Dad's optimistic that they're all past the worst of it. I think a couple of the officers are out there."

"Thank you, ma'am." He nodded as he studied the crew. "Is there someplace more private where I can call my captain?"

"I'll be in the small mechanical room," Hoffman said. He shuffled out the door.

"I'll leave you in peace to call your captain in a minute," I said. "But first there's something I wanted to tell you without an audience."

CHAPTER 33

"There's more?" The idea didn't seem to cheer up Lieutenant Tracy.

"Well, yeah," I said. "You can already see why we were so relieved when we saw your ship."

"Yes, ma'am," the lieutenant said. "Actually, we call it a cutter."

"Even when it's that big?"

"Coast Guard tradition, ma'am. All our vessels are cutters." He glanced over at the door. "You said you had some information you wanted to communicate privately?"

"Yes." I took a deep breath. "And you're probably going to think I'm some kind of paranoid loon or something, but please hear me out."

"Yes, ma'am."

"Someone murdered a crew member and threw him overboard," I said.

"Are you sure about that, ma'am?" He was frowning. And looking at me oddly, just as I expected. "Our information was that it was a woman passenger. And that she jumped overboard."

"Yes, we had that happen, too," I said. "And maybe she committed suicide but my father — the one with the stethoscope — was suspicious of the circumstances, and not very happy with how little investigation the captain was conducting, so we managed to obtain a key card that we could use to search her cabin. He wanted to look for anything that would shed light on her state of mind. Whether she was really suicidal — they call it a psychological autopsy."

"And the ship's captain agreed to this, ma'am?"

"No, he just wanted to sweep the whole thing under the rug," I said. "Which is why we did our search in the middle of the night, and I'm not going to tell you how we managed to get hold of that key card."

"Yes, ma'am." I could tell he was trying to suppress a smile.

"And we found a body in the wardrobe. Not the alleged suicide — a crew member named Anton Bjelica. Dad — did I mention that in addition to being a doctor he's a medical examiner back home? — Dad estimated, from the degree of rigor mortis, that he'd been dead for a few hours, but less than a day. And there were ligature marks around his neck, which to Dad suggested that he'd been killed by ligature strangulation."

The lieutenant wasn't smiling anymore. He was looking at me oddly again.

"And then we heard someone unlocking the door, and we hid in the bathroom — because remember, we weren't really supposed to be there — and while we were hiding, whoever came in threw the body off the room's balcony. We didn't realize he was doing it until we heard the splash, or we'd have tried to stop him."

"And you didn't see who did it?"

"We were in the bathroom with the door open just a crack — maybe this much." I held my thumb and forefinger about an inch and a half apart. "Maybe less. And we were trying not to be seen, so we weren't peering through that crack. But when whoever did it left, we checked the wardrobe again and the body was gone."

"And you didn't tell anyone?"

"Like a member of the crew?" I asked. "Because apart from the fact that most of them were deathly ill, they'd all have had access to the room, and any one of them could have done it. And then faked being sick to have an alibi."

He nodded. But he was looking at me as if he couldn't quite decide whether to believe me or ask what I'd been smoking.

"Ma'am, I don't suppose you have any proof of . . . well, any of this," he asked finally.

"I took pictures." I pulled out my phone, opened up the first of the Anton shots, and handed him the phone.

His eyes went wide. I could understand. There was something about the expression on Bjelica's face, with its half-open, unseeing eyes, that made you realize it was no hoax. He was dead. The facial expression and the odd, unnatural way his head was bent to the side. Although I suspected it was the close-ups of the ligature marks that really convinced the lieutenant.

"Good thing you had the presence of mind to think of taking pictures, ma'am," he said.

"And I can share them with whoever's going to be investigating this," I said. "I have no idea who that would be."

"Neither do I, ma'am," he said. "But I imagine the CGIS might want a piece of it. Coast Guard Investigative Service," he translated.

"I guess you wouldn't routinely bring them along on a mission like this," I said.

460

"No, ma'am. But once I fill my captain in on what you've just told me, I expect he'll put in a request to send out a CGIS team on the double."

"Fill your captain in, by all means," I said. "But not our captain. Or any of his crew. Because Dad and I are still here on the ship. And so is whoever threw Bjelica overboard. It would make me very nervous if word got around that Dad and I knew anything about that."

"Yes, ma'am."

"One more thing — Bjelica was a member of the engineering crew. And whatever went wrong with the ship happened while he was in the middle of doing some kind of maintenance on the emergency generator system that required taking it apart on the engine-room floor. Maybe it's just a coincidence that it was the generator expert who got strangled and tossed overboard. But I understand you're going to send over some of your engineering crew to help us out."

He nodded.

"Tell them to watch their backs."

"Yes, ma'am," he said. "I think under the circumstances the captain will probably detail guards to watch their backs for them. So they can concentrate on their work."

"Good." Armed guards, probably — I

liked that idea.

"This happened last night, is that correct ma'am?" he asked. "Mr. Bjelica being thrown overboard?"

"Yes," I said. "And Desiree St. Christophe the night before that, or more accurately very early yesterday morning. It was starting to look like an oceangoing remake of *And Then There Were None*. We were overjoyed to see your sh— your cutter show up; at the rate we were going we'd have been a ghost ship before long."

I didn't say "what took you so long?" but maybe he deduced that I'd been thinking it.

"Sorry you had such a long wait, ma'am," he said. "We're out of helicopter range here."

"And I know it takes a while to get here from Baltimore."

"Portsmouth, actually. That's the nearest RCC — Rescue Coordination Center. But really, it shouldn't have taken this long except . . ."

He stopped as he was about to say something he shouldn't. And then, apparently, he decided the hell with it.

"The *Wanderer*'s personnel weren't very . . . efficient in their communications. They reported the passenger overboard and seemed to imply that they were stopped

462

briefly for minor repairs. It was only when Dr. Blake sent out his message that we became aware — that anyone not on board became aware — of the extent of the problem. And, of course, we were giving first priority to organizing the search for the missing passenger. Which is still ongoing, of course."

"Very discreetly, I gather."

"Discreetly, ma'am?"

"Well, we haven't seen anyone searching," I said. "I don't suppose they're doing it with submarines?"

"No, ma'am. We've got several Coast Guard cutters deployed, and of course the information went out over AMVER — the Automated Mutual-Assistance Vessel Rescue system. Which means any vessels along the *Wanderer*'s route will be keeping a lookout, and some may even change course to help out with the search."

"Our route?" I was puzzled. "But she went overboard here. After the ship was already stationary."

"How do you know this, ma'am?" He didn't quite emphasize the "you," but I got the point.

"Maybe the captain didn't believe me, but I woke up at four thirty-five A.M. The ship was stopped, and I went outside on the deck to see what was going on. And when I figured out nothing was, I went back to sleep. And sometime between seven fifteen and eight o'clock, while the captain was pretending to brief us on why the ship was stopped and actually saying nothing, a crew member came running into the dining room to say that someone had jumped overboard. They found her shoes, her shawl, and a suicide note right where I'd been staring at the moon a few hours earlier. So unless someone moved her stuff after the fact, all those ships searching between here and Baltimore are wasting their time, aren't they?"

He stood motionless for a few long seconds, looking at me.

"Would you excuse me for a minute, ma'am?" he said. "I should brief my captain. Stay here."

He crossed to the other side of the bridge, taking a radio from its holder on his belt as he went. I stood by the window and watched what was going on down on deck two.

Eventually he put away his radio and came back over to my side of the bridge.

"This is unbelievable," he said. "If your information is accurate, we've got hundreds of personnel searching halfway to Baltimore when they needed to be searching right here. And your ship's captain didn't even notify his salver."

"His what?"

"His salver, ma'am. Any vessel entering U.S. waters is required to have a contract with a marine salvage company that can perform any repairs that are beyond the capabilities of the ship's engineering staff or tow the vessel if they can't get it moving again."

"Kind of like triple A for ships," I said.

"Yes, ma'am." He chuckled at the idea.

"Maybe they forgot about that little requirement. I've been getting the impression that playing by the rules isn't Pastime's strong point."

"Oh, they have a salver, all right." The lieutenant's smile took on a grim cast. "Apparently their salver was surprised not to have heard about this already. Surprised and, I'm willing to bet, not very happy."

"Let me guess: It costs Pastime money if they have to call the salver."

He nodded.

"Then that's probably the reason," I told him. "I've been getting the definite feeling that Pastime is all about cost cutting."

"Keep all this to yourself for the time being, ma'am," he said. "We were already planning to bring on board a couple of petty

465

officers to help with the repairs and also our corpsman so he can report back to the captain on the recovering crew members. After I relayed your information to the captain, he's decided to send a couple of guard details — as I expected."

"Good," I said. "And thanks."

"Thank you, ma'am."

"If Captain Detweiler objects to having guards, you could always explain that you're doing it to keep the rowdy passengers in order. As you may have figured out by now, we kind of stepped in and started doing things the crew were too sick to do. Like tending the sick, repairing the emergency generator, cleaning the ship, cooking meals — stuff like that. I'm sure the captain wants to hang us from the yardarm as scurvy mutineers."

"I'll keep that in mind, ma'am." He was fighting a smile again. I hoped that meant that charges of mutiny weren't in any of our futures.

The rest of the afternoon passed in a whirl. By nightfall, Dad had pronounced all of the crew members out of the woods, and a few of them were back on limited duty — although without the passengers who'd volunteered to help in the kitchen, neither dinner nor the post-dinner cleanup would have happened.

Once the Coast Guard engineering crew figured out that Delaney knew exactly what she was doing, they let her continue to work on repairs, and by bedtime she'd managed to get the ship's Wi-Fi working. The Internet connection was still spotty, but it was lovely to text friends and family on board to find out where they were instead of hunting from floor to floor.

Grandfather gave an energetic after-dinner talk on parasitism, symbiosis, commensalism, mutualism, and mimicry in marine creatures. I'd have to talk to him about finding a catchier title. Nothing wrong with the lecture, which was full of dramatic pictures and videos — clownfish darting around unharmed in the stinging tentacles of sea anemones. Boxer crabs warding off predators by picking up stinging anemones with their claws and waving them around. A mimic octopus changing shape to resemble a stingray or a lionfish. Imperial shrimp avoiding predators by riding around on poisonous nudibranchs. Pearl fish living inside the intestines of sea cucumbers by day and swimming out at night to eat crustaceans. Even the Coast Guard officers who sat in on the lecture — either to keep an eye on what we were all doing or because they'd heard of Grandfather before — applauded enthusiastically at the end.

And after Grandfather's lecture, while Michael and the boys stuffed themselves with cookies and ice cream brought over from the Coast Guard cutter, I actually managed to read three chapters in my book club book. It was a relief to know, whenever problems came up, that I could tell people to take it to the Coast Guard. The cutter's captain left Lieutenant Tracy on board in charge of two guard details — one in the engine room, and one on the bridge.

I wondered if the bridge detail was also keeping an eye on the captain and the first officer. The captain was still sleeping it off — I knew this because the lieutenant called in Dad to examine him and make sure there was nothing really wrong with him — and I hadn't seen the first officer since the Coast Guard's arrival.

Of course, that didn't mean the Coast Guard hadn't been chatting with him.

"All's well that ends well," Michael said, as he was trying to stop yawning long enough to finish brushing his teeth.

I wanted to point out that everything wasn't ended. We still had no idea when the salver would arrive. Or how long it would take to either fix the ship or tow it to port.

The investigating team from the CGIS was supposed to arrive in the morning, but what were the chances that they'd be able to figure out what had really happened to Anton Bjelica? Or, for that matter, to Desiree?

But I didn't want to spoil his good mood, so I just nodded and turned out the bedside light.

If only my brain had an off switch.

Michael fell asleep almost immediately. I tried to match his soft breathing. It didn't help. After a while, I switched to the kind of yoga breathing Rose Noire insisted was an infallible way of falling asleep — breathing in quickly, holding your breath for a count of seven, then breathing out slowly.

My body wasn't having any of it.

I got up, donned my flip-flops, grabbed my Pastime card, and slipped out of the room. I told myself virtuously that it was the considerate thing to do — why risk waking up Michael and the boys? They'd had a long hard day — hauling all those buckets of water.

Which was nonsense. Tired as they were, I could have done a clog dance back and forth between the rooms while blowing an air horn and they wouldn't wake up. I was just tired of watching them sleep while I couldn't.

I hesitated in the hallway. My first impulse was to go out on the sun deck and gaze over the ocean. I even took a few steps that way and then changed my mind. Gazing over the ocean from the deck four sun deck was what I'd been doing just before everything went to hell. Not tonight.

I could go up to the sixth floor and gaze over the ocean from a different vantage point. Or drop down to the third floor and see how the repairs were getting along. I could even go down to deck zero and see if there was anything that needed doing for the recovering crew members — if I couldn't sleep, at least I could make myself useful.

But no. I was peopled out. I wanted some peace and quiet.

"Should have brought my book club book," I grumbled to myself. If anything was going to put me to sleep, that would.

But I had my phone. Delaney had put one of her beloved weresquid books on it, hadn't she? I could read that.

Yes. And I could retreat to the library lounge, which was only a few doors down, and read there until my eyes felt heavy. If the weresquid didn't thrill me as much as it did Delaney, I could search the shelves for something else.

I turned right, toward the library lounge.

So nice to have light back. Only the dim emergency lights, until they finished working on the main power system, but still. Light. Running water. Flush toilets. Life was good.

I was reaching to open the door to the library lounge when I saw something odd. The door to 411 was just closing.

Desiree's room.

CHAPTER 34

I crept silently down the passageway —
which wasn't easy in flip-flops. I stopped at
the door to 411. It was closed now. Maybe
I'd only imagined the brief flash of movement.

I put my ear to the door and listened.

Nothing. Long seconds of nothing.

I was just jumpy. Some sort of delayed reaction to everything that had happened over
the past couple of days. I'd probably imagined the door closing. I'd be fine as soon
as —

I heard a creak. A familiar creak. Someone
was opening the closet door.

Okay, it was unlikely that anyone had
stashed another body there in preparation
for tossing it overboard, but still — no one
should be in there.

I should probably go find the Coast
Guard, I told myself. They were right downstairs.

But whoever was burgling Desiree's room could get away while I fetched them. If I needed the Coast Guard, all I had to do was scream.

First, I'd find out what was going on.

I fumbled at my pocket. In addition to my own Pastime card — yes, I was still carrying around Anton Bjelica's card. I pulled it out, quickly slid it through the lock of 411, opened the door, and stepped inside.

"What the hell are you doing in here? This is my cabin."

Desiree was standing in front of the closet, wearing a chartreuse green-flowered silk kimono over a fuchsia satin nightgown and holding a glass of red wine in one hand and a wine bottle in the other. She wobbled unsteadily on her feet, as if this hadn't been her first glass.

"What the hell am I doing here?" I repeated. "What the hell are *you* doing here? You're supposed to be dead."

I let the door close behind me. I should probably call the Coast Guard on her. In a minute. I wanted to find out what she'd say. I didn't see her as much of a threat under any circumstances, and particularly not in her present inebriated condition.

"Supposed to be dead? What do you mean by that? Are you threatening me?" She clutched the neck of her dressing gown in a gesture straight out of a silent movie — the fragile, wide-eyed heroine threatened by the evil villain. The effect was rather spoiled by the fact that she sloshed half the contents of her wineglass onto herself.

"We found your shawl, your Christian Louboutin shoes, and a suicide note by the railing on the fourth-floor sun deck." Why was I telling her this? She was presumably the one who'd put them there. "We thought you'd jumped overboard."

I glanced around and noticed that the shawl, or one just like it, was draped over the end of the bed. I suspected the shoes were back in the closet. And there was stuff scattered everywhere — bits of clothing and cosmetics. None of that had been here when Dad and I had burgled the room last night.

I focused back on her. She was staring at me. Then, as if figuring something out, she assumed an expression of fear and took a step back.

"They wanted to kill me! That must be it!"

"Who?" I tried not to sound skeptical. I must have failed.

"You don't believe me." She threw herself into the small armchair with a sob. "No one believes me."

"Try me," I said. "Who tried to kill you?"

"I have enemies," she said. "They've been spreading malicious rumors about me, even accusing me of murder. I can't get away from them, not even on this cruise. And now they've tried to kill me. They're insidious!"

"They also appear to be unsuccessful," I pointed out. "You still look pretty much alive. Where have you been the last two days?"

"I'm not sure where I was," she said. "I was out on deck, just gazing at the moonlight. Bathing in the healing light of Mother Luna. And suddenly everything went black." She refilled her wineglass from the half-empty bottle of merlot and took a gulp.

"Then what?"

"I was unconscious for a long time," she said. "And when I woke up I was bound and gagged and blindfolded. And drugged. I kept slipping in and out of consciousness. I had no idea how much time was passing. And then, just now, I woke up and found myself here. In my stateroom. It was horrible!"

She shuddered, lifted the glass to her lips with both hands, took a gulp, and then held it there, as if the wine vapors somehow strengthened her. Then she spoiled the effect by glancing quickly at me from under her brow, as if to gauge whether I was buying it.

If I'd been kidnapped and drugged and suddenly found myself free, I don't think my first reaction would be to put on my nicest silk dressing gown and get sloshed. I wasn't even sure I believed it was Desiree's first reaction. But I tried to keep my face neutral.

"Sounds like a horrible experience," I said. "And you have no idea who did it?"

"Oh, I know," she said. "But I'll save that for the police."

"Probably wise," I said. "We don't have any actual police here at the moment, but we do have some Coast Guard officers down on the bridge. I think some of them are MPs, or whatever the equivalent is in Coast Guard lingo. I'm sure —"

Just then the door opened.

"Oh, great," someone behind me said.

I whirled around to see First Officer Martin standing in the doorway, pointing a pistol at us.

"Just what I need," he muttered, as he let the door fall closed behind him and dropped whatever he was holding in his left hand on the floor with a thud.

"Deal with her," Desiree said — rather

loudly. "I want you to —"

"Shut the hell up," Martin raised the gun slightly. "And hands up. I don't want to have to shoot you."

"I'm paying you —" Desiree began.

"Not enough." Martin's face took on a look of . . . long-suffering patience? No, downright annoyance. "Not nearly enough. This has been the longest two days of my entire life. You too. Hands up." He gestured at me.

I put my hands up. Not way up in the air like a first grader dying to answer the teacher's question. Just up at shoulder height, palms facing him so he could see I wasn't concealing a gun or, unfortunately, the cell phone I'd tucked into my pocket before sneaking down to Desiree's room. But ready to grab anything that looked like a weapon if the opportunity arose.

"You were hiding her in your cabin, weren't you?" I asked.

"It was only supposed to be for a few hours. They find her clothes and the suicide note, and when the Bermudian authorities search the ship they find her bound, gagged, and blindfolded in the cabin of some people she has it in for. She gets the headlines, her enemies are in a world of legal trouble, and Johnnie Martin's just a little bit richer. And then the stupid drunken idiot goes and sets up the fake suicide twenty-four hours too early."

Desiree waved her hand, in a gesture that clearly said "what's the big deal?" She wasn't even looking at him. I like to keep my eye on people who are pointing weapons at me, or even in my general direction. Not to mention the fact that I'd be making more of an effort not to annoy someone who looked as mad as Martin did right now.

And however nice it was to have my curiosity satisfied about what really happened to Desiree, and why, and where she'd been all this time, the fact that he was coming right out and saying all this wasn't reassuring. He was looking at us with calculating eyes. I was pretty sure he was calculating how to dispose of us without making any noise. I had to find some way to turn the tables on him before he figured it out. I suspected that any story he came up with about how we ended up full of bullets would be nearly as lame as the one Desiree had just tried to spin. The police or the FBI or whoever investigated would see right through it, but that wouldn't do me much good if I were already dead.

And that was assuming anyone did investigate. If he managed to toss our bodies overboard and invent a plausible story about the gunshots . . .

I should keep him talking.

"And you got Anton Bjelica to sabotage the navigation system, didn't you?" I asked. "Wasn't that kind of overkill — having both the ship's system failure and Desiree's kidnapping the first night out?"

"None of it was supposed to happen the first night out," he snapped. "She wasn't supposed to pull her disappearing act until we got to Bermuda — the second night out. And Bjelica wasn't supposed to do his thing with the navigation system until we were heading back to Baltimore — after I had had plenty of time to convince both the passengers and Pastime's management that Detweiler had fallen off the wagon worse than usual and kept sailing in spite of some kind of maintenance issue that could bring the whole show to a halt at the worst possible moment. Bjelica was supposed to come up with something subtle — something no one would suspect was sabotage. But no — the idiot jumps the gun and just whacks a few key parts with a ball-peen hammer. Even the idiots in the head office could look at that and realize it was sabotage. But he was impatient — he couldn't wait to start blackmailing me. And before you ask, no, it wasn't my idea to do it while the backup generator was in pieces on the engine room floor. Do you think I enjoy cold showers and half-spoiled food? Idiot! I can still pull it off, though. Convince them that Detweiler was so far gone he failed to spot a dangerously unbalanced crew member. Failed to take proper security measures. Yeah. That should fly."

He seemed to be losing himself in planning how he was going to turn Bjelica's premature and obvious sabotage to his benefit. Maybe I could jump him while he was distracted. Grab the gun and —

"Don't even try it," he barked — although I'd hardly moved a muscle. "Get over there." He gestured slightly with the gun. "Closer to the old cow."

"I don't think so," I said. "I like it right here."

I said it to test him, and his reaction — or lack of it — reassured me. He was smart enough that he wanted to avoid shooting me if he could.

"Old cow," Desiree muttered. "You keep talking to me like that and you won't get that bonus we talked about."

"Ha, ha," Martin muttered. He took another step closer and in passing kicked aside whatever it was he'd dropped when he entered. It looked like a couple of crumpled black plastic garbage bags, and they'd made a heavy clunking noise when his foot had hit them.

I focused back on Desiree. Good. She was frowning at him. But I needed her furious.

"I suspect he's not really worried about the bonus," I said to Desiree. "If I had to guess, I'd say he's trying to figure out whether you can keep your mouth shut about him hiding you in his cabin for the last two days, or whether he should just tie a weight to your foot and toss you off your balcony."

Desiree shook her head slightly, but she was listening.

"He came prepared." I pointed to the garbage bags. "I'm not sure whether he's planning to stuff you in one of those or whether they're for throwing your belongings overboard after you, but he's got some kind of weights in them."

Desiree blinked and looked confused. Confused, and maybe just a little anxious.

"Why would he do that?"

"Because you can tell on him," I said. "If you reveal that he helped you fake your suicide, he'll be in a lot of hot water. With Pastime, and maybe even with the police."

"It wasn't a fake," she said. "It must have

481

been him! He kidnapped me and kept me in his cabin all this time. Who knows what sinister plans he had?"

"Oh, come off it," Martin said. "If I were planning to toss her off a balcony, why bring her back here? I could have just tossed her off my own balcony."

He had a good point. Unless —

"Not really," I said aloud. "Your cabin's on the starboard side, where the Coast Guard cutter is. You don't dare toss her off there. But you figured if you waited until dark and did it off the port side, you could get away with it."

"He wouldn't do that," Desiree said. "In the past few days, we have formed a bond."

"In spite of him tying you up and blind-folding and gagging you?" I asked.

"I have seen through his rough exterior to the noble and tender soul within," she said. "And we have formed a bond forged in adversity, a bond —"

"Will you shut the hell up?" Martin snarled. "I don't want to hear any more of that sickening drivel. The world is not one of your stupid bodice-rippers, lady. Now both of you, lie down —"

Desiree screamed in utter rage and began to stagger toward him waving the not-quite-empty merlot bottle. He instinctively took a step back. He was focused on Desiree, so I hoped he wouldn't notice whatever I did. For a split second, I thought of just letting them fight it out, like the Cats of Kilkenny. Then I dived in, grabbed Martin's right hand, and tried to aim the gun away from me. And away from Desiree, too, and, if possible, toward the outside wall of the cabin.

Martin fired the gun. Two shots. I heard glass shattering. One of the bullets had hit the sliding glass doors to the balcony. Maybe both bullets. Then more glass shattering as Desiree took a swing at his head with the merlot bottle and hit the wall instead.

She shrieked again, tossed the remnants of the bottle aside, and lurched forward, grabbing for his throat. He collapsed under her weight, and I was able to wrench the gun out of his hand on the way down.

I could hear footsteps running up the stairs. The Coast Guard, probably. I didn't want to be standing with the gun in my hand when they came in. I thought of just tossing it aside, but it was still touch and go whether Desiree would succeed in strangling Martin or whether he'd free himself and go looking for his weapon. So I stepped into the bathroom, tossed the gun in the toilet, and slammed the lid closed. Then I stepped around the patch of floor where Desiree and Martin were wrestling and went to open the door for the arriving Coast Guard officers.

CHAPTER 35

Sunday

"Weren't you worried when the Coast Guard ran in?" Janet asked the next morning. "Worried they'd shoot you or arrest you or something?"

"A little," I said. "But I figured with the other two rolling on the floor in a puddle of wine and broken glass, trying to choke each other and shrieking things I wouldn't have wanted the boys to hear, I looked pretty sane and trustworthy by comparison. Not to mention the fact that I opened the door and greeted them with 'Thank heavens you're here.' "

We were standing at the front of the deck six sun deck. Below us, on deck five, we could see Rose Noire leading a group of eighteen or twenty passengers — including Michael and the boys — in a sunrise yoga session. Not that the sun had showed itself so far — the day had dawned cloudy and blissfully cool. Janet and I had opted for the less strenuous delights of experiencing the sunrise over a mug of coffee for her and a can of Diet Coke for me. Hot coffee and cold soda still felt like fabulous luxuries.

And on either side of us, as the wisps of early fog gradually cleared, we could see more and more clearly the shoreline slipping past as the ship cruised up the Chesapeake Bay toward Baltimore. We took turns using a pair of Grandfather's binoculars to study the passing scenery or gaze forward in the hope of being the first to spot the pier.

Yes, we were returning to Baltimore. Shortly after the Coast Guard had transported Desiree and First Officer Martin over to their cutter to be locked up in the brig, the salver had arrived. And, wonder of wonders, they'd brought the right parts to mend the ship. We'd gone to bed in the Bermuda Triangle and awakened to Lieutenant Tracy announcing over the ship's loudspeaker system that deboarding in Baltimore would begin at approximately oh-nine-hundred. I wondered if the Coast Guard would normally have left personnel on board to see the *Wanderer* safely home or if the fact that they'd done so was measure of how profoundly they distrusted

Pastime. Either way, the passengers were happy. The way the Coast Guard ran a ship was a vast improvement over Captain Detweiler's system.

"And apparently that lawyer guy was wrong about crimes at sea not getting investigated," Janet went on. "First the Coast Guard and soon the FBI, from what I hear."

"I think the Coast Guard takes a dim view of people trying to commit murder on their watch," I said.

"And they brought in the FBI?"

"That might have been Horace's doing," I said. "He has a lot of friends at the FBI. Most of them buried in various forensic labs, of course, but still — they seem to have some influence. Although I think Grandfather's webcast might have had some effect, too. Delaney tells me it's gone viral."

"Fabulous. I just hope Desiree doesn't get off too lightly."

"Unlikely," I said. "Since Horace isn't officially on the case, he's been more talkative than usual. According to him, First Officer Martin is so furious with Desiree that he's spilling everything. She really had it in for your writing group — Martin was going to arrange for the Bermudian authorities to find her bound and gagged in one of your cabins, and then she'd accuse you of kidnapping her and planning to throw her overboard when the boat went out to sea again. Fabulous publicity for her, and revenge on a group of people she hated."

"Is trying to frame someone a crime?"

"Pretty sure it is," I said. "And they'll probably also charge her with something in connection with Anton Bjelica's murder. Accessory after the fact or co-conspirator or whatever."

"Good." Janet looked glum. "Because if it weren't for her, that poor man would still be alive."

"Maybe not. According to Martin, that poor man was trying to blackmail him," I said.

"Bjelica found out about Desiree's plot?"

"No, Bjelica sabotaged the navigation system on Martin's orders. Part of the plot to make Captain Detweiler look bad so Martin could inherit his job. If I'd been Martin, I'd have postponed the sabotage until the next trip and focused on making Desiree's plot work — having a kidnapping on board his ship wouldn't look good on the captain's record, either. But Martin got greedy and impatient. And when Bjelica showed himself a blackmailer, Martin decided he had to go."

She nodded, but still looked pensive.

"I just don't get why she targeted us," she said finally. "I know why we hate her — and I think we have good reason. But why did she hate us so much that she'd try to hurt us that way?"

"I bet it will turn out that she thought you knew her secret," I said. "About stealing Nancy's manuscript. And for that matter, taking the credit for Nancy's work. And she assumed you'd try to hurt her with it — because that's what she'd do. So she decided on a preemptive strike."

"Yeah," she said. "That could be it. It's the only plausible explanation I can think of. Thanks for filling me in — but now let's pretend Desiree doesn't exist and enjoy the morning."

"Good plan."

"Morning!" Grandfather boomed, stepping out of the elevator. "Wonderful day, isn't it?"

We agreed that it was indeed a wonderful day and watched as he pulled something out of his pocket. A tin of sardines. He opened it up, spilling a good bit of the liquid in which they were packed on his fisherman's vest. No doubt we'd soon find out if there were any cats on board. Or for that matter in the entire city of Baltimore, once the ship docked.

Grandfather fished out half a sardine and held it aloft, with an impatient look on his face. Although, luckily, he didn't seem to be looking at Janet or me. Not even for the sake of placating Grandfather could I face consuming a sardine this early in the day. Then he looked up at what Rob called "the mast-like things" and frowned.

"Serge said he'd show up pretty quickly," he said. "I wonder if — Aha!"

The injured South American tern fluttered down from somewhere above us and perched on the rail near Grandfather, his glittering black eyes fixed on the sardine. Grandfather tossed the sardine chunk toward him. The tern caught it very neatly and swallowed it whole.

"He trusts you — good!" Serge appeared in the doorway, half leaning on Léonie.

"Terns are very intelligent." Grandfather tossed another chunk of sardine to the expectant bird.

"I think it's being ravenous that's making him trust you," I suggested.

"Hmph!" Grandfather held out another sardine chunk and favored the tern with the sort of smile he usually reserved for people he suspected of being willing to donate large sums of money to environmental causes.

"Bonjour," Serge said, turning to me. "Is it true that you were suspicious of me because of my little feather ornaments? You thought they were evil voodoo fetishes?"

"No, I thought they were charming," I said. "And just to make sure, I had them assessed by an expert who confirmed my gut feeling that there was nothing dark or evil in them, only light. But I was suspicious of you, mainly because I found a feather ornament in your cabin, and the only other one I'd ever seen was lying right beside Desiree's suicide note."

"Ah, that explains it," Serge said. "She took it from me. Well, demanded it of me. I was sitting outside the main dining room, working on it while waiting for the beginning of Dr. Blake's lecture, so I could slip in and sit in the back. And she saw me working on it and said she wanted it. She offered me money, but I did not want to take money from her."

"Me, I would have refused," Léonie said. "And when I heard, it made me so angry I promised I would get it back. But when I searched her cabin for it, it was gone."

"I picked it up at the crime scene." I reached into my jeans pocket and pulled it out. "Here."

"No, keep it," Serge said. "If you wish. I

would be honored if you wished to have it."

"Thank you." I tucked it back in my pocket.

"May it serve as a reminder of the pleasant memories of the voyage." He accompanied his words with a courtly half bow. "There are, I hope, a few."

"Surprisingly many," I said. "Including the memory of how I met so many new friends."

We all beamed at each other. Well, except for Grandfather, who was leaning closer so he could inspect the tern. I'd have been afraid the thing would peck out my eyes, but Grandfather's confidence that animals would know he was their friend was usually justified. And when it wasn't — well, he had the most interesting collection of scars of anyone I knew.

"You did a good job of rehabilitating him," he said over his shoulder to Serge.

"Thank you," he said. "But what is to become of him now? I have given in my resignation, you see," he said, turning back to me.

"We both have." Léonie was beaming at Serge.

"It is possible that Pastime could try to enforce our employment contracts," Serge went on. "But after all that has happened, I think they will be just as happy to see us go."

"And where will you go?" I asked.

"Saint Cyr sur Mer," Léonie said. "It is on the Riviera some forty kilometers east of Marseilles. My parents run a little restaurant there, and they have been hoping I would return home to take it over so they can retire. Serge will see to the cooking, and I will manage the serving staff and the business affairs."

"If you are ever in Provence, you must come and dine with us," Serge said. "I will write down the particulars for you before you leave."

"Which will be relatively soon," Janet said. "I have to say, I have mixed feelings about Pastime canceling the cruise. I think we should hold out for a replacement cruise."

"Not unless it's on some other cruise line," I said. "You couldn't pay me to take another cruise with Pastime."

"Good point," Janet conceded.

"I'm going to see how many of the passengers want to stick around Baltimore and take some nature hikes and boat rides with me," Grandfather said. "As long as Caroline can find us all a nice place to stay and organize the boats or buses or whatever we need."

"That sounds fantastic," Janet said. "Count me in."

I wondered if he'd bothered to tell Caroline about this plan yet.

"Meanwhile, what about this tern?" Grandfather said, turning back to Serge. "If you leave the ship, who's going to look after him?"

"I do not know." Serge's good humor deserted him, and Léonie patted his arm sympathetically. "But I do not think I would be allowed to take him with me."

"Nonsense," Grandfather said. "I'm sure it can be arranged. The Mediterranean coast should be a perfectly suitable climate for him, and clearly you've proven you know how to take care of him. We'll arrange for you to get a *certificat de capacité*. That's the paperwork from the French government that lets you take care of a wild animal. Make sure Meg knows how to find you in this Sur Cyr place and I'll get cracking on arranging the permissions."

He tossed the last bit of sardine into the tern's mouth and stumped off toward the elevator.

"That would be wonderful," Serge said, as we watched Grandfather leave. "But — do you think he can do it?"

"I'm sure he can," I said. "People let

Grandfather get away with the most amazing things. Even the most stubborn bureaucrats eventually figure out that the only way to get him to leave them alone is to let him do whatever he wants."

"Let us hope." Serge held out his arm and made a clucking noise. The tern flapped awkwardly onto his outstretched arm and then walked up until it was sitting on his shoulder, nuzzling the bill of his uniform hat.

"Now what are they up to?" Janet was at the stern end of the sun deck, pointing down toward deck five. I joined her and looked down to see Rob, Delaney, Tish, Kate, and Angie having an enthusiastic conversation about something.

"Let's go down and see," I suggested.

"Hey, Meg," Delaney called when Janet and I emerged from the ship. "We're taking down Desiree."

"I think she's pretty much taken herself down," I said. "When the story of her faking her suicide comes out —"

"Already has," Rob said. "Complete with some very unflattering photos."

"And believe me, it's gone viral in fandom." Delaney looked smug, and I suspected she'd done what she could to make this happen. Making things go viral seemed to be one of her favorite pastimes.

"Then if there's any justice, she's already a laughingstock," I said. "Not to mention the strong possibility that she'll be charged as an accessory after the fact in Anton Bjelica's murder."

"All good," Delaney said. "And we're going public with my proof that Nancy wrote the Were-Knights."

"You're not worried about the non-disclosure agreement?" I asked.

"The non-disclosure agreement was between Desiree and Nancy," Rob said. "Of course, Desiree could go after Nancy's estate if she thought Nancy had broken the agreement."

"She's certainly welcome to try," Tish said. "Nancy was up to her ears in debt when she died. The four of us paid for the funeral."

"And the agreement's not binding on Angie," Rob said. "Always a possibility that Desiree could try suing for defamation, claiming she really did write the books."

"But if she does that, my program will blow her out of the water," Delaney crowed.

"What we really want to achieve is recognition for Nancy," Angie said. "Desiree's welcome to keep the money — but we want the readers to know that no matter who owns the copyright, the Were-Knights were Nancy's creation."

"Well, that's not quite all we want," Tish said. "We're also hoping we can find a way to get Desiree to let us continue the series."

"Together." Kate beamed at the others.

"Not as ghostwriters," Angie said. "Not with her having any control whatsoever."

"But if there's some way we can buy the rights to continue the series, we think we can do it," Janet said. "The publisher will benefit by keeping a popular series going. Hell, even Desiree will benefit — having new books coming out helps sales of the old books, which she will still own."

"I'm going to talk to Festus," Rob said. "If it's not in his area of expertise, I'm sure he can recommend an attorney for them."

"Good idea." Our cousin Festus Hollingsworth was a highly successful crusading attorney, and if he took on the writers' case — or persuaded a trusted colleague to do so — Desiree was in for a hard time.

"And the Were-Knights will ride again!" Delaney exclaimed.

"Good morning!" someone behind me called out. I turned to find Ted Lambert leaning against the rail, lifting a coffee cup in salute.

"Good morning," I said. "You're very

497

cheerful today."

"Positively delirious at the thought of being on dry land again." He looked happier than I'd ever seen him. "And for some strange reason, the wife's taken against cruising. Says if I get the notion to go gallivanting on a boat again I can go by myself."

"I thought she was the one who insisted on taking a cruise," I said.

"Oh, she was." He chuckled softly. "I could prove that if I wanted to. But if I've learned one thing after twenty-four years of marriage it's to shut up when things are going my way. Incidentally, if you happen to have a hankering to own a piece of the Pastime Cruise Company, I heard their stock's going for pennies this morning."

"Thanks," I said. "But I think I'll pass. Although it would be tempting to show up at a shareholder's meeting and ask who hired Detweiler and Martin."

"No idea about Martin," Lambert said. "But according to this morning's news reports, Detweiler's the son-in-law of the president of Pastime."

"Rats," I said. "Then I gather there's no hope he'll lose his job."

"He will if Pastime goes belly up," Lambert said. "And it could come to that."

"Good riddance to the captain, then," I said. "And with any luck First Officer Martin will be locked up until well past retirement age. But what about the rest of the crew?"

"Oh, they'll be okay."

"Easy for you to say," I said. "Pastime has abused and exploited them, and now if it goes bust —"

"Easy for me to say because Caroline Willner has already recruited me to the committee to help all the crew find new jobs," he said, holding his hands up as if in surrender. "I don't anticipate much difficulty. Anyway, I must go and thank your friend Delaney for getting our Internet back."

"You were able to file your brief?"

"Not yet — I plan to do that from the hotel tonight. But I was able to do some amusing legal research. Did you know that there's a penalty of up to twelve years in prison for filing a false "passenger overboard" report? Of course, what case law I could find seems to indicate that the federal courts rarely impose that heavy a sentence, but they are rather likely to require that Ms. St. Christophe pay restitution for some or all of the costs of the search."

"That won't be cheap," I said. "According to Lieutenant Tracy, they had two of their biggest cutters out there looking, and hundreds of crew."

"Then let's hope for her sake that her books are selling really well." He lifted his cup and drained the last of his coffee. "I need to go and pack. My wife wants to be one of the first passengers off the ship. Nice sailing with you!"

"And with you."

"Ms. Langslow?" I turned to find Aarav, the bartender, standing on the deck behind me. He was wearing his white-and-gold uniform, but with a bandage wrapped around his head instead of the customary hat, and under his left arm he was holding a parcel wrapped in a white tablecloth. "I wanted to thank you. For saving my life."

"I didn't do much," I said. "Someone else would have come along to let you out eventually."

"Most probably First Officer Martin, who would no doubt have thrown me overboard," Aarav said. "It was he who hit me over the head. With a bottle of Chateau Petrus Pomerol. The 2010 vintage."

From his shocked tone of voice, I deduced that Martin had picked a particularly fancy bottle of wine to cosh him with.

"Do you have any idea why the first officer would want to kill you?" I asked.

"When I came around and found him tying me up, I asked him why he was doing it," Aarav said. "He seemed to think I had overheard something that would get him in trouble if I reported it. I was in the wine closet, you see, and walked out in the middle of his quarrel with Anton. I tried to convince him that I was trying to resolve a discrepancy in the Bordeaux inventory and was completely oblivious of whatever he and Anton were arguing about, but he didn't believe me. After he left I managed to knock down a bottle — luckily only a modest chardonnay — and use the broken glass to saw through my bonds. But then I found I was locked in the closet, and the loss of blood was making me faint. So I beg to differ — by getting me out of the wine closet you did a very great thing indeed. Without you, either I would have bled to death, or Martin would have returned to finish me off. Please accept this as a small token of my thanks."

He bowed and whipped away the tablecloth to hand me a bottle wrapped in white paper and tied at the neck with a metallic gold ribbon.

"Treat it gently," he advised, before vanishing back into the stairway.

I pulled aside the paper enough to see an

old-fashioned label printed in black and red, featuring an engraving of a stern-faced saint and the words 2010 PETRUS POMEROL GRAND VIN.

I wondered if this was the very bottle he'd been hit with. And hoped it wasn't too expensive a wine. Or if it was, that he wouldn't get in trouble for giving it to me. I'd put Mother in charge of deciding how and when to serve it. In the meantime, I tucked it into my tote and returned to the rail, where Janet was now peering through the binoculars. She'd had a good long turn while I'd been talking to Ted and Aarav. My turn now.

And that's how I managed to be the first to spot the pier. There seemed to be rather a lot of people. Strange, since there were no cruise ships docked. Even if there had been, it wasn't yet nine o'clock. Passengers wouldn't be showing up that early, would they?

As the ship drew closer, I spotted half a dozen trucks bearing the logos of Baltimore-area TV and radio stations. Dozens of people jostled for position on the pier and pointed cameras at the arriving ship — everything from giant news cameras to tiny pocket cameras and cell phones. A mixture of reporters and curious bystanders, I deduced.

"Looks as if our welcome's going to be a bit better than the sendoff." Grandfather joined us at the rail. Serge's pet tern was still perched on his shoulder. Had he deserted Serge for Grandfather? Or did his sudden apparent infatuation with Grandfather have something to with the bits of sardine Grandfather occasionally fished out of the pockets of his fisherman's vest.

"Let me have those things a sec." Grandfather held out a hand for the binoculars.

I handed them over — they were his anyway. Grandfather raised them to his eyes and scanned the pier. But he was still scowling, I noticed — what now? Normally there was nothing he liked better than a large collection of reporters he could charm. Was he under the delusion that our arrival wasn't getting as much coverage as it deserved?

Finally, about the time we got near enough to see the crowd without binoculars, a look of relief washed over his face.

"Ah, good," he said. "Trevor's there waiting for us."

I mentally kicked myself. I'd assumed Caroline would let Grandfather know that we'd finally reached Trevor, who was safe and sound and had never left Baltimore.

She probably thought I'd shared the news. I'd been too busy taking care of Trevor's anguished request that I burn the auto-graphed copy of *The Sharp Claw of Love* that Desiree had thrust into his unwilling hands to thank him for paying off her taxi driver. Although in the end, I didn't actu-ally burn the whole thing — only the title page with its embarrassing inscription. I'd shelved the book itself in the library lounge.

"Were you worried about him?" I asked aloud.

"No such thing," Grandfather retorted. "Just wondering whether the wretch has thought to bring me my ginger beer."

Liar, I thought. But I didn't say it aloud — I just watched as Grandfather fed another bit of sardine to the expectant tern, stepped forward, struck his most dramatic pose, and basked in the knowledge that dozens of cameras were focused right on him.

ABOUT THE AUTHOR

Donna Andrews is a winner of the Agatha, Anthony, and Barry Awards, a *Romantic Times* Award for best first novel, and four Lefty and two Toby Bromberg awards for funniest mystery. She is a member of Mystery Writers of America, Sisters in Crime, and the Private Investigators and Security Association. Andrews lives in Reston, Virginia. *Terns of Endearment* is Andrews's 25th mystery in the Meg Langslow series.

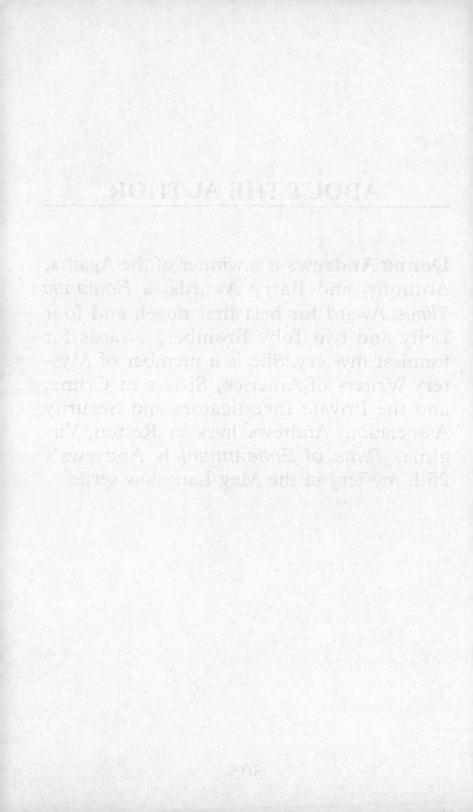